By David Sherman and Dan Cragg

Starfist
FIRST TO FIGHT
SCHOOL OF FIRE
STEEL GAUNTLET
BLOOD CONTACT
TECHNOKILL
HANGFIRE
KINGDOM'S SWORD
KINGDOM'S FURY
LAZARUS RISING

By David Sherman

The Night Fighters
KNIVES IN THE NIGHT
MAIN FORCE ASSAULT
OUT OF THE FIRE
A ROCK AND A HARD PLACE
A NGHU NIGHT FALLS
CHARLIE DON'T LIVE HERE ANYMORE
THERE I WAS: THE WAR OF CORPORAL HENRY J. MORRIS, USMC
THE SQUAD

Demontech
GULF RUN
ONSLAUGHT
RALLY POINT

By Dan Cragg

Fiction
THE SOLDIER'S PRIZE

Nonfiction
A DICTIONARY OF SOLDIER TALK
GENERALS IN MUDDY BOOTS
INSIDE THE VC AND THE NVA (with Michael Lee Lanning)
TOP SERGEANT (with William G. Bainbridge)

STARFIST
A WORLD OF HURT

A WORLD OF HURT

BOOK TEN

DAVID SHERMAN
AND
DAN CRAGG

BALLANTINE BOOKS • NEW YORK

A Del Rey® Book
Published by The Random House Publishing Group

www.delreydigital.com

Library of Congress Cataloging-in-Publication Data

Sherman, David.
A world of hurt / David Sherman and Dan Cragg.—1st ed.
p. cm.—(Starfist ; bk. 10)
"A Del Rey book."
ISBN 0-345-46052-9
1. Marines—Fiction. 2. Life on other planets—Fiction. I. Cragg, Dan. II. Title.

PS3569.H4175W67 2004
813'.6—dc22
2004048853

Text design by Julie Schroeder

Manufactured in the United States of America

First Edition: December 2004

2 4 6 8 9 7 5 3 1

To:
PFCs Tom Purdom
and
J. B. Post
Reluctant Cold Warriors
and old friends

STARFIST
A WORLD OF HURT

PROLOGUE

Samar Volga maneuvered the mule up the forested mountainside almost all the way to the saddle before the steep slope threatened to overturn the machine. He sidled the vehicle against a sturdy tree to keep it in place, then climbed the rest of the way on foot. The saddle wasn't much higher, and he only had to use his hands a few times to help him climb. When he got to the other side of the saddle and looked into the hidden valley beyond, what he saw made his breath catch.

The valley was a long oval, no more than ten kilometers at its widest, close to double that in length. The mountains that ringed it were much steeper on the valley side than on the outer; only isolated bushes and weeds found purchase on their upper slopes.

But what bushes and weeds! He'd never seen their like; not in field trips, in the university's museum and labs, nor in textbooks. Samar Volga believed the valley's life-forms had been isolated from the outside world for so long they had evolved to the point where they were unique to it. He was equally certain that he was the first human to set eyes on them.

A couple of hundred meters down, the slope gentled and more growth had taken root. The floor of the valley was blanketed by a forest dotted with small clearings. Using his glasses at high magnification, he could make out the uppermost leaves in the nearer trees; none looked familiar.

Almost salivating with the desire to begin his investigation, the young botanist looked for a way down to the upper growths. But the slope was too steep, and he knew he wasn't a good enough mountaineer to risk a free climb without someone to back him up if he fell. Momentarily frustrated but glad that he'd thought to bring climbing gear, he returned to his mule. He spent the rest of the day ferrying mountaineering kit, specimen packs, and recording equipment to the saddle.

Finally, exhausted, he made himself eat a light dinner and wrapped himself in his sleeping bag. But tired as he was, sleep was a long time coming. He was going to be the first human to enter the pocket valley, the first to examine its plant life. The honor of naming all its species would be his. Eventually he would go into other hidden valleys.

Maugham's Station was studded with such isolated pockets.

No need to investigate the hidden valleys indeed. He'd show those hidebound Frères Jacques what was what!

A cacophony of avian calls woke him at dawn. He barely took time for his morning ablutions and to bolt down a quick breakfast before heading back up to the saddle.

Quickly, he anchored a rope and lowered three loads of gear down the steep slope, collecting equipment, recorders, food, and water. Then he rappelled down to where the slope was gentle enough so he didn't need the rope. Maneuvering the gear the rest of the way by hand was hot, sweaty work, but when he reached the forest below he knew it was well worth the effort.

His pulse raced as he marveled at the scarlets, pinks, ambers, and blues—*blues?*—and the infinity of greens of the foliage before him. And it was all leaves and stems and vines; there wasn't a flower to be seen.

And it was all his to identify, classify, and name!

With great effort he pulled himself back from his state of awe and looked about for places to site his recording equipment. It wasn't until he picked three spots and began carrying his gear toward them that he realized something an entomologist or zoologist would have noticed immediately—the near utter silence of this forest of unknown species. There was no buzzing of pollinating insectoids, nor sounds of other animal life. The only sound was the rustling of vegetation moved by the wind. Except . . .

Except when he looked up he didn't see any movement in the tree-tops. He froze and listened carefully, slowly turning around, peering between trees, leaves, and vines, squinting into shadows, looking for whatever danger had made the animals and insects go quiet. Surely they hadn't all gone silent because of *him*.

Never mind, he told himself. He had specimens to collect. He set to it with great enthusiasm and filled half of his specimen packs before thirst and hunger forced him to stop for a meal. He sat in the shade of a tree at the forest's edge, in clear view of two of his recorders.

Samar Volga never saw the streamer of greenish, viscous fluid that arced out and hit him in the back. But he felt it. He arched his back away from the burning agony, but it went with him. His mouth stretched wide to scream, but no sound came out—the pain of the first strike knocked the air from his lungs and there was none left to scream with. Not that anyone would have heard anyway.

His knees buckled and he fell forward. His hands didn't move fast enough to break his fall and his face thudded hard onto the ground. Another streamer of fluid lashed at him from a different direction, and he writhed as though violent movement would make the pain go away. A third streamer struck.

Steam rose from his bubbling flesh and his movements became jerky, slower, and after a few minutes ceased altogether.

CHAPTER ONE

Gunnery Sergeant Charlie Bass woke with a groan on the first morning after his return to Thorsfinni's World. His head hurt and his stomach began lecturing him on the need to mend his evil ways. He cracked an eyelid to see where he was, and immediately slammed it shut to block the murderous sunlight that stabbed into his brain. He groaned again, and lay unmoving while he tried to reconstruct what he'd done the night before, in hope that would give him a clue to where he was.

Right. It had been evening and he'd gone straight to First Sergeant Myer's quarters, where he'd found the Top, Gunny Thatcher, Staff Sergeant Hyakowa, Doc Horner, and both the FIST and battalion sergeant majors eating reindeer steaks, drinking Reindeer Ale, and playing cards. They'd all been shocked to see him—except for the first sergeant, who acted like he was expecting him. Bass had joined them for an evening of eating, drinking, and general revelry. He smiled at the memory, but quickly stopped because the effort hurt too much. He vaguely remembered being taken very late to the transient barracks, where newly arrived Marines were quartered when they joined 34th FIST, before being assigned to units.

He listened, but didn't hear any of the normal sounds of Marines performing their duties in Camp Major Pete Ellis. Then he remembered: last night was Fifth Day on Thorsfinni's World. Which meant this must be Sixth Day morning, and nearly everybody was off base on liberty.

He shifted into a more comfortable position—well, a less uncomfortable position—and assayed another smile; that one didn't hurt as much, so he let it linger. It was such a comfort to wake up without immediately worrying about fending off an attack from the Skinks, or the army of Dominic de Tomas.

Comfort. He sighed as he remembered the young daughter of Zachariah Brattle. Well, not *that* young—she was a full-grown woman, after all, which she'd demonstrated to him beyond all doubt. That woman would make a wonderful wife for a warrior. He sighed again. But Comfort was still on Kingdom, probably holding down some important government post, and he was back where he belonged, with 34th FIST on Thorsfinni's World, and he'd never see her again.

Back where he belonged.

He swore, comfort and Comfort forgotten, and rolled up to sit on his rack with his legs over its side.

Right. Back where I belong. He'd been commander of Company L's third platoon for three or four years, ever since Ensign vanden Hoyt was killed in action on Diamunde. But he was a gunnery sergeant, a company level noncommissioned officer; a platoon commander was supposed to be an officer. And last night he'd been told that during the time he was thought dead, an ensign had been assigned to take command of his platoon.

Shit.

He *liked* being commander of Company L's third platoon. Of course, he could get command of another platoon easily enough—all he had to do was accept a commission.

Charlie Bass liked having his own platoon, but had refused a commission every time one was offered to him. In his opinion, officers had to do too much crap. They had to have fancy mess uniforms, act like proper "gentlemen," and not "fraternize" with their subordinates.

Well, senior NCOs weren't supposed to socialize with junior NCOs and enlisted men either, but he'd never let that stop him from playing cards or getting drunk with any Marine he felt like.

And to be an officer he'd have to go back to Arsenault, where he'd gone through Boot Camp so long ago, to that damn finishing school the Confederation Marine Corps called the Officer Training College, and learn which fork to use and how to hold his pinky out while he drank tea from a china cup. He already knew everything a Marine platoon commander needed to know to fight and win a battle and bring his men back alive, with the mission accomplished. Hell, the only fork a fighting Marine needed to know how to use was the one in his mess kit. And holding a pinky out in combat was a good way to lose it.

But there was no way he'd get third platoon back even if he accepted a commission. It was Marine Corps policy that when a Marine completed officer training and got commissioned, he was assigned to a unit he'd never served with before. Charlie Bass knew his only alternative was to accept whatever gunnery sergeant billet in 34th FIST he was assigned to, wait for a platoon commander in the FIST's infantry battalion to get killed, then hope for a reshuffling of officers that would open his job back up.

He grimaced. Marines died, more often in 34th FIST than in almost any other unit, but he couldn't wish death on another Marine, not for his own benefit.

Groaning and huffing with the effort of moving, he set aside his sour mood and struggled out of the rack to go to the head for his morning shitshowershave.

A lance corporal wearing the armband of the duty NCO stopped him on his way back to his room.

"Gunny Bass? Some people want to see you. They're in the office," the Duty NCO said. Awe was audible in his voice and visible on his face. He'd heard about Charlie Bass. He didn't have much trouble accepting that Gunny Bass had somehow survived being captured by the Skinks and managed to escape from them. But to single-handedly overthrow a planetary government! Well, that went a bit beyond what he thought a Marine capable of—even if the Marine in question was *the* Gunnery Sergeant Charlie Bass he'd heard so many stories about, and he had the assistance of a rebel army and a rebellious army general.

"Thanks, Lance Corporal," Bass said. "Any idea what's up?"

"Nossir— I mean, no, Gunny."

Bass shot him a look. Enlisted men "sirred" sergeants major, but all other enlisted addressed each other by rank or the title "Marine." He saw how nervous the unknown lance corporal was and took pity on him. "Thanks," he said, and clapped him on the shoulder. "Keep up the good work, Marine."

"Aye aye, Gunny. Thanks, Gunny."

Bass was wearing only a towel wrapped around his waist. He decided that wasn't appropriate dress for reporting to the transient barracks office, so he stepped into his room and, so as not to jar his aching head and queasy stomach, cautiously pulled on a set of drab-green garrison utilities.

The office was a few steps away. Bass opened the door and entered. Top Myer and Gunny Thatcher were sitting on two unoccupied desks. It was indecent how chipper they looked. Then he saw Captain Conorado, Company L's commanding officer, and Lieutenant Humphrey, the company executive officer. He pulled himself to attention.

"Gunnery Sergeant Bass reporting as ordered, sir," he said to Conorado.

"Relax, Charlie," Conorado said, stepping forward to shake his hand. "Welcome back."

"Thank you, sir. It's good to be back." He repeated the greeting with Humphrey. Only then did he notice that all four men were in undress reds, a much more formal uniform than they normally wore, certainly more formal than they wore on the weekend—much less the one he was wearing. "Undress reds" was a bit of a misnomer, as only the uniform's tunic was scarlet; enlisted men's dress uniform trousers were navy blue and officers wore gold.

"About time you decided to show up!" Thatcher snarled. But he smiled, so Bass knew he was just putting on an act.

"Actually, we aren't the ones who want to see your dumb ass," Top Myer growled. He picked up a garment bag and handed it to Bass. "This is your undress reds. Go back to your room and change into the appropriate uniform."

Bass looked at him, wondering what was going on.

"Here," Thatcher said. "Doc Horner said to give this to you, though I'm damned if I know why he'd want to cure your hangover after your behavior last night."

Bass took the thing Thatcher held out, a tiny box with a hangover pill. He wondered what Thatcher meant. He didn't remember doing anything more outrageous than anyone else the night before.

"Aye aye, Top. Thanks, Gunny." He turned to Conorado. "By your leave, sir?"

Conorado, blank-faced, pointed a finger at the office door.

What the hell? Bass wondered as he headed back to his room to change. The only reason he could imagine for them to wear their undress reds was an award ceremony. But decorations were always handed out at full-FIST assemblies—and those ceremonies called for full dress reds. Besides, he hadn't done anything to rate another medal. His part in overthrowing Dominic de Tomas didn't count, since he hadn't done that in his capacity as a Marine. He dry-swallowed the hangover pill on his way back to his room and was already beginning to feel better by the time he started changing into his undress reds.

They were waiting outside the office when he returned.

"Let's go," Conorado said. He led the way out the front door of the barracks to where a landcar waited for them. "Go," he said to the driver as soon as they were in, and the landcar smoothly moved out.

"Where are we going?" Bass asked. Everybody looked away, but he wasn't left in suspense for long; the landcar took them to the headquarters building of 34th Fleet Initial Strike Team, only a few minutes' drive from the transient barracks.

Conorado again took the lead, and in moments they were in the outer office of Brigadier Sturgeon, 34th FIST's commander. Colonel Ramadan, the FIST executive officer waited for them. Ramadan was also in undress reds. He rapped on the door frame to the inner office and announced, "They're here, sir."

"Bring them in," Brigadier Sturgeon said. He was on his feet at the side of his desk as they came in. FIST Sergeant Major Shiro stood to the side of a row of visitor's chairs in front of Sturgeon's desk. The infantry battalion CO, Commander van Winkle, and the infantry battalion's senior enlisted man, Sergeant Major Parant, were also there.

Conorado came to attention in front of the brigadier and said, "Sir, Company L detachment reporting as ordered!"

"At ease, gentlemen," Sturgeon said. His lips quirked in a cut-off smile and he added, "I'm tempted to say, 'and you too, Charlie,' but that wouldn't be very decorous."

Every reply Bass could think of was even less decorous, so he didn't say anything.

Still looking at Bass, Sturgeon went on, "Everybody but you knows why we're here, Charlie. And you're smart enough, I'm sure you figured it out even before you got here."

Actually, he hadn't until just now, but he wasn't about to admit to the slightest bit of vincibility. So he said, "Ground I believe we've covered in the past, sir."

"Indeed we have, Charlie," Sturgeon said, "and you made me bend Marine Corps regulations every step of the way in order to keep you as a platoon commander." He went behind his desk to sit. "Seats, gentlemen, please." He cocked an eyebrow and added, "You too, Charlie."

Conorado, Lieutenant Rokmonov, and Myer sat on the sofa against the office's side wall, Thatcher sat on the sofa's arm. When Bass began to move to the sofa's other arm, Parant grabbed his arm and pointed at the chair between him and Shiro. Bass's lips pursed, since that chair put him dead center on Sturgeon's desk, directly across from the brigadier.

Gunnery Sergeant Charlie Bass felt more seriously outnumbered than he had when he faced Dominic de Tomas's Special Group.

"Gunnery Sergeant Bass, when you disappeared on Kingdom, we all thought you were dead," Sturgeon said. "Since our return to Camp Ellis, 34th FIST has received enough replacements to fill every vacant billet. One of those vacant billets is—was—commander of third platoon, Company L of the infantry battalion. One of the replacements is an ensign who I can plug into that slot.

"Then you had to come back and complicate matters. Captain Conorado," he nodded toward Company L's commander, "wants you to resume command of third platoon. So does Commander van Winkle," he nodded at the infantry battalion commander. "I concur. That platoon has been outstanding under your command.

"But the billet is supposed to be filled by an officer, and I have an officer to fill it." Bass opened his mouth to say something, but Sturgeon raised his hand to cut him off. "I know, it's within my prerogative as commander of a remote FIST to assign a senior noncommissioned officer to permanently fill a platoon commander's billet. In the past I've done that through the simple expedient of never having an extra officer who would go to waste. But this time, believing that you were dead, I requisitioned an ensign to fill that slot.

"Well, we all want you in command of that platoon, but you've created a problem for me. So this time I'm making you an officer and that's that." He nodded to Bass, giving him permission to speak.

"You can't do that, sir."

"I don't care what you say, Charlie. I'm doing it."

"Sir, with all due respect, you can't. As you said, sir, Marine Corps regulations allow for the commander of a forward FIST to permanently assign a senior NCO as a platoon commander, but they don't allow for a Marine to be assigned to the Officer Training College against his will. Besides, the last I heard, 34th FIST was quarantined and nobody is allowed to be transferred, so I couldn't go to Arsenault even if I wanted to."

"You're absolutely right, Charlie. I can't make you go to Arsenault against your will, and I wouldn't if I could—if I did, I wouldn't get you back after you received your commission. And we *are* still under quarantine, so Arsenault is a moot point."

"Sir?" Bass said, confused. "How can you make me an officer if I don't go to the finishing school?" The pill Doc Horner had provided may have eradicated most of Bass's pain, but his neural pathways weren't quite up to snuff yet, otherwise he wouldn't have called OTC "finishing school" in front of the brigadier.

Shiro and Parant both sharply elbowed him in the ribs, and he bit off a grunt.

Sturgeon bowed his head to hide a smile. Stone-faced again, he looked up. "Gunnery Sergeant, yes, there is some etiquette instruction at OTC, but more than ninety-five percent of it is in matters such as leadership, tactics, weapons, combined arms—courses you're well qualified to teach. Frankly, sending you to OTC would be a waste.

"Do you know what an Executive Order is, Charlie?"

Bass was startled by the abrupt change of subject. "Yessir. It's a law the President of the Confederation makes by fiat, without going through Congress."

"That's right. I have here," he lifted a sheet of foolscap and turned it so Bass could see its ornate calligraphy and ornamentation, "an Executive Order empowering me to grant commissions as I find necessary."

The blood drained from Bass's face.

"You see, Charlie, President Chang-Sturdevant couldn't go to Congress for this legislation. Hardly anybody in Congress knows that 34th FIST is quarantined, much less the reason for it. She also understands that 34th FIST is better off if some replacement officers come from within than if they come from outside and get the shock of their lives when they find out what they're in for only when they get here."

He grinned. "Charlie, this document means I can make you an officer. You don't have to go to OTC for the small amount of training it offers that you're ever likely to need—there isn't that much in the way of 'polite society' on Thorsfinni's World." He shook his head. "Which is a very good thing. I've seen your scandalous behavior in 'polite company.'

"So, Charlie, all you can do at this point is smile and say, 'Thank you, sir!' "

Bass's face went from pale to flushed in a flash. He started to rise, but dropped back onto the chair when he saw Shiro and Parant start to reach for him. "Damnit, sir, I'm a gunnery sergeant, I outrank almost any damn ensign. You're busting me!"

"AS YOU WERE, GUNNERY SERGEANT!" Shiro bellowed.

Parant jumped to his feet and leaned over Bass, his fists clenched at his sides. "You've already been busted a couple of times, Bass. You're bucking for another!"

"But—"

They all turned to Sturgeon, who was almost doubled over with laughter.

"Oh-my-Charlie," he gasped as he struggled to get himself under control. He weakly waved at the two sergeants major to resume their seats. After a moment he gained enough control to assume a stern expression, but wasn't able to hold it and broke up laughing again. It took a few more moments before he calmed down to occasional laughing barks.

"Charlie, Charlie, Charlie," he said, and took a deep breath. "Yes, yes, your final enlisted rank does outrank the final enlisted ranks of most ensigns, but really, an ensign outranks a sergeant major." He held up a placating hand to Shiro and Parant. "*Technically* outranks." Shiro and Parant looked only partly mollified.

"As I was saying. Your pay remains the same, but you get additional allowances. Seniority for ensigns is a bit more complex than it is for other officers; as final enlisted rank enters into the calculation, it's not based simply on date of commission.

"Charlie, you've been doing the job, and in a most exemplary manner." He had enough control now to turn serious. "Any ensign doing as good a job as you've done would be strongly recommended for promotion to lieutenant—I think you know that. You don't lose anything by accepting a commission. Instead you gain. I've got enough officers now, so I have to fill your billet with an officer. I'd rather keep you in it, but there are things even the commander of a forward outpost FIST—even one under quarantine and with an Executive Order in hand—can't do."

"Sir, with all respect," Bass said, speaking more soberly as well. "You were an NCO yourself once. You remember how senior NCOs feel about ensigns. They're mostly kids, even if they were sergeants or staff sergeants before they got commissioned. They need to be nurse-maided and trained. I don't want to be nurse-maided."

Sturgeon shook his head. "That attitude was supposed to change when the Marine Corps decided only to commission officers from the ranks. Sadly, it hasn't, and that leads some senior NCOs who would make outstanding officers to decline commissions, thus depriving both themselves and the Marine Corps." He tapped the Executive Order. "There's something else this does. It authorizes me to promote officers under my command as needed."

"Sir?"

"There's nothing in Marine Corps regulations that says a lieutenant has to be a weapons platoon commander or a company executive officer."

"Sir?"

"There's nothing that says a lieutenant can't be a blaster platoon commander."

"Sir?"

"If I feel like it, I can make you, by rank, the senior blaster platoon commander in the infantry battalion." He nodded to van Winkle. "With Commander van Winkle's concurrence, of course."

"I have no problem with that, sir," van Winkle said.

"It's settled then." He looked at the assembled officers and senior NCOs. "After operations on Kingdom, 34th FIST has quite a few men who merit decorations and deserve promotions. There will be a combined award and promotion ceremony in a FIST formation four days from today." He looked back at Bass. "I'm glad the staff sergeant and the sergeant I'm going to commission then haven't given me the same grief over it that you have, Charlie.

"Now. The new officers will need new dress reds. Thirty-fourth FIST is going to revive a discarded tradition; their first set of officers' reds will be a gift from the FIST's other officers." He looked at van Winkle. "Two of the new ensigns are yours, Commander. Will you take care of that?"

"Yessir, gladly, sir," van Winkle said with a grin.

Sturgeon looked around the room again. "Gentlemen, this is Sixth Day. Why aren't you off base enjoying some liberty? Not you, Charlie. You're going to New Oslo with the other two who are about to be commissioned to get your new uniforms."

On the flight to New Oslo, Bass ignored the staff sergeant from Mike Company and the sergeant from the transportation company who were going with him to Thorsfinni's World's finest men's clothier for the final fitting of their dress reds. Instead he mused over the sequence of events that culminated in his getting a commission.

The scientific team on Society 437, more commonly called "Waygone" because of how far it was from inhabited worlds—an Earthlike planet that was being examined by the Bureau of Human Habitability Exploration and Investigation for possible colonization—had missed two consecutive routine reports. His platoon was detached from 34th FIST and dispatched to investigate. They discovered that Society 437 had been invaded by an alien sentience armed with acid-shooting weapons who wiped out the entire thousand-person team. In a harrowing operation, the platoon met and wiped out the small invading force. On their way back to Throrsfinni's World, their ship was intercepted by a major general from Headquarters, Marine Corps, who ordered them never to speak of what they'd encountered on Society 437. Any slip would result in automatic sentence without appeal to the penal world of Darkside—a prison from which no one was ever paroled.

Not long afterward, third platoon along with the rest of Company L was sent on a secret mission under the command of an army general. This time they went to Avionia, a world that was quarantined, the public was told, because of virulent pathogens that killed all who landed on it. The truth was far, far different. Avionia was home to yet another alien sentience, one that had only reached the cultural level of fifteenth-century Earth. Avionia was quarantined for the protection of its native population. But the world also held a unique commodity—a type of gemstone that became highly prized when some were leaked into the marketplaces of Human Space. Not only were outlaws secretly landing on Avionia and smuggling the gemstones out, they were providing some of its inhabitants with weapons four or five centuries beyond anything the local technology was capable of producing, thereby threatening to disrupt the natural development of the Avionians in ways that could conceivably lead to their extinction. Company L's mission was to put the smugglers out of business and retrieve the weapons from the locals who had them—to kill that technology.

Thirty-fourth FIST was normally a two-year duty station, but transfers had stopped without explanation or notice. Brigadier Sturgeon had made a trip to Earth to find out why. Assistant Commandant of the Confederation Marine Corps, Anders Aguinaldo, found out 34th FIST was quarantined to prevent knowledge of the alien sentiences from spreading. Not only were transfers to other units canceled, so were releases from active service due to end of enlistment or retirement—assignment to 34th FIST had, in effect, very quietly become a life sentence.

Thirty-fourth FIST had recently returned from Kingdom, a human world that had been invaded by a major force of Skinks—the name the Marines had given the aliens who invaded Society 437. They had been joined on that campaign by 26th FIST. Bass wondered if 26th FIST was also quarantined now. And what about Kingdom? Or the sailors of the CNSS *Grandar Bay*, the ship on which the Marines had gone to Kingdom and that supported them in the operation?

For that matter, was the civilian population of Thorsfinni's World also closed off from two-way contact with the rest of humanity?

Ah, thinking about it did no good. All that accomplished was to raise questions and make him think the situation wasn't fair. Great Buddha's balls! One lesson lengthy service in the Marine Corps had taught him was that nothing was ever fair. Anyway, through the window he could see they were on the final approach to New Oslo, the capital city of Thorsfinni's World. Capital city? With its million-plus population, New Oslo was the only *real* city on Thorsfinni's World, and it looked like a village compared to cities he'd visited on other worlds. New Oslo was on the southern part of Niflheim, a fjord-rent island roughly the same shape and size as the Scandinavian peninsula on Earth, and at about the same latitude. That, and the fact that it was the largest island on the continentless planet, was why Ulf Thorsfinni had selected it for his settlement when he'd led the first colonists there.

New Oslo. Bass wondered if Katie still lived there, and if she was still single and available—and still willing to talk to him after he'd been out of touch for so long. He flinched when he realized he hadn't seen her since before the Diamunde Campaign. She was probably a fat, contented hausfrau with three fat, happy babies by now. Still, they'd had a lot of fun together. It wouldn't hurt to look her up. Anyway, she was more pleasant to think about than aliens and quarantines. And certainly more pleasant than thinking about how he was going to walk out of that clothier with an officer's dress reds.

The bloodred tunic with its stock collar was fine; the only difference between it and the dress reds tunic he'd worn through his entire career was it was made of better material and was tailored. Not even that—he'd had his tunics tailored for the past fifteen years! But those gold trousers—the agony! He *liked* the blue trousers with blood-stripe outer seam that showed he was a noncommissioned officer. Like most enlisted Marines, he'd always thought officers' dress reds were entirely too gaudy.

And he had to turn in his hard-earned—and more-than-once-earned—chevrons, rockers, and crossed blasters for the lousy single silver orb of an ensign's rank insignia. They'd let him keep the wound stripes on his sleeve. As if he *wanted* entire worlds to see them and know how many times he'd done something dumb in the line of fire and gotten injured. If the tailor had put the wound stripes on his sleeve, he decided, he'd have him take them off. That was one benefit of being an officer—officers didn't have to show off that badge of error.

The aircraft landed. Bass and the other two soon-to-be officers piled into a waiting courtesy car and were whisked off to the clothier.

The other two were greatly impressed when they saw the mass of decorations and medals already mounted on Bass's waiting tunic; he had more than both of them combined.

In less than an hour they left, each carrying a bundle. On the way to the hotel where they would stay until returning to Camp Ellis in two days, Bass gave his companions directions to a not-too disreputable establishment where they could find decent food, inebriating drink, and willing women.

As for him, once he stowed his new uniform, he got out his personal comm and punched up Katie's number.

She wasn't there anymore, which didn't much surprise him. Comm Central reported that while he was away on Kingdom she'd moved to—

Bronnysund?

Bronnysund—"Bronnys," as the Marines of 34th FIST called it—was a fishing town in the northern reaches of Niflheim. More to the point, it was the local liberty town for Camp Ellis. Why had Katie moved to Bronnys? Had she met and married a fisherman? That didn't seem at all like the Katie he'd known and very nearly loved. Did she go there in search of Charlie Bass? That didn't seem very likely either, but the thought certainly stoked his ego.

Maybe she'd like to come to his commissioning ceremony. *Yessir!* Katie pinning on one of his silver orbs. That would almost make having to go through the stupid ceremony worthwhile!

To hell with his orders to remain in New Oslo for two more days. He caught the next flight back to Bronnys and looked for Katie. He found her too.

CHAPTER TWO

Minister of the Interior Anton Elbrus sighed dramatically. "Where did he go? Do any of you have any idea?" he asked the quintet of Firstborn who stood in a loose group before his desk. Nobody spoke right away. Instead, they cast secretive glances at each other and avoided looking at him.

Elbrus's fingers drummed a brief tattoo on his desk. He was a middle-aged man who looked exactly like what he'd been most of his life—a mild-mannered bureaucrat. So it came as a surprise to the younger people in his office when he slammed the flat of his hand onto his desktop with a sharp *crack*. He further surprised them by shouting, "Come on! You're supposed to be Samar's friends. You know how long he's been gone. You know the last time he contacted any of you. *And you know he's missing!* Don't you care that your friend is missing, that he might be injured or lost and needs help? *You*, Yenisey." He thrust a finger at one of them. "Since childhood you two have always done everything together. I'm surprised you didn't go with him. Where did he go?"

Kerang Yenisey quickly looked around at the others, but if he looked for help, none appeared—the others studiously avoided making eye contact with him. "He said he wanted to find a way into one of the hidden valleys," Yenisey finally mumbled.

"I think we all know that," Elbrus replied dryly. "There are hundreds, maybe thousands, of hidden valleys. *Which one?*"

The young people, all members of the first generation of colonists born in Ammon, the only populated area on Maugham's Station, cast nervous glances at each other, but nobody said anything, even though they all had a general idea where Samar Volga had gone.

"He went into one of the interdicted areas, didn't he?" Elbrus asked. That wasn't a wild guess—most of the land area of Maugham's Station was interdicted. "Well?" he asked when no one spoke up.

Yenisey looked at the others again, and when they still didn't speak up, he said, "He went to Haltia. Almost a month ago."

Elbrus squeezed his eyes closed for a moment; that was even worse than he'd expected. Haltia wasn't far outside Ammon, but it was one of the most rugged of the interdicted areas, and it would be a very difficult area to search.

"Why did he pick Haltia?" he asked so softly it was almost a whisper.

Volga's friends exchanged quick glances, a couple of them nervously licking their lips. They also knew it would be harder to find their missing friend there than in almost any other area on the continent.

"Almost a month," Elbrus said. "I know he's been gone for almost a month." He fixed Yenisey with a sharp glare. "How long did he say he'd be gone?"

"A couple of weeks," the young man mumbled.

"A couple of weeks," Elbrus repeated. "*A couple of weeks!* And how much longer were you going to wait before any of you mentioned he was overdue? Don't you realize how much trouble your *friend* could be in? Didn't it occur to any of you that he might need help?" He stood abruptly and leaned forward, fists planted aggressively on his desktop. "Do you realize he could be *dead* because none of you thought it was important to report him missing?"

"He's been overdue before," Tanah Ob murmured.

Elbrus looked at her coldly. "*Before?* You mean this isn't the first time he's gone into Haltia?"

"No—I mean yes—I mean, I mean—" the young woman stammered.

"He hasn't gone into Haltia before," Yenisey said.

"Then where has he gone before?"

Yenisey hung his head and sighed though not as dramatically as Elbrus had earlier. He was already talking, he decided, so he might as well give up on holding anything back. "He's been to Baltica, Aland, and Ugric before."

"To get into the valleys?" Those three areas, all interdicted, were within an easy day's land travel from Olympia, Ammon's capital city.

Yenisey nodded without looking up.

"Did he get into them?"

Still looking down, Yenisey shook his head. "No."

"So why did he go to Haltia this time?"

Yenisey grimaced, then looked defiantly at the Minister of the Interior. "Because he found a map that showed what looked like an easy way into the valley."

Elbrus opened his mouth to demand to know where Volga had gotten a map with that kind of detail, since the Ammon government hadn't yet begun detailed mapping of Maugham's Station beyond the populated area, but snapped it closed before he asked. Samar Volga must have found it in the archives, left over from when Maugham's Station was an emergency way station for starships.

"He chose Haltia because he wanted to avoid detection," Elbrus said. It was a statement, not a question, so none of Volga's friends bothered to answer. He made another mental note: he needed to go to the Prime Minister and pressure him to get Parliament to approve the launch of a world-girding satellite net. Because all of the population of Maugham's Station was concentrated in the 350,000 square kilometers called Ammon, with most of the rest of the planet interdicted, the government didn't bother to maintain a world-spanning satellite network, and the planet's single geosync landsat was focused on the populated area. Even if it had instruments sensitive enough for the job, it would take weeks to get authorization to maneuver that satellite into position to locate a lost person in Haltia.

He looked away from the five Firstborn and sighed a third time. "Get out of my sight before I have you arrested."

He waited until they left, then sat heavily. He ponderously shook his head at the folly of the self-called Firstborn, the first generation to be born on Maugham's Station. *His* generation, the people who had colonized the onetime emergency way station, understood the hazards involved in colonizing a new world. They had constructed cities and towns to live in, farms and mines and factories to create an economy,

and set about methodically building their world. To ease the development, everything was concentrated in one small area of a middle-sized
continent. The arrangement also gave the colonists a feeling of familiarity—they came from densely populated worlds, and there was a danger
of widespread agoraphobia if they were spread thinly over the new
planet. Later, after a few generations, when the economy was sound and
the local resources were well enough developed that Maugham's Station
was properly self-sufficient and could apply for full membership in the
Confederation of Human Worlds, *then* they could explore the rest of the
planet and expand into its vastness.

As an aid in getting started, no one under the age of twenty-five was
included among the original colonists, and they held off having children for ten years. The thinking—and Elbrus knew it was right—was
that a new colony couldn't afford to have people sidelined with child-
bearing and -rearing. Only when the colony was past the perilous edge
of survival had they built schools. Construction wasn't begun on the
world's first college until the first cohort of the generation that called itself the Firstborn was in secondary school. Now, that first cohort was
through with its schooling and eager to stretch its wings. Unfortunately,
a sizable portion of the Firstborn were too impatient to participate in
the methodical development of Maugham's Station and wanted to expand the colony's physical frontiers *now*. Why? The world wasn't going
to be self-sufficient in their lifetime, they knew that: the methodology
and rationale of colonial development was taught at every level of edu-
cation from primary through undergraduate.

On a hunch, he leaned forward and queried his console. As Minister of the Interior, he had instant access to all but the most sensitive material stored in the world's data banks. In seconds his query was
answered. He let out another sigh.

Elbrus had been a young man, not long out of university, when his
family emigrated. He remembered his father, then a junior member of
Parliament, protesting the founding of a chair in Human Space Expansion in the History department when Olympia College was founded.

Samar Volga and four of the five Firstborn who'd just been in his
office had minored in Human Space Expansion.

Folly, pure folly. His father had been right. The heads of the
younger generation were filled with romantic ideas about exploration,

of "Going where no man has gone before." And now Elbrus was faced with the consequences of what his father had warned against.

Anton Elbrus didn't have jurisdiction over Haltia—nobody did, except, perhaps, some obscure parliamentary subcommittee—and assembling a search party and transporting it outside Ammon itself exceeded his authority. But he knew how many weeks—or months—it would likely take for Parliament to approve and outfit a search. Olympia's chief forensic pathologist informed him that the longer they waited, the less chance there was of finding anything, so he didn't even bother notifying the President or Parliament.

Like everything else on Maugham's Station, the search and rescue mission was organized methodically. There weren't any explorers or frontiersmen, of course, but there were botanists and zoologists who studied the flora and fauna on the fringes of the towns and cities and close beyond the borders of Ammon, and civil engineers who planned, built, and maintained the landways that linked the cities and towns. A team of twenty such specialists was assembled for the search. Of course, there were some oddballs who liked to picnic or camp in the wilds just out of sight of the towns and cities, so a dozen of them were conscripted as "guides" for the search.

Thirty-two searchers, plus four armed policemen; a doctor; and a three-person administration team to coordinate the searchers' activities and maintain communications with Olympia. Elbrus knew that wasn't enough people to search for a missing person in so large an area, but he didn't dare assemble a larger team for fear of attracting notice on a higher level.

It took more than a week to assemble the searchers and gather the equipment and supplies they would need. He used that time to quietly conduct an aerial search and survey the area, using aircraft and crews from Olympia's police department.

The aerial search revealed no sign of Samar Volga or any other person in or near Haltia, though it did update the official map database, which hadn't been done since the Bureau of Human Habitability Exploration and Investigation had completed its cursory examination of Maugham's Station more than two generations earlier. That was better than nothing.

Under the lead of Third Assistant Minister Frans Ladoga, the search party set out thirty-nine days after Samar Volga left Olympia for the wilds of Haltia.

On the third day of the search, Jean Lonnrot knelt to peer closely at fresh growth in the ground cover under the multicanopy forest trees. She brushed her gloved fingers through a tangle of blue-tinged leaves of a type she'd never before seen, wondering what gave them their odd color. An experienced botanist, she slipped her other hand into a pouch on her field belt, where her fingers fell immediately on a specimen pack of exactly the right size and opened it, ready to receive the plant. Gently, she groped through the leaves until she found the main stem and followed it to the ground. Holding the specimen pack in her teeth, she drew the digger from its holder and barely glanced at the control dial as she set it. Guiding the point of the cutter with her fingers, she cut a five-centimeter-radius circle around the stem, where it entered the ground. The circle complete, she returned the cutter to its belt loop and probed into the cut with both hands. Her hands went all the way in; the cutter had gone the exact fifteen centimeters she wanted. Gently, she pushed farther, curving her fingers inward to meet under the plant. After twisting to break the plug free, she lifted it out and lowered it into the specimen pack.

She settled back on her heels and studied the newly exposed ground where the specimen had grown. She pushed aside other top growth and looked some more. After a moment she spoke into her comm unit. "Elias, I'd like you to take a look at this."

"Where are you, Jean?"

"Don't you have me?" She checked the medallion on the left breast pocket of her field jacket. "My tracker seems to be working."

"Oh, right. I've got you. Be there in a few minutes."

Jean chuckled. Elias Sillanpa was a highly regarded zoologist, but tended toward absentmindedness and often forgot equipment that wasn't of immediate use in whatever he was studying at the moment. A crashing in the underbrush announced his approach. She shook her head. When he was stalking an animal, Sillanpa could slip through the densest growth as silently as a slug. At other times he was as noisy as a herd of kwangduks in a spindle forest.

"What did you find, Jean?" he asked as he came close.

She answered with a question of her own. "What kind of large fauna do we have here?" She knew full well the search party hadn't found any game trails larger than those used by the rodentlike animals that were a nuisance throughout Ammon.

His face went blank for a moment while he considered, then turned bright. "None. What did you find?"

She replied with another question. "Then what did this?"

He looked at the exposed growth, then dropped to his hands and knees to examine it more closely. He touched a crushed leaf here, a bent stem there, a broken twig elsewhere. He lowered his head to sniff, turned it as though listening to the trampled foliage, then looked up.

"I'd say that wasn't done by a large animal." Still on hands and knees, he crawled forward a dozen meters, poking and probing at the undercover and the ground as he went. "I'd say," he said, standing and brushing debris off his knees as he looked farther along the line he'd crawled, "it wasn't an animal, it was some kind of landcar."

Once they had a trail to follow, it only took a few more hours to find Samar Volga's mule. It sat where he'd left it, against a sturdy tree high up on the slope of a mountainside. From there it was a simple matter of deduction to climb higher to the saddle, where they found the rope Samar Volga had used to rappel into the valley below.

Jean Lonnrot's eyes grew wide with excitement when she saw the hitherto unimagined flora within the valley, and she could barely wait to descend into it to collect specimens for study.

Once the entire search party descended into the valley, Elias Sillanpa's reaction was equally excited—but for a distinctly different reason: he immediately noticed the total lack of animate life. Not only didn't he see any animals—or even insectoids—on the ground, in the branches, or flying, he saw no tracks, trails, scratches on tree trunks, chewed leaves, or scat. What kind of habitat was it that had no animals?

"Spread out, everyone," Frans Ladoga ordered. When nobody moved, other than the happily gathering botanist, he realized he'd barely spoken aloud and tried again. "Everybody, spread out," he said more loudly. "See if you can find any sign of Volga."

The others jerked, as though snapping out of trances. Lonnrot continued gathering, Sillanpa kept looking for signs of animals, and one of the policemen, Neva Ahvenan, stood listening. The others began looking for signs of the missing man's passage. Nobody bothered to cry out Volga's name. The ground cover looked as if it had never been trod by man's foot, and the rope Volga had used to rappel into the valley obviously hadn't been used in several weeks.

After a few minutes of peering nervously into shadows, Officer Ahvenan sidled over to Sillanpa. "I don't like this," he whispered.

"Neither do I," the zoologist whispered back.

"It's too quiet."

"There are no animals."

They heard a rustling in the branches and looked up toward the sound, but couldn't see what made the noise.

"It's just the wind in the trees," Sillanpa said when he failed to see anything.

"Then how come there's no wind up there?"

Sillanpa looked higher. Ahvenan was right, *nothing* was moving in the trees.

Just then someone called out, "I found something!" and everybody rushed to see what it was.

It was a camera. Within minutes two more were found. There were two trids and a 2-D. All were broken open and plants grew through them. Frans Lagoda told the others to leave the cameras in place, but to retrieve the recording crystals in case they could still be read.

Farther into the undergrowth, the search party found what they were afraid they'd find—human bones. They were still covered with clothing, but all the flesh was gone; they had been more thoroughly scoured than anybody would expect from the likely length of time they'd been there—especially with the clothing relatively undisturbed.

When they attempted to lift the skeleton into a forensic bag, they found they had to cut it free of tendrils that grew from the ground, through the clothing, and into the bones. When they finally picked it up and bagged it, the disarticulated bones slid together into a pile.

"Let's go," Lagoda said. "We found what we came for." He cast a worried look around. They'd found Samar Volga, but they had no idea what killed him—and whatever it was might still be nearby.

There was rustling in the trees as they filed out of the forest, back to the steep slope leading up to the saddle. Officer Ahvenan, the last person out, didn't see the streamer of greenish fluid that arced out from the bush and just missed his heel as he left the trees.

Outside again, Frans Lagoda ordered cameras and other sensors placed to observe the slope leading up to the saddle. If whatever killed Volga was still inside the valley, he wanted a warning if it tried to come out.

In due time forensic pathologists determined that some of the cratering on a few of the bones had been caused by a yet to be determined acid and noted that fact in the Unexplained Expiration report frontier worlds were required to file with the Department of Colonial Development, Population Control, and Xenobiological Studies whenever cause of death was unknown.

They routinely filed an Unexplained Expiration report for the two people who next died in a hidden valley. And for the one after that as well.

CHAPTER THREE

Nobody had ever officially bothered to give 43q15x17–32, an uninhabited planet orbiting a smallish, nondescript G-2 star, any formal name other than its alphanumeric designation in the *Atlas of Non-Habitable Planetary Bodies of Human Space*. The Bureau of Human Habitability, Exploration, and Investigation—commonly called by the acronym "BEHIND"—had taken one quick look at the planet and summarily rejected it as a candidate for human colonization. They didn't even think it worthwhile for mineral exploitation.

The planet 43q15x17–32 certainly wasn't much to look at. It was a blotchy brownish-red with occasional scabrous splotches of cobalt blue or washed-out green. The blue wasn't water (its seas were a sickly gray) and the green wasn't plant life—it was exposed mineral veins. So were the other surface colors. The only land-based plant life on the planet was scraggly mattings of algaelike bacteria at the fringes of its oceans. There wasn't any terrestrial animal life. No one other than xenobiologists studying the origins of life had any interest whatsoever in the plants or animals that might eke out a living in the planet's oceans. The atmosphere was too thick to breathe, but that didn't matter, since the air was mostly ammonia and methane anyway. The surface was hot and the atmosphere crackled constantly from permanent lightning storms.

The planet 43q15x17–32 was uninviting enough that no one ever casually visited it. Even among life-origins xenobiologists, only the most enthusiastic, or the most desperate for a paper devoted to something on which nobody else was working, ever bothered to come to study—and few of them were willing to stay very long. When the xenobiologists who did visit later mentioned the planet, they called it the "Rock" in a tone that strongly suggested it was unpleasant.

Then there were the miners, who also called 43q15x17–32 the "Rock," though more in a tone of despair. They didn't count as visitors, though, and so far as the Confederation of Human Worlds knew, they weren't there at all.

The miners were convicts from St. Helen's, serving sentences anywhere in duration from five years to life. "Life" was a nominal sentence, though; the environment was so harsh and the work so onerous that almost nobody managed to survive five years. Even the soldiers and sailors who guarded the mining operation were disciplinary problems who were posted to the Rock in lieu of court-martial and prison. In order to prevent mutiny, the soldiers and sailors were billeted on an orbiting space station and spent only one week in four planetside. More, they were promised that upon successful completion of a tour of duty, negative entries in their records would be fully expunged and they would be honorably retired on pensions equal to eighty percent of St. Helen's median income—which was considerably more than most of them could ever hope to earn through any activity that wouldn't put them at risk of serving as miners on the Rock themselves.

The St. Helen's mining operation on the Rock was a tightly held state secret. It had to be—the original evaluation of St. Helen's by the Bureau of Human Habitibility, Exploration, and Investigation had determined that the planet didn't have desirable metals and rare earths in sufficient quantity to make mining commercially viable—information that was easily accessible to anyone who felt like checking. So it was generally known among those who traded with St. Helen's for refined metals that the mining operations were somewhere off-planet. Exactly *where* was a state secret. After all, the mining operations were highly lucrative, and there were four human worlds closer to the Rock than St. Helen's. Any of them could make a strong case that 43q15x17–32 was in its legitimate area of possession, and that by exploiting the Rock's mineral wealth, St. Helen's was engaging in interstellar piracy.

There was precedent for such a claim. In the twenty-third century, Steinenborg brought a similar charge against Alhambra for mining an inhospitable world called Hell. The Confederation Supreme Court found in favor of Steinenborg, though by the time the court passed judgment, there had been a rebellion on Hell and the world gained independence. Nonetheless, Alhambra was required to pay reparations severe enough to impoverish it for a generation.

Unfortunately for St. Helen's, We're Here!—a planet settled by one of the first waves of colonists from Earth, and the planet nearest to the Rock—found out.

"I'm picking up some anomalous EMR, Skipper," Lieutenant Hope Bluebird said. She was the communications officer of the We're Here! navy heavy cruiser, *Goin'on.*

"Tell me about it," replied Commander Moon Happiness, captain of the *Goin'on.*

"Looks like bleed from a focused burst-comm."

"Where?"

"Seems to be coming from the Rock. I'm also picking up what looks like kinetic drive signals along the burst-comm track. But it doesn't look right for drive engines. Too small, more like a shuttle. Too far out for a shuttle, though. A couple of AU."

Captain Happiness thought about that for a bit. A couple of AU out from the Rock would put the shuttle at a distance similar to that between Earth and Sol's asteroid belt. Bluebird was right, that was *way* too far out for a shuttle. Unless it was an orbital body that wasn't on the *Goin'on's* charts, which he seriously doubted. He asked the radar officer, Ensign Freelion, if he had picked up any such. He hadn't.

"Sir," Freelion said, "the shuttle's moving on an intercept path toward the Rock."

Captain Happiness thought a bit more, then asked, "Have either of you read up any on cloaking?" Neither had heard of cloaking.

"The Confederation Navy's working on it," he told them. "It's supposed to make starships show up as something smaller."

"Stealth technology?" asked Bluebird.

"Similar," Happiness confirmed. "Stealth doesn't work on anything bigger than a Bomarc 36V. Cloaking is supposed to."

"I've seen stealth," Freelion said. "This isn't stealth."

"Hmm. Con, can you tuck us in behind that ship?"

"I've got a read," Lieutenant Sunshine Stems'n'seeds chirped. "Can do, sir."

Captain Happiness smiled tightly. If the *Goin'on* was directly behind that vessel, whoever she was, the *Goin'on* would be invisible to her and could follow wherever she was headed—unless she jumped into Beamspace. Which she wasn't likely to do unless her captain didn't realize she was on a collision course with a planet and needed to make an emergency jump in order to avoid catastrophe.

He didn't believe for a second that the cloaked ship didn't know she was on an intercept course for a planet.

Though she was a heavy cruiser in her current life, the *Goin'on* had been a Confederation Navy Omaha-class light cruiser before the Confederation Navy sold her to We're Here! shortly before the end of her scheduled service life. They'd included all of her existing systems, and to juice the sale a bit, thrown in a service-life extension. Which made the *Goin'on* one of the most sophisticated military starships owned by the local navy of any individual world in Human Space, and by far *the* most sophisticated in We're Here!'s navy.

The craft with the shuttle drive signals, when the *Goin'on* got close enough to see her on visual, was a good deal bigger than a Bomarc 36V, which was the smallest ship capable of interstellar travel. She was an ore freighter, ten times the size of the *Goin'on.* The registration markings, which by Confederation statute were required to be clearly visible on the freighter's stern, had been painted over—the ship was unidentifiable. Except to someone who had the latest updates to *Jane's Commercial Starfleets of the Confederation,* which We're Here!'s navy made sure to keep updated on all its starships.

The freighter appeared to be the *Broken Missouri,* registered in St. Helen's as part of United Express Freight's starfleet. The *Broken Missouri* had been reported lost to pirates three years earlier. A drone sent by the ship carried jerky, mostly out-of-focus 2-D vids of the pirate attack. No pirate band was ever identified as being behind the attack, and there had been no reports of the ship or any member of her crew being seen since. Neither had there been an acknowledged ransom demand. The *Broken Missouri* had been dead-heading when she was attacked, so there was no cargo to show up on either the black market or the gray.

When it became clear that the *Broken Missouri* was indeed headed for rendezvous with the Rock, Captain Happiness backed off the *Goin'on* far enough that the possibility of detection from either the planetary surface or orbit was near enough to zero to make no difference, and he observed and considered the implications of the missing freighter approaching an uninhabited planet along the plane of the ecliptic.

Starships coming out of Beamspace had two priorities: avoiding gravity wells, and allowing for margin of error in their exit to Space-3. That typically meant several days' transition travel above or below the plane of the ecliptic, as unanticipated gravity wells and small objects were more likely to be encountered along the plane. Contact with a sizable gravity well or an object much larger than a grain of sand could be catastrophic for a ship making the transition. Anyone watching for a ship to transit into Space-3 would, therefore, look above and below the plane of the ecliptic, not along it.

Captain Happiness came to the only conclusion that made sense: someone didn't want the freighter's arrival to be noticed. Which meshed tightly with the fact that the *Broken Missouri*'s kinetic drives were cloaked.

The next question Happiness had was: Who? Followed immediately by: Why?

Passive observation of the *Broken Missouri* in the visual, comm, and radar bands after she reached orbit made it clear that the freighter was loading cargo ferried up from the Rock. The only cargo Happiness could think of that might be worth uploading was minerals. The very minerals the *Goin'on* was there to investigate—the *Goin'on* carried a geological survey team that they'd planned to land on the surface. Obviously, they'd been beaten to it.

Captain Happiness considered what to do about the unexpected situation and concluded he had three choices. One: he could close with, board, and commandeer the freighter, then quarantine the planet while he sent a drone back to We're Here! for further instructions. Two: he could wait until the freighter left orbit, then intercept and capture her. Three: he could wait until the freighter jumped into Beamspace, land a boarding force, and take the planetside mining operation, then send off a drone requesting further instructions.

He didn't like any of those options.

In the first, it wasn't likely that the *Broken Missouri* was still a pirate vessel—pirates didn't engage in trading for minerals and ores—and taking her could well cause a major interstellar incident. The same applied in the second, in addition to which he didn't know what defenses, if any, the ship had. Neither did he know what defenses the planet might have.

He decided on a fourth choice. Send a drone to We're Here! and stay in place observing until further instructions arrived.

A week later, when the freighter finally left orbit and headed out to where she could jump, he was glad he'd decided on his fourth choice. The *Broken Missouri*'s hull had masked a military space station, to which she had been docked, from detection by his ship. Had he attacked, the space station might have caused severe damage to the *Goin'on* even if he'd been able to win a battle with it, which, while probable, wasn't certain.

Like the *Broken Missouri*, the space station had no identifying marks.

It took the *Broken Missouri* six days standard and a couple of hours to get far enough from gravity wells along the elliptic to make a jump into Beamspace. Only then did the *Goin'on* launch a drone. After little more than one day in Beamspace, it jumped back into Space-3 less than two days out from its destination and immediately began broadcasting its arrival. It was picked up the next day by a We're Here! coast guard cutter that downloaded its message and tight-beamed it to Navy HQ, where it was loaded into the Fleet Intelligence section comp and decoded.

Lieutenant Stardust had the duty. When he saw the message was classified "Urgent Highest," he nearly panicked; he'd never before seen that classification on a live document and didn't immediately know what to do with it. Other than not read it; neither he nor anyone else in his duty section held the necessary security clearance. He punched up the board to see whether anybody with a sufficiently high clearance happened to be in HQ. Such a person was.

Admiral of the Starry Heavens Sativa Orange, the We're Here! Chief of Naval Operations, was in his office. Lieutenant Stardust immediately routed the message to Admiral Orange and, to make sure it wasn't overlooked, placed a voice call to the admiral's office. Admiral Orange was alone, so there was nobody to take the call, but he dutifully noted a call had come in and made a mental note to see what it was before he left, which he planned to do in just a few minutes—no one would send a voice message to his office on an off-day unless it was very important.

The few minutes passed and Admiral Orange finished with the few logistics details he'd come in to check on—he was a notorious micromanager—and listened to the voice message. He heard with surprise the excitement in the voice that informed him of the arrival of an Urgent Highest message. Curious—he'd seen very few Urgent Highest messages in his entire career—he called up his in-box. There it was. He lifted his eyebrows and turned down the corners of his mouth at it, then read. He read it again. He pressed the panic button as he read through it a third time.

It was a literal panic button. Behind a sliding panel on the edge of his desk was a red button, about twenty millimeters in diameter and protruding ten millimeters from the back of the recess hidden behind the panel. Pressing the button sent a message to his senior staff ordering them to drop whatever they were doing and assemble immediately in the staff briefing room adjacent to his office.

Admiral of the Starry Heavens Orange had never had to press the panic button before, so an hour later he didn't know whether to be pleased that his senior people had gathered so quickly or furious that it had taken them so long. He opted for neutrality, as though the occasion was a regularly scheduled staff briefing and everybody was right on time.

"Do any of you know anything at all that will shed light on this?" Admiral Orange asked, and tapped the key that displayed the Urgent Highest message on the console in front of each of his people.

All of them did their best to keep their expressions blank as they read, but other involuntary reactions made their shock clear. Captain Head, Chief of Personnel, nervously brushed fingertips across her throat. Commodore O'Wow, Head of Intelligence, turned pale. Vice Admiral Toke, Operations, turned red. Rear Admiral Crashpad, Logistics, developed a severe tick in his left eyelid. Commodore Hitme, Civil Actions and Control, began trembling.

One by one, and with obvious reluctance, they turned their heads toward their commander. None of them was immediately willing to say anything.

"Commodore," Orange said, looking at O'Wow, "I believe this falls under your primary responsibility. Is there anything you haven't been telling me?"

"Nossi—" O'Wow squeaked, then tried again. "Nossir. Th-This is a complete surprise. It must have happened since the last time we surveyed 43q15x17–32." He looked to Toke.

Toke moved as though to tug her collar loose, caught herself, lowered her hand, and, mindful of O'Wow's squeak, cleared her throat before speaking. "Sir, it's been three years since our ships visited that system. This operation must be more recent than that."

"We haven't had any observation there for three years?" Orange demanded incredulously.

"Nossir," Toke croaked. She wasn't about to remind the Admiral of the Starry Heavens that ignoring the outlying systems in We're Here!'s sphere of influence had been his idea.

Orange shook his head and stood theatrically taller. "You realize what this means, don't you?"

His staff shook their heads.

"It means war."

Before the moment of stunned silence stretched long enough to become too uncomfortable, Rear Admiral Crashpad asked, "Against whom, sir?"

"Well, that's what we need to find out, isn't it?" He looked pointedly at Commodore O'Wow.

In his half century standard of service in We're Here!'s navy, Admiral of the Starry Heavens Sativa Orange had never gone to war. For that matter, We're Here! had never had a war in its entire history. We're Here! had originally been settled by counterculturists, back-to-earthers, feminists, and others who thought everybody should simply be dreadfully nice to one another. And it was far enough out of the way that it didn't have any nearby neighbors to annoy or be annoyed by.

Admiral Orange was head of the navy, and the purpose of a navy is to fight wars. It didn't occur to him that he had to notify the President of the situation, and the President had to take the matter up with the planetary congress before any action could be taken, or that the appropriate first step was for We're Here! to make an appeal to the Confederation of Human Worlds. The main thing on his mind was: *I have under my command a heavy cruiser that, by Confederation Navy standards, is less than a full generation away from being a state-of-the-art light cruiser!*

And what was the point of having such a modern warship if you never get to use it to fight a war?

CHAPTER FOUR

Brigadier Sturgeon and Sergeant Major Shiro stood on the reviewing stand that was centered along one side of the parade ground at Camp Major Pete Ellis. With them stood Colonel Bankey, the Camp Ellis commanding officer, and his top people; Rear Admiral Blankenvoort, commander of the navy supply depot on Thorsfinni's World and senior Confederation military officer; Stor Edval, mayor of Bronnysund; and other distinguished visitors. Even a half-dozen members of Thorsfinni's World's legislature were present. The men and women—Marine, navy, and civilian—who constituted the Camp Ellis base personnel, sat in bleachers flanking the reviewing stand, as did the few military family members allowed to accompany their spouses to the hardship post, and a significant number of interested civilians from Bronnysund.

The steady *tromp-tromp-tromp* of marching feet reverberated off the parade ground and echoed from the surrounding buildings as the Marines of the infantry battalion, composite squadron; headquarters company; transportation company; and the artillery battery that comprised the FIST marched onto the parade ground. The units marched in a straight line from the right of the reviewing stand. Company by company by squadron by battery, they halted at their designated positions and faced left. When they finished, the entire FIST, standing at rigid attention and resplendent in dress reds, was centered on the reviewing stand, facing it.

Admiral Blankenvoort stepped to the front edge of the reviewing stand and made some innocuous remarks about the courage and loyalty of the 34th FIST Marines, how proud everyone was of them, and finished with a remark about how well deserved were the decorations and promotions about to be given to so many. Colonel Bankey remarked about how proud he and his base personnel were to be host to one of the Marine Corps' most honored and decorated units. Mayor Edval then said much the same, though from a civilian's point of view and in fewer words. And, of course, the politicians from New Oslo all had to have their say, so the Marines had been standing at attention for nearly an hour by the time it was Brigadier Sturgeon's turn.

Sturgeon knew all about standing at attention in the ranks for outrageous amounts of time while windbags spouted off about things of which they had precious little knowledge and even less feeling. He scrapped the remarks he had planned to make and ordered, "FIST, PARADE *REST*!" Parade rest, feet at shoulder width and hands clasped behind the back, was still a formal position, but less strenuous and easier to hold than attention.

"Marines," he said, "I am about to award decorations to some of you for heroism displayed during our recent campaign on Kingdom. At the same time I will promote those of you who have been serving in billets above your rank.

"Some of the decorations I will award today are interim. A few of you performed acts of heroism on Kingdom that merit higher decorations than I am authorized to award. In those cases, today I will award you the highest decoration allowed by my authority. Be assured that recommendations have been forwarded to the appropriate authorities and that should those authorities concur, at a later date the award I give you today will be replaced by the decorations you deserve.

"Remain at parade rest unless you hear your name called. If your name is called, come to attention and march to the reviewing stand."

He turned to Shiro. "Sergeant Major, call the roll!"

"Aye aye, sir!" Shiro unrolled a scroll he held clutched in his left hand and began reading names. At each name, someone in the formation came to attention and broke ranks to march to the reviewing stand, where a master sergeant from the base headquarters company directed him to the stairs to the stand. After calling each name, Shiro either read the citation that described what the decoration was and why it was being awarded to the Marine, or gave the rank to which the Marine was being promoted.

Brigadier Sturgeon pinned decorations on those being awarded medals and handed promotion warrants to those being promoted. He was assisted by the family members or special friends of each Marine who had such people present.

The final three people to be called were the three being commissioned, and Charlie Bass was the last of them. They took off their enlisted tunics and donned their new officers' tunics, then had ensigns' silver orbs pinned onto the epaulets; changing into the gold trousers of the officer dress reds would come later.

Newly commissioned Ensign Charlie Bass grinned like an idiot as Katie helped Brigadier Sturgeon button his new tunic and pin on his new silver orbs.

After Bass returned to his position at the front of Company L's third platoon, Brigadier Sturgeon called the FIST to attention, then ordered, "PASS IN REVIEW!"

Commands were shouted and, as one, the Marines faced right and began marching. Almost immediately, the lead company turned a corner to the left, marched forty meters, turned left again, and marched past the reviewing stand. As each company reached the stand, its commander shouted out, "EYES RIGHT!" and heads in the marching formation snapped toward the reviewing stand, only the rightmost rank continuing to look forward. "EYES FRONT!" came the command as each company in turn completed its pass. The military personnel on the reviewing stand raised their hands in salute to Commander van Winkle as he and his staff marched past at the head of the infantry battalion. They held their salutes as the battalion's headquarters company and all three of its line companies marched past.

Seconds later they saluted again as the FIST's composite squadron marched by. Then they saluted the artillery battery and the transportation company. The FIST headquarters company brought up the rear, and was saluted in its turn.

"ATTENTION ON DECK!" Staff Sergeant Wang Hyakowa's call boomed loud enough to echo off the walls and reverberate the length of third platoon's squad bay.

Corporal Rachman Claypoole, on his way back to his fire team's room from the squad leaders' quarters, was facing in the right direction to see for whom the platoon sergeant called attention. His face lit up and he repeated the call, "ATTENTION ON DECK!"

Sergeant "Rat" Linsman, Claypoole's squad leader, was standing in the doorway of the squad leaders' quarters and saw the reason almost at the same time. "ATTENTION ON DECK!" he bellowed so quickly his voice and Claypoole's sounded almost as one.

At the opposite end of the long passageway, Lance Corporal Isadore "Izzy" Godenov poked his head out of his fire team's room, snapped to attention, and echoed the cry.

"AS YOU WERE, PEOPLE!" newly commissioned Ensign Charlie Bass roared. His face turned red. His men had snapped to attention for him before, but always because of respect for him personally—this was the first time Marines had been called to attention for his rank, and he wasn't sure he liked that.

Then he saw the expressions and heard the voices of the Marines who boiled out of their rooms to crowd around him, and realized they were indeed responding to him, not his rank.

"Welcome back, Gu— ah, sir!" Sergeant Lupo "Rabbit" Ratliff, the first squad leader, said, pushing his way through the Marines in his way. He thrust out his hand to shake his platoon commander's hand. "And congratulations on your commission!"

"Outta my way, Rabbit, I saw him first," Linsman said, elbowing his way next to Ratliff. "I'm so damn glad to see you back, ah, sir!"

"Yeah, but I've known him longer. Welcome back—sir!" Sergeant "Hound" Kelly, the gun squad leader, forced his way between the other two sergeants.

Then Bass lost track of exactly who was welcoming him back to third platoon, crowding too tight, forcing Hyakowa and the squad leaders out of the way, pumping his hand, slapping his back. After a couple of moments he managed to free his hands and raise them above his shoulders, palms out.

"All right, people. Back off, will you?" He shot a glance at Hyakowa and the squad leaders, as though accusing them of abandoning him to fend off a serious assault by himself. Then his face split in a broad grin and he looked around at his platoon again. "It's good to be back—right where I belong."

He looked from face to face, remembering names, remembering actions he'd been through with them, *his* Marines! Then he saw six Marines who were hanging back, faces he didn't know, but he knew they were the replacements for Marines who had been killed or were too seriously wounded to return to duty during the campaign on Kingdom.

In his mind's eye he saw the faces of the Marines who weren't there to welcome him home: Lance Corporal Dupont, his longtime communications man, who was killed at the same time Bass had been captured; Corporal Stevenson, from the gun squad, who'd been a PFC when Bass first joined third platoon; Lance Corporals van Impe and Watson, who had also been with the platoon about as long as he had; PFC Gimble, who'd joined the platoon after they first encountered the Skinks on Society 437; Lance Corporal Rodamour and PFC Hayes, for whom Kingdom was their first and only deployment with 34th FIST. Sergeant Bladon and Corporal Goudanis weren't there either—they'd both been so severely wounded on Kingdom they'd been evacuated and nobody knew whether they'd ever be able to return to duty.

His eyes misted over as he remembered them, those men, Marines all, who'd given the last full measure in defense of people they didn't know. He almost shouted angrily at the excited Marines who surrounded him, still enthusiastically welcoming him back, ordered them to knock off their grab-assing and show respect for their dead. But he didn't. He remembered in time that old Marines don't die, they go to hell and regroup. He knew those dead Marines would live forever in the collective memory of the Corps. They'd already been mourned by the platoon, the company, the battalion, the FIST. *He* was the only one who hadn't properly mourned yet. And just then wasn't the time for mourning. He could hold that off until later.

He fixed the new men with a gimlet eye and said firmly, "I'm Gunnery Ser—" Well, he *tried* to say it firmly. He started again, speaking above the raucous laughter of his men. "I'm Ensign Charlie Bass and this is my platoon. Who the hell are you?"

Those nearest the new men stepped aside and pushed them forward so they could meet their new platoon commander.

First a big lance corporal came to attention in front of him. "Sir, I'm Tischler. Gunner, first gun team."

Another lance corporal said, "Zumwald, first fire team, sir."

A barrel-chested PFC of slightly less than average height was next. "PFC Gray, sir. Blasterman, first fire team, first squad."

Next was: "PFC Little, sir. Second fire team, second squad."

Another: "PFC Shoup, sir. Second fire team, first squad."

Finally: "PFC Fisher, sir. Second fire team, second squad."

"Lance Corporal Tischler, PFC Gray, PFC Shoup, PFC Little," Bass said, fixing the names he already knew to the faces he was now seeing for the first time. "I'd say welcome to third platoon, but it seems you've already seen action with us. Gray, Shoup, Little, Fischer, how are your wounds?"

The four looked at him, surprised that he knew they'd been wounded on Kingdom when they hadn't joined the platoon until after he'd disappeared and was presumed dead.

"Fine, sir," each replied. "All healed."

"Glad to hear that. We never know when we'll have to go out again, and it doesn't do to have Marines on light duty heading into harm's way.

"Staff Sergeant Hyakowa tells me you're all settled in your fire or gun teams and there's no reason to move anybody, so I'll accept that." He paused and looked at them. Twenty-nine Marines who depended on him to lead them to successful completion of whatever mission was assigned to them—and bring them back alive and whole. He knew from his experience he could rely on twenty-three of them to do their jobs well enough that he'd be able to fulfill their expectations. Everybody in the company chain of command from the Skipper on down to Hyakowa told him the six replacements the platoon had received on Kingdom were just as good—and that they all had combat experience even before they joined the platoon. Just then, he'd take their word for it—anyway, he had no reason to suspect they were misleading him.

"Well," he said before his thoughts kept him silent long enough to cause discomfort or concern among his men, "I just wanted to come in to say hello and that I'm glad to be back. Now, if nobody else has done it yet, I'm sounding liberty call. Get out of here. I don't expect to see any of you again until morning formation tomorrow." He turned and headed back down the stairs with Hyakowa right behind him.

"COMP-ney, a-ten-HUT!" Gunnery Sergeant Thatcher bellowed the following morning.

" 'TOON, ten-HUT!" the platoon sergeants cried out in turn.

The 110 or so Marines standing in formation behind the barracks snapped to.

" 'TOON sergeants, re-PORT!" Thatcher called.

The platoon sergeants about-faced and called, "Squad leaders, re-PORT!"

"First squad, all present and accounted for!" the first squad leader roared back.

"Second squad, all present and accounted for!"

"Gun squad, all present and accounted for!"

When their squad leaders had reported, the platoon sergeants again faced front.

"First platoon, all present or accounted for!"

"Second platoon, all present or accounted for!"

"Third platoon, all present or accounted for!"

"Assault platoon, all present or accounted for!"

Thatcher ticked them off on his clipboard as the platoon sergeants reported all their men present or accounted for. Finished, he about-faced himself.

The rear door of the barracks opened and Captain Conorado, the company commander, marched out, followed by the company's other five officers. First Sergeant Myer and the company clerks, as usual, didn't attend the morning formation, nor did Supply Sergeant Souavi.

Conorado stopped in front of Thatcher, who brought his right hand up in a crisp salute. Conorado returned the gesture just as sharply and held it. The officers formed a rank to his rear.

"Sir, Company L all present and accounted for!" Thatcher announced loud enough for every man in the formation to hear, even though the man he addressed stood only a pace in front of him.

"Thank you, Gunnery Sergeant," Conorado replied in a voice that carried just as far. "The company is mine. You may take your place." He cut his salute.

"The company is yours. Aye aye, sir!" Thatcher cut his salute, stepped a pace to the rear, pivoted to his right and marched to his place in the formation, just in front of the lead rank of first platoon.

Conorado stood silently for a moment, looking over his company. *His* Marines, who he was so proud of. Again, they had faced that implacable enemy known only as "Skinks," and again they'd defeated them, even though the Skinks had come up with new and horrendous weapons. He'd almost lost this company once, thanks to the machinations of a bureaucrat-scientist he'd offended, but now it was his again, and it seemed it would be his for the rest of his life. If he might never rise above the rank of captain, well, at least he'd be the commander of the best company he'd ever served with.

"At ease!" Conorado finally said. He didn't roar or bellow; still, his voice carried clearly to every man in the formation.

"I have two announcements this morning.

"First, Headquarters, Marine Corps, has notified us that a medal is being struck for the Kingdom campaign. Which is too bad for those of you who are already top heavy and were hoping for just another campaign star on your Marine Expeditionary Medal. You'll just have to find room for another medal." A smile threatened to break out on his face as he looked at several of the senior Marines as he spoke, though he didn't turn around to include Ensign Bass, who had been on more campaigns than most other Marines.

"Second, in light of our most recent experience, next week we will deploy south for training in swamp and jungle warfare. And don't even think of liberty in New Oslo while we're away; we're going farther south, leaving Niflheim and headed for an uninhabited equatorial island called Nidhogge." He allowed the muffled groans to run their course. Swamps and jungles, right. Train for the last war.

That wasn't completely fair—Marines more often than not fought in heavily wooded or watery terrain, and the Skinks seemed to prefer swamps and bogs, so there was a high degree of validity in keeping those wetland skills sharp.

"That is all. COMP-ney, A-ten-HUT!"

The Marines snapped to attention.

"Comp-NEY . . . dis-MISSED!"

The Marines broke from their positions of attention and began moving in controlled chaos, commenting to each other on the announcements, the previous night's liberty, and any of the myriad other things Marines talk about when released from formation. Above the hubbub, the platoon sergeants' voices rang out with last minute orders, followed by the squad leaders' orders and fire team leaders' commands.

They filed back into the barracks in semiorderly manner and headed to their platoons' assembly areas.

There was something Ensign Charlie Bass had to do before the FIST headed for Nidhogge. He didn't say anything to anyone before he left the company area, but First Sergeant Myer saw him go and guessed from his direction where he was headed. Myer gave him a few minutes, then headed out himself.

He found Bass right where he expected to—at the Stones.

Five large, igneous boulders, each standing three meters high and two wide, stood in line along a flagstone walkway. Hillsides covered by a dense grove of firlike trees wrapped behind the Stones from side to side, protecting them from the elements. The front face of each Stone was cut flat, slightly off vertical, and polished until it gleamed like a gem. The faces of the first three, and the top three quarters of the fourth, were engraved with the names of Marines who had died in combat while serving with 34th FIST. Bass squatted in front of the fourth stone, gently brushing his fingertips over the bottom rows of names; the Marines who had given their last on the Kingdom campaign. His fingers paused over one name and a chill ran up his spine.

The name was his.

"But I'm not dead," he whispered.

Padding softly, Myer came up behind him unheard and heard what Bass whispered.

"Damn straight you're not," the Top said gruffly. "I told them not to put your name up there, I *told* them you were too ornery and ugly to get killed by any damn Skink rail gun. But would they listen to me? *Nooo!* Now they have to take it off and mess up the whole Stone."

Bass turned his head and looked up at Myer; his eyes seemed to gleam like the face of the Stones. The Top looked away from him, back at the Stone. There must be something in the air at the Stones, he thought, something that got into his eyes to make them water like that. The same thing had happened to him when he last visited there, and watched as the stonemasons carved the names.

"Can they do that?" Bass asked. "Remove a name, I mean."

Myer pointed at a spot just over head high. There was a gap between names, wide enough for another name. It rippled slightly in the smoothness of the Stone's face, and was sunk a bit below the surrounding surface. Bass stood to look at the gap and nodded.

"They'll do the same thing on your name, Charlie."

"Until it goes back for real."

"Maybe. But they'll be carving on the fifth Stone before that happens."

Bass dropped back to a squat and brushed his fingertips over the newest names once more.

"Marines don't die, we go to hell and regroup. I'll see you again, then," he promised the Marines whose names he touched. He stood and in a thick voice said to Myer, "Let's head back to the company and do what we can to make it a long, long time before any names go onto that fifth Stone."

Anatoly Sibir called his boss and told him he was too sick to come into work. In fact he wasn't sick, except perhaps from love. Or maybe it was just infatuation, one could never quite tell with people so young. He was in love with Sonja Koryak. Or maybe it was simple lust. Sonja was a year and a half younger than Anatoly and still a university student, though she was going to graduate in the spring. It was not at all happenstance that she skipped classes on the same day Anatoly called out sick. The two lived in the city of Neu-Kiev, near the southern border of Ammon, and planned to meet and spend the day together in the wilderness without any of their elders—those stuffy original Frères Jacques—lecturing them on how dangerous it was outside the borders of Ammon.

When you're young and in love, there is no risk too great to take to be alone with your love.

Their rendezvous was at the southern edge of town. Anatoly added Sonja's basket to the blanket and wine bottle he'd already stored in his scoot's trunk, then she mounted behind him; the scoot was just the right size for two, if they were friendly enough. The road ended abruptly five kilometers south, where the foresting operation had recently been terminated until the tree farm within its boundaries became mature enough to harvest. But the land was level and recently cleared, so they continued another ten kilometers, to the edge of the forest, then turned along it toward the cliffs of the Salainen Mountains, a short distance farther to the west, where Anatoly had recently found a secluded glade. It was just a brief walk up the slope of the mountainside, and he thought it was exactly right as a trysting spot for two young lovers such as Sonja and himself.

When they got there they discovered he wasn't the only one who'd found the glade and thought it was ideal—it was already occupied by another young couple, who were so engrossed with each other they didn't notice they had company.

Anatoly and Sonja discreetly withdrew and decided to climb higher. Surely that would place them far enough from the possibility of interruption.

Right at the foot of a slope the trees bent away to form a cozy cul-de-sac, and they set out their picnic. After they ate, they excused themselves to go politely behind bushes for relief. Anatoly came back excited, and insisted Sonja come see what he'd found.

He'd gone uphill a short way and found a saddle from which he could see into the valley beyond. She was reluctant, but he was insistent. He took the blanket when they went to explore.

On the saddle's other side was virgin territory. It truly looked as though the foot of man had never trod there. The foliage of the trees and other growth was scarlet, pink, amber, blue, and all of the ten billion greens. The trees were spaced as if in an orchard, and the undergrowth was almost polite in the open spaces between them. The ground cover was spongy underfoot.

Sonja's eyes glowed as she took in the natural beauty that surrounded them. Anatoly's eyes gleamed as he took in the natural beauty of his love.

It wasn't long before they had the blanket laid on the ground, themselves laid on it, and their clothing disheveled and then some.

They broke from a blissful clench and Sonja opened her eyes to drink in more of the beauty of their surroundings. Instead, her eyes opened wider in horror and her mouth opened in a soundless scream. Anatoly's eyes were too busy drinking in the beauty of her breasts to notice, so he was unaware of their danger until a stream of greenish fluid splashed across both of them and he arched his back in agony. It may have been a kindness that he was in too much pain to see the acid that splashed across Sonja's face and breasts and ate them away.

CHAPTER FIVE

Three months after the discovery of the remains of Samar Volga in the Haltia region of Maugham's Station, Tarah Shiskanova, an analyst third class in the Development Control Division of the Department of Colonial Development, Population Control, and Xenobiological Studies, was surfing through routine reports from recently colonized planets—those that could reasonably be called "frontier worlds" even though many of them were well within the outer boundaries of Human Space—to determine where to file them when she stopped to read an Unexplained Expiration report all the way through. The report detailed the curious and somewhat gruesome death of two young colonists on the colony world called Maugham's Station.

There wasn't anything all that unusual about the report; colonists did occasionally meet death in unexpected and sometimes spectacular manner. But something about that one niggled at her. She read through it again, wracking her brain in search of what it was. Oh, *yes*! It was the second Unexplained Expiration report from Maugham's Station that had crossed her desk in recent weeks. But, no, three unexplained deaths on a colony world over a period of several weeks was hardly far enough out of routine to catch her attention, so what was it about this one?

She went into the files to retrieve the earlier report. The first report gave details of the demise of one Samar Volga, a botanist on a solo study of the flora of an unexplored area of Maugham's Station. She paused at that, wondering if it was routine for biologists to venture alone into unexplored areas, decided it didn't matter, then compared the two reports.

This time she noted a detail that had seemed insignificant when she'd seen it in isolation. The remains of the young couple and the earlier biologist showed signs of having been eaten by acid. The type of acid wasn't noted.

Odd, she thought. What was it that seemed significant about that? She read through the two reports again. Another mental synapse clicked and she remembered something else that, at the time, had seemed to have no bearing whatsoever on her job.

A year or so earlier she had been engaged in a passionate affair with an army colonel who worked in the Heptagon. One night, after a particularly enthusiastic bout of lovemaking, he'd said something about a mysterious danger that had struck a couple of frontier worlds—human worlds, but on the fringes of Human Space. Invaders who used acid weapons.

At least that's what it sounded like he said; he was rather vague about it, and she wasn't listening all that closely. When she'd asked for clarification, he quickly backed off and told her to forget he'd said anything, it was classified Ultra Secret, Need to Know, and he wasn't supposed to know anything about it himself. She was so filled with an excess of afterglow from the sex, she'd readily forgotten about it.

Until now.

What *had* he been talking about? A rebellion? No, he said a couple of worlds. A war between human worlds? No, she would have heard about a war between human worlds if there'd been one, no matter how obscure were the worlds involved. An alien invasion?

She snorted a laugh. Everybody knew there was no other sentience anywhere humanity was likely to make contact, maybe not even in the entire galaxy. Well, maybe somewhere in the other spiral arm, but humanity wouldn't encounter *them* for many millennia to come. If they even existed. In reality, alien invasions only happened in some of the more lurid trids and books.

Still, the colonel had said the business of acid weapons was classified Ultra Secret, Need to Know, so it must be somehow significant. He *had* said something about acid weapons, hadn't he?

Tarah Shiskanova decided that her reports were, possibly, something the military should know about.

So instead of uploading the new file into the Open Directory of

Unexplained Expirations, where reports of odd fatalities normally went, she annotated it as of possible military interest, attached a copy of the earlier report to it, and queued it up the line for review.

It was a slow month, and Fourth Assistant Director for Control Himan Birkenstock was seriously bored. It was three more weeks until his scheduled holiday—he was taking his wife and children to the dizzney on the moon's far side—and he wasn't sure he could last three more weeks without going completely vacuum-crazy. He desperately needed something to do, something to get him out of the office for an hour or three. Thus it happened that, without reading beyond her annotation recommending referral to the Heptagon for disposition, he jumped on the report Tarah Shiskanova had forwarded.

A distant cousin of Birkenstock's was a lieutenant commander in the Confederation Navy who had been posted to the Heptagon six months earlier. Ever since, the two had been promising each other they'd get together for lunch some day "soon." Some day soon hadn't come yet.

Birkenstock immediately punched up the Heptagon directory and did a search for Lieutenant Commander Stewart "Soupy" Gullkarl, CN. In less than a second a listing appeared in the Directorate for Orbital Weaponry Assessment and Evaluation. He touched the comm link in the listing, and in only a few more seconds got a response.

"Lieutenant Commander Gullkarl. How can I help you, sir?" The gray in the neatly trimmed beard shown in the projection belied the youthful features of the barely remembered oval face.

Birkenstock blinked in surprise; he hadn't realized his cousin was old-fashioned enough to wear spectacles instead of having his eyes corrected.

"Soupy? It's Himan," he said.

"Himan?" Birkenstock distinctly heard an unspoken *Who?* after his name before Gullkarl's face lit up in recognition. "Himan Birkenstock! Good to hear from you, cousin. You know, we really do need to get together for lunch sometime."

"Well, cousin, that's why I'm calling. How about today?"

"Don't know." Light reflected off the lenses of Gullkarl's spectacles as he shook his head. "I've got quite a bit of work here." That was their usual excuse for not meeting; one or the other always seemed to have a lot of work to do, though that was hardly Birkenstock's problem just now.

"And I want to add to it."

"You do?" Gullkarl looked at him with a mix of interest and curiosity. He wasn't really busy with work, he had a tentative "discreet" luncheon meeting planned with a lieutenant commander—female—in the Directorate of Pregnancy and Sexually Transmitted Disease Prevention and Control. He was hoping that the "meeting" would actually happen and turn into a *very* long and intimate luncheon.

"Yes. One of my analysts flagged a"— he looked at the report to see what it was and where it was from— "an Unexplained Expiration report from Maugham's Station as being of possible military interest. I don't know who to route it to, and I was hoping you could give me some direction."

"All right. Queue it over to me and I'll take a look when I get a moment."

Birkenstock leaned toward the projection and lowered his voice. "Soupy, I need to get out of the office; I'd rather walk it over."

Gullkarl surreptitiously glanced at a clock and saw he had enough time. "Can you come over now? I can't promise lunch, though."

"I'll let you know when I'm five minutes out."

"Make it six minutes. Come to the southwest entrance." That was how long it would take him to check with the lovely lieutenant commander and get from his office to the southwest entrance to the Heptagon to verify his visitor.

Hiram Birkenstock and Lieutenant Commander Soupy Gullkarl reached the guard station at the Heptagon's southwest entrance almost simultaneously. Rather than begin the verifications and other formalities involved in securing a visitor's pass for Birkenstock and admitting him through the guard station, Gullkarl came out.

"My meeting got canceled," he said sourly. "Let's go to lunch."

Sixty thousand people worked in the Heptagon and its immediate annexes, and a small city of shops and eateries had sprouted up around it to service them. Gullkarl steered them to a medium-size place that advertised a traditional Eastern European menu. Birkenstock let

Gullkarl order for both of them, since he was unfamiliar with Eastern European cuisine, preferring traditional British himself.

They made small talk about seldom seen relatives while they waited for their meal, and even smaller talk while they ate. Only after the dishes were cleared away and they were enjoying a cup of real coffee did they get to their ostensible reason for meeting. Birkenstock popped a crystal into his reader and handed it to Gullkarl.

The navy officer read through the report and looked up at his cousin. "What's supposed to be of military interest in this?" he asked.

"Tarah, Tarah Shiskanova—she's the analyst who flagged it—thought she saw something." He took the reader back and scanned the report beyond its what and where for the first time. "Here it is," he handed it back, "the bit about acid."

Gullkarl studied the minor note for a long moment, wondering why on earth anyone would think the military would be interested. Then he blinked. Right. He'd heard something, a vague, whispered rumor. There was somebody out there using acid guns. He nodded and almost snorted. Right. An alien invasion. Absurd. Absolutely absurd. And that was being kind. *Everybody* knew there was no such thing as sentient aliens. Still, there was that whispered rumor.

"Can I have the crystal?" he asked, returning the reader. "I'll check it out."

Birkenstock nodded. "It's a copy." He popped the crystal and handed it over.

They chatted over a second cup of coffee, wrangled over who would pick up the check—Birkenstock won, he was certain he could charge it to his division as a military liaison expense—and went their separate ways, vowing to get together soon for another lunch. Maybe Gullkarl could come to dinner sometime and, yes, he could bring a lady friend.

Lieutenant Commander Stewart "Soupy" Gullkarl, fully aware of the pun, stewed over the report and what to do about it for two days before deciding to go upstairs with it. He didn't literally go upstairs—"upstairs" was the glass-walled office at the end of the row of desks of which his was one. Captain Wilma Arden occupied the glass-walled office. She sometimes mused over the irony that an office with walls she could see through in all directions was a career dead end.

She didn't realize it when Gullkarl rapped his knuckles on the frame of her open door, but her career was about to take a very dramatic change in direction and progression.

"Enter!" she called.

"Excuse me, ma'am," Gullkarl said as he took the seat she waved him toward. "Someone at Colonial Development passed a report to me and I can't figure out what to do with it." He gave her the crystal when she extended her hand.

Arden morphed the console out of her desktop and popped the crystal into it. "I don't see anything about orbital weaponry. Why would anyone give it to us?"

Gullkarl lifted his hands in embarrassment. "He didn't know who to queue it to. We're distant cousins, so he asked if I could direct him to the appropriate office."

"Hmm." She read through the reports again and this time noticed the bit about acid. She'd heard the rumor too. She looked up and swiveled her chair to look out the window toward . . . toward . . . She knew all the constellations and could name every major star she saw in the night sky, but she was no astrogator and had no idea what stars or constellations lurked invisibly in the daytime sky where she looked.

Wilma Arden was a navy captain. She wasn't supposed to wonder what to do, she was supposed to act like she knew exactly what to do—even if she hadn't the foggiest notion. She spun back to Gullkarl and slapped the palms of her hands on her desktop. "Thank you, Lieutenant Commander," she said firmly. "Your 'distant cousin' was right in referring this to the military, and you were right in bringing it to my attention. I'll take care of it from here."

"Yes ma'am." He stood, understanding that he was dismissed, and came to attention. "By your leave, ma'am?"

She nodded curtly, and he marched out of his commander's office, glad to have that crystal off his hands. A few minutes after he sat back at his desk, it occurred to him to wonder whether he'd promised cousin Himan he'd get back to him on the final disposition of the report. Then he shook his head. No, Birkenstock hadn't seemed to have any notion what the report was really about and had probably forgotten all about it.

He was right.

*　　*　　*

Commander Moon Happiness liked to think he had the best job in the We're Here! navy—commander of the heavy cruiser *Goin'on*, We're Here!'s most advanced starship. Just then, though, he wasn't as happy about his command as he had been. Admiral of the Starry Heavens Sativa Orange, Chief of Naval Operations for We're Here!, had taken personal command of the mission to locate the current home port of the *Broken Missouri*, the pirate freighter that was hauling rare ores from the planet designated 43q15x17–32—at least Admiral Orange and Commander Moon had independently concluded that's what the unmarked-but-nonetheless-identified *Broken Missouri* was doing, though Moon kept to himself his opinion that she wasn't a pirate ship—and made the *Goin'on* his flagship for the mission.

Happiness was unhappy because Orange was unhappy. Not because he commiserated with Admiral Orange, but because the admiral was unhappy with *him*. Admiral Orange believed that the *Goin'on* should have already located the *Broken Missouri*'s home port, and had made known his suspicion that her failure to do so was due to either dereliction or incompetence on the part of her commander. So Commander Happiness was justifiably concerned that instead of being promoted to captain, as he should be as commander of We're Here!'s most advanced warship, he might be relieved of his command, which would effectively terminate his career.

Admiral Orange, in expressing his displeasure with Happiness, said more than once that he had forgotten more about being a ship's commander than the *Goin'on*'s current commander had learned. Which was true as far as it went. Unfortunately for the sake of accuracy, what Admiral Orange remembered was less than what Commander Happiness knew. One detail that Admiral Orange had forgotten was, once a starship jumped into Beamspace, it was impossible to follow.

When the *Goin'on* reported back to We're Here!, the admiral had come aboard with his primary staff and ordered the starship back to the Rock, which he called by its official designation. They'd only waited for nine days standard before the *Broken Missouri*, still cloaked, reappeared and headed for the planet. Admiral Orange wasn't impressed by the freighter's stealth capability or by the skill demonstrated by the *Goin'on*'s crew in spotting it.

"Why didn't you pick her up earlier?" he growled when he realized the starship must have been in Space-3 for three or four days before she was detected.

They watched as the unmarked starship docked with the equally unmarked space station. They waited while the freighter took on its cargo. They followed discreetly when the *Broken Missouri* headed out-system for her jump into Beamspace. When she jumped, Admiral Orange waited with growing impatience for the *Goin'on* to follow. He finally demanded to know what the delay was.

Commander Happiness did his best to control his expression, but wasn't able to keep some astonishment from showing. "But, sir, we can't follow a ship in Beamspace!"

"Of course you can," Admiral Orange admonished Commander Happiness.

"Sir?" Happiness asked, confused. Everybody knew starships couldn't be tracked in Beamspace.

"It's simple. You enter Beamspace on the same trajectory your quarry enters it. That is how you find its destination."

Commander Happiness blinked. That wouldn't work, but he wasn't about to tell the only admiral of the starry heavens in the entire history of his world that he was thinking from the wrong end of his spinal column. "Yessir," he unhappily replied. He ordered his astroga-tor, Lieutenant Sunshine Stems'n'seeds, to plot the course.

"Aye aye, sir," replied Lieutenant Stems'n'seeds. "How far do you want us to jump?"

Therein lay the rub. The *Broken Missouri* could jump back into Space-3 anywhere from one light-year distant to twenty or more lights, and nobody had any way of knowing without being informed by some-one privy to the freighter's astrogation plan. Even then, the vagaries of Beamspace were such that where a starship returned to Space-3 would vary to some extent from a true straight line. If that wasn't enough, when she made her jump back into Beamspace following the brief course correction for which she reentered Space-3, the *Broken Missouri* could jump in any direction. Again, there was no way for anybody to know—or even make an educated guess—without, again, access to her astrogation plan.

Commander Happiness was in a very bad position. No matter what he told his astrogator, he was going to be wrong. He swallowed, wondering if he'd be allowed to wear a spacesuit when he was keel-hauled, and asked, "Sir, how far does the admiral want us to jump?"

The look that Admiral of the Starry Heavens Orange gave him was one that had sent many a staff officer scurrying back to quarters for a quick shower and change of undergarments. The voice in which he replied was cold enough to fracture continent-size ice sheets. "This is your ship, Captain. How far do you normally jump?"

How far the *Goin'on* jumped depended on how far she was going, how great the need for precision was, and whether she had any escort destroyers. Happiness glanced at the starchart to see where other gravity wells were relative to the evidently mineral-rich planet they had under observation and picked a destination midway between it and the next major gravity well that could have a negative impact on the starship's reentry into Space-3.

"Make it four point one lights," he ordered.

"Four point one lights. Aye aye, sir," Stems'n'seeds replied. "Jump in five minutes."

Happiness turned to Orange. "If the admiral will return to his cabin, sir."

"The admiral will remain on the bridge, Captain," Orange said in a barely less frigid voice. He proceeded to strap himself into the Skipper's jump couch.

Commander Happiness unhappily looked about the bridge. The other jump couches were all occupied by officers and crew who actually had jobs to perform during the jump. He came to the sad conclusion that he was the only person present on the bridge whose presence wasn't vital during a jump, and headed for the executive officer's cabin, which he was sharing since Admiral Orange occupied his.

Ten minutes later, no worse for the experience of a jump than usual, Happiness emerged from his cabin, wondering why the officer-of-the-deck hadn't restored ship's gravity. He found out—and almost lost it—when he entered the bridge.

Essential crew were carefully selected for their ability to withstand the gut-wrenching effects of jumps. Admiral Orange hadn't made many jumps since he'd been assigned to planetside duty as deputy G1 of the previous CNO fifteen years earlier. The single jump the *Goin'on* had made between We're Here! and the vicinity of the Rock had, purely coincidentally, come as the admiral was taking a nap. This was the first jump he'd made while conscious in a decade and a half. That, combined with the null-g required during jumps, had a powerful effect on the admiral, and the entire contents of his upper digestive tract ejected themselves rather spectacularly into the close space of the bridge. That caused two of the bridge crew to eject theirs, and that in turn set off the regurgitative reflex in everybody else.

The air and effluvia scrubbers were working as hard as they could to clear both stench and floating globules from the bridge, but with the contents of six stomachs wafting about, it was going to take a while.

Happiness wasted no time. He picked up a comm unit and pressed the appropriate button. "Med, Captain. We have six class-one jump accidents on the bridge. Get appropriate personnel and equipment up here to deal with the situation. Do it now."

"Captain, Med," came the reply. "Six class-one jump accidents on the bridge, aye. Appropriate personnel and equipment are on their way." The ship's surgeon managed to say all that without a hint of the incredulity she felt at the—in her experience—unprecedented event.

Nearly two hours standard later, all the members of the bridge crew were fully recovered. Admiral Orange was still being attended to in his cabin.

There's not much for a starship's crew to do in Beamspace. Collisions with space debris were unlikely, as no debris was known to exist in Beamspace. Some astrophysicists believe space debris does exist in Beamspace and collisions with such debris is why infrequently a starship that enters Beamspace never returns to Space-3. So the loss of the bridge and its crew for two hours constituted no more than a minor annoyance. It had the beneficial side effect of giving the med section something to do. Once he ordered gravity restored, Commander Happiness put the rest of the crew to work on policing the starship and routine maintenance.

A few minutes less than sixteen hours after jumping into Beamspace, the *Goin'on* jumped back into Space-3. This time, sedated at his own request, Admiral Orange stayed in his cabin.

Lieutenant Stems'n'seeds double-checked the astrogation computer's calculations and informed Commander Happiness they'd reentered Space-3 no more than three light-minutes from their target point.

Commander Happiness complimented her on the accuracy of her astrogation—three light-minutes was very precise over 4.1 light-years.

Then everybody waited anxiously while Ensign Freelion worked his magic with the sensors. Their anxiety wasn't caused by what they expected Freelion to find, but rather Admiral Orange's reaction when he learned that Freelion didn't find anything. But Ensign Freelion surprised everybody.

"Sir, traces of recent passage!" Freelion yelped.

"What?" Happiness squawked. He pushed himself out of his jump couch and managed to grab the back of Freelion's before his momentum carried him past. He looked over the radar officer's shoulder at his displays.

There it was, signs of rapidly dispersing electromagnetic radiation showing where a starship returned from Beamspace, burned its forward thrusters to cut its velocity, and turned 68 degrees high starboard onto a new trajectory.

"Get a lock on that pattern," Happiness ordered before he could be overcome with sheer incredulity at the unlikeliness of jumping out of Beamspace in the same location as the ship they were following.

"Aye," Freelion said, and did something with his controls. "Locked, sir," he said a few seconds later.

"Lieutenant Stems'n'seeds, take the con and get us a pursuit vector."

"I have the con," Stems'n'seeds replied, awe in her voice. "Will maneuver to a pursuit trajectory."

"I'm going to tell the admiral." Happiness left the bridge.

"See? I told you it was easy," Admiral Orange said when told of the track they'd found. "You may return to the bridge, Captain. I will stay here until after the jump into Beamspace." He fumbled on a shelf beside his bed for the buzzer that connected him with the med section—he wanted to be sedated again before the jump.

Their luck ran out. There was no sign of a starship transiting into, out of, or through Space-3 when they reemerged into it seven light-years farther along. The only occupied world in range was the colony world of Maugham's Station, seven lights beyond their present position. A quick check of the *Atlas of the Populated and Explored Planets of Human Space, Nineteenth Edition* showed that the government and populace were not the sort to engage in the piracy that had taken the *Broken Missouri*.

Admiral Orange was convinced that the failure to find the freighter's second jump point was entirely due to the incompetence of either Commander Happiness or Lieutenant Stems'n'seeds. He ordered a series of one-light jumps along the trajectory of *Broken Missouri*'s last jump, beginning from the place where the freighter had entered Beamspace and continuing six lights beyond Maugham's Station.

Naturally, they found no traces whatsoever.

Admiral Orange ordered a return to We're Here! to assemble a destroyer escort. The next time, they'd have a far better chance of following the pirate ship no matter where she went.

CHAPTER SIX

The preparations for the FIST's movement to the uninhabited equatorial island of Nidhogge were complete and the Marines were just waiting for transportation.

"Waiting" was the key word.

"Hurry up, hurry up, hurry up," Lance Corporal "Wolfman" MacIlargie groused. He was sitting at his tiny desk in third fire team, second squad's room, positioned so he could look out into the passageway beyond without having to turn his head. A reader was on his desk, loaded and lit, but he wasn't reading. Everything else he wasn't taking on the training exercise was secured in the company supply room, along with everyone else's belongings. Everything he was taking was in his pack or attached to his gear webbing, both of which, along with his helmet, were in a ditty bag under his rack. The ditty bag was necessary, because the pack and webbing were chameleoned but the bag wasn't— he wouldn't have to grope to find his gear when it was time to move out.

Lance Corporal "Hammer" Schultz was sitting at his own desk. Unlike MacIlargie, however, the big man was hunched over his reader, studying Fingshway's recently published analysis of the classic *Technology and War*, by the twentieth-century military scholar Martin van Creveld. While part of him wished he'd read the original before the Diamunde war a few years earlier, he still found it useful because the Skinks kept coming up with technological innovations. He ignored MacIlargie's complaints.

Corporal Rachman Claypoole, like his men, sat at his desk. He was working on a problem in the Marine Corps Institute's squad leaders' tactics course. He hadn't planned on making a career of the Marines, but he was stuck, along with everyone else in 34th FIST, possibly for life. If he had to stay in anyway, unlike Schultz, he wanted to get promoted, maybe even get commissioned someday.

"Marines always have to hurry up to get ready to go. Then we sit here with our thumbs up our asses waiting for the navy to get around to picking us up," MacIlargie continued.

"That's why when I'm a staff sergeant, you'll still be a lance corporal," Claypoole said without looking up from his problem. Then he remembered and shot a glance at Schultz. "Not that there's anything wrong with being a career lance corporal, of course." Schultz was adamant about not getting promoted; he liked being a lance corporal.

MacIlargie snorted. "You, a staff sergeant? Sure. You'll be old and gray by then and I'll be a brigadier. I'll promote you just because I remember how hard you tried to be a good fire team leader. Then I'll put you in charge of issuing athletic equipment, or something else where you won't be able to screw things up too badly."

Claypoole slowly turned his head to look at MacIlargie, then equally slowly turned back to his reader.

"'The independent worlds of Frump de Dump and Spangle have been waging war against each other on the unpopulated world of Ratatat,'" he read aloud. "'After several unsuccessful diplomatic attempts on the part of the Confederation of Human Worlds to bring about a cessation of hostilities, 17th FIST, embarked on the CNSS *Corporal S. A. Jones*, an amphibious landing ferry, has been deployed on a peace-making mission. After a week of fierce fighting, 17th FIST has been successful in forcing a cease-fire.

"'You are a squad leader in first platoon, Alpha Company. First platoon, reinforced by a UAV team, is providing security for the commander of the Frump de Dump forces, which is en route through heavily wooded hills to a meeting at FIST headquarters with the Spangle commander to make the cease-fire permanent. The UAV scouts the way. Halfway to FIST HQ, the UAV's infrared sensors show what could be a company-size unit in position next to the road five kilometers ahead of your current position. The platoon commander has the UAV investigate more closely while he prepares to assess the threat and makes a plan to, if necessary, neutralize the possible threat. The UAV clearly shows a company of Spangle soldiers in ambush position in a saddle between two hills overlooking the road from the left side.

"'The platoon commander alerts the Frump de Dump commander, and deploys the platoon ahead. He assigns the gun squad to set a base of fire on the military crest of the hill overlooking the saddle. He takes second squad to the gun squad's left, from which he will assault the ambush from the flank. Your squad, first squad, is sent across the road from the ambush to catch the ambushers in a cross fire. Your squad is not to open fire until you receive the platoon commander's signal.

"'You are nearly in position when you hear on the platoon net that the gun squad is approaching the hill's military crest. Suddenly, two things happen simultaneously. One: you hear a firefight begin beyond the gun squad's position, where you think second squad is maneuvering to its assault position. Two: you lose all communications except for your squad net.

"'It is absolutely essential that the commander of the Frump de Dump forces reach FIST HQ without being ambushed. Sergeant, what do you do now?'" Claypoole turned from his reader and looked at MacIlargie. "All right, brigadier-to-be, what *do* you do now?" he asked smugly.

"*What?*" MacIlargie squawked.

"You heard me. That's a problem in the squad leaders' tactics course. I have to come up with a solution that will allow the convoy to make it through. If you're brigadier material, you must have a solution to the problem. So what would you do?"

"I—I . . . No comm?"

"That's right. Except for squad comm."

"I . . ." He looked at Claypoole, appalled.

"That's why I'm going to be a staff sergeant when you're still a lance corporal." Claypoole turned back to his reader.

He flinched when Schultz rumbled: "Break up the ambush."

MacIlargie wasn't the only one having trouble with "hurry-up-and-wait," but Ensign Charlie Bass's problem had absolutely nothing to do with waiting for the navy to provide the promised transportation to Nidhogge.

"Sir," he said to Captain Conorado, "the brigadier commissioned me as an ensign."

"Yes he did, Charlie." Conorado smiled. "Congratulations. It's well past time you became an officer." They were in the company commander's office.

"But, sir, I'm a . . . I'm an ensign."

"That's right." Conorado cocked an eyebrow in question.

Bass worked his jaw. This was proving harder than he'd expected. "But, sir—"

"Charlie, we're alone." Conorado nodded toward the closed door. "My name's Lew."

"Yessir, I know that," Bass said, confused.

"So use it."

"Sir?" A light blinked on. "Oh. I mean, right. Lew."

Conorado was mostly successful in keeping his amusement at the difficulty Bass had saying his first name to his face. "When officers are alone we generally use first names."

"First names. Yessir—ah, Lew." Bass had spent entirely too many years calling officers "sir," or in the case of junior officers, "mister," to be immediately comfortable calling his company commander by his given name. But he was a Marine, he was accustomed to accomplishing the merely difficult immediately, and just needed a clarification.

"Does that mean the next time I run into the brigadier in the officers' club, I should call him Ted?"

Conorado had to laugh at that. "Discretion, Charlie. I think for now you should restrict your familiarity to company-grade officers. Unless, of course, the brigadier invites you to call him Ted."

"Yessir—Lew." The corner of Bass's mouth twitched at his slip, but he managed to get the captain's first name in immediately.

"So what was it you wanted to see me about, Charlie?"

"Well, s— Lew, I'm an *ensign*—"

"So you are." Conorado was pretty sure what was coming and was having trouble not laughing.

"Well, Lew—" Why was the Skipper making this so difficult? "—I don't *like* being an ensign. I was a gunnery sergeant, a senior NCO—"

"Three different times, as I recall." Conorado gestured for Bass to continue.

Bass briefly gave him a hard look; he hadn't needed to be reminded he'd twice been busted from gunnery sergeant. "Well, Lew, the thing is, I feel like I'm starting over again. I've been in this man's Marine Corps for too long to have to start over again."

"You *are* starting over again, Charlie. You're starting as an officer."

"But—But . . . You know, Lew," he shifted his chair closer and leaned his elbows on the desktop, his hands raised almost as though he was going to clasp them in prayer, "ever since I was a salty corporal, I figured I outranked most ensigns—at least, I knew as much as most, and more than a lot of them."

Conorado couldn't help it, he broke out in laughter. After a moment he managed to say, "I've been there, Charlie. I thought the same thing when I was a salty corporal." He lowered his face and shook his head. When he looked back up, he wasn't smiling. "But we both know better now, ensigns—*Marine* ensigns—*do* know more than most corporals, no matter how salty."

Bass tried so hard not to glare he looked sullen instead. "I'm sure you remember, Lew," he kept to his point, "the brigadier said he would commission me a lieutenant."

Conorado clasped his hands behind his neck and looked up at the ceiling while he reconstructed in his mind just what the brigadier had actually said. He lowered his hands to his desktop and his eyes to Bass. "As I remember it, Charlie, he said he *could* do that."

"But—But, sir—Lew, he *knows* I don't want to be an ensign."

Conorado leaned forward earnestly. "He also said he was making you an ensign no matter *what* you wanted."

"But—"

Conorado raised a hand to cut him off. "Charlie, you're right, the brigadier did imply that he'd promote you to lieutenant. I'm sure he will. Either at what he deems to be an appropriate time or when he *has* the time. A FIST commander is a very busy man, you know that."

"Yessir—Lew. I know he's very bus—"

"I'm not going to go to Commander van Winkle with this, Ensign."

"But—" Bass's jaw snapped as he bit off whatever he'd been about to say. The Skipper had just called him *Ensign*. That made their conversation official, brought it into the sphere of strict military discipline, and meant no further discussion was permitted.

"Yessir. I understand, sir." Bass stood. "By your leave, sir?"

Conorado nodded. Bass turned and left the company commander's office. He remembered to leave the door open behind him.

"So how'd it go, Charlie?" Top Myer asked.

Bass snapped something inarticulate and left the company office without even looking at the first sergeant.

Myer watched him leave, then pushed himself to his feet and went to the door to Conorado's office. He suspected he knew what Bass's visit was about. "He'll get over it, Skipper."

"I know he will, Top," Conorado replied.

The navy finally got its act together, as it always does, no matter how unlikely it seems to the Marines who have to wait, and a fleet of twenty-two Essays landed at Boynton Field, the Camp Ellis airfield. They dropped their ramps, and forty-two navy Dragons powered off, to form up with the twenty-four Marine Dragons waiting in formation. The Marines of 34th FIST, waiting to board the Dragons, exchanged knowing glances and looked toward the navy men. The navy may have finally shown up, but they *still* didn't have their act together; the navy Dragons simply weren't as sharply lined up as the waiting Marine Dragons. The Marines had seen sailors march. They weren't very sharp at that either.

The navy thought the Marines were arrogant. The Marines looked at how the Dragons lined up not quite on plumb, remembered all the bouncing in the sailors' nearly ragged ranks when they marched, and thought that what the sailors perceived as arrogance was simply an expression of natural superiority. Some semithoughtful Marines thought the navy always made them wait out of pure spite. Others, more thoughtful, maintained that Marines always had to wait for the navy because the navy, being so much larger, was cumbersome and naturally took longer to perform the most basic functions than the lean and mean Marine Corps.

Whatever the cause of the waiting, the navy was there with its Essays and Dragons, and the Marines began boarding. The Marine formations were well lined up and their movements crisp. They boarded in short order. They'd show those squids what sharp looked like.

The sailors, of course, knew what the Marines were thinking, and didn't do a thing to give their cargo—they wouldn't dignify the Marines by thinking of them as "passengers"—a smooth ride, either during the Dragons' boarding of the Essays or the three-hour suborbital flight to equatorial Nidhogge.

By the time the Essays touched down on the ocean beyond the horizon from Nidhogge, the Marines, who had suffered the bumpy journey in the cramped, uncomfortable, dimly-lit-with-no-view-outside Dragons, were ready to fight and kill just about anybody. Enemy soldiers, Skinks, sailors, they didn't care; though most of them would have taken squids as their first pick.

The Dragons roared off the Essays on their air cushions and raced in waves for the unseen shore. The first ashore were the blaster companies of the infantry battalion. The first wave of Dragons, more than half of them Marine, sped inshore half a kilometer before stopping to drop their rear ramps long enough for the Marines to race off. The Raptors of 34th FIST's composite squadron roared overhead as the infantrymen ran to form a defensive perimeter. The first wave of Dragons turned about and sped back to shore, to be replaced in moments by the Dragons carrying the battalion headquarters company and the artillery battery. The third wave was ground elements of the composite squadron, which immediately began preparing an expeditionary airfield, and the FIST headquarters company. As soon as the last Dragons were out of the way, the squadron's hoppers landed behind the budding airfield. The Marine Dragons remained on the beach when they got back there, while the navy Dragons returned to the waiting Essays for return to their home at the Naval Supply Depot on Niflheim.

The time from when the first Dragon dropped its ramp to when the last Marine stepped off the last Dragon of the third wave was hardly longer than the time it had taken the Marines to board the Dragons back at Camp Ellis.

Brigadier Sturgeon checked the reports that came in from his subordinate commanders and nodded. His FIST had arrived for this simulated combat assault in three elements: the ground forces, which came in via Essays and Dragons; the Raptors, which had departed Camp Ellis some hours earlier to make the flight on their own; and the hoppers, which had left home the day before. All arrived in good order. Had they landed against a live opponent rather than on an unpopulated island, they would have achieved the desired surprise and struck with shocking force. He was going to have to give everyone a "Well done." Even the navy performed well.

Now for the next phase of the exercise: infantry movement by companies deeper into the wetlands, where each company would set up a fire base in an area with very little in the way of dry land.

The next time 34th FIST encountered the Skinks—and Sturgeon had no doubt they would—his companies might have to spend extended periods in wetlands hunting them, and he wanted his men to be familiar with the necessary techniques to avoid immersion injuries and fungal infections.

And they hadn't stressed men or equipment in a true equatorial climate in a while.

"It's too hot," Corporal Doyle complained.

Corporal Kerr stopped scanning the swamp and looked at Doyle. It was hard to tell using his infra, but Doyle's head seemed to be pointed straight ahead—his staggering was easily visible. "Which flank are you supposed to be watching, Doyle?" he asked.

There was a pause before Doyle replied. "Dunno. Too hot. Can't remember." His voice came through the air to Kerr's helmet pickups, the same as before, instead of over the radio. He raised his screens and looked at Doyle in visual—his screens were up and his uniform's atmosphere was escaping.

"Why are you hot, Doyle?" Kerr said softly. "Think about it. Why are you hot?" He used his infra to look back. His new man, PFC Summers, was walking more steadily than Doyle. He raised his infra and the image of Summers vanished from sight. He quickly scanned the right flank, then looked toward Doyle again. "Your left, Doyle. Watch the left flank."

"Left flank," Doyle repeated. The reddish blur of Doyle's infrared image flared bright on the left side of the lump that showed where his helmet was. Kerr knew it shouldn't flare like that. He raised his infra. Damn, he could see Doyle's face. He pushed forward through the water to Doyle's side.

"What's wrong with your climate, Doyle?" Kerr slipped off a glove and put his bare hand on Doyle's shoulder; it was only slightly warmer than the air temperature.

"It's too hot," Doyle mumbled.

Kerr looked closely at Doyle's face. It was flushed and he was sweating copiously. His eyes weren't focused. Kerr touched Doyle's face. His skin was cold and clammy. He called up Doyle's uniform and personal diagnostics. His chameleon's cooler control was off; his body temperature was elevated, his pulse was thready, and there were indications of dehydration.

"Rat," he said into the squad command circuit, "I've got a heat casualty. Doyle. He's still ambulatory, but I don't think for long." He began looking for a tussock of ground above the water where Doyle could lie down.

"Roger that," Sergeant Linsman, the squad leader, replied. "Get him someplace where he can lie down." Kerr thought he heard the squad leader mutter "Doyle" before he switched to the platoon command circuit and say, "Corpsman up. Heat casualty. Doyle's down."

"Third platoon, hold up," Ensign Bass said as soon as he heard the report. "Set a perimeter."

The voices of squad leaders assigning positions to their fire teams came over the platoon command circuit. On the squad circuit, Kerr heard Corporals Chan and Claypoole assigning fields of fire to their men.

There: it wasn't dry land—he didn't see any ground above water— but a tangle of small buttress roots looked big enough for a man to recline on; if not comfortably, at least out of the water.

"Come with me, Doyle." Kerr took Doyle's blaster and slung it over his own shoulder, then he took Doyle firmly by the arm and guided him to the roots. "With me, Summers," he added. Behind him, he heard splashing as Summers hurried to catch up.

"Give me a hand here," Kerr ordered. Between them they got Doyle recumbent on the tangle of roots. Kerr groped for one of Doyle's canteens and pulled it from its carrier—it was full. He handed it to Summers. "Trickle this down his throat. Don't pour, just give him a small stream until he's able to drink on his own."

"Right," Summers said, taking the canteen.

Kerr checked Doyle's other canteen. It was also full. The water reservoir in his pack was less than a quarter emptied. He shook his head. Doyle had more than twice as much water as he did. If he'd been drinking all along, he wouldn't be suffering from heat exhaustion.

"Kerr, where are you?" HM3 Hough's voice came over Kerr's helmet radio.

"Over here, Doc," Kerr said. He slipped a cuff out of a glove and raised his arm to let the sleeve slide down. The sudden exposure made his arm feel like he'd just stuck it in an oven; sweat broke out all over it and started flowing down.

"I have you," Doc Hough said, and Kerr gratefully covered his arm and resealed the cuff into the glove. He checked the indicators; the ambient air temperature was over 40 degrees centigrade. No wonder Doyle was sweating so heavily. Why didn't he have his cooler on, and why hadn't he been drinking? If he didn't replace fluids and lower his temperature, he could be in serious trouble.

Hough sloshed up to them and quickly checked Doyle's diagnostics. "Classic heat exhaustion," he said, shaking his head. He didn't raise his shields, but did keep the clear screen down so the three Marines could see his face. "How much of that have you given him?" he asked Summers.

"Not much, Doc. He doesn't want to swallow." Most of the water trickling into Doyle's mouth dribbled back out of his lax lips.

"Stop for now. If he swallows suddenly he might choke on it."

Summers withdrew the canteen.

"Help me prop him up." Kerr helped Hough shift Doyle so his head and shoulders were elevated. Most of the water in his mouth flowed out. "I've got to open him up, get access to his throat," the corpsman said. "Take his helmet."

Kerr removed Doyle's helmet while Hough unfastened the neck of his chameleons, exposing his neck and upper chest.

"Hold his shoulders like this," Hough told Kerr, and positioned Doyle the way he wanted him. "Give me the canteen." He took it from Summers and held it to Doyle's mouth. "Take a swallow, Corporal, you can do it." He tipped the canteen so a light flow of water went into Doyle's mouth. He tilted the canteen up and said, "Close your mouth and swallow. You can do it, Marine."

Doyle rolled his head from side to side.

"Yes you can, you're a Marine, Corporal. You can do anything."

Doyle closed his mouth and worked his jaw, but his throat was still, he wasn't swallowing.

"Swallow, Corporal. You can do it." Hough massaged Doyle's throat and he suddenly gulped. His mouth dropped open; the water was gone. "Have another drink." Hough poured more water in Doyle's mouth, and he swallowed it. "Good man." He slipped a hand into his medkit and checked the label on the medpack he pulled out. "We've got to replace your electrolytes." One-handed, he opened the pack and withdrew a capsule. "I'm going to put this on your tongue, then give you more water. I want you to swallow it. Understand?"

Doyle's eyes wandered, but he nodded.

Hough dropped the resealed medpack back into its place in his medkit and put the capsule on Doyle's tongue, then tipped the canteen over his mouth again. "Now close your mouth and swallow."

Doyle did as he was told.

"Drink some more water." Hough visually examined Doyle as the corporal took another drink. He was still sweating copiously; his temperature needed to be lowered. "I'm going to close you back up and I want you to turn your cooler on. Do you understand?"

"It was too cold," Doyle said weakly.

"You can adjust it." Hough resealed the chest and neck of Doyle's shirt. He added to Kerr, "Put his helmet back on, all shields up." When Kerr did, he reached inside to make sure the nipple from the pack water reservoir was in Doyle's mouth, then toggled on the cooler unit. "Let me know when you start to get chilled," he said, and settled back to watch Doyle's diagnostics.

Staff Sergeant Hyakowa had joined them while Doc Hough was working on Doyle, but he stayed back and kept quiet so he wouldn't interfere. Now it was all right for him to say something, and he did.

"How did this happen?" he asked Kerr.

Kerr looked at the platoon sergeant's hovering face through his own clear screen and shook his head. "I don't know. I checked, his cooler was working properly before we moved out this morning. He never said anything about a problem with it."

"Can you hear me, Doyle?" Hyakowa asked, turning his face to the reclining man.

"Yes," Doyle said weakly.

"What happened?"

"I was cold. Turned it off."

"Don't you know how to adjust the cooler?"

There was a pause while Doyle took a sip of water. "Yes."

"Why didn't you adjust the temperature instead of turning the cooler off?"

"Too cold. Off was faster."

Hyakowa bit off a disgusted response and turned to Hough. "How long will he be down?" he asked.

Doyle was still sweating heavily, but not quite as much, and his pulse was a bit stronger. "Half an hour, maybe," the corpsman answered.

"Does he need to be medevacked?"

"No, he'll be all right."

"Can you get him up and moving sooner than a half hour?"

"I don't know. Maybe. It depends."

"Do what you can."

"Aye aye."

The platoon was on the move again twenty-five minutes later. This time, Doyle kept his uniform's cooling unit adjusted for comfort, instead of turning it off when it got too cold.

Corporal Doyle wasn't the only member of the infantry battalion to have a heat problem. He wasn't even the only one to turn his cooler off instead of adjusting it. None of the units failed. And that was important to Brigadier Sturgeon: he had to know whether the cooling units would function properly in a wetland environment after not having been used for so long, and whether his Marines remembered how to properly use them.

Thirty-fourth FIST, like most Marine units, relied very heavily on its junior noncommissioned officers to conduct patrols and other missions without the supervision of senior NCOs or officers, so the exercise included training specifically designed for the fire team leaders. Each fire team was taken to an isolated position, given a map with a starting point and a destination marked on it, and told to go from "here" to "there." They were instructed not to initiate any radio contact with company headquarters unless they had an emergency that required a medical evacuation. And their satellite-based geosync positioning systems were taken away from them—they had to rely on the inertial guidance system built into their maps.

CHAPTER SEVEN

Mud, mud, and more mud. Nothing but mud. And it seemed like all of the mud was underwater. Not deep underwater, like under the ocean. No, if it was under the ocean, they wouldn't have to be slogging through it. This mud was under boot-top water, ankle-deep water, knee-deep water, crotch—*oof!*—deep water. *That* was why they had to slog through all that mud—it wasn't under the ocean, so they *could* slog through it. Mud that clung to their boots, clutched at their trousers—tried to suck their damn boots right off their feet! They didn't dare drop anything, or the mud would suck it straight down to the center of the world, never to be seen again until it went through the entire geologic cycle of tectonic plate subduction and came back in an upwelling of volcanic magma! Try explaining that to the supply sergeant!

If the mud wasn't bad enough by itself, the local trees shot out roots at all kinds of improbable angles, ready to trip unwary feet and drench the men who tripped over them. It wasn't as if the Marines could see the roots—the trees were heavily canopied, and moss hung from branches in thick mats, blocking out most of the light. At high noon the place looked like dusk. Some of them tried to use their infra shields, and the damp, moss-covered roots didn't show up through them at all. Not as well as the naked eye showed them, anyway, and the naked eye hardly showed them at all.

The water itself was murky and almost felt alive. That was likely because of the life that abounded in it, though hardly anybody wanted to think about what kind of life flourished in water like that. They suspected that the fish, eels, aquatic land animals, and the amorphous stuff that drifted with the sluggish currents were all poisonous, or at least too vile for anyone to eat.

And the swamp stunk like an ill-kept sewage system.

It was—by Buddha's great green balls!—worse than Quagmire, and Quagmire was nothing more than an overgrown mud ball!

"What's the name of this island again?" Lance Corporal MacIlargie asked.

"I don't know," Corporal Claypoole snarled. "Something dumb out of Norse mythology." He wiggled his heel to break the mud seal around his foot that threatened to pull his boot right off.

"Nidhogge," Lance Corporal Schultz said.

"What?" Claypoole asked, surprised that the big man said anything.

"Nidhogge," Schultz repeated. He paused behind a root tangle in thigh deep water and rotated his shields through infra, light gatherer, and magnifier, picking a course through the next section of swamp.

Claypoole snorted. "Got the 'hogge' part right. This is worse than walking through a pigsty." He stopped at a respectable distance behind Schultz and rotated through his shields, looking for whatever Schultz was looking for. He couldn't see anything different enough in any direction to see any point in rotating through the shields.

"You'd know all about pigsties, Rock," MacIlargie snorted. "City boy like you." He stopped behind Claypoole and turned to watch their rear. He also cycled through his shields.

"I know about pigsties because you're in my fire team and I get stuck living in one because of you," Claypoole shot back. Schultz moved out and Claypoole tapped MacIlargie, then followed. "Aargh!" he snarled as he hauled himself out of the water to clamber over the root tangle.

"I am not!" MacIlargie protested.

"Are too! You can't even talk right. *Oof!*" The water on the other side of the root tangle was deeper than he'd expected, and he went in waist deep. He felt about with his feet, found the higher ground Schultz had stepped on, and wondered how the big man had found it while he didn't. "I didn't say you *are* anything," he continued to MacIlargie, "I said you live in a sty."

"Not me." MacIlargie grunted as he maneuvered over the roots. "Never me. My mama didn't raise no slob."

"Your mama didn't raise you at all. She took one look and turned you in for a model that wasn't defective."

MacIlargie, having watched Claypoole's progress more closely than Claypoole had watched Schultz, eased himself over the roots and into the less deep water on the other side. He was working on a riposte that would top Claypoole's last remark when Schultz stopped again.

"Map," Schultz growled.

"You want to see the map?" Claypoole used his light gatherer and looked around. There wasn't anything that would show up on the map, so there wasn't any point in looking at the map except to see where the map's inertial guidance system claimed they were. And they'd made so many turns and doglegs, he wouldn't be surprised to find the inertial guidance system put them on entirely the wrong side of Nidhogge.

Schultz raised all shields so Claypoole could see his face and fixed a baleful look on him.

Claypoole swallowed. "Map. Right. You want to see the map." He turned his head so the map would be oriented with the ground—he hoped his compass was functioning right—and flipped it on.

Schultz stood next to him and studied the projected image. A small rosette showed their starting point and a larger one their destination; a simple X indicated their current position.

After a few moments the big Marine grunted and set out again. Claypoole stood uncertainly watching him, then said, "Ah, Hammer? Shouldn't we be going this way?" He pointed on a tangent to Schultz's direction.

"Inertial's wrong," Schultz said and kept going.

"But . . ." Claypoole began, his distrust of the inertial guidance system of just a moment earlier completely forgotten.

MacIlargie had also studied the map projection. "As much as we've been slipping and sliding," he said, "that map's got to be wrong. I'm going with Hammer."

"But . . ." Claypoole stood there, watching MacIlargie follow Schultz. "I'm the fire team leader, I'm supposed to be in charge here," he finished to himself. He sloshed through the water to overtake MacIlargie and resume his place between his men. After all, inertial systems *did* slide off course from time to time, and Schultz *was* one of the best Marines he'd ever heard of at land navigation.

Schultz damn well better be right! he thought.

A half hour later they hauled themselves out of the mud onto an islet of compacted vegetation. Schultz had been right. Only two other fire teams had beat them. They were in garrison utilities that were so clean and dry Claypoole wondered if they had actually made the trek through the swamp. Sun broke through the overhead in a few places. About twelve minutes later the squad leaders showed up, dripping wet and muddy enough that the chameleon effect of their uniforms was negated.

"What are you doing sitting around in your muddies?" Sergeant Ratliff asked as he dropped his pack. He opened it and pulled out a fresh set of garrison utilities and a towel. He and the other squad leaders stripped down, dried themselves off, and changed.

Claypoole and MacIlargie looked at each other, Claypoole with embarrassment for not realizing that was why they'd had to lug the clean uniform and towel in their packs, MacIlargie with anger because his fire team leader had let him sit around in his wet, muddy uniform. Schultz ignored it; he was asleep.

The rest of the platoon arrived over the course of the next hour and a half. The command group—Ensign Bass, Staff Sergeant Hyakowa, and Lance Corporal Groth, the comm man—were the sixth of the ten trios to arrive.

Once they'd dried themselves and changed, Bass and Hyakowa went aside by themselves and reported in to company headquarters. Then Bass chatted briefly with each of the teams already in and each of the others as they arrived. When the last of them were in, he stood up and called the platoon together.

"Could be better," he told them. "It took five hours and seventeen minutes for the last team to make it in. For comparison, second squad's first fire team made it in three hours and four minutes. That's a wide difference, but the fire team and gun team leaders also have a wide difference in land navigation experience. Corporal Kerr has more experience than any of the other team leaders." He looked at second squad's first fire team leader. "And more than some of the squad leaders." Several of the Marines looked at Corporal Doyle and remembered how the platoon had to stop when Doyle became a heat casualty. They wondered how his fire team had managed to come in first. None of those who wondered, however, had been with the platoon when Doyle, Company L's chief clerk until 34th FIST's most recent deployment, had been on the "Bass patrol" that navigated across the Martac Waste on Elneal while surrounded by hostile locals. Corporal Kerr knew what the looks meant; he hadn't been on that patrol, but had heard about it. He clapped a hand on Doyle's shoulder and gave it a comradely squeeze. The former chief clerk had a hard time keeping up, but he'd done it. Now, Doyle did his best not to flush, and almost succeeded.

"But that was the purpose of this exercise," Bass continued. "To give all of the fire team and gun team leaders experience at land navigation in difficult terrain." He looked out at the swamp. "And this certainly qualifies as difficult terrain.

"I know that some of you team leaders think this was more difficult than it needed to be because you had to use inertial guidance systems on your maps instead of using GPS." Some of the fire team leaders—including Corporals Claypoole and Dean—glared at him; they thought exactly that. "But as some of you know from hard experience," he looked pointedly at Dean and Claypoole, "we don't always have a GPS, or even inertial guidance." Claypoole and Dean sheepishly looked away. They'd gone through the Martac Waste with him, an unscheduled, long distance patrol where they hadn't even had a map, much less a GPS unit.

"But the big thing is, all of you made it here on your own. Nobody had to call for assistance, nobody had to be rescued. For that, I give everyone a 'well done.'

"Just so none of you latecomers think some of us were taking it easy here while the rest of you were humping your way through the swamp, the command group made it back in four hours and twenty-seven minutes, and the squad leaders took three hours and forty-nine minutes.

"What I should do now is send those of you who took more than four hours back out to do it again." He raised a hand to cut off the groans. "But it's too late in the day, and there's no time anyway." He glanced at Staff Sergeant Hyakowa, who nodded. "Hoppers are on their way now to pick us up and take us to the company area." He let the cheers at that news run their course.

"Now secure your gear and get ready to saddle up. We'll be moving out in . . ." He looked at Hyakowa.

"The hoppers are less than ten minutes out," the platoon sergeant said. "You heard the boss, secure your gear."

The Marines of third platoon scrambled to pack their dirty chameleons, which were now drier than they'd been, and get their gear ready to take when they boarded the hoppers.

Corporal Doyle paused halfway through his preparations and looked into the treetops. "Wait a minute," he said. "How are hoppers going to land here?"

Schultz gave him a look that turned him away. "They aren't," he rumbled.

"Oh." Doyle looked confused—not a difficult thing, since he was confused more often than not about being an infantryman—and resumed packing.

Minutes later they heard the roar of hoppers hovering over the trees above them and four weighted ropes dropped through the canopy. As soon as the ropes touched down, a Marine in a harness slid down each of them. Three of the Marines stood by the ends of their ropes while the fourth detached himself to confer briefly with Bass and Hyakowa. Then Hyakowa ordered, "First squad, over there," and pointed at one rope. "Second squad, that one. Guns, there."

The squad leaders lined their men up at the designated ropes and helped the four Marines who anchored them attach their men to harnesses that were spooned at the bottom of each rope. As soon as each Marine was securely attached, his harness climbed the rope. Bass sent Lance Corporal Groth up the fourth rope. When the last men of the platoon were ready to be harnessed, Hyakowa followed Groth. Bass waited until the last of his men was rising before he let himself be harnessed. The four Marines who'd ridden the ropes down were the last to ascend.

The only signs third platoon left of its presence on the islet were indentations in the mud that quickly filled with water.

A hot shower, the first they'd had in four days, and plenty of soap, were waiting for the men of third platoon when they reached the company area. The Marines gleefully cleaned themselves; for a while they'd felt they'd never get the miasma of the swamp out of their pores. The hot shower was followed by a hot meal, also their first in four days. It wasn't immersion-heated field rations, but reindeer steaks, baked potatoes, and salad flown in from Camp Ellis and grilled over charcoal on the spot by cooks who accompanied the food.

All that was lacking were a few kegs of Reindeer Ale.

The sun had set by the time they were all cleaned and fed. Gunnery Sergeant Thatcher assembled the company in formation.

"AT EASE!" Captain Conorado shouted when he stepped front and center. "Close in on me, then sit down and get comfortable." He waited a moment while his men pulled in more tightly and sat on the ground. He looked them over and mentally shook his head, thinking he must look like a counselor in front of a bunch of happy campers.

"Listen up," he said when they were settled. "This is good news, bad news time. The good news is, we're almost finished with the training we came to Nidhogge for, and we've done it all successfully so far." He paused while his Marines laughed or cheered or happily poked each other in the ribs. "The bad news is, we have to cut it short and head back to Camp Ellis. We leave at dawn."

This time there were fewer cheerful expressions. The more experienced Marines knew that cutting a training exercise short usually meant a deployment, and wherever they went was likely to be bad.

"We aren't going anywhere, not right away," Conorado said to cut off worries. "We're going back early because we have a distinguished visitor coming and you'll need a couple of days to prepare for him. That is all." He turned to Gunny Thatcher.

"Gunnery Sergeant, dismiss the company."

"Aye aye, sir." Thatcher saluted and held it even after Conorado returned it. He didn't cut until the Skipper walked away.

"All right," he addressed the company, "don't anybody ask me who the 'distinguished visitor' is, I can't tell you what I don't know. Reveille will be at oh-dark-thirty, so you'll have time to chow down before we leave. Platoon sergeants, taps is in forty-five minutes. Make sure your troops are bedded down, I don't want any sleeping beauties missing the flight out of here in the morning.

"COMP-ney, dis-MISSED!"

A hundred kilometers east of Olympia a blue-backed yort fled for its life. Its spindly legs seemed to ricochet off the ground, sending it in a different, unexpected direction with every bound. The pursuing storkatt didn't always guess right at the yort's direction changes and wasn't able to close on its prey. But the predator was determined, and knew it had strength and speed to outmatch the yort's endurance and unpredictability. When the antelopelike animal bounded, its lithe body had to go between branches and bushes, between tree trunks and treelings. The bigger, stronger storkatt could easily crash through the bushes and brush the branches and treelings aside; if necessary, in hot pursuit, it could carom off the tree trunks.

Fliers flapped their wings to gain perches safely above the ground-bound high-speed chase; long-limbed tree dwellers scampered higher, out of reach of the catlike animal. Other prey animals had already scattered to safer environs, leaving their fleeing brothers and cousins to make the sacrifice that would save them all for another day.

The storkatt's determination began to turn the tide, and the blue-backed yort felt the predator's hot breath on its rapidly contracting and expanding haunches, felt the ground tremble with each impact of its pursuer's feet. Desperate before, now the yort panicked and raced up-hill, and its legs ricocheted it through a screen of dangling branches—

—and over the edge of an unseen drop. The yort bleated in terror as it bounced down the steep slope, skidding and flipping. Behind it, the storkatt saw the yort unexpectedly fall from sight and jinked into a slender tree trunk to help it stop before it too might fall. The catlike animal shuddered and *whoofed* at the sudden pain caused by its aided stop, then bounded to where the yort had disappeared. It saw its dinner struggling to its feet far below, looked about for a way down but didn't see anything that looked safe. The storkatt screamed in frustration, then turned about and stomped angrily away to find another dinner to chase down.

The blue-backed yort shakily regained its feet. The fur of its sides was scraped down to the abraded hide in places, and it was copiously bruised, but no bones were broken or tendons sprung. Timorously, it looked back up where it had come from, but the storkatt wasn't following—the yort heard the predator's cries recede as it went in search of other prey. Saved, its chest heaved and legs trembled as its body labored to regain its breath, to quell its terror. It took a few tentative steps toward the forest that stood a few bounds in front of it and felt strength and steadiness return. It calmly walked into the safety of the trees, where it found many strange things to see and smell, but familiar ones as well. There, dangling from a low-hanging branch, was food. It took two confident steps and stretched its neck out to nibble at the succulent fruit. The fruit's juice reminded the yort it was thirsty after its energy-expending flight. It listened for the sound of water bubbling in a brook and heard it. Moments later it stood lapping its fill.

Fully refreshed, the blue-backed yort lifted its head and sniffed the air, twitched its ears from side to side and front to back, listening. It scented no predators. That was good. Neither did it scent its own kind, which was strange, since the forest was where its kind lived. Nor did sound carry a hint of predators, which was equally odd. No fliers flapped their wings, or glided bough-to-bough, nor did tree-clamberers screech from above.

Then another dangling fruit caught its eye and it went to feed anew.

The yort was halfway through the second fruit when an unexpected sound caused its ears to perk up. It whuffled at the air but smelled nothing threatening. There was another sound, and it began to turn its head to look for the source, but it looked too late and never saw the streamer of greenish fluid that arced through the air and splashed across its body. The blue-backed yort bleated in agony and bucked to the side, but was splashed by another arc of greenish fluid. It dropped to its knees, bleating . . .

No Unexplained Expiration report was ever filed on that incident. After all, it was just a blue-backed yort, not a human being. Nobody had looked for it and nobody knew how it had died.

CHAPTER EIGHT

"Send her in," Admiral Joseph K.C.B. Porter, Chief of Naval Operations, snarled when his aide opened his office door and announced that the officer he'd sent for had arrived. He didn't bother to look up from his console.

Captain Wilma Arden marched smartly to a spot two meters in front of the CNO's desk and stood at attention. "Captain Arden reporting as ordered, sir!" she said as smartly as she'd marched. On the outside she was as calm and determined as a navy captain should be. On the inside she was quaking so badly that she wondered if she'd be able to survive the meeting without collapsing. Certainly, she'd reported to any number of admirals in the past—she'd once harbored dreams of becoming an admiral herself. She'd even met the CNO before, as well as his predecessor.

But this was the first time she'd ever been ushered into an admiral's presence under armed guard.

Admiral Porter ignored her for a few moments while he read through the Colonial Development, Population Control, and Xenobiological Studies report one more time. He'd caught reference to acid the first time he read the report. Unlike everybody else who'd read the report, he hadn't heard a rumor, but rather, he *knew* about the hostile aliens and their acid guns. Finally, he looked up at Arden and fixed her with a glare like a mad entomologist holding a pin over a still living butterfly. She barely noticed when he flicked his fingers in dismissal to her armed guards.

He swiveled his console so she could see what it showed. "Where did you get this?"

She glanced at the console and recognized the report. "One of my people, sir. Lieutenant Commander Gullkarl." She swallowed.

Porter looked past her to his aide, who was standing at parade rest in front of the closed door. "Get him."

"Aye aye, sir." The aide snapped to attention, then opened the door only far enough to slip through. He closed it firmly behind him.

Porter returned his glare to Arden. "Tell me everything you know about this, and why you thought it was worth taking to Admiral Sung."

She had to swallow before she could speak. "Sir, it says something about acid damage to the remains. I heard a rumor . . ." Her face flushed. Now that she was facing the CNO, it all seemed so ridiculous.

"Speak up, Captain. I don't have all day. What was the rumor?"

"Aye aye, sir." She cleared her throat. "Sir, I heard a rumor that aliens have invaded several outlying worlds. They were armed with weapons that shot acid. I know," she continued hastily, "that's not possible, there aren't any aliens, but there must be some truth in there somewhere. Maybe one of the worlds has developed a new weaponry and has embarked on a campaign of conquest. If that's so . . ." Her voice trailed off again.

"Yes?"

"Sir, if one of the Confederation worlds has begun attacking its neighbors, the navy needs to know when they strike again, because we'll most likely be called on to do something, whether it's fight the attackers or otherwise protect Confederation interests. That's why I took it to Admiral Sung, sir."

Porter leaned back in his chair and drummed the fingers of one hand on his desk while his eyes continued to bore through Arden. After a moment he stopped drumming and asked softly, "So you think the idea of hostile aliens armed with acid guns and rail guns is ridiculous, do you?"

"Yessir." She hoped her voice didn't sound as girlish to the CNO as it did to her. And what was that about rail guns?

He sat up straight and planted both hands on his desktop. "Well, Captain, you managed to stumble across the first uncontrolled piece of evidence I've seen on these hostile aliens. You now know about something that's so secret *I'm* barely cleared to know about it."

"Sir?" This time she was positive her voice squeaked.

"What do you think would happen if knowledge of a hostile alien sentience became public knowledge?"

"Sir?"

"Yes, Virginia, there really is a Santa Claus."

She blinked, not understanding the arcane reference.

"Captain, on two different occasions in the past few years, Confederation Marines have engaged in combat against an implacable alien sentience that seems bent on, if not conquest, at least annihilation of *H. sapiens*."

"Ohmygod."

"Oh my God is right. Can you imagine the public's reaction if that became public knowledge?"

"There would be panic, sir."

Porter nodded slowly. "That's why their existence is one of the most tightly held military secrets in the Confederation."

"Yessir. I understand, sir."

"Good. Then you understand the decision you have to make."

"Decision, sir?"

"Yes. We can't risk having this get out. I will give you your choice, Captain. Darkside or permanent assignment to the CNSS *Grandar Bay*."

Arden staggered, but managed to regain her balance and stiffen herself. Darkside, the penal colony from which no one ever returned, or—

"Sir, the *Grandar Bay* was lost."

"Have you heard any rumors to the contrary?"

"Nossir."

"Good." He smiled. At least something was working right. "We want everyone to believe the *Grandar Bay* was lost." He almost smiled at her shocked expression. "The *Grandar Bay* was involved in a major campaign against the aliens on a world that is now quarantined. It has been marked in the records as lost in Beamspace, and its crew is frozen. None of them will leave that ship for the duration." The *Grandar Bay* was the Crowe-class amphibious battle cruiser that carried the Marines of 34th Fleet Initial Strike Team to the outlying world called Kingdom.

"Sir?"

"We can't afford to have anybody who has had contact with these aliens to ever have contact with the Confederation's general population.

You know about them now, so the same goes for you. What's your choice, Captain? Darkside or the *Grandar Bay*?"

"The *Grandar Bay*, sir," she said without hesitation.

"Good! That's the response I expect from a navy officer. You're not married, are you? No children? No 'significant other'? No one with powerful political or news connections who can cause major problems if you vanish without explanation? Good." He didn't wait for answers because he knew them before he asked the questions. "Don't worry, you won't be alone on your new assignment. Gullkarl will be going with you. Unless he chooses Darkside."

He touched a button on his desk. "Send them back in."

The door opened and the two armed guards entered.

"Take her to segment Alfa."

"Aye aye, sir." The guards—one a lieutenant commander, the other a very burly master chief petty officer—flanked Captain Arden and marched her from Admiral Porter's office. They didn't know where she was going once they delivered her to the prisoner transit office, all they knew was she wasn't to speak to anybody—including them.

They passed Lieutenant Commander Gullkarl in the corridor. He recalled the horrified look Arden gave him when he stood before Admiral Porter. He had made the same choice Arden had.

Himan Birkenstock and Tarah Shiskanova, as civilians, weren't given the choice. They were quietly taken on their way to work the next morning and shipped to Darkside. Their families were told they'd been killed in a freak traffic accident, their bodies burned beyond recognition.

Once he was sure that everyone in the Heptagon who knew about the Unexplained Expiration reports from Maugham's Station had been identified and safely removed from circulation, Admiral K.C.B. Porter leaned back and pondered his next move. He hadn't known about the incidents until Vice Admiral Sung, Assistant CNO for Weapons R&D, under whose auspices the Directorate for Orbital Weaponry Assessment and Evaluation fell, brought the Unexplained Expiration Reports to his attention. Sung knew about the Skinks and their weapons; he was responsible for R&D into countering and duplicating the alien weaponry.

Of course, Porter knew he had to take the matter to the Combined

Chiefs. Otherwise he risked being accused of overreaching his authority in shipping two civilians to Darkside. But if the Skinks were on Maugham's Station, he had to take action *immediately*, not when the Combined Chiefs got around to doing something about it. He pushed a button on his desk.

"Yessir," his aide-de-camp responded immediately.

"Give my compliments to Commandant Aguinaldo. Tell him I would be pleased if he could receive me in, say, half an hour." That was how long it would take for him to get from his Heptagon office to his landcar, and be driven from there to the Headquarters, Marine Corps, complex elsewhere in Fargo, the capital city of the Confederation of Human Worlds.

"Aye aye, sir."

Thirty-one minutes later he was ushered into the office of the Commandant of the Marine Corps.

"Ken." Aguinaldo was already standing next to his desk. He strode forward with hand extended.

"Andy." Porter shook his hand. "Thanks for seeing me on such short notice."

"It's not every day a fellow member of the Combined Chiefs wants to drop in on me. Have a seat, please." As he led Porter to one of a pair of leather armchairs facing each other across a low table, Aguinaldo couldn't help notice how strained the CNO looked. "Can I offer you some refreshment? I'd offer coffee, but Marine Corps coffee isn't up to the standards of navy coffee." Navy coffee was reputedly used to scour old paint off starship hulls. "Would you settle for a glass of something potent in a different way? I happen to have an unopened bottle of Invergordon."

Porter raised a hand to shake off the offer, then realized what Aguinaldo was offering. "White label?" he asked.

Aguinaldo nodded. "One of my people recently returned from a visit to the ancestral manse on Highlands. She brought back a case and was gracious enough to gift me with a bottle."

"I hope you've promoted her," Porter said. "That is certainly above and beyond the call."

"I'm giving that all due consideration in her next fitness report."

Porter chuckled, and eagerly watched as Aguinaldo broke the seal on the bottle and poured two fingers into each of two glasses.

The commandant sat across from the CNO and they toasted each other's health and happily sipped the scotch. Finally Aguinaldo returned to business. "What brings you to see me today, Ken?" He knew it wasn't a social call; he and Porter had never been close.

Porter turned serious. "I don't imagine you've heard anything about this." He handed over a few sheets of flimsy.

Aguinaldo skimmed the first Unexplained Expiration report; Porter knew where he was when his eyes stopped moving. Then the commandant quickly flipped to the second report. He looked up.

"So soon," he said softly. More than a year and a half had passed between the first contact with Skinks on Society 437 and their appearance on Kingdom. But just months had passed since 34th and 26th FISTs had driven them from Kingdom.

"Thirty-fourth FIST is closer to Maugham's Station than 26th FIST. Can you deploy them without raising undue notice?" Porter asked.

"Where is the *Grandar Bay*?"

"I can have her on station off Thorsfinni's World in about three weeks."

Aguinaldo sighed. "The timing is impeccable," he said. "I'm about to leave on a tour of hardship bases, to show the Marines their commandant knows and cares about them. Thirty-fourth FIST is my first scheduled stop." He smiled tightly. "I'll be there in three weeks. I can deploy them without anybody outside Thorsfinni's World knowing about it." He gave Porter a hard look. "We have to tell the Combined Chiefs and President Chang-Sturdevant."

"Do you want to tell them before you depart, or would you rather I took care of it after you're safely in Beamspace?"

Aguinaldo barely had to consider his reply. "The military answers to civilian authorities," he said. "I have to get the President's approval before I deploy Marines on this mission."

"I thought you'd say that. I made an appointment for us for tomorrow morning. The Combined Chiefs can wait."

Aguinaldo nodded.

Commander Moon Happiness was very happy, in a confused sort of way. He was still captain of the *Goin'on* despite Admiral of the Starry

Heavens Orange's evident unhappiness with him. And Admiral Orange had personally chosen him to captain the starship on its next cruise, even though the admiral had also chosen to personally command the fleet he'd ordered assembled around it and again chosen to use the *Goin'on* as his flagship. Of course, Admiral Orange continued to express his opinion that Commander Happiness was somewhat less competent than one might desire.

The fleet the *Goin'on* led was a fleet only insofar as it was the largest assembly of navy starships ever put to space by We're Here!'s navy. In addition to the flagship, it consisted of three Mallory-class destroyers, long obsolete by Confederation Navy standards, one supply tanker, and a tug. Because the astrogation equipment on all but the *Goin'on* and one of the destroyers was aged and not in good repair, the fleet had to be more cautious than normal in approaching the Rock—there was no telling just where they'd come out of Beamspace, so they had to reenter Space-3 not only at a safe distance from gravity wells, but from each other as well. A greater margin of safety was also required because of the gas giants with far-reaching electromagnetic fields that lived in orbit around the Rock's star.

The fleet jumped back into Space-3 in tighter formation than anybody had a right to expect; none of the starships was more than ten light-minutes from the *Goin'on*, and all seemed to have avoided the Rock's surveillance.

Once roused from his sedated slumber, Admiral of the Starry Heavens Orange checked the disposition of his forces relative to the recorded path of the *Broken Missouri* on her departures from the Rock and once again gave his ships their picket orders—assigning the positions from which they would follow the freighter when she made her next departure. The picket positions had been assigned before the fleet left We're Here! and needed to be changed only in the event a starship returned to Space-3 too far from its assigned position to be able to reach it without risking detection from the distant planet.

While the admiral was issuing his redundant orders, Commander Happiness directed his crew to surveil the Rock for signs of the presence of the *Broken Missouri*. She wasn't there then, but did show up two days later, farther out from the Rock than when she'd been spotted the last time.

"That's better," Admiral Orange grumbled when apprised of the sighting. "More ships, more eyes in the sky to find her."

But it wasn't any of the additional "eyes in the sky" that found the *Broken Missouri*, it was the *Goin'on*, the only starship in the fleet with equipment sophisticated enough to detect her through her cloaking. Of course, this time the cruiser was closer to the *Broken Missouri*'s reentry point into Space-3.

In due time the *Broken Missouri* departed the unmarked orbital station and headed out-system. One by one the starships in We're Here!'s fleet followed her into Beamspace. Four point one lights was farther than the fleet's final jump into the Rock's system, and the starships were accordingly more widely spread when they returned to Space-3, up to twenty light-minutes from the *Goin'on*. That made no practical difference by then; each starship had her orders: wait for a signal from the *Goin'on*, then jump a predetermined distance along the vector assigned in that signal.

The *Goin'on* quickly determined that they were again at the *Broken Missouri*'s jump point, and she'd changed vector the same as last time. Admiral Orange gave the order, and signals were sent to the other starships, all of which made independent jumps to their predetermined points.

Each starship made the most detailed investigation it could of the area of space into which it jumped, then jumped again to a predetermined rendezvous point, where all reported the same results: no one detected any sign of a starship making a jump anywhere within five light-hours of where they reentered Space-3. Which didn't really mean anything, since the *Goin'on* was the only starship in the fleet with equipment sufficiently up-to-date to detect the passage of any starship at that distance, much less a cloaked starship.

Reluctantly, Admiral Orange sent the fleet home—but had the *Goin'on* make a side trip back to the Rock to deposit an intel drone to detect and record the next visit of the *Broken Missouri*.

Hansik Vaelta was angry. Ever since that botanist had gone off alone and died from an accident in a hidden valley in the Haltia region, the government had been bombarding everybody with tales of how dangerous it was to leave the borders of Ammon. Vaelta, like all the other First-born—well, like *many* of the Firstborn—knew Maugham's Station beyond the borders was just as safe as most of the unpopulated areas within the borders. If those stodgy old Frères Jacques had a hint of how many Firstborn routinely went exploring, they'd probably all suffer massive coronaries.

The Frères Jacques could preach all they wanted; Vaelta easily blocked them out, as most of his generation did. What had made him angry this time was the fact that they'd stepped up border surveillance, planting an almost solid ring of cams with overlapping fields of view around the colony, so it was almost impossible to go into the beyond without being spotted and stopped. He himself had been turned back three times by the police before he'd gotten ten kilometers.

It wasn't right that he be turned back when all he wanted to do was go out and enjoy the beautiful sights of his world, hike its prairies, and climb its mountains. He wasn't hurting anybody. He wasn't even putting himself in any danger! Before going out, he always went into the library archives to search for information on where he was going. Sure, neither the emergency way station nor the BEHIND survey had done exhaustive work, but he never went anyplace where there wasn't enough information to give him a solid idea of the conditions he'd encounter and what he'd need to survive. The maps and survey data he found were always accurate enough so he'd never run into trouble. And he always left a detailed journey plan with trusted Firstborn friends. The lack of communications satellites didn't bother him; his HF transceiver bounced signals off the ionosphere, and he would use it to call for help if he ran into trouble.

So why were the Frères Jacques so determined to stop him and everybody else?

But they couldn't stop him every time. He'd made more thorough preparations this time, and found a gap in the cam-ring on the southwest border of Ammon, through the coastal mountains. There were no roads through those mountains, of course, but that didn't bother him; his scoot was ruggedized and easily able to handle terrain that would cripple the standard street model.

Two weeks standard after he left, after he'd missed two consecutive twice-daily radio reports, Hansik Vaelta's friends went searching for him. They had his detailed route plan and copies of his maps and other data, so they knew how to mount their expedition. All six of them were experienced in the wild. They didn't pause to explore or enjoy along the way; they were on a rescue mission. It only took them two days to travel the distance Vaelta had required ten to cover. There, they found his camp and his scoot at the foot of an ancient volcano in the middle of a plain.

Vaelta's journey log lay on the bedroll in his tent. Its last entry said he was leaving to climb the mountain.

His trail was well marked and easy to follow, all the way up to the saddle and halfway up the ridge to the saddle's left, where it disappeared entirely. Not only were there no more markers, there weren't any marks left by a climber. They checked carefully for signs that he might have tumbled over the side of the ridge, even though the ridge top was too broad for an experienced climber to lose his balance and fall.

One of Vaelta's friends, looking over the far side to see if he had fallen that way, was struck by the beauty of the valley hidden there. As his eyes swept back and forth, he spotted a splash of orange at the edge of the forest far behind them.

"I see something," he said. The others looked where he pointed.

"He must have backtracked from here," one of them said.

They backtracked to the saddle and clambered down into the valley. The splash of orange they'd seen from the ridge was Vaelta's jacket. Up close, they were surprised they'd managed to see it from such a distance—it was overgrown with vines and covered with leaves. At first they thought it was just his jacket, since it looked empty at a quick glance, as did the brown trousers that stuck out from the waist of the jacket. But his body was in the clothes, or what was left of it. They had to hack the vines away from the corpse in order to free it. They worked quickly because, so close to the forest, and as beautiful as the valley had looked from above, it felt eerie now, somehow hostile.

Maybe it was just finding their friend's half-dissolved corpse.

As they were hurrying away with the body, anxious to get out and on their way home, one of them screamed and fell, clutching at her calf. She screamed again as her fingers came into contact with the greenish fluid that was eating a hole in her leg.

"Run!" someone shouted.

They dropped Hansik Vaelta's corpse and ran, two of them dragging the injured woman between them.

Back where they'd left their scoots, they paused to treat their casualty. Nothing in their first aid kit worked. Fortunately, one of them thought to use a knife to scrape away the acid that still bubbled in her flesh. They bandaged the injuries and gave her a sedative, then headed back to Ammon as fast as their scoots would take them.

Several days later a police team from Olympia uneventfully re-trieved Vaelta's remains. More of the flesh was gone by then, and they had to cut the remains free of vines.

An Unexplained Expiration report was duly filed.

CHAPTER NINE

Thirty-fourth FIST did it again; another formal formation followed by a pass in review. But the FIST was followed by the companies of the base battalion, which in turn was trailed by the officers and sailors of the Confederation Naval Supply Depot on Thorsfinni's World. All military personnel at Camp Major Pete Ellis were on the parade ground except for those few who were required to maintain essential systems for the length of time the parade took. As were all the navy personnel save those needed to run essential systems at the facility.

Civilian employees of both bases packed the stands. The parade ground, normally spacious for the FIST, was barely adequate to hold the Marines and sailors and allow them the room they needed for the maneuvers of a pass in review. It was a most unusual parade, but it was a most unusual occasion: the first time a Commandant of the Marine Corps had ever visited Thorsfinni's World. But the crew of the CNSS *Northumberland*, the cruiser that brought the commandant on his visit, wasn't there—the men had been given shore liberty in New Oslo.

Commandant Anders Aguinaldo hadn't come empty-handed, he'd brought with him the medals earned on Kingdom that he was authorized to award, as well as the Kingdom Campaign Medal—struck for the peasant revolt that never happened. He presented each medal and shook the hand of each Marine who'd participated in the bloody operation. Then he presented 34th FIST with the Marine Unit Citation, the second highest of the Confederation's unit awards.

The presentation ceremony had been long by the time the first Marine stepped out to pass in review; Aguinaldo had to hand out nearly two thousand decorations, medals, and ribbons.

"Sir, it will go a lot faster if you simply pin the medals on the major subordinate commanders and let them handle giving the medals to their men," Colonel Newton Helms, a newly appointed member of his staff, had advised when Aguinaldo announced his intention to pin the medal on each Marine who'd earned it.

"I'm fully aware of that, Colonel," the commandant had replied dryly. "But those Marines did something extraordinary, and they deserve to receive their medals in an extraordinary manner." He didn't say anything more on the subject, but did make a mental note to transfer Colonel Helms to a hardship post as soon as they returned to Earth—the man had obviously forgotten how important enlisted Marines and junior officers were.

Everyone agreed that to receive a medal from the hands of the commandant himself was most decidedly extraordinary. But Aguinaldo agreed that pinning the medal on every man who'd earned it would take far too long, so he agreed to a compromise, merely handing the medals to the men marching up to him in a line.

At length the parade passed into the history of Camp Ellis, 34th FIST, and Thorsfinni's World. That was only the first of the formalities. It was followed by a reception in the Bronnysund town hall, to which every local dignitary was invited, as well as everybody who could lay the remotest claim to prominence in Bronnysund or the surrounding communities. The town hall quickly became so tightly packed that Mayor Stor Edval started moving people in and out of the hall in a reception line. The procession through the line was remarkably orderly, and no more than a dozen fights broke out over accusations of cutting in or undue pushing. Next came celebratory parties in the Officers' Club, the Noncommissioned Officers' Club, and the Enlisted Men's Club, each of which was attended briefly by the commandant.

Then it was off to New Oslo for a formal reception with the President, the Althing, the national judiciary, and local dignitaries.

It was the fourth day of his visit before Commandant Aguinaldo was finally able to sit down with Brigadier Sturgeon to discuss the other reason for his visit to Thorsfinni's World. Neither their staff nor aides attended. They met alone because the Skinks were part of the discussion. The FIST staff could have met with the commandant without compromising security because they knew full well about the Skinks, but Aguinaldo's people weren't cleared for that knowledge, and they'd have too many questions he either couldn't or didn't want to answer if he met with the FIST staff and excluded his own.

"Congratulations, sir," Sturgeon said. "And here I thought Assistant Commandant was a terminal appointment."

"Thank you, Ted," Aguinaldo said modestly. His use of the first name signaled that the meeting was informal and off the record. "It always has been, but President Chang-Sturdevant believes I can serve the Confederation better as commandant than as commander of a special task force. It happened right after I sent you that last back-channel."

They were in Sturgeon's office. He served tea for them both from a pot on a side table. Aguinaldo had brought two kilos of Earth-grown tea as a present. Sturgeon set the cups down on a coffee table and sat opposite Aguinaldo.

"But you knew when you wrote that, didn't you, Andy? Or did you plan to retire and visit on your own?" The message had concluded with, *Be patient, I'll fill you in when I see you—which will be sooner than you expect,* and this was certainly sooner than he'd expected.

Aguinaldo nodded. "I knew, but wasn't at liberty to say. This trip," he gestured vaguely, "well, it's been several administrations since a CMC toured any but the installations closest to Earth."

Sturgeon briskly nodded. It took too long to visit remote Marine bases, and most Commandants of the Marine Corps were political animals who didn't like to spend any more time than absolutely necessary away from the center of power.

"So I'm breaking with recent tradition." He paused to sip at his tea. "I'm actually taking this tour to visit you, but it would be too obvious if Camp Ellis was my only stop. Thorsfinni's World is the first of four 'hardship posts' I'm visiting." His mouth twisted into a wry smile. "Showing the troops their commandant really does care about them."

Sturgeon simply nodded and waited for Aguinaldo to get to the reason for his visit. He didn't have to wait long.

"Kingdom's been quarantined."

"I suspected it would be."

"As has 26th FIST."

Sturgeon merely nodded. He'd thought that was a foregone conclusion.

"And the *Grandar Bay* has been reported lost in a Beamspace jump."

"She was a good ship, a good crew," Sturgeon said. "Commodore Borland and I formed a strong working relationship, even a friendship, during the Kingdom campaign. How did it happen?"

"Ted, I said 'reported.' Right now, the *Grandar Bay* is on station a couple of light-hours from Thorsfinni's World."

Sturgeon looked at him sharply. "Are are you saying what I think you are, Andy?"

"I'm sure I am. Someone far enough above me that I don't know who decided it was easier to 'lose' the *Grandar Bay* than to quarantine her."

Sturgeon sat back and slapped his hands on the arms of his chair. "Well! The powers that be are certainly trying to contain knowledge of the Skinks."

"They are indeed. I have to wonder how much longer the secret can be kept. The Skinks' next incursion probably won't be the one that breaks the news into the open, but the one after that could be."

Sturgeon cocked an eyebrow. "Do we now have intelligence about their plans? Do we know what their next incursion will be?"

Aguinaldo shook his head. "No. What we *do* have is reports from a colony world that sound like the Skinks are present and doing something, maybe setting up a staging area the way they did on Quagmire." He looked Sturgeon in the eye. "I'm sending 34th FIST to Maugham's World aboard the *Grandar Bay* to deal with the situation there. Whatever it is."

"How soon?"

"The *Grandar Bay* can be here in days. How well are your new men integrated?"

"Well enough to do the job." He chuckled. "They've had time to acclimate to the shock of being assigned here for the duration, even if they aren't over it. We can be ready to embark as soon as she arrives."

"You don't need to go that soon. Take two or three weeks. You'll need the extra time to sort out the other present I brought you."

Sturgeon cocked an eyebrow. "Yes?" A "present" that would need a week or two to sort out wouldn't be something on the order of a two-kilo block of tea.

"I have, still on board the *Northumberland*, another hundred Marines for 34th FIST. You can assign them however you like, but I convinced President Chang-Sturdevant to go outside channels to get them to you for use as a Whiskey Company, to supply immediate replacements for combat losses. Another fifty Marines should arrive in a few days, certainly before the *Grandar Bay* reaches orbit."

For long moments Brigadier Sturgeon simply looked at the Commandant of the Marine Corps. Getting replacements for combat losses *before* a deployment was unheard of. "How bad is it on—where did you say, Maugham's Station?"

Aguinaldo shrugged. "All we have is two seemingly routine Unexplained Expiration reports about isolated individuals who died under mysterious circumstances. Some kind of acid seems to have been involved. The reports didn't include the results of lab analysis, so I have no way of knowing whether they were killed by Skink acid shooters."

"So it could be something as big as Kingdom, or it could be nothing."

"Exactly."

"And we don't know what reports might have come in since you left Earth—or might be en route now."

Aguinaldo didn't bother to reply.

Sturgeon smiled the wry smile Aguinaldo had earlier. "Well, we're Marines. Half the time when we go on deployments, we don't know what to expect when we get where we're going. The other half of the time, what we expect to find is no longer the case when we get there."

"Anything else I can get for you?"

Sturgeon thought for a moment, then said, "I hate to do this to anyone, but there was a surveillance and radar tech on board the *Fairfax County* when one of my platoons first encountered the Skinks. I understand his work was instrumental in locating their base for my Marines to destroy. I'm sure it would be extremely helpful if he was assigned to the *Grandar Bay*."

"If you can get his name and rating for me, I'll get a drone off to the CNO before I leave tonight."

"I'll have it. Excuse me, sir." He reached for his comm. "Lieutenant," he said when his aide came on, "Contact Captain Conorado. Tell him I need the name and rating of that SRA tech on the *Fairfax* when his third platoon went to Society 437. I need it ASAP."

He barely had time to ask if the commandant wanted another cup of tea before his comm unit sounded an incoming message. He answered, said "Thank you," then turned to Aguinaldo. "He was SRA3 Hummfree. It's been long enough that if he's still in the navy, he's probably been promoted."

"If he can be found, I'll get him for you. There's no telling how long it'll take to get him to the *Grandar Bay*, though." He stood up.

"Thank you, sir. I know that you'll do everything possible, and quite a bit that isn't."

Aguinaldo smiled. "I may be spending nearly all of my time in Fargo now, but I'm still a Marine."

Sturgeon smiled back. "I know. We're Marines; the merely difficult we do immediately, the impossible may take an extra day."

Hours before the *Northumberland* left orbit, one hundred Marines made planetfall and were transported into a vacant, isolated barracks. Their barracks was doubly isolated: not only was it set somewhat apart from the others on base, it was surrounded by a hastily erected fence, and the single entrance was guarded round the clock by two military policemen. The MPs neither talked to the Marines behind the fence nor allowed anyone through it without a pass signed by Brigadier Sturgeon—and the FIST commander signed only one such pass. FIST Sergeant Major Shiro used it only after the hundred Marines had been joined by another fifty off the CNSS *MacAninley*, when he came to escort them to the base theater for orientation.

The Marines off the *MacAninley*, who had only been incarcerated for a few hours, were merely curious about being locked away. The Marines off the *Northumberland*, having been locked up for six days, were in a state of controlled fury—particularly those who had already served a tour of duty elsewhere and knew how replacements were normally treated upon arrival at a new duty post.

"COMP-ney, a-ten-HUT!" Sergeant Major Shiro's voice rang out through the base theater.

The buzz of conversation ceased and there was a clatter of feet and the harsh rustle of cloth as the 150 Marines in the theater's front rows jumped erect, heels together, feet at a forty-five degree angle, legs and backs straight, heads facing forward, arms along their sides. Their eyes should have looked straight ahead, but all tracked the Marine who strode onto the stage to the podium at its center front. He wore undress reds, khaki shirt over gold trousers. The silver nova of a brigadier adorned his shirt collars. Surprisingly few ribbons for someone of his rank were arrayed above his left breast pocket—surprising until the observers realized every one of the ribbons was a decoration for personal or unit heroism in combat, none were campaign or service medals.

The brigadier gained the podium and placed his hands on its sides as he looked over the Marines standing before him and made a mental note of the fact that some—many—appeared unhappy. He understood their unhappiness; he would feel the same way in their situation. After a moment he ordered in a crisp voice, "Seats!"

There was another rumble as the Marines resumed their seats. None slouched, none lounged, all looked alert, all were quiet. The most experienced prepared themselves to demand an explanation for their treatment if one wasn't forthcoming.

"I am Brigadier Theodosius Sturgeon, commander of 34th Fleet Initial Strike Team, Confederation Marine Corps. Thirty-fourth FIST is one of the proudest units in the Corps. We have been on more deployments and seen more combat than any other in the modern history of the Corps. Thirty-fourth FIST is more often than not on deployment, fighting in major wars, minor wars, peacekeeping missions, peacemaking missions, search and rescue missions, and show-of-force missions.

"Those of you who have been around for a while know that when a large number of replacements joins a FIST, the commander gives brief 'welcome aboard' remarks, then hands them off to his staff, who provide whatever further orientation is necessary.

"I would like to do that, say, 'Welcome to 34th FIST and I'll hand you off to my staff,' but I won't." He paused for a few seconds, then repeated, "I won't say 'welcome to 34th FIST.'

"Some of you, I know, are angry about the fact that you have been locked away for six days, as though you had been tried and convicted and nobody told you what the charges were. To you, I offer my apologies for that treatment. But I wanted to give all of you your briefing at once, and didn't want you to hear things from someone else before you heard them from me.

"You see, 34th FIST has another kind of mission in addition to those that FISTs are normally assigned. I believe I would be derelict if I didn't tell you about it myself.

"I'm sure many of you have heard rumors of hostile alien sentiences on the frontiers of Human Space." He ignored the surprised gasps of some of the men facing him. "I'd be very surprised if any of you have not at one time or another seen vids or trids, or read novels about intrepid Marines, sailors, or soldiers fighting hostile aliens; such entertainments are rather popular. I'm sure most of you who have heard the rumors that hostile aliens are real discounted them as the products of overheated imaginations. After all, there are never any confirming news reports, and the Confederation has long held the position that there are no sentient aliens, hostile or otherwise." He paused a beat to read the audience. Nervous rustling was increasing throughout the theater.

"I am going to disabuse you of what you think you know. There *are* alien sentiences—34th FIST has been in contact with three of them— and at least one is hostile. Thirty-fourth FIST has gone to war with that sentience—which we call 'Skinks'—and an element of the FIST has also engaged the Skinks on one other occasion." The nervous rustling stopped. It was as if the Marines seated before him had turned to stone. "Because 34th FIST, by chance, became the first Confederation military unit known to have encountered hostile aliens, we have been designated the unofficial military first-contact unit when aliens are encountered. To the extent possible, we will be the *only* unit to make contact with aliens, hostile or otherwise." He didn't bother to mention that 26th FIST was now also a "first-contact" unit, nor did he say anything about the navy ships and crews that supported them in such operations.

"There is official denial, and there are no news reports, yet 34th FIST or its elements have been engaged with a hostile alien sentience on two occasions. That lack of information to the general public is because the existence of the aliens is a tightly held state secret. As a step in holding that secret, 34th FIST has been removed from the normal duty rotation of the Marine Corps. Assignment to 34th FIST is for the duration. There are no transfers, no retirements, no releases from active duty, no off-world leave.

"You are here until the existence of the Skinks and other sentient aliens is no longer a closely held secret, or until you die, whichever comes first."

The quality of the silence changed; the Marines were no longer as stone, now they were somehow red. Not the red of flushed faces or elevated blood pressure or even the red of anger, but the blue-tinged red of stunned speechlessness. Sturgeon waited for it to change again. When a lance corporal in the second row suddenly stood and sounded off, "Sir, permission to speak!" the floodgates broke and everyone burst out with shouted questions.

The Marines were all on their feet, but they kept their places, so Sturgeon let them shout for a few moments—better to let them blow off steam than risk them blowing up later.

Eventually he said, loudly enough to cut through their voices, "As you were, people! *Seats!*" It took a few seconds for them to quiet down, but they retook their seats immediately.

"Yes, I know," Sturgeon said drily when all but a few soft voices had stilled, "that's quite a shock." His voice turned harsh. "But at least someone stood up and told you outright what's going on. Those of us who have been here for a while had to find out the hard way—when we noticed nobody was being transferred out of 34th FIST on normal rotations.

"I know you're angry—especially those of you who did not plan to make a career of the Marine Corps. That's only natural. But you signed a contract when you enlisted. There is a clause in that contract that says you will serve at the convenience of the Confederation of Human Worlds. The Confederation finds it convenient that the term of enlistment for anyone assigned to 34th FIST be extended for the duration.

"This is tough, but it isn't as bad as it could be. You were selected for assignment to 34th FIST because none of you have families or close childhood friends waiting on your home world for your return."

"Sir, permission to speak, sir!" It was the same lance corporal in the second row who had requested permission before everyone began shouting.

"Yes, Lance Corporal, you had a question before we were interrupted. What was it?"

"Sir, you answered that question, but now I have another one."

Sturgeon nodded for him to go ahead.

He looked grim. "Sir, this means we're expendable, doesn't it?"

"No Marine is expendable, Lance Corporal. We're all valuable. But within the context of being valuable, yes, you could say we are expendable; no individual Marine is irreplaceable when we go in harm's way. Does that answer your question?"

"Yessir, thank you, sir." The lance corporal didn't sound fully satisfied with the answer, but he sat back down and remained quiet.

Another Marine called out, "Sir, there are more than enough of us here, all replacements, to form a full line company. Does this mean 34th FIST has an exceptionally high casualty rate?"

Sturgeon thought for a moment about how to answer. Finally he said, "Yes and no. The first time we met the Skinks, it was a single platoon from Company L of the infantry battalion on detached duty. Casualties were modest—especially when you take into account that the contact was totally unexpected and the aliens were armed with weapons of a kind unknown to humanity. Thirty-fourth FIST recently returned from fighting a major campaign against this foe. Again, they had new weapons we had never encountered before. Before we learned how to counter the effects of those weapons, yes, we suffered serious casualties. But once we learned, our casualty rate dropped to almost zero.

"We suffered heavy casualties in the early months of that campaign, but most of them were replaced during the course of the campaign, and the rest shortly after we returned to Thorsfinni's World. None of you are here to fill vacant billets. You are here as a reserve force to fill billets caused by illness or injury in the future, so the FIST doesn't have to wait months for HQMC to send us replacements."

"Sir, what are these unknown weapons?" a PFC shouted without asking to be recognized.

"Please hold all questions about the Skinks, their weapons, and tactics for now. When I'm through, FIST Sergeant Major Shiro will brief you on those topics.

"I doubt you've ever heard of the world where we just fought the Skinks, the Kingdom of Yahweh and His Saints and Their Apostles. 'Kingdom,' as it's more commonly called, has been quarantined in order to prevent word of the aliens from spreading throughout Human Space. Thorsfinni's World, however, has not. Which brings me to a dire warning I must issue to you.

"Under no circumstances are you to say anything to anybody outside your own company, battery, or squadron about the Skinks or other alien sentiences. I'm sure you've all heard of Darkside. Darkside sounds bad enough to be a myth, but it's not; it's real. The penalty for informing anybody about the existence of alien sentiences is summary sentencing to Darkside. Whoever you tell will also be summarily sentenced to Darkside." He paused to let that sink in. "If you heard that consignment to Darkside is a life sentence without parole, you heard right. There are people there—not Marines—who are there because they have unauthorized knowledge about the existence of the alien sentiences. I don't want any of my Marines to join them.

"Tomorrow the CNSS *Grandar Bay*, a Mandalay-class Amphibious Landing Ship, Force, will arrive in orbit. Within a week 34th FIST will embark on her and head out for a colony world called Maugham's Station. We don't know what we're going to find there. It might be Skinks. It might be nothing.

"Now if there are no other questions, I will hand you over to the ministrations of Sergeant Major Shiro." He ignored the hands that shot up and turned from the podium.

"A-ten-SHUN!" Shiro bellowed.

The Marines snapped to.

"Sit down and listen up good," Shiro roared as Sturgeon strode through the theater wing to the exit—the sergeant major wasn't about to let the new men dwell on what they'd just been told. "What I'm about to tell you *will* save your lives one fine day. Look at the display. That ugly character is what we call a 'Skink' . . ."

CHAPTER TEN

True to his word, Commandant Aguinaldo dispatched a drone to the CNO before he left Thorsfinni's World. Admiral Joseph K.C.B. Porter, Chief of Naval Operations, was not pleased when he received the message the drone brought him.

The Skinks and the need for secrecy were increasingly complicating his job. The *Fairfax*? How had the *Fairfax* slipped through the cracks, why wasn't she quarantined, or "lost" like the *Grandar Bay*? Her officers and crew knew more about the Skinks than anyone in 34th FIST other than the one platoon did, yet all of 34th FIST was quarantined, and the *Fairfax's* officers and crew were allowed to go on with their lives. By now most of the people onboard her were scattered throughout the fleet; some may even have retired to civilian life.

Obviously, when the decision for quarantine was made, someone overlooked the *Fairfax*. He breathed deeply. Obviously, the someone who overlooked the *Fairfax* was him. As CNO, it was his responsibility, and he had totally muffed it.

What to do about that was a problem for another time. The immediate problem was Commandant Aguinaldo's request for this—what was his name?—SRA3 Hummfree. Where was he now? Was he even still in the navy? As a sailor, Porter knew he should bristle at a Marine telling him how to assign sailors. But the Skinks were a problem that transcended interservice rivalries.

Admiral Porter pressed a button on his desk. While he waited for the person he summoned, he jotted what little information he had on Hummfree on a slip of paper. Master Chief Petty Officer of the Navy Hiram Jiminez rapped on the frame of Porter's office door just as the admiral finished. He waved him in.

"You called, sir?" Jiminez said as he took a seat by the side of Porter's desk.

"I need a sailor found." He slid the slip of paper to his top enlisted man.

Jiminez looked at it. "Can do. What do you want him for?"

"I want him assigned immediately to 34th FIST on Thorsfinni's World, transportation there by the most expeditious means possible."

Jiminez looked at his boss with mild surprise. "Will do. Two questions. One, why do the Marines need a surveillance and radar tech? Two, what if he's been released from active duty?"

Porter's lips tightened. "Second question first. He is to be found and recalled to active duty and given no more than three days to put his affairs in order. As for your first question, I'm sorry, Chief, but that's so secret even *I'm* barely cleared for it."

The Confederation Navy's top enlisted man gave his boss a steady look. That level of secrecy could only mean one thing: Skinks. He didn't say that, though, since he wasn't supposed to know the damn things existed. Instead he merely said, "This Hummfree is as good as on his way."

"Thank you, Chief, I know I can depend on you."

Jiminez stood and left Admiral Porter's office to begin tracking down this Hummfree. And while he was at it, he'd use his own sources to find out what was so special about this particular SRA that he had to be assigned to the *Grandar Bay*. That was something else he wasn't supposed to know about. But it's impossible for any service to keep secrets from its top enlisted man.

Hummfree was indeed still in the navy, and had been promoted to SRA2. What's more, he was on the CNSS *Philadelphia*, a Nelson-class cruiser en route to the Mars Port navy yard for an overdue upgrade of its weapons systems. Master Chief Petty Officer of the Navy Hiram Jiminez skimmed the cruise orders of the ships in-system and those along the probable route of the *Philadelphia*. One, the *HM3 Gordon*, a newly reoutfitted fast frigate, was about to depart Mars Port on a cruise to that part of the outer reaches of Human Space that just happened to include Thorsfinni's World. Better yet, the *Gordon's* chief of ship was Master Chief Petty Officer Wondun I'wazari, who Jiminez had known since they were third class petty officers together.

He wasted no time putting a radio call through to I'wazari. The time lag between Earth and Mars orbit made for a hesitating conversation, but both men were used to the inconvenience, and kept a record of what each other said while waiting for replies. And they both had other things to keep themselves occupied during the waiting times.

"Wazi, are you ready for Earthside duty yet?" Jiminez sent, once the connection was made. "You know I can get it for you, almost anytime you want. But I hope you don't say you want it right now, because there's something I need for you to do first. How's this Skipper of yours? I don't know him."

The reply, in I'wazari's oddly cultured voice, came about an hour later. "I'm fine, thanks for asking. How's your salty ass? It's a good thing you've got something you need me to do out here in deepest darkest space, because hell no, I don't want any damn Earthside duty. That'd turn me into a deskbound old geezer, just like you. May as well retire to the old sailors home as do that. The new Skipper's okay. He's new on the *Gordon*, but this is his third cruise as boss, and he knows to listen to his chief of ship. What do you need? How are the wife and kiddies?"

Jiminez smiled when he heard the reply. It was the reaction he'd expected to the offer of Earthside duty. Sometimes he was sorry he'd taken it himself; he missed being a chief of ship. "You would want to go to the old sailors home," he said. "The food there tastes just as bad as the swill you fix for yourself in your cabin aboard ship. I can't believe anybody can eat that shit and not die from it. Alice is fine. She goes shopping all the time and spends so much money I can't afford to retire. The kids are grown and on their own, which is a damn good thing—if I had to support them too, I'd need to get into honest work in order to pay all the bills. How are your children?" He didn't ask about a wife; I'wazari was married to the navy, and his "children" were the sailors on board his ship. "I'm getting orders cut for a diversion in your cruise. The first thing I need from you is to make sure you don't break orbit before the orders arrive. The orders are coming from BUPERS"—Bureau of Personnel—"but they're really from Uncle Joey"—the nickname given

Admiral Porter by most enlisted sailors. "You need to intercept a starship, the cruiser *Philadelphia*, and transport a petty officer from it to Thorsfinni's World. I need you to make sure you get that done without any delay whatsoever."

The reply this time took a bit longer than an hour. Jiminez wasn't surprised. He'd dumped something fairly heavy on his former shipmate, and I'wazari probably had to think about its implications.

"Well, if that's what Uncle Joey wants, and you concur, I don't see any problem. But what's so damn important that we have to go that far outside standard procedure for a personnel movement? My kids are doing fine. I had a couple problems that some other starship wanted to dump on somebody else, but they've got their acts straightened out now." He chuckled evilly. "I saw to that."

Jiminez had his answer ready. "Uncle Joey says he's barely cleared to know the why of this, so you know I'm not supposed to. But I've got my suspicions. Someday, after you accept Earthside duty, I'll tell you what I think over a few brews. Then I'll probably have to kill you to make sure the secret is kept. Otherwise, I'll visit you in the old sailors home and tell you then." He snorted. "If I tell you in the old sailors home, I won't have to worry about security, because you won't remember what I tell you. Not that you'd remember it if I told you now. One more detail about this petty officer. It might be a very good idea if he has limited contact with your crew.

"All right, Wazi, we've both got work to do, and these interplanetary calls cost more money than the navy wants to spend on a couple of old chiefs like us. Jiminez out."

He leaned back, satisfied that the orders he had BUPERS cutting and transmitting would be executed. Now to find out what was so important about SRA2 Hummfree.

It took less than two days standard for BUPERS to cut and transmit the orders for the *HM3 Gordon* to intercept the *Philadelphia* and transport SRA2 Hummfree to Thorsfinni's World for duty at the convenience of Commander, 34th FIST, Confederation Marine Corps. A second set of orders was cut and transmitted at the same time. It was to be given to the executive officer of the *Philadelphia*, and gave a different reason and destination for Hummfree's departure.

The *Gordon* successfully intercepted the *Philadelphia* at a scheduled jump point.

"Hummfree, front and center!" Chief Kem bellowed over the intercom.

"Hmmm?"

"Wake up, Hummfree, the chief wants you." SRA1 Kisegito, the senior of the petty officers who shared the compartment, shook Hummfree's shoulder.

"G'way. M'zleebin'." SRA2 Hummfree had just finished a twelve hour shift a couple of hours earlier and had been asleep less than an hour.

"Not when the chief wants you, you're not!" Kisegito ripped the sheet off Hummfree.

Hummfree rolled over and flopped out an arm, pawing for his missing sheet. "Zleebin'," he murmured.

"Not any more you aren't," Kisegito told him. "You don't get up right now, I'm dumping you on the deck."

"Mmmrph." Hummfree curled himself into a ball.

"Don't say I didn't warn you." Kisegito slipped his key into the control panel for Hummfree's acceleration couch, which was flattened into a bed for travel under gravity, and pressed the button that flipped it upside down.

"Awk!" Hummfree yelped when he thudded onto the deck. He started to spring to his feet to face whoever had attacked him, and slammed straight into his couch, which was now above him—the collision knocked him back down.

"On your feet and get dressed, Hummfree. The chief wants you."

"Wha'?" Hummfree looked bleary-eyed at the senior petty officer. "Whazza chief wan'?"

"You, though why anybody would want you is beyond me."

Hummfree grumbled as he crawled out from under his upside down bunk, the linen trailing from it to the deck, and looked at it. "Whoever did that better put it back by the time I get back," he said, giving Kisegito a dirty look.

While Hummfree was pulling his uniform on, Kisegito turned his key again and the couch returned to its normal position. "Who did what, Hummfree?" he asked innocently, ignoring the sheets that hung from the bunk to the deck.

Hummfree looked at the bunk and made a noise in his throat. "I want my sheets back in place too," he said. "Where is he?"

"In his quarters. Where do you expect to find a chief off shift?"

Hummfree made another throat noise. Dressed, if not totally squared away, he left his compartment.

"Took you long enough, Hummfree," Kem snarled when Hummfree reported.

"I was asleep."

The chief gave him a hard look. "Time enough for that when you die." He scowled at Hummfree for a long moment, then asked, "What the hell did you do?"

"Chief? What do you mean?"

"I mean, you had to have done something. The chief of ship wouldn't want to see you if you hadn't done something."

"Th-The chief of ship?"

"Did I stutter? What did you do?"

"I didn't do anything! What's the chief of ship want to see me for?"

"It may come as a surprise to you, Hummfree, but the chief of ship doesn't always confide in us lowly division chiefs. Why the hell do you think I'm asking what you did?"

Hummfree looked at Kem aghast. The chief of ship never sent for a petty officer unless the PO had done something wrong and was going to get reamed a new one. "I swear, Chief, I didn't do anything."

Kem shook his head. "Well, I guess I just have to wait until you get keelhauled to find out. Report to the chief of ship immediately. If you get there fast enough, maybe he won't add to your punishment for being as late as you already are."

"Right, Chief. Immediately." Without waiting for further encouragement or permission, Hummfree took off at a sprint. He hoped he wouldn't encounter another chief on his way—sprinting in the passageways was forbidden except when General Quarters was sounded.

The chief of ship was in his office-cum-quarters, adjacent to the executive officer's quarters. The hatch was open and Hummfree rapped on it.

"Chief, SRA2 Hummfree, reporting as ordered," he said in as strong a voice as he could muster.

Master Chief Petty Officer Underhaven looked up from his reader and crooked a finger for Hummfree to enter.

Hummfree stepped inside and stood at attention, eyes fixed on a 2-D of a sailing ship on the bulkhead behind the chief's desk. Chief Underhaven stood and casually walked over to Hummfree. He leaned toward his face and sniffed.

"You've certainly done a good job of cleaning the smell," he growled.

"Chief?" Did the chief of ship think he'd been *drinking*? Onboard a starship in space?

"Have you wondered why we've been at jump point for nearly a full day standard when we should have jumped back into Beamspace after only an hour or so?"

"Ah, nossir, Chief, I've been on duty and wasn't paying attention to that."

"Because of you, that's why. I expected to smell turd breath when I leaned in. You had to be doing some serious ass-sucking for this." Underhaven turned his reader so Hummfree could see the document on it.

Hummfree read with increasing interest and confusion. The document was orders transferring him to Headquarters, Third Fleet, as a surveillance and radar instructor. "Is this why . . . ?" he asked.

Underhaven nodded. "This is why we were intercepted at a jump point, yes. It's why you just came off a twelve hour shift guiding us through space debris to a rendezvous." He shook his head. It happened sometimes that a starship on cruise was intercepted at a known jump point. Not often, but sometimes. Usually it was for a change in orders, the starship had to go in harm's way, or maybe the harm's way it was headed for had been dealt with and she no longer needed to go there. The only other time Chief of Ship Underhaven had ever seen an intercept to take a man off the intercepted starship, it was to arrest him for a capital crime that hadn't been discovered until after the ship sailed. He didn't quite know what to make of it, other than it was going to deprive him of the talents of the most skillful SRA he'd ever seen. "So get your shit together and say your good-byes. You're transferring in," he checked the time, "eighty-seven minutes."

"Aye aye, Chief." Hummfree started away, then turned back. "Ah, Chief, sir? It's been good working on the *Philadelphia*. I've learned a lot here, this is a good ship."

Underhaven looked at him and wanted to shake his head, but didn't. He didn't think Hummfree had learned a damn thing on his ship, but Hummfree had taught the other SRAs a lot. "You did good for us. We'll miss you. Now scoot, son."

Hummfree grinned. "Aye aye, Chief." He turned again.

"Hummfree!" Underhaven's voice stopped him again. "You know, the SRA trainer's billet at Fleet is a first class billet."

Hummfree nodded, suddenly unable to speak.

"In my opinion, you deserve it. Now get out of here before you miss your transit and we have to do it again."

Farewells were brief. Most of the people he worked with were sleeping, and the women were in their own quarters, where men weren't allowed. He was all packed and ready at the bo'sun's chute in plenty of time. Two ratings strapped him and his gear into the deep-space skiff and a first-class checked their work. The skiff launched at the designated second, and its coxswain gentled it into the docking bay at its destination less than fifteen minutes later.

A chief with a holstered sidearm met him at the docking bay, led him to a small, unoccupied compartment and locked him in. Hummfree spent several days wondering what was going on. He hadn't expected to be locked in the brig! And transit to Third Fleet Headquarters shouldn't take so long. Meals were slid through a slot in the hatch three times a day. Twice a day he spent an hour in required physical exercise, though nobody else was in the small gym he was allowed to use. He also had access, only partly restricted, to the starship's library of vids, trids, books, and journals.

After two weeks' incarceration, he felt the starship fall into orbit around a planet. A few hours later the hatch to his isolation compartment opened and the same armed chief met him and escorted him to the bo'sun's chute, where he was hustled onto a waiting Essay.

"What's going on, Chief?" Hummfree asked, but the chief wouldn't say anything to him.

He and his gear were strapped into the webbing of the otherwise unoccupied Dragon that was the only one on the Essay. Moments later the Essay launched and went into the first-ever combat assault landing Hummfree had ever experienced. Of course, he thought the Essay was out of control and he was going to die. But it wasn't and he didn't. The Essay splashed down on water and the Dragon emerged, to speed over the ocean to the distant shore. When the Dragon stopped and dropped its ramp for him to exit, a burly Marine master sergeant was waiting for him. Using an absolute minimum of words, the master sergeant walked him through an abbreviated in-processing, followed immediately by a transfer in which he was handed over to a chief petty officer. The chief escorted him to another otherwise unoccupied Dragon waiting aboard an Essay, which launched as soon as he and his gear were strapped in and the hatches closed.

The flight back to orbit was much less violent than the descent had been. The Essay docked in a welldeck. When atmosphere was restored and the ramps opened for him to exit, he was met by a burly chief who was chewing on a stub of one inch hemp cable, the same way Hummfree had seen other chiefs chew on cigar butts.

"Your name Hummfree?" the chief growled.

"Sure is, Chief. What's going on?"

The chief stuck out a hand that could well be called a paw and growled, "I'm Chief Nome. Welcome to the *Grandar Bay*, the worst assignment in the Confederation Navy. Your ass belongs to me."

CHAPTER ELEVEN

"Come on, Sergeant Ratliff, you can tell me, you know I won't blab it all around," Corporal Dean said. He and his squad leader were alone in the squad leaders' quarters.

"Even if I believed you wouldn't blab," Ratliff said without looking up from the gear he was cleaning, "which I know better than to believe, I wouldn't tell you because higher-higher has decreed that you aren't cleared to know."

"But—"

"Besides which," he looked at Dean, "higher-higher hasn't bothered to enlighten the best squad leader in the FIST."

Dean opened his mouth to say, *I don't care if Sergeant Linsman doesn't know, it's you I want to hear from*, but thought better of it—Ratliff didn't look all that happy about the cleaning he was doing and just might welcome a chance to take it out on one of his fire team leaders. Instead he asked, "What about Gun—ah, Ensign Bass?"

Ratliff shrugged and turned back to his cleaning. "He says he doesn't know either." He paused, looked at what he was doing, then said, "Is your fire team ready to pass an inspector general's inspection?"

"It's not an IG. The commandant himself was just here. An IG wouldn't come right after the commandant."

"That doesn't answer my question, Corporal."

Corporal. His squad leader had addressed him as "Corporal." That must mean he was getting annoyed. "Just about, Sergeant."

" 'Just about'? They better be completely ready by the time I finish here and go to conduct my own inspection."

"Ah, right. They will be, Sergeant Ratliff." He hurriedly headed for his fire team's room.

"He doesn't know," he told Lance Corporal Godenov and PFC Quick when he entered the room. "And he's pissed. He's coming to conduct an inspection, so let's make sure everything is ready." He began inspecting his men's uniforms and equipment to double-check that everything was shipshape.

An hour later Ratliff looked in.

"Oop," Godenov said. He was the first to see the squad leader.

"We're ready for your inspection, Sergeant Ratliff," Dean said sourly. He thought it was very unfair that Ratliff was going to inspect them now.

"You sure you're ready?" Ratliff asked.

"Yes, Sergeant."

Godenov and Quick stood at attention.

"Well, I'm too damn hungry to conduct an inspection. I want to go into Bronnys and scarf a reindeer steak, and wash it down with a few gallons of Reindeer Ale. You want to come with me? We'll see who else wants to go." He looked at Godenov and Quick as though seeing them for the first time. "What's the matter with you, Corporal? Chow call's already been sounded, dismiss your men."

Godenov and Quick broke into smiles, relieved they didn't have to stand an inspection.

Dean glared at Ratliff. "One of these days I'm going to be a sergeant too, you know," he said. "Then I won't have to put up with this mickey-mouse from you anymore."

Ratliff nodded. "Yeah, one of these days when no one's looking you just might sneak by and make sergeant. By then, of course, I'll be a staff sergeant. And you know, a staff sergeant can dump a lot more mickey-mouse than a sergeant. Come on if you're coming, I'm hungry. And you two, get out of my barracks."

Godenov and Quick scrambled to change into their civvies; just because they weren't going with their squad leader and fire team leader didn't mean they were staying on base.

*   *   *

Big Barb's, a combination ship's chandler, bar, restaurant, and bordello in Bronnysund, the town just outside the gates of Camp Major Pete Ellis, was third platoon's unofficial shore liberty headquarters. Nearly every night when they weren't on a field exercise or a deployment, at least a few members of the platoon could be found there; on weekends very often they could all be found in Big Barb's. Which made it very convenient for the duty NCO if an emergency arose and they had to be called in from liberty.

Big Barb's was where Sergeant Ratliff and Corporal Dean—along with Corporals Dornhofer and Pasquin, the squad's other two fire team leaders—headed when they left the barracks. So did Lance Corporal Godenov, PFC Quick, and the rest of the squad, but the four NCOs formed one group and the junior men another. Nobody minded the exclusionary nature of the caste system; there were other nights when all the members of a fire team—or even the entire squad—went on liberty together without regard for rank.

Second squad and guns were already in Big Barb's when first squad showed up—neither Sergeant Linsman nor Sergeant Kelly had felt as much compulsion to overclean his gear as Ratliff had, so they'd sounded liberty call for their squads earlier.

"Joseph!" a familiar voice gleefully shrieked.

Dean grinned and shouted, "Carlala!" He opened his arms to the broadly smiling young woman who ran at him. He didn't notice the local fisherman from whose lap she had just leaped. The fisherman quickly took in the number of Marines who'd just entered Big Barb's, added that number to the number already there, and wiped the scowl off his face and sat back down. He wouldn't have to go alone into a fight for Carlala's favors, but there were simply too many Marines who'd just returned from a major campaign. People might get killed. Besides, another comely lass was winking at him. He winked back and put Carlala out of his mind.

Dean didn't brace himself when Carlala threw herself into his arms—why should he? She was slim, almost skinny, so she couldn't hit with much of an impact.

Or so he thought.

Carlala met Dean with enough momentum to stagger him, and only Pasquin's quick reflexes and his shoulder kept the corporal from toppling backward. As it was, being hit fore and aft drove all the air from Dean's lungs and he had to quickly extricate himself from her kiss to keep from being suffocated.

"Carlala!" he wheezed.

"Joseph, you're back!" she squealed, then said with a pout, "Don't you like my kisses anymore?"

"I love your kisses!" he said, and planted one on her—but made sure he took a deep breath first. "Let's find a table," he said when they came up for air.

Carlala looked back at him and leaned into his face. "Not a room?" she asked, her lips almost brushing his.

"I'm hungry—" he began, then stopped when her lips pressed against his and her tongue darted between them. "Well, maybe . . ." he gasped when she broke away. As she led him away, he managed to maintain enough awareness of his surroundings for his eyes to pop when he saw Corporal Kerr sitting like an Oriental potentate in a captain's chair.

The reason Kerr looked like an Oriental potentate was the two lovely young women sitting on the arms of the captain's chair. Each had an arm around his shoulders and held a schooner of ale for him in her other hand. Both were busy alternately buzzing into his ears and pecking at the sides of his face.

Kerr looked mildly embarrassed by their attentions. They were Frieda and Gotta, one blond and fair, the other dark and sultry. At the blowout party Brigadier Sturgeon had thrown for the FIST on its return from Kingdom, Big Barb had assigned them to bring moody Kerr all the way back to the living. Since they hadn't been satisfied with their progress that night, they assigned themselves the job of making him forget the time when he'd almost died from his wounds. They managed to get part of the story from him that night, and the rest from others in third platoon who'd been with him when they all thought he was killed.

The two were enough of a distraction that Kerr wasn't brooding on the subject of death as often as he had been. Corporal Pasquin understood Kerr's mood. He hadn't been with third platoon when Kerr was almost killed, but he'd had his own ghost to lay to rest, and fully approved of what Frieda and Gotta were doing.

Not that Pasquin was paying much attention to Kerr's healing; he

was fully occupied himself. He sat at a table with a two-inch-thick reindeer steak already cut into bite-size chunks, devouring it, along with a
couple of baked potatoes swimming in butter and a double-size serving
of broccoli on the side.

Pasquin was sitting sideways at the table because Erika was
perched on his knee. Erika grasped a schooner of ale in both hands,
which she tipped for him every time he wanted a quaff. She giggled
each time, because some Reindeer Ale dribbled down his chin onto his
shirt with every gulp.

Pasquin laughed right along with her, it *is* funny, he thought. He
also thought it would be funnier when he simultaneously chewed on a
particularly juicy chunk of steak and butter-drowned potato, and slob-
bered a kiss that left juice and butter dribbling down her face onto her
chest.

Erika gave out a startled laugh, then yelped as ale sloshed from the
schooner and drenched the front of her blouse.

"Oh, what have you done?" she wailed. "Now I have to bathe and
change my clothes."

"Gimme a few minutes to finish here and I'll help," he replied as he
shoveled more food into his mouth.

"Oh, Raoul, you say the nicest things," she breathed as she leaned
close to his ear.

He yelped and sprayed the table with a mouthful of half-masticated
steak and broccoli when her teeth sharply nipped his earlobe.

Across the table, with as much savoir faire as he could muster,
Claypoole used a napkin to pluck a globule of Pasquin's ejecta off his
shirtfront.

"I'm sorry, Jente," he apologized to the young woman who sat next
to him. "You'll have to excuse my friend. He was in Recon before he
came here and doesn't know how to behave in polite society."

Jente looked amused rather than offended. She lay a hand on his
wrist and said, "It's all right, Rock, I understand. He's a Marine infantryman, just recently returned from a major operation where he was
wounded again. That gives a man both a need and a right to let off
steam." She gave his wrist a squeeze before removing her hand. "Very
few men can display as much gentility as you do after an experience like
that." She had no idea what the operation had been or who the foe

was—nobody in Big Barb's except the Marines did—only that the fighting had been fierce and the casualties heavy. "It's a marvel that you can be so sweet after an experience like that must have been."

Claypoole preened at her praise. It was the things she said, things like that, that allowed him to be so polite and "sweet" when what he really felt like doing was letting off steam the same way Pasquin was. But Jente was so . . . so . . . He couldn't describe what she *was*, only what she *wasn't*. She wasn't loud and raucous and free with her body like the other young women in Big Barb's. Of course she wasn't; she wasn't one of Big Barb's girls.

She was one of the young women from Brystholde, a village forty kilometers down the coast, who had been brought in to help the Marines party when they got back from Kingdom. Gunny Thatcher had been very firm when telling the Marines of Company L that the young women from the remote villages who came to party were nice girls, and woe to the manjack who didn't treat them the way he'd want his sister to be treated. Of course, some of those young women had ideas of their own that had absolutely nothing to do with being treated like anybody's sister.

Jente was one who wasn't interested in being treated as if her big brother was watching. At twenty-four, she had decided it was time she got married. She wasn't interested in the fishermen from Brystholde or the other villages in the area, so she'd gone to the party to see if the Marines were any different from the men she knew. In ways she couldn't describe, this Rachman Claypoole was not only different from the men she knew at home, he was different from the other Marines. She knew he didn't behave any better, because she'd seen him when he didn't know she was there, and he was just as loud and reckless as the rest. Except when he was with her.

When he was with her, his behavior changed radically. He was nice, he was gentle, he was attentive, he was . . . *sweet*. No other man had ever treated her the way he did; it seemed he never wanted whatever he could get from her, but instead wanted to give her what *she* wanted.

What she wanted most, though, was something she hadn't told him. She wanted a husband. Rock—she thought that nickname was so charming for such a gentle man—was the best potential husband she'd met. There was only one thing wrong about him in that regard. Once in a while he had to go away, and every time he had to go, there was a chance that he'd come back maimed or crippled—or that he wouldn't come back at all. If he got out of the Marine Corps at the end of his enlistment and settled on Thorsfinni's World, that would be no problem. Or she could go with him wherever he wanted to go; that would be fine with her as well.

But he wasn't going to get out of the Marines at the end of his enlistment. She didn't understand why, all she'd managed to get out of him on the topic was, "I'm in for the duration." She'd asked around and found out all the Marines of 34th FIST were "in for the duration"—whatever that meant.

Well, he seemed confident about his ability to come back whole every time he went on a deployment, and since she first came to meet the Marines of 34th FIST, she'd met several who'd gone on far more deployments than he had and come back whole from every one of them.

Which left only one barrier to marrying him.

She leaned close and whispered, "I'm through eating, you're through eating. Do you think your friends will be upset if we leave?"

Claypoole looked at the other Marines of third platoon. Would they *mind*? They were all so busy eating, drinking, or paying attention to their women he doubted anybody would even notice if he and Jente left.

"If we leave quietly, we'll be okay," he whispered.

They took each other's hand as they stood and headed for the exit.

Outside, the closing door cut off the roar of Marines on liberty, dropping them into near silence. Their ears briefly rang from the abrupt absence of loud noise.

After a few steps Jente quietly asked, "When will you be promoted to staff sergeant?"

Claypoole barked a short laugh. "I have to be promoted to sergeant first, and I haven't been a corporal for very long." He shook his head at the silly notion. He would have been appalled if he'd made the connection: Marine Corps regulation forbade marriage for enlisted men under the rank of staff sergeant, a fact that Jente had found out.

"Are you interested in becoming an officer?" she asked, pulling his arm close so it pressed against her breast.

"Me, an officer?" Neither did he make the connection there; he was distractingly aware of the warm pressure of her breast against his arm.

In the background they heard Big Barb's bellow, audible even through the soundproofing of her outer walls, "Vere's Charlie? I vant Charlie!"

They couldn't hear Sergeant Kelly's roar in reply: "Charlie's an officer now, he doesn't pull liberty with the likes of us enlisted pukes!" Kelly's roar was loud enough to be clearly heard above the rattle of both of his squads' guns, but he wasn't nearly as loud as Big Bertha in full voice. Big Bertha came by her name honestly. She was huge, with rolls and slabs of fat around her belly, under her chin, hanging from the backs of her arms, and sliding off everywhere else they could establish a hold.

"I don't care Charlie's no stinking ossifer, I vant him!" Big Bertha's rolls of fat bounced and jiggled with every word she shouted, and she shimmered hard enough to knock away anyone who stood too close when she spoke up.

The Marines laughed uproariously. Most of them knew what then–Gunnery Sergeant Bass had done to secure Big Barb's big upstairs private room for the last promotion party he'd thrown.

"You can 'vant' all you want," Dornhofer roared, "but Katie might have something to say about whether or not you get him!"

"Katie! Katie ain't half da voman I am! Katie ain't a turd da voman I am!"

"Big Bertha, nobody's anywhere *near* as much woman as you are!"

CHAPTER TWELVE

Admiral of the Starry Heavens Orange finally figured it out. It was inevitable that he would, of course. Members of his staff, along with Commander Happiness and *his* top staff, had said it either directly to him or in his presence often enough that it finally sank in—just deeply enough for him to believe the idea originated with him, of course.

"We've tracked that pirate ship three times," he announced to his staff and Happiness in the *Goin'on*'s senior officers' wardroom, which he'd commandeered as his operations center, "and each time she came out of her jump from 43q15x17–32 in the same place, made the same turn, and then we lost her. What we'll do this time is place picket ships along her vector. One of them will have to spot her when she returns to Space-3, and we'll get a fix on her next vector and follow that scoundrel to her home." He positively beamed at the assembled officers. His staff, knowing him well enough, heaped fulsome praise on the admiral for the brilliance of his idea.

Admiral Orange cut off his beam and glowered at Happiness, the only officer in the wardroom who hadn't thrown glory at him. "Do you have a problem with that, Commander?"

Happiness did his best not to quail under Orange's glare. "Not with the basic plan, sir. I think the basic plan is exactly what we need to do, and I wish we had done it earlier. But we only have six starships, including a tug. That's not nearly enough to form a proper picket line—the *Broken Missouri* can return to Space-3 anywhere along a twenty-light path."

Orange grunted. Happiness's praise of his brilliant idea wasn't as enthusiastic as his staff's, but the *Goin'on*'s captain *had* praised it nonetheless. And he pointed out the one flaw in it, a flaw his own staff had evidently not seen. He briefly glowered at them, then turned back to Happiness and bestowed a beatific smile on him.

"Captain Happiness, that is one of the benefits of being Chief of Naval Operations for a peace-loving world. The citizenry, and most of the government, is happiest with its military when its military is out of sight. I can order out the entire fleet for this picket duty, and everyone will be so happy to see our ships out of planetary space that nobody will pay much attention to where we've gone or what we're doing, so long as I don't tell them we're invading a sovereign world. Which, of course, we aren't, although we may invade a pirate den when we find where that pirate ship makes planetfall." He beamed again.

This time Commander Happiness joined in the fulsome praise, even though his praise wasn't voiced quite as enthusiastically as that of the staff officers.

All twenty-one of the We're Here! navy's starships fit for interstellar duty left planetary space and took up positions along the vector the *Broken Missouri* turned onto at her first jump point after leaving the Rock. The fleet consisted of the same Omaha-class light cruiser, three Mallory-class destroyers, one supply tanker, and the one tug of the original task force that tracked the pirate ship, along with the *Groovy*, a King-class dreadnought, two Fremont-class light cruisers, three destroyer escorts of various classes, three more supply ships, two more tugs, and four auxiliary assault landing ships, infantry. All of the additional ships were at least two generations behind current Confederation Navy standards, and one of the auxiliary assault landing ships had been decommissioned by the Confederation Navy nearly a century earlier.

Admiral of the Starry Heavens Orange spaced his fleet at half-light-year intervals along the *Broken Missouri*'s vector, beginning one light from her jump point and extending out to twelve lights—skipping the vicinity of Maugham's Station.

Initially, the *Goin'on* lurked near the Rock to verify when the *Broken Missouri* left the space station, then she jumped to the first jump point/course change to verify that jump. She then jumped far to her assigned picket post in the center of the picket line.

After waiting for seven days standard, Admiral Orange dispatched drones to the other ships of the picket line, ordering them to assemble and report. It took one day for the drones to reach the farthest picket ship, a day for the farthest picket ship to rendezvous with the *Goin'on*, and another for that farthest ship to maneuver through Space-3 to get close enough to communicate without undue delays between transmissions. All pickets reported the same thing: no sighting of their quarry.

Admiral Orange stewed for a while but couldn't come up with a plausible way to blame the failure on any of his subordinates. Instead, he ordered one aged destroyer to take post near the Rock, and the rest of the fleet to return home. When the *Broken Missouri* returned to the Rock, as he was certain she would, the sentry would send a drone to We're Here!, then take her place on the picket line, a quarter light-year from her earlier position. On receipt of the drone's message, the rest of the fleet would resume picket duty, this time with fifteen of them spaced at half lights beyond the earlier picket, with the remaining five at other intervals in the earlier line.

Commander Happiness wasn't surprised that they'd failed to locate the *Broken Missouri*. Even though her jump point had to be along the line of pickets, she could have made her jump anywhere between them. Light and other radiation from her reentering Space-3, maneuvering, and jumping again could take more than ninety days standard to reach one of the picket ships, yet none of the ships was on station for more than ten days standard. More, he suspected the equipment on most of the ships of We're Here!'s fleet were incapable of detecting such light and other radiation at a range of more than several light-days, and several could only detect the proper frequencies at a distance of a few light-hours. More, none of them was capable of detecting a cloaked starship unless within five light-minutes of her.

He wasn't about to bring all that to Admiral Orange's attention, though. He knew he was not one of the admiral's favorite officers, and didn't want to risk the CNO's wrath—he liked having command of the *Goin'on* too much.

In due time a drone message arrived at navy headquarters on We're Here! and Admiral of the Starry Heavens Orange ordered his fleet to interstellar space once more. The navy took up station on its picket line. And once more failed to spot the *Broken Missouri* returning to Space-3.

After two more failed attempts, when Commander Happiness saw that the direction of Admiral Orange's displeasure had spread to his staff—indeed, seemed *more* directed at his staff than at anyone else, most particularly including Commander Happiness—he decided to approach the admiral with his misgivings. Still, he might not have broached the subject had he not begun to fear that he would remain on futile picket duty until Admiral Orange retired—and who knew when that would be?

Now how to phrase it so Admiral Orange thought he'd had a brainstorm instead of believing he was facing an insubordinate officer?

"Sir."

"Captain."

"I realize the admiral is extremely busy, sir."

Orange came perilously close to preening at this unsolicited recognition of his importance. "I am, Captain. Make it short."

"This article in the April 2438 issue of *The Proceedings of the Naval Institute* may not have come to the admiral's attention." Commander Happiness showed his reader to Admiral Orange. "I have highlighted the relevant passages."

Orange curled a lip at the reader; he was entirely too busy to bother reading articles, even those published in *The Proceedings of the Naval Institute*. "Just give me a verbal abstract, Captain," he sneered.

"Yessir. Sir, it says the radiation detection equipment on Mallory-class destroyers can pick up a ship exiting or entering Beamspace at ranges up to fifteen light-days."

"Yes?" Utter boredom dripped from his voice.

"Our pickets are currently arrayed at ninety-plus light-days." Happiness hesitated, but the admiral didn't appear to see the relevance of that fact, so he continued. "Our Mallorys are each currently responsible for a forty-five light-day radius, but can only cover fifteen light-days."

Boredom vanished from Orange's face and his jaw set. "Elucidate."

"Sir, the Mallorys' equipment is second only to that on the *Goin'on* in the fleet."

Orange turned a baleful eye on Happiness. "You mean . . . ?"

"Yessir. Most of our ships can't see as far as the Mallorys."

"I've been wasting my time out here?" Orange's voice cracked at the peak of his roar.

"Sir, there is a solution," Happiness said in rapid attempt to calm the admiral down.

"What?" Orange snapped.

"The pirate's first jump was 4.2 lights. It's likely her next jump was in the same range. If we position our pickets, bracketed around 4.2 lights from the first jump point, so their fields of view overlap—"

"Yes, I see a solution now. Captain, get me the effective ranges of all the ships in the fleet."

"Yessir. Here they are, sir." Happiness handed over a data crystal.

"Good work, Captain. With this data," Orange held up the crystal, "which you compiled on my instructions, I can position my starships so their fields of view overlap, bracketed on the most probable jump point of the pirate ship. This time I will catch her." He fixed Happiness with his gaze like an entomologist about to pin a beetle into a display case. "Do you see why *I* am Chief of Naval Operations, and *you* are but a starship's captain?"

Happiness swallowed. "Yessir."

"But you show promise, Captain. Whenever you have the opportunity, observe me, see how I solve problems. If you learn enough and apply it properly, then someday you might make captain in rank as well as position."

"Thank you, sir."

"That will be all, Captain."

"Thank you, sir." Happiness gratefully left Admiral Orange to wallow in his own brilliance.

The ping of the *Goin'on*'s proximity detector announced the arrival of a drone. Commander Happiness dispatched a longboat to retrieve it. It was from the tug *Annie*, and marked for the immediate attention of Admiral of the Starry Heavens Orange. Happiness hand-delivered the sealed message himself—it came to *his* ship, so he believed he should be one of the first to know its contents. He burned with curiosity about what information the tug *Annie* might have found that was important enough to send a drone with a sealed message for the CNO. After all, she had the shortest field of vision in the entire fleet, and was consequently posted just outside the planetary space of Maugham's Station, which Admiral Orange believed to be the least likely place for the *Broken Missouri* to reenter Space-3.

He rapped on the bulkhead along the side of his—the admiral's—cabin.

"Come!"

Happiness entered the small cabin and found the admiral sitting at the desk. The admiral's reader sat on the desk, turned so it didn't face the entry hatch, but not so far that Happiness couldn't read the running header: *Raidar's Revenge*. He barely managed to swallow a groan before it broke past his larynx. *Raidar's Revenge* was the latest installment of an interminable series of potboilers about a galaxy-spanning empire that was constantly at war with itself.

And Admiral Orange claimed to be too busy to read anything in *The Proceedings of the Naval Institute*!

"Sir, a sealed message has arrived from the *Annie*." Happiness extended the crystal.

"The *Annie*?" Orange looked distastefully at the crystal without taking it.

"The *Annie*, yessir."

"What in heaven's name could the *Annie* have to say that's so important?"

"I'm sure I don't know, sir." Happiness still held out the crystal. "But Captain Main thought it was important enough for your immediate attention."

Admiral Orange's lower lip puffed out in a pout. He turned to his reader, marked his place in *Raidar's Revenge*, and closed the file. Only then did he accept the crystal from the *Annie* and pop it in. He scanned the message, then jerked as though jolted by an electric charge. "What!" He reread the message, then showed it to Happiness. "Can you confirm this, Captain?" he asked.

Happiness read the message, blinked, reread it. His voice was tight as he said, "Short of going there, nossir."

"Well," Orange said after a brief pause, "what are you waiting for?"

"Sir?" He blinked in surprise, then said, "I'll send a skiff immediately, sir."

"*Take* it, Captain."

"Sir?"

"This is not something I'd trust to a bo'sun, Captain. This mission requires someone I can trust implicitly. "*Take* the skiff and report back as soon as you have confirmation or denial."

"Aye aye, sir." Happiness left his—the admiral's—quarters and headed for the bridge, his mind spinning. He had to leave someone else in command during his absence, and didn't have a proper executive officer. That meant either Lieutenant Bluebird or Lieutenant Seeds'n'stems would be in command of the *Goin'on*. He shuddered to think of how easily Admiral Orange could ride roughshod over either of them—what kind of shape would his ship and crew be in on his return with nobody to stand between them and the CNO? Or would the admiral keep to his cabin during his own absence? Well, *Raidar's Revenge* was a very long book. Happiness could only hope the admiral's lips did not get too tired; If they cramped up, he'd have to leave the cabin for medical help. Not only would that give him a chance to foul up Happiness's ship, he'd probably end up pestering BuPers to authorize another wound bar for his uniform.

It was a short hop from the *Goin'on* to the *Annie*, less than a hundred light-days distant. It felt as if the skiff had barely jumped into Beamspace before it jumped back into Space-3. It was certainly less time than the boat had taken getting far enough from the *Goin'on* to make the jump. The bo'sun's mate who coxed the boat was good, and it came out a mere four hours' flight from the *Annie*.

"Welcome aboard, Commander," Captain Main growled, after a startled look flashed across her face so rapidly Happiness wasn't sure he'd actually seen it. "I didn't expect the ackshul cap'n of the flagship t'come visitin'." She was far too old and grizzled to be an ensign, and the ensign's rank insignia on her collars looked far too new for someone of her age. What she looked like was a grizzled, old, chief petty officer. Happiness guessed she'd been exactly that, and had accepted the commission just to get command of her own ship, even if it was only a tug—or maybe she *liked* tugs.

"Thank you, Captain," he replied more calmly than he felt. He was concerned that Captain Main's growl expressed displeasure at a higher ranking officer coming aboard her tug unannounced—he noticed she didn't stick out a hand for him to shake. In an attempt to placate her, he made a self-deprecating gesture and said, "The admiral said he wanted someone he could trust to verify your message. You *did* say you saw the *Broken Missouri* make planetfall on Maugham's Station?"

"Aye, I did," she growled. "Got 'er clear on visual and radiation sig'natur. C'mover here, I'll show ya."

Happiness didn't have to come over anywhere to see what Captain Main wanted to show him since the *Annie*'s bridge was small enough that he could see everything from where he stood.

"Show 'im," she growled at the petty officer third seated at an array of sensor displays and monitors. The array was impressive for how many were jammed into such a small space—yet more impressive was how easy they all were to view or read.

"Aye, ma'am." The PO3 was long and lean, and so was his dour face; the name tag on his shirt read KETTLE. He seemed to move slowly, but his fingers danced over the controls. "Watch the big one on the top left, sir," he added to Happiness.

The indicated monitor blinked from its visual of Maugham's Station, then showed an unmarked freighter that was clearly the *Broken Missouri*, and he said so. PO3 Kettle touched his controls again and another image blinked onto the monitor, the eerie ghost image of a starship's radiation.

"Compare it to this," Happiness said, and drew a crystal from his jacket pocket.

Kettle took the crystal and popped it into a receptacle on his console, then his fingers did their incongruous dance again. So did the ghost image on the monitor. When the dancing stopped, he said, "Ninety-nine point seven six percent match, sir," then popped the crystal out and returned it. His fingers danced briefly, and the view of Maugham's Station returned.

Happiness nodded. "That's her. Good work, Captain."

"Ah, ain't nothing any tugboat driver and crew cain't do, Commander," Main growled. "We gotta be able t'spot and identify starships, part o' the daily grind." Happiness blinked. Had she actually blushed at the mild compliment? "What we're lookin' at here," she said quickly, "is Maugham's Station and its inner satellites. Its moon's orbit's highly elliptical, right now it's out'n our view."

The monitor showed the planet with two dots of light on opposite sides. The *Annie* was located well below the plane of the elliptic, so anything near an equatorial orbit would show.

"T'one on the sunside limb is their geosync," Main growled. Happiness decided a growl was her normal voice. "T'one on the nightside limb is the starship." She nodded approvingly. "Planet's only got one satellite, geosync above the populated area. *Broken Missouri* stationed herself in t'opposite geosync, where she's out of sight from the geosync or anyone planetside."

"What's she done since you've been on station?"

"She's been sending shuttles planetside." She shook her head and looked perplexed. "You ever see Confederation Marines make planetfall, Commander?" she asked. He shook his head. "I did oncet. They do it strangelike, what they call a 'combat assault planetfall.' 'Stead of orbiting to the surface like civilized folk, they go straight down under power." She looked at him, her brow furrowed in bewilderment. "The *Broken Missouri's* shuttles go straight down."

Happiness didn't let his surprise show. "Captain, are you suggesting—"

Her head shake cut him off. "Commander, I ain't suggestin' nothin'. Alls I'm doin' is reportin' what this old star-dog seen."

Shuttles going straight down, just like a Confederation Marine combat assault planetfall. What could that mean? This was a problem he was going to be glad to dump on the admiral.

"Contact, Cap'n," Kettle broke in.

"Show me," she growled, leaning forward to peer intently at the upper left monitor. A dot of light appeared in the middle of the otherwise blank screen; Kettle had blanked out all known stars so only the alien contact would show. "Max mag," she ordered.

"Max mag. Aye, ma'am." A starship jumped to fill half the display.

"Get an ident," Main ordered the petty officer on comm. Most of the volume of the *Annie*, as well as her mass, was devoted to the massive power works she needed to grapple and move disabled starships, so all ships' functions except engineering, berthing, and galley were crammed into the bridge.

Happiness couldn't tell, nothing showed on the monitor, but for some reason he suspected the new starship hadn't come in on the same vector his longboat had.

"Captain, may I see the contact's course relative to our picket line?" he asked.

"Do it," Main growled.

Kettle had already entered the commands to display the intruder's position and course relative to the We're Here! picket line, and only had to touch one button for the display to change.

The schematic that popped up showed the approximate location of the fleet's starships, centered on the *Goin'on*. Maugham's Station was clearly marked; the contact was indicated by an arrow showing her vector. The arrow ran at an oblique angle to the picket line, pointed away from its base.

"Can you show me what's along that axis?"

"How far out?"

"Can you show a hundred lights?"

She nodded. "Do it."

Kettle had already started keying in the appropriate commands. A new schematic appeared. Human occupied worlds in the schematic were labeled. None of them were directly on the contact's vector, though that didn't necessarily mean anything. More significant, Happiness thought, was the fact that no planet with a Confederation Navy base was anywhere near the vector.

"I have her, ma'am," said the comm petty officer. Main just looked at her. She cleared her throat and said, "I don't see any markings, so I had to check *Jane's Commercial Starfleets of the Confederation*. She's the *Heavenly Mary*." Her voice cracked on the name.

"The *Heavenly Mary*! Are you sure?"

"Yes ma'am." She leaned aside so Main could see the *Jane's* entry herself.

Captain Main didn't bother to check for herself, she knew the history of the *Broken Missouri*. If it was true for the freighter, then why not for this legendary passenger starship? The *Heavenly Mary* was a luxury liner. She had been ferrying passengers in a great arc through Human Space three years previous and vanished between worlds. Because of the identity of some of the passengers—politicians from half a dozen powerful worlds, a number of superwealthy playboys and -girls, and several major industrialists—an exhaustive, two-year search had been launched to find her. The search failed to turn up anything. Neither did any of the observation buoys stationed along her route detect anything during that time or since.

Happiness thought about that. First the *Broken Missouri*, and now the *Heavenly Mary*. Yes, that fit pirates better than the Confederacy. And if Maugham's Station was a relay station . . . They wouldn't want to be seen making planetfall, and Maugham's Station's entire population was conveniently located in a limited area of the otherwise largely unpopulated planet, which would explain the Marine-style landings.

He looked back at the schematic still displayed on the large monitor. "Mark the Rock," he said.

Kettle tapped a couple of times and the Rock appeared. He gauged the distance from the Rock to Maugham's Station, then looked the same distance in the direction of the *Heavenly Mary's* vector.

There were two human worlds within a radius of two and a half light-years of the point. But the *Broken Missouri* made a sharp vector change between the Rock and Maugham's Station. Who was to say the *Heavenly Mary* hadn't also changed vector at a mid-course jump point? Happiness wondered. And why should the pirates put their transfer station almost exactly between their illegal mining operation and their home base?

"Commander?" Main growled, and Happiness realized she and Kettle had been conversing while he was thinking, and she'd asked him a question.

"I'm sorry, Captain, I was trying to figure something out."

"I asked how long you plan to be here."

He'd momentarily forgotten he was supposed simply to verify the *Annie's* message and return to report to Admiral Orange. He looked back at the display, at the arrow and the dot that indicated the *Annie* and the *Heavenly Mary*. It would be a good five days or more before the *Heavenly Mary* reached Maugham's Station, and he had to get back to the *Goin'on* long before then. Could his skiff make a jump without being noticed by her? He had to take the chance.

"I'm going to leave as soon as my skiff is ready," he answered. "Watch that starship and report what she does when she reaches orbit. Send a copy of the report to me in the same drone."

"Aye aye, Commander." She grinned broadly and winked at him. If he had to guess, Happiness would have said she didn't have a tremendously high opinion of the CNO.

CHAPTER THIRTEEN

Something less than a full day standard after heading out in his skiff to verify the *Annie*'s report, Commander Happiness was back aboard the *Goin'on*, reporting his findings to Admiral Orange.

"Splendid, Captain. Absolutely splendid work." He rattled Happiness's speculations back at him as though they were his own ideas, including a thought Happiness had on the trip back to the *Goin'on*; that instead of rendezvousing with the *Broken Missouri* to exchange cargo, the *Heavenly Mary* might be bringing back plunder from yet another planet, and the entire operation was being run sub rosa from Maugham's Station, either hidden from the planetary government or, covertly, by the government.

"I will leave the *Annie* on station for now," Admiral Orange announced. "Send a message to the rest of the fleet to assemble here for a meeting of starship captains!"

"Aye aye, sir," Happiness said. "The text of the order?"

"You know what I want to say. Say it—but don't tell them why." His expression reminded Happiness of the ancient story in which a cat gradually disappeared until only its smile was left. As he remembered the story, that cat couldn't always be trusted.

Happiness kept his expression blank. "By your leave, sir."

The admiral nodded, quite pleased with his newly favorite officer.

The *Goin'on*'s captain headed for the bridge, quietly fuming about the admiral's order—and having to compose it himself.

Don't tell them why, he'd said. Then what was he supposed to say? *The admiral requests the pleasure of your company for high tea?* There was no need to assemble the fleet for the captains to meet with the admiral, he could easily communicate with them via drone, but Happiness knew in his gut that Admiral Orange wasn't about to ask for advice or opinions from the captains. As short as the picket line was, half of the captains could simply come on their skiffs, the same way he had gone to the *Annie*. Worse, if there was anything the slightest bit wrong with the written order, or the slightest misunderstanding—or if Admiral Orange changed his mind—the blame would belong to him, not the admiral; he could be scapegoated.

Half of the fleet was spread out along a line less than a half light-year long. In less than one day standard, the last of those starships were closing on the *Goin'on*. The others, stationed beyond the end of the previous picket line, took several days to receive the message and assemble. When the last starship arrived, the captains transferred to the *Goin'on*.

The *Goin'on*'s wardroom was packed. Even with the table collapsed and stowed away, there wasn't room enough for anyone to sit, and Admiral Orange had to stand in the wardroom's entrance, facing the twenty assembled captains. He was mildly annoyed that there wasn't enough space in the wardroom to accommodate his senior staff; but then, he wasn't very happy with them just then anyway. Why hadn't *they* come up with any of the advice or intelligence like this ship driver Happiness had? His staff jostled each other for favored position in the passageway behind him. If the captains hadn't assembled by height, shortest in the front, most of them wouldn't have been able to see their commander, nor he most of them.

Admiral Orange's gaze lingered as he looked from captain to captain, not quite making eye contact with each of them. The officers shuffled no more than necessary to ease muscles cramping from standing so long in such tight quarters, except for one, who liked the press of another captain's front against her back. She shifted backward to increase the pressure; she could tell that he liked it too, and decided to turn around to see who he was when they were dismissed.

"I have located the pirate base and most of their fleet!" Admiral Orange suddenly declared. "I will lead our gator ships to home port and embark a landing force to take that base."

"What's a 'gator' ship?" a captain in the back whispered to the men next to him.

"Amphibious shipping," his fellow captain whispered back.

"Thank you." Why hadn't the admiral said that? And what did the word "gator" mean?

"The remainder of the fleet," Admiral Orange continued, oblivious to the brief exchange, "will take positions to blockade the pirate fleet when the gator task force returns. My staff will give you your orders before you return to your ships. That is all."

He stepped back from the wardroom's hatch, causing his chief of staff to nearly fall over, getting his toes out of the way of the admiral's heels, and strode toward his cabin. His staff trailed, looking questions at each other: What were gator ships? Was the pirate base really on Maugham's Station? The pirate fleet had to consist of more than one captured freighter and one captured luxury liner, but what? Were they supposed to position the warships to blockade the pirate ships from leaving Maugham's Station, or to prevent them from reaching it?

None of them entertained any illusions that Admiral of the Starry Heavens Sativa Orange would provide the answers.

Commander Happiness was the last to leave the wardroom. Not because he was the tallest and therefore in the rear of the room, but because he was stunned by Admiral Orange's announcement.

He knew most of the "pirate fleet" had not been located. He did not know that the "pirate base" was on Maugham's Station—the *Annie* hadn't yet reported on what the *Heavenly Mary* did when she arrived at Maugham's Station; he would have received a copy of the message if there was one, which there couldn't be because the liner could not have reached the planet yet. They had no intelligence as to what defenses there might be planetside, or what defenses or armaments the two ships they knew about might have. They didn't have any firm idea who was behind the smuggling. If, indeed, they were smuggling. There was nothing to tell them what they might be up against when they took action. The only thing they did know was, the starship they'd seen dock with an unidentified military space station orbiting the Rock was now in geosync orbit around Maugham's Station, opposite that world's sole geosync satellite.

Commander Happiness was so stunned by the news that Admiral Orange planned to form an amphibious task force immediately and launch an attack that he was the only one of the assembled captains who didn't notice the excited, promising looks being exchanged between two of the captains who had stood back-to-front during the briefing.

A day later the four auxiliary assault landing ships, infantry, the dreadnought *Groovy*, two of the three Mallory-class destroyers, one of the Fremont-class light cruisers, the *Goin'on*, and two of the four supply ships—the latter for replenishment—jumped into Beamspace to return to We're Here! In the absence of the specific orders Admiral Orange's staff had failed to provide them with, the remaining light cruiser, destroyer, destroyer escorts, supply ships, and tugs remained in position, fully confused as to where they should be.

The one productive thing they did manage to do was establish communications with the *Annie*. She reported that the *Heavenly Mary* also sent shuttles planetside in the manner of a Confederation Marine combat assault landing.

It took longer than Admiral Orange had anticipated to assemble and embark a landing force on his four obsolete amphibious landing ships and the five warships he'd brought back to carry assault troops.

It wasn't that he encountered serious problems with We're Here!'s politicians. To the contrary, they were quite happy to have their navy's infantry head off-planet for maneuvers—Admiral Orange told them he had ordered the naval infantry's first amphibious training exercise in more than a generation. The only difficulty he had in freeing up the funds available in the military budget was that several legislators were accustomed to diverting the unused portion of We're Here!'s annual military budget to pet projects in their own districts. But those naysayers were quickly hooted down by legislators who saw the departure of a fleet crammed with naval infantry as a splendid opportunity for speechifying and grandstanding, and passing legislation that would direct funding to their own districts.

No, the problems that delayed him had to do with purely naval matters. First, the warships had to be reoutfitted to accommodate troops so they would be alive and fit enough to survive planetfall at their destination. Then there was the matter of the naval infantry itself.

Since an amphibious combat assault had not occurred in more

than a generation, nobody on active duty in the We're Here! naval infantry had ever made one. So it was necessary to search through the records to locate living veterans who had the requisite experience. Then they had to be tracked down and recalled to active duty to instruct the current naval infantry on amphibious combat assault tactics and assist them in drawing up plans for the operation.

Admiral Orange had occasion to wish he hadn't ordered the first training assault to take place before an audience; legislators and citizens interested in what promised to be an exciting display of military prowess watched in shock and horror as one orbit-to-surface shuttle broke apart mid-stratosphere and two more failed to pull out of straight-down assaults in time to land. More than a hundred naval infantrymen were killed in the three failed shuttles. Had the admiral's afteraction report to the legislature included the fact that five more shuttles were damaged beyond immediate repair by landings that were too hard, it is probable that more legislators would have demanded a cessation of the training pending a full and independent investigation. The admiral certainly wasn't about to tell them six more naval infantrymen and a coxswain were killed in those hard landings, and two dozen more men were seriously injured. As it was, he had to proceed cautiously for a week while making preparations for the second training session.

No shuttles were lost or men killed in the second training assault, though four more shuttles were badly damaged and more than a dozen men severely injured. The third training assault had no particularly serious mishaps.

So, at long last, the supply ships were replenished, the naval infantry more or less trained in amphibious assault tactics and embarked aboard ship, and the amphibious task force could head out of We're Here!'s gravity well to jump into Beamspace. The politicians were glad to see them off; many of them were concerned about facing their constituents if there was another public landing debacle. And everyone was happy when the military was out of sight and mind.

When the amphibious task force assembled beyond the reach of Maugham's Station's geosync satellite, Commander Happiness read the Annie's latest report and whoofed out a sigh of relief. There was simply no way now that Admiral Orange would go through with his planned assault on Maugham's Station.

During the time the admiral and half his fleet were at home, a Mandalay-class Amphibious Landing Ship, Force, of the Confederation Navy had taken station in orbit around Maugham's Station and landed what had to be an entire Confederation Marine Corps Fleet Initial Strike Team.

Happiness didn't know if the Confederation was there because of the pirates or for some other reason. What he did know was, one Mandalay-class amphibious landing ship with its embarked Marines was more than enough to defeat We're Here!'s entire military.

So he nearly went into cataleptic shock at Admiral Orange's reaction to the report.

"I knew it!" the admiral crowed. "The Confederation is behind this piracy! They think that just because they're big and strong and we're small and pacific, they can steal our riches right out from under our noses and we'll just huddle on our little world and let them do it. Well, Captain, the Confederation is *wrong*! We are going to land, and we are going to wipe out their little pirate den, and we are going to bloody their noses in a way the Confederation won't forget for a long, long time!

"Mess with We're Here!, will they?"

CHAPTER FOURTEEN

The Confederation Navy starship, the CNSS *Grandar Bay*, a Mandalay-class Amphibious Landing Ship, Force, reached orbit around Thorsfinni's World. After conferring with Brigadier Sturgeon, Commodore Boreland, her captain, gave his crew seventy-two hours shore liberty—their first since before the Kingdom campaign—in Bronnysund. The townsmen, most particularly the tavern owners and merchants, were thrilled to have the sailors visit—and spend their money. They even enjoyed the many fights, which broke out with a frequency that people elsewhere would have found distressing.

While the crew was busy drinking, chasing (and often catching) young women, eating, fighting, and—mainly—spending money, the sailors of Rear Admiral Blankenvoort's Naval Supply Depot replenished the stores of the starship and otherwise prepared her for a cruise of indefinite duration. Rotating through the watches and departments, it took a full week for the entire crew to get their shore liberty, and even the most senior chief petty officers and the commissioned officers got the full seventy-two hours planetside.

Part of the *Grandar Bay's* replenishment was two new crew members who arrived directly from Earth via fast frigate.

Captain Wilma Arden and Lieutenant Commander Stewart Gullkarl stood at rigid attention in front of Commodore Boreland's desk. The commodore lounged back in his swivel chair and examined them over fingers steepled in front of his face. This was a problem he'd never considered when he received the bad news that his starship and he and his crew had been lost in Beamspace: he understood now that he was in danger of being saddled with every navy officer and sailor who learned too much about the existence of the Skinks, whether he could use them or not. He finally lowered his hands and sat up.

"I'm sure you like being here even less than I like having you," he said. "I already have a full complement of officers, so what am I going to do with you?" He looked from Arden to Gullkarl and back, but wasn't bothered when neither replied; his question was rhetorical.

"Lieutenant Commander Gullkarl, you're up to date on orbital weapons development?"

"Yessir."

"I'll assign you to the weapons division in a supernumerary capacity. You will assist whatever officer or chief petty officer requests your assistance, but you are not in the division's chain of command and are not to issue any orders without my express permission. Do you understand?"

Gullkarl swallowed. "Yessir." He could hang out in the weapons division, but he had nothing to do unless someone needed an extra hand for something. Every officer wanted assignment to a warship, but not that kind.

"Captain Arden, you present a greater problem. No matter where I assign you, you will probably outrank the division commander, and that will be very awkward. I've reviewed your record. Unlike Mr. Gullkarl, you haven't served on a warship before, which means you have no understanding of the realities of your situation. That's a major problem in integrating any officer above the rank of Lieutenant, j.g.. You probably know as much, possibly more, about orbital weaponry as Mr. Gullkarl—excepting for your lack of warship experience—so one might think you could fit in there. But the division head is a commander, which could promote second guessing and might cause morale problems. So, assigning you there won't do.

"So," he leaned back again, "just what *do* I do with you?" He glanced at his console monitor, then sat back up. "I see you have experience in communications. How current are you?"

"Sir, I took a refresher course on my own time last year."

Boreland nodded. He knew that, he wanted to see how she expressed it. She didn't say anything to inflate what her record showed. "As it happens, I am in temporary need of a communications officer. My comm officer suffered injuries in an accident the other day and should be transferred planetside to be tended in the navy hospital. I can slot you in there until he returns to duty the next time we come to Thorsfinni's World. It's a lieutenant commander's billet, but it's the best I can do." He looked at her for a reaction.

"Thank you, sir. I'll do my best to live up to your expectations."

"Just remember, Captain, you'll be an acting lieutenant commander. Act like one."

"Yessir. Aye aye, sir."

"You're dismissed. I'll have someone show you to your duty stations."

"Thank you, sir," Arden said. She about-faced and marched out of Boreland's office. Gullkarl followed close behind.

Rooster tails flew up behind the twenty-four Dragons of 34th FIST's transportation company, each bearing a full complement of Marines, as they roared in line onto Boynton Field at Camp Ellis. When it reached the loading chief's stand the lead Dragon—the company commander's—pulled out of its position and turned to face the remaining air-cushioned, armored, amphibious assault vehicles as they passed by. They in turn followed the markers they were directed to by the landing chief. Three by three, the Dragons headed for the eight Essays; three by three, they faced about and backed into the Essays. When the last of his vehicles passed, the company commander ordered his driver to follow the loading chief's directions; his was the last Dragon to board the last Essay.

Ground crews oversaw the raising and securing of the Essays' ramps. On board, the coxswains checked their systems to assure the ramps were raised and secured and their craft were sound and ready for launch. The loading chief waited for his subordinates to report that each Essay's ramp was up and secure, then ordered them to assemble on him. When his people were all present and accounted for, he turned control of the Essays over to the control tower.

The tower communicated with each Essay—voice between human

controllers and coxswains, digital between the control comp and the Essays' comps. When coxswains, human controllers, and comps were all satisfied with communications, the controllers cleared the first Essay for launch. It fired its engines and sped along the airstrip a short distance before shooting sharply upward at a high speed. Fifteen seconds after it began its movement, the second Essay followed. The others trailed at fifteen second intervals.

The first Essay leveled off at three thousand meters and swung into a wide orbit. Less than two minutes later all eight Essays were circling high above Boynton Field. The tower called for a final system check. When all eight Essays were orbiting and the coxswains and their comps were satisfied with their systems and with vehicle performance, the control tower cleared them to head for orbit. The chief coxswain gave the final order, and one by one the Essays rolled out of the orbit and shot upward at increasing speed until they reached escape velocity.

The *Grandar Bay*'s coxswains gave the Marines an even rougher ride on their Essays than had the Essay coxswains on the trip to Nidhogge. As far as the *Grandar Bay*'s crew was concerned, it was the fault of the Marines that they were stuck on their starship "for the duration," reported as lost in Beamspace.

Not that the Marines were happy to be back aboard the *Grandar Bay*; most of them had unhappy memories of all the time and energy they'd expended doing "squid work"—cleaning the starship—when they rode her back to Thorsfinni's World from Kingdom. This time the Marines wouldn't have to do any squid work; they were on a mission of unknown severity and had to prepare for it.

Ten minutes after breaking orbit, the formation leveled off again, in sight of the looming bulk of the *Grandar Bay*. They maneuvered in closer, heading for the gaping maw of the open welldeck. Under it, the comps fired forward vernier jets to bring their velocity down to that of the ship, then fired gentle puffs from ventral jets to lift themselves into position for the clamps and grapples to grab and hold them in place. The welldeck hatch ponderously closed snug against the bottoms of the Essays, which lowered their hatches. Atmosphere flooded the welldeck, and crewmen in spacesuits with open faceplates, tugging guidelines, scrambled aboard the Essays, and the Dragons in turn lowered their ramps. Weightless in the null-g of a starship in boarding operations, the sailors attached the Marines in the Dragons to guidelines and escorted them from the welldeck.

In moments the two companies of Marines who'd risen to orbit in the placental Dragons borne within the Essay-wombs were out of the welldeck, being led to the compartments they would call home during their cruise to Maugham's Station.

Then the welldeck was sucked dry of atmosphere and reopened to space, and the Essays were launched for the return trip to Boynton Field. Another flight of eight Essays was already waiting a couple of kilometers away to enter the welldeck. A third flight of eight Essays launched from Boynton Field at that same moment.

Four hours after the first Essay fired its engines to begin its launch, 34th FIST was fully embarked. Sixteen Essays, each with three Dragons, were snugged in their places in the *Grandar Bay*'s welldeck, readying to launch an assault force of Marines and their killing power on whatever target they were aimed at. The starship commenced final preparations to leave orbit for transit to its first jump point, some three days out from Thorsfinni's World and perpendicular to the plane of the elliptic.

The Marines studied up on Maugham's Station—not that there was much to study. They could have stopped with what they learned in the briefings given by Captain Conorado and First Sergeant Myer, who simply regurgitated what they'd learned at Brigadier Sturgeon's Commanders' Call the day before they launched, because there wasn't all that much to know about a colony world such as Maugham's Station. But there were things about Maugham's Station that bothered the more experienced Marines, which made them want to know more—and that bother conveyed itself to the less experienced, so they also wanted to know more.

Most of them spent the best part of their days—at least those hours when they weren't engaged in physical exercise, fire team, and squad drills in the virtual reality chambers, or maintaining their weapons and other gear—with their readers plugged in, ransacking the ship's library to glean every scrap of information it held regarding their destination. Those who didn't spend the best part of their free time at it spent *all* of their free hours during the day and many of their night hours ransacking the library.

What mainly bothered the more experienced Marines was that Maugham's Station was largely unexplored and had neither a globe-encircling satellite system nor much of a sensor array that could be deployed outside the limited populated area. Which effectively made Maugham's Station a virgin planet. Most of them had recent experience on a virgin planet, when they pursued the fleeing Skinks from Kingdom to the abandoned exploratory world called Quagmire. Quagmire had presented them with things they'd never encountered, or even heard of, much less trained for. They could have made serious mistakes and suffered unnecessary casualties because of their ignorance. Who knew what they were going to encounter on Maugham's Station? Skinks, probably. Maybe. Nobody knew for sure, though it looked like it. If they did, the enemy had been there for a while, long enough to gain some degree of familiarity with what Maugham's Station had to offer. Certainly they'd know more about it than the Marines knew. And long enough to prepare booby traps, ambush sites, defensive positions, and other nasty surprises.

The Marines didn't like that one little bit.

They were so engrossed in their study and other preparations that few of them noticed how much better the food was in the starship's messes than it had been the last time they'd sailed on the *Grandar Bay*.

By the time the *Grandar Bay* made her second jump the Marines had absorbed every scrap of information on Maugham's Station the library held. Some of them were even able to understand the more esoteric reports filed by BEHIND, the Bureau of Human Habitability Exploration and Investigation, during its brief exploration and investigation of the world, and to translate it into standard English for the benefit of those who had less extensive scientific educations. Even that didn't tell them anywhere near as much as they wanted to know.

Not even First Sergeant Myer managed to cast much light on the situation during the unofficial briefing he delivered the day after the last jump.

"A-ten-SHUN!" Top Myer barked, and the Marines of Company L jumped to their feet and stood at attention while Captain Conorado stepped away from the lectern at which he'd delivered his final briefing.

All he'd had to tell them was that communications had been established with Maugham's Station, where another death had been reported, which was similar to two incidents that triggered 34th FIST's deployment. Brigadier Sturgeon and a few members of the FIST staff, along with the battalion and squadron commanders and a couple of their top people, would make preliminary planetfall to meet with Maugham's Station's leadership before making final plans. Conorado left the compartment via the hatch nearest the small stage, followed by the company's other officers.

Top Myer remained on the stage, watching as they left. When the hatch closed and he was certain they wouldn't return, he nodded. Gunnery Sergeant Thatcher dogged one hatch, Staff Sergeant Hyakowa the other. Now they wouldn't be interrupted by anybody simply walking in unannounced. Myer had another reason for waiting before he began his unofficial briefing: the officers didn't know he knew that when they left the official briefing, they would assemble in their wardroom to listen to his briefing on a circuit they believed he didn't know about.

Hmmpf! As if *anything* that went on in his company was unknown to any first sergeant worth his salt. He *wanted* them to listen in; they might learn something that would help them save the lives of some of their Marines.

But what could he say today that could save Marine lives? They were blind! He didn't even know if they really were up against Skinks; the limited transmissions they'd had from the planet since yesterday's jump had been singularly unilluminating on the subject. If Skinks were there, most of these Marines who stood looking so expectantly at him knew more in detail about fighting them than he did.

Well, he was a Marine. When in doubt, act decisively.

"Siddown," he growled. He glowered at the 121 Marines plus navy corpsmen who resumed their seats, then clasped his hands behind his back and began pacing the width of the small stage.

"I imagine you know I don't have squat to tell you about this place," he finally said. "You've had full access to the same BEHIND reports I have, you've seen the same transcripts of the Unexplained Expiration reports I have, your briefings have covered the same ground in the same detail mine have. I've never been to Maugham's Station and I don't know anybody who has."

He stopped pacing and faced front, arms akimbo, fists jammed into his hips.

"What this means, people, is the only thing we can expect when we make planetfall is the unexpected. Are Skinks waiting for us, like they were on our last deployment? Are any Skinks even there?" He gestured vaguely. "I don't know, and neither does anybody else.

"Are the Unexplained Expiration reports accurate? Hell, all I know is they're incomplete." He shook his head. "In my experience, most colony worlds, no matter what they say about needing and wanting Confederation support, don't want anybody to know too much about what they're doing, what kinds of problems they're having, and they either deliberately leave out essential information or are simply careless in their reporting. And this Ammon country didn't even ask the Confederation to send Marines; they have no idea how much trouble they *might* be in for.

"The way this has shaped up so far, we could be walking into the middle of a personal vendetta, a family feud, a civil war, a Skink trap, or—nothing. And we aren't going to know which until we're in the middle of it. The one thing I *do* know is, the unexpected can kill you.

"Most of you remember in our last operation, Mike Company didn't expect the Skinks to wait in ambush underwater and rise up to hit them from the rear. That cost Mike Company almost an entire platoon.

"In the late twentieth century, Marines on a peacekeeping mission in a Middle Eastern country called Lebanon didn't expect suicide bombers. That lack of expectation killed 241 Marines, soldiers, and sailors.

"When I was a PFC, I was a member of a ceremonial detail representing the Confederation at the coronation of the Raja of Kotte on Burgher. We knew the new raja's outcast brother was organizing an insurrection, but we didn't expect the insurrection to begin with the assassination of the raja and massacre of the guests at the coronation." His eyes suddenly went out of focus and his voice dropped so low only the Marines closest to the stage heard what he said next. "Half the Marines in the detail were killed before we were able to load our weapons and begin to fight back." He stood silent for a moment, looking into a place only he could see, then shook himself and refocused on the Marines. When he resumed speaking, his voice was once again strong.

"So you see, what you don't expect can rear up and bite your ass right off. When we go planetside, be alert and be ready for anything. Be especially alert for the unexpected."

With that, he turned and marched off the small stage to the hatch through which the company's officers had exited. He had to fumble with the dog before he could open it and leave.

The compartment was silent for long seconds after the first sergeant left. Finally someone in the back shouted out, "What did he say after 'massacre of the guests'?"

Commodore Boreland, with Brigadier Sturgeon concurring, decided not to radio a notification of the *Grandar Bay*'s arrival to Maugham's Station until the starship was in position to land the landing party. They didn't know what kind of security the Skinks—or whoever might be causing the deaths on the colony world—might have. The closer the *Grandar Bay* could get without being detected, the better, and a radio broadcast from several days' out would certainly be picked up by the foe.

The welldeck was ready to receive the Marines before the communications officer made his first contact.

"Maugham's Station Central, this is the Confederation Navy Starship *Grandar Bay*," Captain Wilma Arden said into her transmitter. "Do you hear me? Over." She waited a moment, then called again. "Maugham's Station Central, this is the CNSS *Grandar Bay*. Is anybody monitoring your communications? Over." The voice that replied sounded distinctly surprised.

"CNSS *Grandar Bay*, this is Maugham's Station Central. We are monitoring. Where are you?" He was so surprised to be talking to someone he didn't know was in orbit he forgot radio procedure.

Arden smiled wryly. "If your geosync is functioning, you should be able to see us. Over."

"You're in orbit?" the monitor at Central squawked.

"That's affirmative, Central. In orbit and about to launch a Marine landing party. Over."

"Now?" The monitor's voice cracked.

"Within moments. The first wave of Marine Dragons will cross the beach in less than an hour. We would appreciate it if you notified your president that visitors are about to drop in. Over."

"Notify the Pres . . . I'll do it right away, CNSS . . . What ship did you say you are?"

"The *Grandar Bay*, a Mandalay-class Amphibious Landing Ship, Force. Over."

"A Mandalay-class . . . Is that good? Uh, over?"

"The Mandalay-class Amphibious Landing Ship, Force, is one of the most powerful warships in the Confederation Navy. So, yes, that's good. Over."

"I'll notify President Menno immediately, *Grandar Bay*. Maugham's Station Central, over and out."

Arden shook her head. The communications tech at Central forgot all about communications procedure until almost the very end, then garbled it. "Over and out" literally meant, "It's your turn to talk, but I'm breaking the connection and won't listen."

The Marines filed into the welldeck of the *Grandar Bay* and onto the Dragons that waited, already in the Essays that would ferry them planetside. They strapped themselves into their webbing stations; the webbing swung into launch position, lifting their passengers into horizontal positions, tested their mass, and adjusted their tension to keep them from slamming against the deck, overhead, or sides of the Dragon during maneuvers and acceleration. Fire team leaders checked their men's strapping, and squad leaders checked the fire team leaders. Each Dragon crew chief came through and made his own inspection—no crew chief wanted a Marine injured on his vehicle. As each Dragon filled, its ramp rose and sealed. Each Essay's ramp did likewise as its three Dragons battened down. The Essays' computers reported when they were ready, the coxswains double-checked the computers and verified. At last they were ready to go.

The *Grandar Bay* turned off her gravity field, and everything and everybody not secured began drifting in free fall. The air was sucked from the welldeck, and the hatch that moments before had been its deck ponderously rolled out of the way. Most of the Marines didn't listen to the carefully modulated, computer-generated female voice that warned of the loss of gravity, the evacuation of the welldeck's atmosphere, the opening of the welldeck's hatch. Nor did they pay attention to the countdown to launch; the experienced Marines wanted to be relaxed at launch, not tense. They knew they could get injured if they were rigid when the Essays were plunged out of the welldeck and then fired their engines to maneuver away from the starship before the precipitous dive planetside.

Then came the "fast ride on a rough road" that was the straight-down descent through the gradually thickening atmosphere of Maugham's Station to splash-down in the ocean a hundred kilometers beyond the horizon of Ammon's coast.

As soon as the last Essay launched, the *Grandar Bay* made one orbit of Maugham's Station, laying her string-of-pearls ring of observation and communications satellites in low orbit. Then she climbed to a geo-sync orbit, above the longitude of Ammon's capital city of Olympia.

CHAPTER FIFTEEN

The first wave of eight Essays ferried Brigadier Sturgeon and his initial contact party to the surface. The Dragons on one of the Essays carried the FIST commander and his party, consisting of Commander Daana and Captain West, respectively the FIST intelligence and logistics officers; Commander van Winkle, the infantry battalion commander; Commander Wolfe, the composite squadron commander; an aide or assistant for each of them; and the FIST headquarters' security platoon. The FIST's recon and Unmanned Aerial Vehicle squads were aboard another Essay. Company L came along to provide ground security beyond the immediate environs of the brigadier's contact party. Two Raptors and four hoppers, one a gunship, also came down in the first wave.

Those residents of Ammon who lived close enough to the ocean and happened to look up at the right time were treated to a pyrotechnic display such as they'd never seen before—the descent of Confederation Navy Essays bringing Marines to planetfall. Those citizens had seen other shuttles make planetfall, via as many as three leisurely spiral orbits. But the Marines always made planetfall in combat assault mode—straight down at the highest possible speed. The Essays' heat shields glowed with heat so high it rivaled anything short of the sun, creating a lingering line of brilliant light down from the thermosphere to beyond the horizon. The line ended beyond the horizon because the Marines always made planetfall over the water, beyond the horizon from land.

After their precipitous plunge from orbit, the Essays settled gently on the ocean surface and dropped their ramps. Three Dragons roared off each Essay, got in formation on line, and sped toward the distant shore.

President Menno and Minister of the Interior Elbrus led the hastily assembled welcoming delegation of ministers, legislators, judges, city administrators, and other dignitaries who zeroed in on Sturgeon and the other Marines clad in dress reds when they debarked from their Dragons near a gaily colored pavilion that was erected for the occasion over a permanent reception stage. Every planetfall on Maugham's Station was an occasion for formal greeting and celebration because there were so few of them. But the arrival of Confederation Marines was a truly special occasion that called for an extra measure of pomp. The Olympia Symphony Orchestra, minus three violins, a cello, its tenor saxophone, and one Irish harp—those musicians couldn't reach the beach fast enough—struck up the Confederation anthem as soon as the lead Dragons stopped and dropped their ramps.

Brigadier Sturgeon didn't show it, but he was not pleased at the un-expected open air reception—or any public reception for that matter. There was the potential of severe danger here. The Skinks had made it quite clear on Kingdom that they were willing to do anything, includ-ing the slaughter of civilians, to lure Marines to where they were, and they were adept at setting ambushes. If the Skinks were on Maugham's Station, they would be very happy to take advantage of a reception to wipe out the top Marine command, along with the planet's major leadership. But Sturgeon understood the way local authorities would react to the unannounced arrival of the *Grandar Bay* and his Marines, and that certain formalities would have to be observed. That was why he and some of his people wore their gaudiest uniforms.

As soon as the main introductions were complete, Sturgeon said, "Pres-ident Menno, I suggest we retire immediately to a more secure loca-tion."

"But we can't go yet, General! There are many important people waiting to meet you," the President said, gesturing at the dignitaries standing in line. "And the people!" He swung his arm widely. "They all came here to see you and your splendid Marines. They'll be so disappointed if we don't continue the ceremony here! Your visit is such a surprise, we haven't had any time to arrange for you to meet everybody in a more leisurely and seemly fashion."

"Mr. President, I apologize for our abrupt arrival, but we don't know what we're up against—"

Menno blinked. "Yes, why *are* you here? This is so unexpected. We didn't request Confederation Marines, and nobody told us you were coming."

"Those unexplained deaths in the interdicted areas, Mr. President, that's why we are here."

Menno blinked. He had no idea why the accidental deaths of a few disobedient adventurers would interest the Marines, and he said so.

"We don't know that we do have an interest here, but we do have an idea of what killed those people," Sturgeon replied. "If we're right, and I hope we aren't, these people," he indicated the gathered throngs, "could all wind up dead very soon if we don't cut off this open air reception now."

"But General—"

"Please, Mr. President." He took Menno by his elbow and firmly turned him toward the stairs on the back of the stage. Later, he'd correct the President about his rank.

"But—" Menno shook his arm loose. "Let me at least make an announcement." He turned back to face the gathered dignitaries and citizens and spoke into the microphone. "Legislators, judges, other dignitaries, citizens! We are going to adjourn and continue the reception in Congress Hall. All of you, of course, are welcome to attend."

A susurration of disappointment rushed through the crowd; Congress Hall wasn't large enough to accommodate more than a small portion of the people who had gathered to see the off-worlders. Some of the dignitaries in the reception line shouted objections, insisting they were too important to have to wait until they reached Congress Hall to meet the Marine commander.

Sturgeon ignored the disappointment and indignant cries. "Mr. President." He took Menno's elbow once more.

Menno brightened when he saw he was being led to a Dragon rather than his own presidential limousine; he suspected a ride in such a powerful beast would be thrilling.

* * *

There was no help for it, Brigadier Sturgeon had to spend an hour being introduced to everyone who was anybody on Maugham's Station. Well, nearly everyone. If President Menno or Minister Elbrus noticed the absence of Casper Bilisi, Ammon's Deputy Director of Public Safety, and Olympia city's First Assistant Coroner Kara Kum, along with a few other key members of the two departments, neither gave any indication. Those worthies were absent from the reception because they were closeted with Commanders van Winkle and Daana.

Brigadier Sturgeon may have had to spend his time being greeted by what seemed to be half the population of Olympia, but that didn't mean his intelligence chief and the infantry commander couldn't be on the job. That was why van Winkle and Daana had worn garrison utilities rather than their dress reds—they were able to slip away without undue notice.

"Commander." Commander van Winkle, 34th FIST's infantry commander, nodded to Commander Daana, indicating that he should ask the first questions.

"Thank you, sir." Even though they were the same rank, van Winkle was senior, both in time, in grade, and in having a command rather than being a staff officer. Daana looked at the two Ammonites. "Dr. Kum, would you begin by telling us about the bodies?"

First Assistant Coroner Kum nodded. "Call me Kara, please," she replied, and without waiting for a response, handed each of them a hard copy flimsy of an autopsy report. Her office in Olympia Central Hospital was a small room, and the four of them were almost uncomfortably crowded. Shelves crammed with cases of data crystals and, surprisingly, hard copy books and journals, lined the walls. Bones and jars of unidentified but obvious bits of once-live organisms were scattered about.

The report was brief and included only a few paragraphs of text and a few diagrams. "What it says—" Kum began, but van Winkle interrupted her.

"That won't be necessary, Kara, we know enough medical terminology to follow it."

The report said that the clothed skeleton of a man in his late twenties had been thoroughly cleansed of all flesh and other soft tissue, including all the skeletal marrow and dental pulp. Tentative identification was made through dental records. More positive identification was made by matching the molecular structure of the femur with that of a missing man, Samar Volga, who was known to have traveled alone to the Haltia region. Examination of the surface of the bones indicated the scouring of soft tissue had not been made by toothed animals, but by dissolution. The pitting that appeared on parts of the bones appeared to have been caused by acid—of a type not specified, nor was there any indication of testing to identify the acid. Each bone and tooth had been penetrated at least once by a floral tendril, which seemed to have absorbed the marrow and dental pulp. The calcium in the vicinity of the penetrations was missing, along with a few other trace elements, and the remaining structure was considerably weakened. The implication was that in a short time the entire skeleton would have been dissolved to dust.

"This happened in a standard month?" van Winkle asked when he finished reading.

Dr. Kum nodded. "Yes."

Daana looked at the flimsy front and back. "There are no images," he said. "We'd like to see how the remains looked, please."

"Commander—"

"Call me Shalom, please."

"Yes, Shalom. Thank you." She cleared her throat. "The images are, well . . . they're unpleasant. Most people find them too disturbing to look at."

"Doctor—Kara—my name, 'Shalom,' might translate to 'peace' in an ancient language, but I'm a Marine. I assure you, I have seen more disturbing sights than anything your images could show me."

She looked at van Winkle, who said, "We can take it," then at Bilisi, who nodded. Dr. Kum morphed a console from her desktop and tapped a brief series of commands.

A quarter-scale trid appeared off to the side; the office was too small to permit the four to walk around to examine the trid from all sides, so Kum rotated it. The image in the trid was of the patch of ground where Samar Volga's remains had been found. The bones and tatters of clothing were highlighted for easy viewing. A few of the tendrils that penetrated the cloth and anchored the skeleton to the ground were visible. The scene continued until the body bag closed over the remains.

Van Winkle and Daana exchanged a glance. While neither said anything, both were surprised by the tendrils that anchored the remains. Neither had ever seen anything quite like that before, though between them they'd been on nearly half of the human occupied planets during their Marine careers.

Dr. Kum touched another button and the trid was replaced with a view of a laboratory. "This is the autopsy room," she explained. The still-clad skeleton lay on an examination table.

"Can you give us a close-up?" Daana asked.

"What would you like to see?" she replied.

"Focus on that large rent on the shoulder."

She twiddled the controls of the trid and the image shifted until the shoulder was centered, then enlarged to life size. The Marines exchanged another wordless glance—the burn pattern around the edges of the rent was very similar to what they'd seen in the chameleons of Marines who were hit by the Skinks' acid guns before the Marines had received acid-proof uniforms during the Kingdom Campaign.

"Continue, please," Daana said.

They watched as two people clad in one-piece hazard suits cut off the garments. "That's me with the cutter," Kum said, identifying the person leading the autopsy. Daana wanted a close-up of where a tendril penetrated bone. Then the trid closely scanned the surfaces of the skeleton, showing clearly that it had been thoroughly cleaned of soft tissue. Shallow pitting was visible where the clothing had been eaten away. The trid went on to show the interior of bones, through cams inserted through holes in the bones, cross sections cut from them, and long bones sliced open. Close-ups showed the bones so thoroughly cleaned of marrow the insides looked as if they'd been scrubbed.

"Have you ever seen its like before?" van Winkle asked at the end of the presentation.

"Never," Dr. Kum replied soberly. "Not in nature. Even after a body has been eaten by carnivores and scavengers, there is some soft tissue left. And animals break bones open to get at the marrow. I've seen plants send shoots into bones, but only through breaks something else made in them."

Deputy Director Bilisi agreed that he'd never seen anything similar.

Except for the damage clearly caused by acid, neither had the Marines. But they didn't comment on that.

Kum shook her head. "It appears—don't look back at the reports, I didn't include this in them—as if the soft tissues were devoured by plants." She looked perplexed. Carnivorous plants existed, but she'd never heard of any that consumed large animals so thoroughly. "We need to send an expedition out to investigate these plants," she said softly, as though to herself.

"Were the other bodies the same?" Daana asked.

"Almost exactly," Dr. Kum answered. "The only differences are consistent with the length of time between death and recovery."

The Marines didn't look at each other, but they were thinking the same thing. When they went in, they'd have to be on the alert to hostile plants as well as Skinks—or other enemies. It wasn't a prospect either welcomed.

"What about the places?" van Winkle asked. "Do we need to go to your office, Director?"

Bilisi shook his head and withdrew a crystal from his shirt pocket. "I have everything here," he told them, then turned to Dr. Kum. "If I may, Kara."

"Yes, do," she said, moving from behind her desk.

Bilisi took her place and popped the crystal into a slot on the side of the console. He briefed them on its contents while he tapped the commands to bring up displays on a 2-D screen. "This crystal has maps of the areas where the bodies were found. Topological, geographic, microclimate, what we know of flora and fauna, geothermic. It's got vids and trids of the flora found near the remains in each of those areas, and the fauna found outside them."

"Outside?" van Winkle asked. "What about the fauna *inside* them?"

Bilisi shrugged. "We never saw any. They must have fled when we were on our way in." He shook his head. "The odd thing was, we didn't see any tracks either." He looked at the Marines as if he was asking them to explain why there didn't seem to be any animals in the interdicted areas where the bodies had been found.

The Marines studied the topomaps with great interest for several minutes before asking for the geological maps. All three areas, ovals more than ten kilometers along the long axis, formed steep-sided, irregular bowls with walls of uneven height resembling huge volcanic calderas.

"What causes that topography?" van Winkle finally asked. It vaguely resembled the basin-and-plain formation found in the southwestern quadrant of North America on Earth, except for the bowl-like valleys contained within them.

"Nobody knows."

Van Winkle looked at him.

"There's never been a full geologic study."

"Why not?" Van Winkle looked briefly at Dr. Kum. "I know why BEHIND never made much of a survey of Maugham's Station, but you don't seem to have done one either. That doesn't leave you well prepared for surprises." He left unsaid, *Surprises like what happened to those people*, but the question hung between them anyway.

"We are developing our world methodically, Commander," Bilisi said coldly. "If those people had stayed out of the interdicted areas like they were supposed to, nothing would have happened to them." Clearly he wanted to cut off that line of discussion by shifting blame for whatever happened to the people who had died so horribly.

Van Winkle reminded himself that it was their world, to do with as they wished so long as they weren't in violation of Confederation laws. Not exploring wasn't a violation, so if they didn't want to . . .

They resumed studying the maps and images. The only questions the Marines asked now had to do with details of what they were looking at. Neither commented on it, but both were surprised at how little the planetary Deputy Director of Public Safety knew about his world outside the borders of Ammon.

Van Winkle's comm signaled about the time they ran out of questions to ask. It was Lieutenant Quaticatl, Brigadier Sturgeon's aide. The reception was over, and the brigadier requested the pleasure of their company at their earliest convenience—which was the military way of politely saying "right now."

When he told his hosts they had to leave, van Winkle added, "May we have a copy of that crystal?" He didn't care about the maps—the *Grandar Bay*'s string-of-pearls could provide better maps—but the images of the ground and flora inside the "interdicted" areas could be valuable.

"You can have this one, it's a copy," Bilisi said as he popped the crystal from the console and handed it over.

The Marines thanked Bilisi and Kum for their assistance and took their leave.

Commanders van Winkle and Daana found Staff Sergeants Wu and Cunningham, the FIST's recon and UAV squad leaders, with Brigadier Sturgeon, Commander Wolfe, and Captain West in the office suite President Menno offered to FIST to use as its operations center.

"What did you find out?" Sturgeon asked as soon as the door closed behind them.

While van Winkle began briefing their commander, Daana popped the data crystal into a console so the recon and UAV squad leaders could study the maps and life data during the briefing, then joined in with the infantry commander. It took them a lot less time to bring Sturgeon up to date than the two civilians had taken to impart the information.

"Three areas," Brigadier Sturgeon mused when the briefing was completed, "three recon teams, three UAV teams." He looked at Daana and the two squad leaders. "Can you do it?" His eyes flicked at van Winkle; the infantry battalion also had a scout/sniper squad and UAV teams that had experience working with the FIST intelligence gatherers.

"I've been thinking about exactly that, sir," Daana said. "Those areas are large. It will take days for one recon team and one UAV team to thoroughly investigate them. But if Skinks are present in any numbers, it won't take long to find them. And if they are there in numbers, the less intrusive we are, the better chance we have of finding them without being discovered ourselves."

"I concur, sir," van Winkle said.

"Good enough. Commander Daana, I want to see your plans inside two hours. Commander van Winkle, I want you to observe the development of the FIST intelligence plan and prepare a plan of your own based on it. Your immediate objectives will be to coordinate additional intelligence assets with FIST intelligence, prepare a ready force to rescue any recon team that gets into trouble, and prepare a ready force to strike at any target of opportunity disclosed by F2.

"Commander Wolfe, your aircraft are grounded except in emergency situations. When they do fly, they are to remain below the altitude of the valley crests. I want your Raptors armed and prepared to launch Jerichos if needed.

"Questions?"

"Nossir!" the three said.

As soon as Sturgeon and the others were gone, Daana grinned at Wu and Cunningham. They grinned back. Van Winkle and Wolfe recognized the feral expressions of men about to embark on a dangerous mission, men who intended it to be far more dangerous to those they were going up against. If the officers had looked into a mirror, they would have been surprised to see their faces bore the same grin.

CHAPTER SIXTEEN

The corner of Brigadier Sturgeon's mouth twitched as he read over Commander Daana's operation plan, but as FIST commander, it was inappropriate for him to wear a feral grin. Later, when he ordered his FIST into combat, he would look like an alpha wolf about to assert his dominance. He liked the plan and approved it with no changes. Shortly afterward, Commander van Winkle presented his trio of proposals. Sturgeon approved them as well, and released the infantry commander to prepare Company L for the initial stages of the operation.

From its beginnings in hot-air balloons in the mid-nineteenth century, military commanders have found aerial observation and intelligence gathering a valuable pursuit. But aerial observation has always been vulnerable to defeat. As soon as an observer is spotted by the object of its search, steps can be taken to hide or put out decoys. Even orbital satellites can be deceived by such measures. And aerial observation platforms, weather balloons, manned aircraft, and unmanned aerial vehicles have always been vulnerable to fire directed at them from the ground. Even orbital satellites were vulnerable to jamming or destruction by ground, air, or orbital-based weapon systems. And an enemy's intelligent use of camouflage just added to the problem. Those are simple facts that commanders who use aerial observation have always had to live with.

The Confederation Marine Corps, on the other hand, being Marines, didn't believe they had to accept limitations just because everybody else did. And, as Marines, they believed firmly in taking care of their own. They wanted the use of UAVs for battlefield intelligence gathering, and didn't want the craft to be fooled or lost just because they could be seen by an enemy on the ground. So they came up with their own form of UAV, one that could be disguised as any manner of native flier that approximated its size. *Sizes*, actually; the Marines used two different UAVs that could variously look like bird, mammal, or large insect analogs—whatever flying creature was appropriate for where they were deployed.

Not only could the Marine UAVs mimic the look of local flying fauna, they could mimic their actions. Some birds or their analogs constantly flap their wings in flight, while others use their wings sparingly and glide mostly on thermals. The same was true of flying mammals and their analogs. The bodies of flying insectoids commonly bop up and down between their wings, and jitter from side to side in flight.

So could the Marines' UAVs, which could even adjust their thermal output to mimic the infrared signals of real fliers.

As soon as the Confederation Marines adopted their new UAVs, their UAV combat losses dropped dramatically.

The Confederation Army, which was still using UAVs that looked and acted like UAVs, continued to suffer heavy UAV combat losses and became intensely jealous. The Marines, being Marines, smiled smugly and basked in the army's jealousy. After a few campaigns and wars in which the Confederation Army lost a goodly number of UAVs, the army's then–chief of staff broke down and said "pretty please," and the Marines graciously allowed the army to license their UAV design.

Confederation Army UAV losses dropped dramatically.

That didn't mean the army stopped swearing about "those damn Marines." After all, didn't the army have an ancient tradition of bestowing its castoffs and obsolete equipment on the Marines? One should expect *some* gratitude, they thought. But no, not from "those damn Marines"; they were too arrogant by more than half.

For initial operations on Maugham's Station, the Marines disguised their larger UAVs as the Joseph's coated papukaija, a largish, nut-eating bird with riotously colored plumage; and the smaller ones as varpuna thrushmockers, a midsize, drab-plumage, insectoid eater that flitted swiftly from tree to tree.

Three UAV teams, three areas to observe—fortuitous symmetry.

* * *

The FIST-level UAVs were much more sophisticated machines than those used by the infantry companies. The company-level UAVs needed to be constantly controlled and observed, so if both of a blaster company's UAVs were flying simultaneously, both members of the UAV team had to focus on them, one Marine flying each. FIST-level UAVs, on the other hand, had low-level AIs capable of enough independence that an experienced operator could easily control two simultaneously. FIST UAVs were even smart enough to recognize not only the patterns they were programmed to look for, but patterns that didn't match anything they'd already observed on their missions, and to draw their operator's attention to them.

Staff Sergeant Geiger monitored his displays with only a part of his attention during the flights of his two varpuna thrushmockers to the strange, calderalike valley north of Ammon. He paid far more attention to the instruction he was giving Lance Corporal Hawker, the most junior and least experienced man in the FIST UAV squad. It was only Hawker's second live operation. Admittedly, the previous operation—against the Skinks on Kingdom—had been quite a baptism of fire.

"We have to do this a lot differently," Geiger explained. "On Kingdom, we had to search an entire planet, with lots of open landscapes and swamps. Here, we're going to be looking in small areas with very definite boundaries and dense forest—and we don't even have any clear definition yet of what ground level is, or how the ground lays."

That was why Geiger operated the thrushmockers while Hawker handled the two mock Joseph's coated papukaijas. Usually, the senior team member had the larger UAVs. Here, Geiger expected most of the intelligence they gathered to come from deep within the tree cover where the larger UAVs would have more trouble maneuvering, and he wanted personal control of the vehicles that could go deep.

"I want you to stay high," Geiger said, "one in the treetops and the other above them—"

"You already told me that several times, Staff Sergeant," Hawker interrupted.

"And I'm going to keep telling you until you can repeat it in your sleep." Geiger wasn't annoyed by the interruption, he expected it; Hawker wasn't the first Marine he'd broken in as a UAV operator, and

they'd all reached a point where they got so sick of having their instructions repeated to them that they objected. He'd done the same
thing when he was a lance corporal just starting out as a UAV driver.
Just wait until this youngster had to start repeating his instructions after
only hearing them one time—and keep repeating them until the mission was over.

"As I was saying, you stay high, I go low. You look for clearings,
even breaks in the canopy that are just large enough for a hopper to
drop a man-line through, anyplace that gives access between the top of
the canopy and the ground below the trees. And pay attention to your
infra views. Close attention. You've seen the records of the Skink infra
signatures. They don't show much in infra, but they *do* show—you
have to look sharp to spot and recognize them."

Geiger grinned behind the expressionless mask of his face at the
way Hawker grimaced when he mentioned the Skinks. During their
major assault on Haven, before 34th FIST was reinforced by 26th FIST
on Kingdom, one Skink squad had made it all the way to FIST headquarters, and most of the UAV squad—including Hawker—had to take
up blasters and fight them off.

"Remember to keep track of where my birds are so we can coordinate when one of us spots something that needs investigation."

Hawker tuned Geiger's voice out and watched his displays. Especially the visual. He hadn't been on many planets, so every new world
was still a marvel to him. He'd originally applied for UAV school because he thought flying the observation birds would give him lots of
opportunity to see new worlds in ways the infantry or squadron ground
crews never could. So far he hadn't been disappointed. Flying UAVs
was as much fun as he'd thought it would be, so much so that he didn't
even mind all the hours he had to put in on maintaining the birds—or
listening to his team leader repeating instructions he knew well enough
to recite in his sleep.

He did his best to forget fighting the Skinks on Kingdom.

He enjoyed the swooping flight of the mock Joseph's coated
papukaijas. The birds had evolved for short flights in the upper canopy,
with short forays into the understories, but they were capable of extended journeys so long as they could make frequent stops. These two
papukaijas were launched from the UAV tower and glided several

kilometers, using their wings only occasionally to move from updraft to updraft. They didn't follow a straight path from the launch tower to their destination. Instead, they zigged and zagged from copse to copse, and stopped for occasional "rests."

Similarly, the "thrushmockers" that launched when the "papukaijas" were halfway to their area of operations, wings beating constantly, flitted this way and that as though snatching insectoids on the fly, and stopped to perch now and again.

The UAVs reached their AO near enough to simultaneously be in coordinated formation, but with just enough staggering to appear natural and random to an observer. Surely if that hypothetical observer noticed that they seemed to be paired—one papukaija and one thrushmocker in each pair—the pairing would seem random. By then Lance Corporal Hawker was droning his instructions aloud in harmony with Staff Sergeant Geiger's repetition.

The four birds perched on the topological crest of the strange valley's walls and cocked their heads from side to side, swiveled about, aiming one eye here, one eye there, looking over the terrain.

Back in the operations center, Geiger and Hawker studied their displays, paying particular attention to the visual and infra views. Hawker's eyes widened at the sight of the lush vegetation that spread before them, and it made him eager to fly his papukaijas over and into the canopy. Geiger likewise noted the lushness with pleasure, but he also noticed the absence of birds flying above it. Both noticed that no large, heat-producing bodies were visible in infra, and the motion detectors showed nothing that indicated moving masses that couldn't be accounted for by air currents in the trees.

"Let's do it," Geiger murmured. He pushed a button, and one at a time the thrushmockers launched themselves into the air and darted, wings flitting, into the trees.

Next to him, Hawker also pushed a button, and a second after Geiger's birds, the two papukaijas flung themselves off the cliff edge and spread their wings to swoop on the air currents above the treetops.

"Where is everybody?" Hawker suddenly blurted.

"It's about time you noticed we aren't crashing somebody's party," Geiger came back. "Turn on your proximity sensors and threat detectors."

"Aye aye," Hawker replied, tapping the commands into his console. "This is weird. Did you ever see empty air like this anywhere before?"

"Once," Geiger said, keeping most of his attention on his displays. "On an exploratory world that wasn't ready for human habitation. We were searching for lost prospectors who weren't supposed to be there in the first place. Photosynthesis hadn't had enough time to pump sufficient oxygen into the atmosphere, and avians hadn't evolved yet."

"That's different, that's a young planet. What about one like this, a world that has birds, with an area where there aren't any fliers?"

"Only where local conditions make the atmosphere poisonous." Geiger checked his displays. "That's not the situation here; that air's breathable."

Hawker flew one of his UAVs higher and ratcheted up its visuals, then coasted the bird in a circular pattern. "Plenty of birds in the sky," he murmured, "but they're all on the other side of the wall."

"Do you see me?"

Hawker checked a display. "Got you in a pretty picture."

"I'm going to the deck for a closer look. Watch me."

The two fake thrushmockers had been flitting through the middle canopy; after the first few minutes, Geiger had stopped their insectoid-catching charade—there didn't seem to be any flying insectoids in the middle canopy. The two disguised UAVs, nearly a quarter klick apart, darted groundward. Neither landed. Instead they flew just a meter above the ground, as slowly as possible for a thrushmocker. Their infras showed nothing but the faint background glow of the rotting vegetation that covered the ground. Light gathering visuals showed what looked like the normal detritus that blanketed a deciduous forest floor: leaves, twigs, rotted branches, bark flakes, trailing vines, with saplings and weeds poking through all over, straining to reach sunlight.

Geiger checked Hawker's displays, then asked, "See anything odd on my visuals?"

Hawker looked at the other's visual displays for a moment and shook his head. "Looks like a hundred other forests I've flown through."

"Look harder." Geiger flicked his eyes between his own and Hawker's displays while the lance corporal searched his visuals for something out of the ordinary.

"Nothing," Hawker finally said, a question in his tone. Obviously, Geiger saw something and he was missing it.

"No bones," Geiger said. "Animals die in a forest. Their bodies rot away, but bones are left behind because they take longer to decay away or subsume. There are no bones."

"But—"

"The native bones here aren't quite the same as ours, but they decay the same as ours. And there aren't any in this forest— Wait a minute, what's that?"

One of the thrushmockers veered toward something that poked out of a tangle of vines and shoots. It was the first sign they'd seen of animate life inside the bowl. Geiger double-checked his displays to make sure nothing was lurking nearby, then hovered his UAV about thirty centimeters above and to one side of the protrusion.

"Bone," he whispered. "It's a bone. He magnified the vision of the eye fixed on the bone—it was curved like a rib—and blinked. A tendril had bored through its surface. He looked down the bone, into the tangle of vines. By gathering more light, he was able to peer deeper into the tangle and see more bones underneath the vines. He blinked again; several of the bones seemed to have tendrils poking into them.

Suddenly his view spun about as something struck the UAV from its blind side, then the view went blank. His fingers danced over his console as he looked quickly from display to display—all of the UAV's sensors were down!

As he switched to the other thrushmocker and sent it to the lower canopy, heading toward the dead bird, he asked, "Did you see what hit me?"

"There wasn't anything there!" Hawker squawked. "My motion detector picked up something faint, but there isn't anything where it came from."

"Show me," Geiger snapped. An arrowed line traced on the overview. He simultaneously angled his remaining bird toward the line's point of origin and increased the magnification on the overview. "How could someone get that close without us spotting him?" he demanded—the arrowed line was only ten meters long. Hawker wisely decided against attempting an answer.

The thrushmocker circled above where the overview showed the shot had come from, and Geiger focused all its sensors on the place. Nothing. Not even the highest magnification and light gathering showed any sign of a depression on the ground cover where a body might have lain in ambush.

"Are you sure that's where it came from?" he growled.

"According to the motion detector, that's where."

"Damn," Geiger muttered. He drew a vector through the vine tangle where he'd been examining the bones and the spot where Hawker's motion detector showed the silent shot had come from and beyond, and sent his remaining UAV along it, searching for any sign that the shot originated farther out, or sign of someone withdrawing. "Send one of your birds inside the canopy and follow me," he ordered.

"Aye aye." Hawker left his high papukaija orbiting and dropped his low one into the middle canopy, trailing the thrushmocker. *"Right front!"* he shouted, and threw his UAV into a rapid climb, jinking from side to side in evasive maneuvers.

But his warning was too late as a string of viscous, greenish fluid arced out and spattered the thrushmocker, tumbling it into a tree trunk. The UAV crunched and plopped to the ground.

"It came from that tree!" Hawker sent his bird into an Immelmann, and came out of it swooping at the tree the stream had come from. He didn't see the stringer that barely missed his UAV's tail feathers. Seven meters from the tree he twisted his UAV's body to vertical and spun its wings in a braking rotation. The wings blocked his peripheral vision, and he didn't see the second streamer that hit his UAV's side, spinning it out of control. A third streamer blinded it and sent it careening toward the ground.

"Get that last bird out of there, *now!*" Geiger barked.

Hawker canceled his remaining UAV's motion-mimic and sent the false bird climbing for altitude at speed before turning it to head for home.

In little more than two minutes, three of the flight's four UAVs were gone—and they didn't know what had killed them.

In the *Grandar Bay*'s real-time intel section, SRA2 Hummfree watched the three Marine UAVs die. He made sure he'd programmed his console for instant replay of what he was watching, then leaned back and rubbed a hand over his eyes. He'd seen the UAVs go down, had even seen faint flickers that might have been the flight paths of whatever it was that killed two of them. What he hadn't seen was anything at the other end of the flight path of the killer.

He leaned forward again and replayed the scene. And replayed it again, and again. But no matter how he diddled the dials and tickled the buttons, no matter how he merged visual, infra, X and gamma ray—it didn't matter that he was able to clarify the flight paths of the killer strokes that took down the UAVs—he couldn't find any signal that would show him the shooter.

He increased the long baseline interferometry he was using from three satellites to four, then five, and finally six. With the resolution he was able to tweak out of that, he could make out individual leaves in the upper canopy. But he still couldn't find the shooters.

What was going on down there?

CHAPTER SEVENTEEN

Corporal Sonj and Lance Corporals Makin and Zhon flicked off their HUD displays and glanced toward where Sergeant Steffan was squirreled out of sight on the north side of the shallow depression in which the recon team lay hidden; their infra signals were muted. The recon team leader kept his HUD on and reran what he and his men had just observed. The navy's string-of-pearls had relayed scrambled visual signals to them, with infra overlay, from the quartet of disguised UAVs flying through the interdicted area they were about to enter over the ridgetop fifty meters away.

Steffan concentrated, determined not to miss anything that would help them accomplish their mission, anything that would allow them all to report back to the FIST F2, intelligence section, alive and uninjured. He watched as the first fake thrushmocker spun, lost vision, and went dead. He saw the greenish streamer slam into the second thrushmocker and kill it. He shrugged off vertigo as the first papukaija went into its defensive maneuvers, braked to look at the tree the streamer had come from, and then spun out of control itself from a blindside hit before its transmission went blank and died. None of the four UAVs had picked up anything in infra other than the subtle warmth of decaying vegetation on the forest floor. The summary of other data collected showed no movement other than the faint lines of the streamers that killed the three UAVs and another that missed the papukaija. Whoever had shot them down did it from very close proximity to the birds, none much more than ten meters from their targets.

Steffan had seen those greenish streamers before. So had Sonj and Zhon. Makin hadn't; he was one of the new men who joined 34th FIST after the return to Thorsfinni's World from Kingdom. It was the stream from Skink acid guns. Steffan took a slow, deep breath to keep from shivering; the Skink weapons were horrible, but the acid gun was the worst of them. He was glad he and his men were wearing chameleons impregnated with acid neutralizer. Before they went over that saddle, he'd have to double-check his men to make sure none of them had exposed skin, or poor seals where acid could get inside their uniforms.

He blinked. He was assuming they'd have hot contact with the Skinks, which was the worst thing a recon Marine in this kind of situation could have—detection by the enemy on an intelligence gathering mission usually meant the mission failed.

He knew the Skinks had some sense that allowed them to detect chameleoned Marines, almost as though they could see in infrared. They couldn't see in infrared, though, he knew that. Whatever sense it was that they did have gave them a general location, not the exact position of a Marine invisible in his chameleons. But whatever that sense was, it shouldn't have recognized the disguised UAVs for what they were. Did the Skinks have new equipment, something they hadn't used on Kingdom, that allowed them to see through disguises? Would it allow them to locate the exact position of chameleoned Marines? The Skinks' rail guns had caught the Marines by surprise on Kingdom, so they might have something new now. The team would have to be alert for that possibility.

"Inspection," he said into the team circuit of his helmet comm. Unlike the helmet comms of Marine infantry—which were difficult to intercept because their weak signals wouldn't travel far—Recon's helmet comms used spread-spectrum burst transmissions in addition to weak signals. Moving faster than he had at any time since they'd gotten away from Dragon at their insertion point several kilometers and five hours earlier, Steffan went from Marine to Marine, checking for exposed skin or loose closures on their chameleons.

Good, he thought when he was finished with the inspection. They were all tight, no place for the acid guns to injure them. He checked their weapons while he was at it. All four had their knives and hand-blasters secured, but where they could be quickly and easily drawn. Their blasters were fully charged and the safeties were on. He checked his own microwave sniper rifle, a weapon seldom used by FIST-level recon, to make sure its safety was on. He was less concerned with whether it was fully charged, since he didn't expect to find a target he couldn't resist—and if he did have the opportunity to take out an enemy commander, all it would take was one shot from his silent weapon.

"If they spot us, we shoot and scoot. You know what we're doing," he said. "Let's go."

Silently, invisible to casual observers, the four Marines rose from their places and drifted on an angle toward the slope fifty meters away. Their destination was a split in the ridgetop at the side of a saddle four klicks west and north of where the doomed UAV flight had crossed into the valley. They knew it was unlikely any human opponents could spot them, but unlikely didn't mean impossible, so recon Marines always moved carefully—other Marines thought preternaturally so—to avoid detection. This time they weren't positive who they were up against or what their capabilities were. This time their careful movement was so cautious they seemed nearly preternatural even by recon standards. Once they started angling up the slope, they only had to climb eighty meters to reach the split, but it took them more than a half hour standard to do it.

Steffan eased himself closer to the crack in the ridge next to the saddle and stopped less than ten meters from it. He reached into a side pocket of his pack and drew out a minnie, disguised as a native rat-size marsupialoid. He uncovered the control panel on his side and lightly touched the controls.

"HUD check," he said, and flicked his on. Immediately, a minnie's-eye view superimposed itself on his vision.

"I see it," Sonj said.

"Got it," Zhon concurred.

"It's clear," Makin said, speaking for the first time since infiltration.

Steffan touched a series of commands on the control panel and the minnie skittered forward, scooting under bushes and fallen leaves whenever possible. It paused at the edge of the split, its nose twitching as it sniffed the air moving through it, checking for vagrant molecules that could indicate human presence somewhere out of sight. A graph on the side of Steffan's HUD showed nothing out of the ordinary—as if anyone knew what was ordinary inside the interdicted valleys. He touched new commands and the minnie eased away from the edge and into the split. It paused and hunched its back; any observer who didn't know better would think it was defecating. But it was just dropping a comm relay to maintain its connection with Steffan. The patrol leader released it, and the minnie skittered along the bottom of the split on auto.

Flakes and chunks of rock had fallen from the sides of the split in the untold time since the top of the ridge had first cracked. Grains and clods of dirt fell from the top, as had leaves, twigs, and shootlets that failed to gain secure purchase above. The bottom was as uneven as such random falls could make it, and the scree sloped down from the center to the outsides so that standing men on opposite sides couldn't see each other over it. Much of the cracked floor was loose; flakes and chunks of rock balanced precariously one upon another. The minnie scootched through temporary tunnels, scrabbled over loose rocks, burrowed through dirt and plant fall. Up and down the minnie went and from side to side, climbing the uneven, undulating floor to its peak.

At the midway point Steffan had it pause behind a screen of fallen foliage that roofed a small hollow between two chunks of rock. The minnie sniffed for telltale molecules, peering in visual and infra at the narrow wedge of ground it could see beyond the split's far side. It used its magnifier and light gathering capabilities to see deeper than a man could into the trees beyond. Its motion sensor, which could track the progress of a gnat at more than thirty meters, quivered with the effort of picking up movement. It perked and transited its ears, listening to the forest sounds that funneled its way.

Not a single sensor detected anything that didn't belong to forest flora.

Odd, Steffan thought. What pollinates the plants? According to the minnie's reports, there weren't even any insectoids in the forest's fringe.

He sent the minnie skittering forward to pause again when it reached the far side of the split and repeat its midway investigation. Still no sign of anything animate.

"Let's go," he said.

Corporal Sonj rose from where he'd hunkered invisibly against the rock wall, slipped past his team leader and into the split. Steffan followed him, with Makin coming third. Zhon brought up the rear. All but Steffan turned off their HUDs. Ahead of them the minnie skittered from rock to rock, bush to bush, staying as much out of sight of unknown lurkers in the forest as possible.

The Marines went through the split fast; the jumbled surface was too loose for them to stealthily crawl over or walk across, so they needed to get through fast, before anybody could spot the movement of the scree and react to it. On the other side they spread to the sides, two to the left, two to the right; fanned out, frozen, almost totally invisible. Even their infra signals were muted. They lay looking, listening, smelling the air. Their eyes drank in the riot of pinks, scarlets, ambers, blues, and manifold greens before them. They listened to the wind in the trees. Scents of alien flora wafted to their noses. They used every amplifier they had, looking and listening for any hint of anything they couldn't see or hear with their own eyes and ears.

There was less than they'd ever seen in any forest before; no sign of animate life—not even hungry or thirsty insectoids seeking to enter their chameleons.

Strange, stranger, strangest, Steffan thought. He did his best to ignore the sensation crawling along his spine.

They waited a quarter hour standard, a half, then an entire hour standard. Steffan and Sonj watched the progress of the minnie on their HUDs as it crept through the forest fringe and penetrated beyond where they could see from outside of the split.

"Sonj, minnie," Steffan finally said.

"Roger," Sonj replied, and momentarily busied himself releasing the team's other minnie.

"HUDs up," Steffan ordered when Sonj's minnie and its input appeared on his HUD. He transmitted a map to his men. Little of the interior of the geologically bizarre valley was clear on the map—there were no local maps, and the string-of-pearls hadn't yet managed to map surface detail with much accuracy through the dense forest cover. The route he traced on his map instantly appeared on his men's HUDs. So did the dots he indicated as rally points should they get separated. The route he sketched followed an irregular arc to a point four kilometers into the forest, where they would laager for the night, then back out again on a different irregular arc that led to a saddle three kilometers north and a bit west of their current position. Their you-are-here and the two minnies were also marked.

"Got it?"

"Got it," Sonj confirmed; the map was stored in his HUD for recall if needed.

"Check," Zhon replied.

"Stored," said Makin.

The four Marines eased into the forest, taking advantage of every bit of concealment, just as they would if they weren't in infra-damping chameleons. Trying to follow in each other's unseen footsteps, they formed into a straighter line than infantry would. Their interval was also greater than the infantry would maintain in this denseness, just close enough for them to pick up the ultraviolet tags on the back of the helmet and boot heels of the man to their front. The minnies scooted ahead of them, ranging up to twenty-five meters to the flanks.

There were watercourses on the forest floor, a lot of them, most merely thin trickles a man could step across without stretching. They came across very few with pools deep enough for a prone man to lay in submerged. That bothered Steffan; Skinks favored swamps and marshes, or at least streams deep enough for them to swim or crawl through as underwater pathways. Except when they used their small armored vehicles. But the armor required relatively open terrain, and the trees here were too close together for the Skink armor to easily maneuver. The way the soft ground oozed under his boots, he suspected it might be too soft for the armor even if the trees were spread widely enough—Skink armor had wheels and tracks, instead of being air cushioned like the Marine Dragons.

It took several hours of slow, cautious movement through the increasingly weird forest for the recon team to reach its laager point. It remained lush all the way, but they never heard an avian sing or saw a flying insectoid. The ground was barren of animal tracks and spoor. The only animate life they saw was tiny mites crawling on occasional tree trunks or the vines that sprawled across the occasional open area. And the open areas, none as large as ten meters along any axis, had been odd. In other forests, a patch opened when a tree fell, and didn't stay open for long before weeds, bushes, and saplings sprouted and grew in quest for sunlight. Here, the open areas looked like they'd been reserved for low-lying scrub brush and scattered weeds, as though trees had never grown in them. Was there something in the ground that made those patches inhospitable to the forest's trees? Then why hadn't a tree evolved that could take advantage of them?

They had questions but no answers. And not the slightest evidence of Skinks—or any other possible foe.

Steffan and Sonj sent their minnies up trees next to the open patch Steffan had chosen to mark as their laager. They wouldn't spend the night in the open, but alongside it. The minnies climbed the trees to recharge their batteries before the sun went down over the valley wall, and to briefly act as relays for communication with the string-of-pearls; comm had been broken and sporadic during their forest trek. The only download Command had for them was a slightly improved map of the forest floor. Neither of the patrols in the other two areas being reconned had reported sighting any enemy.

The minnies came back down after only a few minutes and were set to patrolling around the laager. The Marines ate cold rations and settled in for a fifty percent overnight watch—two sleeping for two hours while the other two remained up and alert. Steffan and Makin took the first watch.

The strangeness of the forest during the day only deepened after the sun set. The only sound was the soft sighing and occasional rattling of air currents in the trees; no hoo's of night-flying predators could be heard, nor buzzing nocturnal insectoid blood suckers, nor cries of night hunters or the squeals of captured prey.

Steffan looked around through his infra screen. The prone bodies of his men hardly registered against the constant background heat given off by decaying vegetation on the forest floor. The heat-muting function of the recon Marines' chameleons was functioning exactly as it should. They weren't even as visible in infrared as the Skinks he'd seen on Kingdom had been. Almost subconsciously, he tracked the minnies on his HUD; sometimes, when he looked carefully at where they were, he caught a quick infra flash of one of them as it skittered past his view.

Nothing else gave off infra signals. In some atavistic corner of his mind the faint glows became noncorporeal, ghostly. He shivered and raised his infra, opting for the light gatherer and magnifier shields instead. The moon was still below the top of the valley, but some starlight diffused through small gaps in the canopy. There wasn't much light for his screen to gather, but at least he wasn't blind. And even the flattened,

depth-perception-deprived view of darkest night seen through his light
gatherer and magnifier shields was better than the eerie sights seen in
infra.

What was that?

A sudden rustle, as of something moving in the brush along the opposite edge of the small clearing. He saw nothing with light and magnification, switched to infra and still saw nothing.

"See anything?" he murmured into his comm.

"No, what was it?" Makin replied, his voice edgy but quiet. His posture, barely visible in infra, showed he had his blaster pointed in the direction of the sound and his fingers wrapped around its firing lever.

Steffan redirected one of the minnies to the area the sound had
come from and flipped his "all hands alert" toggle. In seconds Sonj and
Zhon responded. He slowly shifted his sniper rifle until it was in his
shoulder and pointing at where he'd heard the sound. He flashed a half-
second infra beam at it. Both clicked to acknowledge his point.

"Zhon, rear," the team leader ordered.

Zhon rolled to face into the forest and cover the team's rear.

The redirected minnie scooted through the area of the sound, pausing here and there for just a second or two to sniff and peer about, but
found nothing. The four Marines waited in silence for long minutes.
Steffan wondered if what he'd heard had been a rotten piece of wood
collapsing. But no, it had sounded like movement. And he couldn't see
anything that might have moved.

There it was again! And this time he'd seen it! Almost saw it. In his
peripheral vision. Something had definitely moved. He slithered backward, took the safety off his sniper rifle, and directed the nearer minnie
to investigate.

Nothing again. He sent the other minnie. Working together rapidly,
the two minnies quartered the area. Nothing. Steffan's hair stood and
the skin of his shoulders and back crawled. He *knew* he'd seen something move, but the minnies weren't able to find anything. What was
going on?

There was the sound of movement in a third place. Steffan turned
to look toward it just in time to see a streamer of viscous fluid, gray in
the gathered starlight, arcing toward him.

"SKINKS!" he shouted, twisting out of the streamer's path and
pointing his sniper rifle at its source. He pressed the firing button, and

a line of air seemed to shimmer from his muzzle to the clump of brush the streamer came from. The sniper rifle was no good in a pitched battle; it needed half a minute to recharge between shots. He drew his hand-blaster and sent a bolt of plasma into the same brush.

"They're over here!" Makin shouted, and fired his blaster in the direction of the original sound.

Another *crack-sizzle* sounded as Sonj fired.

More streamers came out of the forest and from the fringe of the small clearing. One of the minnies squealed its distress signal, and its data transmissions stopped.

"They're all around!" Sonj screamed, echoed by Makin.

"Zhon, report!" Steffan ordered.

"Clear to my front," Zhon reported.

"Go!" Steffan had no idea how many Skinks there were, but even though their chameleons were protecting them from the acid now, given time and enough hits the acid would eat through. And they were too few to beat off a charge if the Skinks closed with them. He grabbed the sniper rifle with his free hand and radioed in a report as he ran.

The four recon Marines leaped to their feet and barreled into the forest, away from the clearing, firing to their rear as they went. The remaining minnie continued to skitter through the area, seeking out the foe and transmitting data until acid streamers spilled over it, first blinding then silencing it.

They raced through the forest, disturbing its quiet. But no startled forest fauna was there to add their noise to the Marines' crashing progress—and there was no sound of any pursuit.

Five hundred meters from where they'd been attacked, Sergeant Steffan checked all his sensors. They showed him nothing.

"Stealth right." In response to Steffan's order, the Marines stopped running and turned perpendicular to the direction in which they'd been moving, maneuvering slowly, silently. "Down." They stopped and lowered themselves to defensive positions, senses alert, weapons ready. He studied his map; where they'd been attacked, where they'd entered the valley, where their point of egress was. Their you-are-here jittered a bit; the string-of-pearls didn't have an exact fix on their location. He swore silently—if the string-of-pearls didn't know exactly where they were, there was no telling what else it was missing.

He quickly sketched a route on the map, toward the nearest saddle, added a couple of rally points, ordered, "HUDs up," and transmitted. His men clicked back that they'd received and saved the map.

"Move out."

They rose and headed out along their new route. On rear point, Zhon's eyes flicked toward the sound of movement near where they'd just stopped, but he saw nothing and there were no more sounds. He didn't mention it.

After the patrol was returned to Olympia by the Dragon that picked them up three kilometers outside the valley, the debriefing was both exhaustive and exhausting. Commander Daana debriefed Sergeant Steffan. Corporal Sonj was queried by CWO Ripley, the intelligence platoon's senior analyst. Captain Tamara, the assistant F2, quizzed Lance Corporal Zhon. And Staff Sergeant Wu talked to Lance Corporal Makin. When they finished their individual debriefings, the four compared notes, then brought the four Marines in together.

Daana ran the joint debriefing.

"None of your sensors detected anything." It wasn't quite a question, despite its wording. All four had already said so, and the data records downloaded from their comps and the string-of-pearls all failed to show anything. "And none of you saw a Skink or anyone else shooting at you?" This time he looked to them for confirmation.

"Nossir, I never saw one," Steffan said. The others voiced agreement.

"You were fired on from multiple directions, and all your motion detectors picked up was the acid streams, not the shooters."

"That's right, sir."

Wu looked at Daana for permission, and when he nodded, asked Zhon, "You heard something move when you began your exfiltration run, but couldn't detect anything when you looked for it. Is that right?"

"Yes."

"And you didn't mention it to anyone. Why not?"

Zhon shrugged, the shrug visible now that they'd changed out of their chameleons into garrison utilities. "We were on edge—*I* was on edge. I didn't want to start shooting at ghosts."

"So you assumed what you heard was natural, or maybe imaginary? Even though you already knew whoever was in there could get close enough to ambush you in your laager without being detected?" Wu asked, obviously unhappy with Zhon's answer.

"That's about it. But I kept a sharp watch—rotated through my shields so I wouldn't miss anything, turned my ears all the way up, set my motion detector on shake so I wouldn't have to look at its display. If there'd been another indication, I would have caught it and reported."

Wu grunted, still not satisfied, but he let it go when he saw the look Steffan shot at Zhon. Yes, better to let the team leader deal with it so it wouldn't become a command problem.

They asked a few more questions. Each of the patrol members' answers were the same as when they were debriefed individually, and each backed up what the others said. And there was nothing in the data dumps to contradict anything any of them claimed.

CWO Ripley had a question for all of them. "Even though you didn't see them, you are convinced it was Skinks that attacked you?"

Sonj, Zhon, and Makin said yes. Steffan hesitated before answering. "I'm not sure."

Everybody looked at him, surprise on all their faces, except those of Daana and Ripley, who thought they already knew what Steffan was going to say.

"Even though we couldn't see who we were shooting at, I know some of our shots had to be hits—a couple of times I saw an acid spray jerk away in mid-shot right after a plasma bolt was fired at it. There weren't any flares. Skinks always flare into vapor when they're hit by plasma bolts." He shook his head sharply. "Unless they've come up with something that keeps them from flaring when they're hit by plasma, even when they're wounded or killed." He paused to take a deep breath. "We weren't attacked by Skinks."

"The Skinks are the only ones who use acid guns," Captain Tamara blurted.

Steffan looked at him levelly. "Before Company L first encountered the Skinks on Society 437, we never heard of acid guns. Maybe they're more common in the galaxy than we think."

Everybody stared at him. They all knew about the medieval bird-like sentients of Avionia, the paleolithic headless centauroids of Quagmire, and the Skinks. The Skinks were the only known starfaring sentience humanity had encountered—and the only automatically hostile one. None of them wanted to think about the implications of encountering yet another hostile, spacefaring sentience.

CHAPTER EIGHTEEN

Hoppers were out of the question. Thirty-fourth FIST had learned the hard way on Kingdom how deadly the Skinks could be to aircraft; not even the Confederation Army had air defense weapons as potent as the rail guns the Skinks had used against Kingdom's forces and then against the Marines. And air was the only way the Marines could get their Dragons into the valley they knew the Skinks were in. That, or burn tunnels right through the forests lining the mountainsides outside the valleys. But burning holes through the forests would tell the Skinks where to aim their rail guns.

Well, they were Marines, not the army. They might travel between worlds on navy ships especially designed to carry them, and they might travel from a base to a battlefield in Dragons or hoppers, but Marines had always moved about battlefields on foot. The army, those lucky dogs, could move about battlefields in cushy armored vehicles, but the Marines always did it on foot. Hell, the army had more vehicles to move their soldiers around than the Marines had to fight their battles. An army unit the size of a FIST not only had enough vehicles to move all its troops at the same time, it had spares in case some of its vehicles broke! A FIST had barely enough vehicles, Dragons and hoppers combined, to transport its infantry battalion. And if it used them all to move its infantry, its composite squadron, artillery battery, and FIST headquarters company were on their own.

But they *could* use the Dragons to get *to* the valley, and they could use their hoppers as well—so long as the hoppers stayed below the valley's walls. The maps the *Grandar Bay* had made were good enough for the transportation company and squadron staffs to draw approach routes that kept their Dragons and hoppers out of line-of-sight from the saddles on the valley sides.

The FIST recon squad went first, along with the infantry battalion's scout-sniper section, which had been reorganized into two recon teams. They infiltrated the valley under cover of night. Company L, transported from Olympia to the west side of the valley by hoppers, slipped through before dawn. So did Mike Company, which reached the valley's south side by Dragon. Kilo Company stayed outside in reserve. Brigadier Sturgeon ordered all UAVs to be readied for use, but held them back; he didn't want to risk losing any more of his UAVs unless he needed them to save his Marines' lives.

Lance Corporal Schultz rotated through his shields, checking the view from behind a tree on the top of the saddle with his infra, light gatherer, and magnifier. He cranked up his ears all the way for a moment, listening to the sounds of the forest in the valley. He turned off his ears and raised all shields except the chameleon one that kept his face as invisible as the rest of him. He neither saw nor heard anything, and not hearing anything other than the sounds of air moving through leaves and branches bothered him more than not seeing any sign of mobile life. He took a deep breath, let it out slowly, then murmured into the platoon circuit, "Ready."

"Go," came Ensign Charlie Bass's reply.

Schultz tossed the coiled rope down the near cliff on the inside of the saddle, tugged on it to make sure it was firmly anchored, then rappelled down to the valley floor. What he did then was up to him; he chose to sprint.

Why me? Corporal Rock Claypoole wondered for the umpteenth time as he rappelled behind Schultz. Why did *he* have to have that madman in his fire team? Why couldn't Schultz have stayed with Corporal Kerr when the platoon was reorganized? Or gone to Corporal Dornhofer, or Corporal Pasquin? Both of them were a lot more experienced as fire team leaders than he was and could do a better job of controlling Schultz. For that matter, so was Corporal Chan. But *no-o-o*, Bass and Staff Sergeant Hyakowa had to give Schultz to him. Sergeant Linsman, his squad leader, even thought it was funny, giving the craziest Marine in the entire FIST to his most junior and least experienced fire team leader.

And when Company L moved, that crazy Schultz *always* had to have the point. Which was why Claypoole was the second member of third platoon to enter the valley.

Schultz hit the slope where the valley wall began to level out, and it looked to Claypoole as though he violated one or more laws of physics, the way he turned to his right and kept going without slowing when he let go of the rope. He went from near free-fall in one direction and just like that—*bang*—he was running on a ninety-degree tangent. Claypoole's feet almost slid out from under him when he tried the same maneuver. But he managed to keep his balance and kept going, skidding just a meter or so when he released the rope. From the broken thudding he heard behind him, Claypoole could tell that Lance Corporal MacIlargie had as much trouble making the turn on the slick ground cover as he had.

Somehow, that failed to reassure him.

Schultz stopped a hundred meters from the saddle and went down, given cover by a ripple in the ground so gentle it was barely noticeable in the night. Claypoole dropped three meters shy of him and aimed his blaster into the forest. He looked to his left and saw MacIlargie take his position three meters away. Good, his men were in position. He saw another form go down beyond MacIlargie, one of the men from Corporal Taylor's gun team. He knew that Sergeant Linsman was next after the gun team. Then Corporal Kerr's first fire team, with Corporal Chan's second fire team closest to the saddle. Using his infra, he saw the splotches of first squad running along the valley side in the other direction. He returned his attention to the forest so close to his front and waited.

He didn't have to wait long. As soon as the platoon command group was off the cliff and in position between the two squads, Bass gave the order over the all-hands circuit, "Third herd, move out."

As one, the thirty Marines of third platoon rose to their feet and rapidly advanced on line into the waiting trees.

"Dress and hold," Bass ordered over the all-hands circuit when the platoon was fifty meters inside the trees.

Each Marine checked to his left and right, making sure he was in line with the Marines to his sides, then went prone, blaster to shoulder, pointed deeper into the trees. One man in three used his infra, one in three his light gatherer. The squad leaders and most of the fire team leaders rotated between shields and included their magnifiers in the mix.

Claypoole wasn't completely comfortable using his magnifier screen at night; it distorted distance too much, made things look closer than they were. He used it during the day with no problem, but during the day he used the magnifier to look more closely at something he saw with his bare eyes. The nighttime forest was eerie enough without distance distortion, so after a couple of cycles, he turned the magnifier off. In infra he saw a faint, ground-hugging glow peeking through the trees in the distance. Through the light gatherer he saw all details of the forestscape in a monochrome so monotonous it defied his ability to perceive depth.

The loss of depth perception, however, was preferable to distance distortion, so he continued to use the light gatherer.

Nothing moved in his vision except foliage lightly ruffled by minor air currents. He turned his ears all the way up. All he could hear was the minor rustling of the foliage moved by the occasional breeze and the muffled noises from his rear made by first platoon as it entered the valley and got into position to move up to third platoon's left flank. The near total silence was odd. Animals should be fleeing, making noise in their flight. Unless something else had frightened them away.

But he couldn't see anything other than vegetation.

Then he let out a silent sigh; he knew what was wrong. There was no buzzing of flying insectoids flitting or bumbling about, looking for skin to light on, flesh to pierce, blood to suck. He didn't recall hearing anything unusual about local insectoids in any of the briefings 34th FIST had on board the *Grandar Bay* or seeing anything about them in the reports he'd read.

So where were the flying, buzzing, salt-licking, blood suckers? Their absence only added to the eeriness of the forest.

"Third platoon, move out," Bass said on the all-hands circuit. "Maintain interval, maintain contact. Don't get too close to the Marines to your sides, don't get ahead of them or fall behind. And *don't lose contact* with them!"

Three meters apart in the predawn dark of the forest. Most of the Marines had been in places where even with their vision-enhancing shields they couldn't see that far in a forest at night. Some of them had been in places where they couldn't see that far during the *day*. But the forest around them was thin enough to allow vision farther than three meters. When Claypoole looked left with his infra, he saw MacIlargie and the gunners beyond him. When he looked to his right, he didn't see *anybody* beyond Schultz—Schultz was on the extreme right of the company's line.

Claypoole shuddered. There was only one Marine between him and whoever or whatever might be on his right flank. But if he could have only one Marine there, Schultz was the one he wanted—the big man seemed to have a supernatural sense for where danger lurked.

And he reminded himself to look to his rear too. He remembered too well what happened to Mike Company in the Swamp of Perdition during 34th FIST's first operation on Kingdom. Mike Company's second platoon, bringing up the company rear, didn't pay enough attention to its own rear. When the Skinks rose from the water behind the platoon and opened fire with acid guns, most of second platoon's Marines were killed or wounded.

Claypoole walked backward a few paces, watching his rear as he maintained his advance with the company line.

"Watch your six," he said on the fire team circuit when he faced front again.

"Roger," MacIlargie responded; he sounded as if he didn't need the reminder.

Schultz made a small noise that might have been a soft grunt, the kind of response he made when someone else might say, "What, do you think, I'm too stupid to do something that basic?" Yeah, Schultz didn't need to be told to watch his rear. He was probably spending more time looking to his right and his rear than to his front.

Something moved under Claypoole's foot and he hopped away from it, leveling his blaster toward whatever it was.

All he saw was a vine, twisting as it slowly rebounded from being trod on.

Twisting? The vine was slowly *writhing*. The longer he looked at it, the more it looked like a sluggish snake.

He backed away from the freakish vine, then looked for Schultz and MacIlargie and quickly made up the couple of meters he needed to put himself back in his place between them.

"What was that about?" MacIlargie softly asked over the fire team circuit.

"Weird-ass vine, that's what."

"How weird?"

"It moved after I stepped on it."

"I saw one," Schultz said. Schultz never wasted words but he sometimes didn't use enough to make what he had to say perfectly clear. But Claypoole was used to him and knew that he meant he'd seen a vine that moved, not that he'd seen a Skink—if he'd seen a Skink, he would have let his blaster do his talking.

Claypoole shivered. He'd stepped on a vine that moved more than a vine should move, and Schultz had seen a moving vine too. What else did this forest have to surprise them with? If he and Schultz had seen moving vines, other Marines must have seen them as well. And that was a surprise, because if he was correct, everyone had good enough fire discipline that nobody shot at a vine. He looked toward Schultz again before checking his route, then turned to walk backward a few paces.

Claypoole had been wrong about Schultz spending more time watching his right flank and rear than watching his front—he was watching equally in all directions, including his left.

There was something very wrong in this forest; Schultz felt danger from everywhere. The danger was diffuse, no more concentrated in one direction than in any other. He put a hand over his lower face and raised his screen far enough to get a good sniff of the air; the chameleoned glove on his hand kept the bottom of his face invisible from the front.

He didn't know what the forest was supposed to smell like, so he couldn't tell if any of the scents that reached him were out of place—except for the faint smell that reached him from Claypoole's direction. There was fear in that smell. Schultz nodded internally. It was good that Claypoole was frightened—that meant he'd be extra alert. The scent wasn't strong; Claypoole wasn't so afraid that he'd do something stupid. Schultz couldn't have told how he knew how much fear-scent meant "too frightened"; he just did.

There, off to his right rear, another of those vines moved when it wasn't stepped on. It didn't move much, nothing that seemed deliberate, more like it had been twisted and was unwinding. But even that was strange. What would have wound it in the first place?

Schultz looked up and saw sunlight in the treetops, even though it was still night on the ground. The line was moving east; the light would reach the Marines shortly. Direct rays from the sun would probably even reach all the way to the ground in some of those strange open spots in the forest.

Schultz used his infra for a moment of looking around. A faint haze showed on the ground; decaying vegetation, he decided. Still, his skin crawled with the feeling of danger.

Where are you? He tried to project his thoughts at the unseen foe. *Give me a hint, so I can kill you.*

The company command group was between and a little behind first and third platoons. It consisted of Captain Conorado, the company's executive officer; Lieutenant Humphrey; Gunny Thatcher; Lieutenant Rokmonov of the assault platoon; Staff Sergeant DaCruz and his assault section; two communications men; and the four medical corpsmen assigned to the company. Second platoon trailed them with the other assault section attached to it.

Conorado was concerned. The forest was far too quiet. It was dawn, sunlight rapidly climbing its way down the trees. The forest should be alive with the screeches of avians. Every forest he'd ever been in had raucously greeted the dawn—unless there was a good reason for silence. His Marines were moving stealthily enough that they shouldn't be disturbing the treetop dwellers. But there weren't any fliers singing welcoming hosannas to the local Apollo. He'd have to wait until dawn reached the ground to see for himself, but he didn't imagine he'd see any animal tracks where the recon team that came into this valley had not.

And he remembered what Sergeant Steffan had said about no flashes of flaring Skinks when his team had to fight its way out. And what Steffan had said about maybe acid guns being more common in the galaxy than the Marines had imagined.

He looked at his Universal Positionator Up-Downlink. The string-of-pearls had a good fix on his company; the UPUD's real-time download showed first and third platoons moving in good order. He shrank the scale to show a larger area of the forest. The hundred and more dots that represented his Marines shrank and consolidated into a smaller area toward the left of the screen. No matter how he adjusted the UPUD's contrast and brightness, it didn't show any dots or even smudges that would indicate a warm-blooded animal or anything large and exothermic.

Maybe the Skinks—or whoever it was that attacked the recon team—had left the valley. But if they did, why hadn't the string-of-pearls spotted them leaving? Had they gone to ground in tunnels? The string-of-pearls maps weren't good enough yet to show underground spaces in the heavily wooded valleys. Damn, tunnels. The Skinks had made good use of tunnels and natural caves on Kingdom. And the Skinks that third platoon had encountered on Society 437 also had a tunnel system. He hoped they weren't underground again; the Marines had had some hairy fights in the tunnels and caves.

But if they were aboveground, where were they?

He was changing the scale on his UPUD again to check on Mike Company's progress from the south when the *crack-sizzle* of distant blaster fire came to him.

Before he could give an order to his battalion-net comm man to relay Mike Company's reports to him, he heard a sharp yell from someone to his rear, the direction of second platoon, and the *crack-sizzle* of a blaster from the same place. Then all of second platoon opened fire.

CHAPTER NINETEEN

"Everybody *down!*" Captain Conorado snapped into the all-hands circuit, then switched to the command circuit. Everyone in the company except second platoon, which was already down and fighting, went to ground and took defensive positions, ready to open fire. He looked back and saw the dawn dimness of the forest to his rear brilliant with the strobing of blaster fire in time with the repeated *crack-sizzle*.

"Two, Six. Report. Second platoon, this is the company commander. What's happening?"

"Six, Two. The Skinks are behind us!" came Ensign Molina's excited reply. "We're holding them."

"Two, how many are there?"

"Six, I can't tell. At least a squad, maybe a platoon. They're close, well inside their range."

The Skink acid guns had a range of about fifty meters. How could the Skinks have come up from behind to closer than fifty meters without any of the company's UPUDs picking up their motion?

"Casualty report."

"No casualties, Skipper, our chameleons are working."

Conorado spared neither time nor energy for a sigh of relief that the impregnated chameleons were proof against the acid. "Enemy casualties?" he asked.

"We don't seem to have hit any." Molina sounded surprised. "No flares, anyway."

Conorado remembered the recon briefing; Recon hadn't seen any flares either. He looked at his UPUD's screen. Every Marine in second platoon showed up, but there were no dots indicating the locations of the enemy shooting at them.

"I see you on my UPUD. Where are they relative?"

There was a brief pause before Molina said, "They don't show on my UPUD!" There was another brief pause, then he added, "I see the acid streamers. Some seem to be coming from within ten meters. The farthest are forty meters away. Scattered formation," he added unnecessarily.

"How wide is their front?" Conorado wanted to send a squad on a flanking maneuver to catch the Skinks in a cross fire, but needed to know where their flanks were.

"Wait one." Molina was back quickly after checking with his squad leaders. "Their flanks seem to be fifteen to twenty meters beyond ours."

"Volley fire, clear them out. I'll have first platoon send a squad to hit them on your right flank."

"Aye aye, Six." The *crack-sizzle* of blaster fire from second platoon's position changed from a din to measured, loud reports as the Marines shifted from firing independently at targets of opportunity to firing simultaneously in disciplined volleys that struck on line.

"One, did you hear that?"

"Roger, Skipper," replied Ensign Antoni. "My first squad is ready to move."

"Send a gun team with them. Volley fire. Go."

"One squad with gun team. Aye aye, Six."

But before first platoon's first squad had time to get to its feet to move onto the attacking enemy's flank, the *crack-sizzle* of blaster fire broke out all around the company and first and third platoons reported in:

"Fire coming from our rear!" they both said.

Then Molina reported Skink fire coming from his flanks.

"Up and at 'em!" Corporal Joe Dean relayed Sergeant Ratliff's orders to his fire team to begin the flanking maneuver. He was halfway to his feet, turning around to face the rear, when a streamer of greenish fluid shot out of the forest to his rear and slapped him in the leg hard enough to sting. Without thinking, he continued his turn, making it a downward spin, pointed his blaster in the direction the acid streamer had come from and pressed the firing lever before he hit the ground.

"Down!" he shouted over his fire team circuit as his back thudded onto the ground. "Down!" he croaked again, not sure if his first command had gotten out before his landing jarred the air from his lungs.

The *crack-sizzles* to his sides told him his men, Lance Corporal Godenov, and PFC Quick were down and firing to the rear.

It was still dark at ground level, but the viscous arcs of acid were visible as snaky shadows moving through the night. Dean snapped his aim to where one came from and fired a bolt, then swore when there wasn't an answering flare. He fired several more bolts at the same place, moving them about to cover the entire area, before deciding the Skink must have moved as soon as it fired. He saw another shadow-arc and fired four or five bolts at its source, again without the reward of a flaring Skink.

Vaguely, he was aware of fire coming from all of Company L's platoons, but the only fire he was immediately interested in was his own fire team's. "They're shooting and maneuvering," he said into his fire team circuit. "Watch my spot, then saturate the area where I hit."

Without waiting for a response, he shot another plasma bolt at the source of another acid shot, and fired again and again. Godenov and Quick followed his example, and an area nearly five meters in radius was strobed with little bits of star-stuff.

No flaring Skink answered the deluge of plasma, but neither did more acid fly from that area. A small fire started from the concentration of plasma bolts.

Corporal Rachman Claypoole of third platoon's second squad also had his men firing on his spotting shots, with the same maddening lack of flaring Skinks.

"SECOND SQUAD, SECOND SQUAD!" Sergeant Linsman's voice boomed on the squad circuit. "Volley fire, seven meters. NOW!"

Ten blasters fired simultaneously, the bolts striking the ground a scant seven meters in front of the Marines and the damp ground erupting in veils of steam as the Marines moved their aiming points from side to side and kept firing. Some bolts sank into the moist dirt and slowly fizzled out; others smacked into trees, thick roots, or vines, and lanced heat into drying wood, raising its temperature to ignition point; other bits of star-stuff ricocheted and arced farther into the forest. All that plasma fire hitting so close caused steam to rise from the uniforms of the Marines and raised copious sweat on their bodies.

But there were no flashes of vaporizing Skinks.

"Second Squad, volley fire, ten meters!" Linsman ordered, and the Marines shifted their fire farther from their positions.

The acid arcs coming at second squad decreased, and Linsman shifted the aiming line again.

What's going on? Claypoole wondered. Why aren't they flaring? Who are we fighting?

Captain Conorado followed his company's fight with everything at his command. On his squad override circuit he heard the commands and questions of every one of the squad leaders as well as those of the platoon commanders and platoon sergeants. His UPUD visual showed the positions of every one of his Marines, as did its motion detector—but the thing didn't give a hint of the enemy positions, except for the brief tracks the motion detector showed of the acid streams arcing at his men. In less than a minute the entire company was fully engaged. There wasn't anybody he could send on a flanking maneuver—even if he could find an enemy flank to maneuver to.

Where had the Skinks come from? The attack first came from ground the Marines had already walked over. This wasn't a marsh or swamp like the Skinks liked to hide out in; they'd only passed a few trickles of water so narrow and shallow they barely deserved to be called waterways. Was the floor of the valley honeycombed with caves? Had the Skinks dug a tunnel network? Were they hiding in spider traps, individual fighting holes with camouflaged covers? Small fires were breaking out in the forest where the firing was heaviest.

Something smacked into his left side. He rolled away and looked to his left. Liquid glistened in the growing light where he'd lain on the forest floor; it looked faintly green in the dim light.

As he looked he saw a line of viscous, greenish fluid arc through the air at HM3 Hough, one of the company's corpsmen. The Skinks were inside the company formation!

One of the assault gunners, closer to where the arc came from than Conorado was, also saw the acid arc and sent a spray of plasma pulses at the ground fifteen meters from the gun. The heat from the assault gun strike washed over Conorado.

"DaCruz!" he shouted into the command group circuit. "Cease assault gun fire!"

Staff Sergeant DaCruz was already ordering his assault gunners to hold their fire. "Blasters and hand-blasters only!" he ordered, but not before the assault gun had caused flames to begin licking up the trunk of the tree that had taken the brunt of the assault gun's burst.

"Plasma shields up!" Conorado ordered over the all-hands circuit. He couldn't remember the last time he'd had to order his company to power up the shields that protected them from plasma bolts, but if the Skinks were inside the company's perimeter, there was danger of his Marines shooting each other by accident.

He saw an arc of acid and fired several shots at where he thought it came from with his hand-blaster.

Then he heard another report that chilled him: first platoon was under fire from its flank and rear. Seconds later third platoon also reported it was under fire from all directions.

Company L was totally surrounded and the enemy was inside their perimeter! He ordered DaCruz to deploy his assault gun section in support of first and third platoons, leaving one man from each gun squad as a blasterman to support the headquarters element.

Corporal Claypoole reacted violently when something liquid slopped across his calves—he jerked and rolled and spun about, his hand pressing his blaster's trigger lever repeatedly as soon as its muzzle cleared Schultz.

No flares met his fire and he saw no bodies charging at him through the trees.

In his peripheral vision he saw a viscous line arcing toward Schultz. Before he could shout a warning, the big man twisted out of the way and fired back.

More acid arcs came at Claypoole, Schultz, and MacIlargie. Rapidly, almost frantically, the Marines returned fire, seeking targets, seeing none except where the arcs came from. But no one was there when they fired.

Claypoole turned his head to his left when he heard footsteps

pounding toward him, and his eyes widened when he didn't see anyone. Then he thought to use his infra screen, and saw two Marines with
an assault gun stop to set up between MacIlargie and Linsman.

"Third fire team," Linsman said on the squad circuit, "heads up! An
assault gun is going to fire over you."

Claypoole was already flat on the ground. He wiggled and managed
to lower his profile a few more nanometers. The assault gun began to
fire a steady stream of plasma pulses that began in front of first squad
and swung around the front of second squad, around its side, and to
the rear, completely enveloping its perimeter before the gunner paused
to change barrels before his overheated barrel melted. When he resumed firing, it was in shorter bursts that wouldn't quickly melt the
gun's barrel.

The incoming arcs of acid ebbed until only a few continued to
come, and those from greater distances than the earlier streamers. Small
fires licked here and there where plasma bolts and the larger pulses of
the assault gun struck dry wood. The smell of smoke began to mask
other odors.

"Second platoon," Ensign Molina called on his all-hands circuit, "cease
fire! Second platoon, cease fire!" The acid streamers had stopped arcing
in. "Squad leaders, turn half of your men around to support the command group!"

In seconds the fire from second platoon was cut by more than half,
as half of its Marines held their fire and prepared to repel another assault, and the others turned about to deliver slower, more disciplined
fire at the force attacking the company command group. There were a
few brief strobes of light as plasma bolts hit Marines, but none of them
took enough hits for their shields to be overwhelmed, and the command group suffered no casualties from friendly fire.

Heavier fire erupted from the lead platoons as the three assault
guns of Staff Sergeant DaCruz's section joined in their fight. Captain
Conorado continued to monitor the company's situation while directing the defense of the command group. In only a few more minutes fire
ebbed from all Marine positions. Smoke from burning trees and brush
was beginning to obscure vision.

"Cease fire," he said into his all-hands circuit. "Company L, cease fire." When three seconds passed without a *crack-sizzle*, he said, "Platoon leaders report."

"First platoon, no casualties. Enemy situation unknown, but I've got some fires out here," came Antoni's report.

"Second platoon, no casualties," Molina reported. "We've got a lot of fires in front of us. Enemy sit unknown."

"Third platoon," Ensign Bass replied, "no casualties. They're gone for now, but we've got fires too."

Conorado considered briefly. His company was whole and suffered no casualties, thanks to their acid-proof chameleons and the fact that all of their plasma shields worked. But he had no idea what kind of harm they'd done the enemy or where that enemy had gone. Given that, they should get to their feet and search the ground they'd just fought over for enemy casualties, cast-off equipment, or signs of where they'd gone. But everywhere he looked, he saw only small blazes started by the intense fire thrown out by his Marines. If the company stayed where it was, it was possible they'd be trapped in front of a rapidly moving forest fire.

A retrograde was the better move. They'd be out of the way of a possible forest fire. If the Skinks who attacked them from the rear had withdrawn, the Marines might catch them in that narrow open area between the forest edge and the sides of the valley. Or chase them out of the valley altogether, to where they'd have to face Kilo Company.

He checked the battalion net. Mike Company was withdrawing in the face of a growing forest fire. That merely reinforced what he'd already decided to do.

"Company L," he said into his all-hands. "Retrograde movement. First and second platoons, in the lead, lines of squad columns. Third platoon, bring up the rear behind the command group, squad columns. Assault squads, remain with the platoons you're with. One, let me know when you're on line with Two." Having the squads in line parallel to each other wasn't a very efficient formation for putting out fire power, but it allowed the company to move faster with more cohesiveness; also, if an ambush came from the flank, the company could respond to it better than if it was spread out on one line, as they'd been when they entered the forest. Conorado checked his map and drew their route while he waited for the platoons to get into position.

A couple of minutes after he gave the marching order, first and second platoons were on line and ready to move out. "Here's our route of march and rally points," Conorado said on the command circuit, and transmitted the map overlay he'd drawn. "Acknowledge receipt."

In a moment all platoon commanders acknowledged receipt of the route order.

"We're heading back to where we came in," Conorado said on the all-hands circuit. "Be alert, they're probably still out there, and they might be sitting in an ambush waiting for us. Move out."

The Marines of Company L began their retrograde. They started by moving to the side, around the fire growing between them and the valley wall.

Bushes and saplings snapped and crackled as flames chomped at them, and bark popped as fire ate its way up tree trunks. Smoke hung in the air, eddying until breezes caught it and swirled it away. Steam began rising from damp mud heated by the growing blazes. Full day had come to the forest floor, but the smoke and steam combined to reduce visibility to what it had been when only the treetops were in sunlight. The fires made the Marines' infras worthless. Flame glare reduced the ability of the light gatherer shields to see into shadows. The Marines were forced to rely on their naked eyes to see in the dimness, to search for danger. And the growing denseness of the smoke forced them to keep chameleon screens in place so they'd have some clear air to breathe, further limiting their vision.

Conorado kept his UPUD set on the visual download from the string-of-pearls so he could monitor the progress of his company—and the growing forest fire. The fire didn't progress en masse or in surges; it jumped hither and yon and shot a line here and a line here, making narrow lanes of fire. Conorado had seen forest fires before, not only in trids and vids, but nearby on the ground. He'd never seen one that spread the way this one was spreading.

"Keep it moving, second squad," Sergeant Linsman ordered. "You can step over that, it won't hurt you."

"Go ahead, Summers," Corporal Kerr said.

PFC Summers, on his first combat mission, hesitated a second longer, looking at the burning vine that lay across his path. It looked so damn *strange*! Its surface visibly knotted in moving swells under the flames that danced on it; not moving in regular pulses, like blood pumping through an artery, but in irregular humps, like a liquid was sloshing—or bubbling—inside a flexible tube. But no steam rose from the vine. And it had just been lying there until all of a sudden fire zapped along its entire length. *Weird.* He then stepped forward and over the vine.

Corporal Kerr followed quickly, and Corporal Doyle stepped over the vine almost timidly. Linsman resisted the temptation to step *on* the burning vine; the flames that ran its length were only inches high and couldn't possibly burn through his boot in the second or so he'd be in contact. But he'd been around long enough and been on enough missions in enough strange places to know that the most innocuous-seeming things could prove deadly.

Lance Corporal Schultz, walking backward on the squad's rear point, only occasionally looking around to check his path and make sure he was still in contact with Corporal Claypoole, was the only one to see what happened when the skin of the vine finally burned through and spilled its contents on the ground.

Fire spread to the sides of the vine, igniting the surrounding brush. He nodded to himself, but didn't say anything.

Sparks flew when bark popped, tongues of fire wafting in the breezes as burning leaves broke free from branches and lifted into the air. Most of them landed in places still too damp to catch fire and harmlessly went out. Some set down on dry places and smoldered until they spread to living wood and foliage. The thick vines that curled across the ground, or dangled, wrapping around the trees, acted like lines of flammable liquid when they ignited—inches-high fire shot their entire lengths so fast a casual observer might not be able to tell from which end the burning started. The vines burned until the flames ate through to their cores, then they broke open and spread their contents, spreading fire to anything they were near. Vine-cluttered trees lit up like gas torches. The fire spread in patches and chunks and lines, mostly along the ground-covering vines. The fire totally engulfed the area where Company L had its firefight, shot veins deeper into the forest, wide to the sides of the battlefield. Racing lines sped ahead of the Marines toward the edge of the forest and the valley's side.

Smoke thickened, blocked sight, infiltrated the acid-tight seams of the Marines' chameleons, seeped into their helmets where they began choking as they breathed it. It gave them an ersatz visibility, hollow ghost figures, partially visible, moving through the white drifts of smoke.

Captain Conorado looked at the real-time download on his UPUD and saw fire growing to the company's front, blocking the Marines' way. But there was a passage—if it held open. He drew another route on his map and transmitted it to the platoon commanders and platoon sergeants.

"Column of twos, close it up, pick up the pace," he ordered; this was no longer a time they needed to be alert for ambush, not until they reached the forest edge, where the Skinks might be waiting. "Alternate sleeves."

The Marines rolled up their sleeves, right for the men in the left file, left for those in the right file, so they could see each other in the firescape where their infras were useless.

First platoon took the lead, the command group mixed in with second platoon as third platoon continued to bring up the rear. The Marines moved quickly into a line two abreast mere meters apart, front to back almost within arm's length.

The company commander looked at his UPUD again and saw the break in the fire beginning to close. "Double-time," he ordered.

Company L started running. Not a sprint, but at a ground-eating pace that men could maintain over a distance.

First platoon made it through the slowly closing gap in the fire. Second platoon and the intermixed command group made it through the more rapidly closing gap.

There was a ten meter gap between Lance Corporal Godenov and PFC Quick, in the lead of third platoon, and the trailing men of second platoon. The gap in the fire slammed shut in front of them, sending them reeling back from its heat.

CHAPTER TWENTY

"Third platoon, fall back!" Ensign Charlie Bass shouted over the all-hands circuit. He rapidly pulled back thirty meters from the closed gap in the wall of flame to a swatch of ground that was bare of vegetation. "Form on me!" He raised his right arm and slid the sleeve all the way down so his Marines could see where he was.

"First squad, form defense right," Staff Sergeant Hyakowa ordered. "Second squad, form defense left. Assault gun, in the middle." First squad drew a half-circle around the platoon command group's right side, second squad mirrored it on the left. The two Marines with the big gun from the assault platoon joined Bass, Hyakowa, and Lance Corporal Groth in the center of the outward-facing circle. The bare ground they were on was so small they knelt almost shoulder-to-shoulder. Glowing embers drifted down around them from the flames in the branches above. The Marines' plasma shields, designed to safely deflect the sudden star-heat of plasma bolts, struggled to dissipate the rippling, steady wash of heat from the forest fire.

"Third platoon, sitrep," Captain Conorado's voice came to Bass over the company's command circuit.

"No casualties," Bass replied. "We're in an open space thirty meters back from the main fire." As he talked, he looked around for someplace free of fire where he could take his platoon.

There was a brief pause before Conorado said, "My UPUD shows a narrow passage to your left. Do you see it?"

"No." Curtly.

"I see you on my UPUD, the passage starts fifteen meters to your left and wends its way a hundred meters to another break in the leading fire. Now do you see it?"

"No." Bass could see a fire-free place where Conorado said there was one, but he didn't see a passage clear of fire beyond it.

"Charlie," sharply, "are you looking at your UPUD?"

"I don't trust the damn thing."

"Ensign Bass," Conorado snapped, "do you remember what happened the last time you didn't trust your UPUD?"

Bass's jaw clenched. The last time he ignored something his UPUD showed, he was wounded and the other Marine and several Kingdomite solders with him were killed by the Skinks the UPUD's motion detector had shown nearby. He was taken prisoner and didn't get free until after the Skinks were driven off Kingdom. Worse, when he did get free, he suffered from amnesia, and it was several months before he regained his memory. By then 34th FIST had given him up for dead and returned to Thorsfinni's World, leaving him to make his way home on his own.

"Well, *Ensign*?" Conorado sounded furious.

Bass ground his teeth, but snatched the UPUD from Groth and looked at its real-time display, downloaded from the string-of-pearls. "I see the passage," he snarled.

"Do you see the break in the fire wall?" Conorado still sounded angry, but not as much.

"I see it."

"Get to it. Use your UPUD. *Now*. Six out." Conorado wasn't going to brook any argument. Charlie Bass might be an excellent leader of fighting men, but he was sometimes far too obstinate.

It was not the time for Bass to dig in his heels, and he knew it. He called up his map, drew the route from the UPUD onto it, and transmitted the map to his squad and fire team leaders.

"Move out, second squad in the lead—"

"Second squad trails," Lance Corporal Schultz broke in. He was the one man in the company, probably the entire FIST, who could be more stubborn than Charlie Bass. Bass opened his mouth to order him to take the point, but Schultz spoke first. "No Skinks in front of us," he said.

Bass looked at the UPUD display again. If it was right in showing where the flames were, then Schultz was right and there weren't any Skinks in front of them—if anyone was in front of them, they were too busy fleeing the fire to ambush his platoon. But much of the ground behind them hadn't yet caught fire, and some suicidal fools could be approaching from that direction.

"First squad, lead off," Bass snarled. "Schultz, take the damn rear point. Closed ranks. Everybody, keep a sleeve rolled up so we can have visual contact. Do it."

"First squad, three, me, gun, two, one," Sergeant Ratliff said. "Go."

Corporal Joe Dean called up the map on his HUD display and made sure both his you-are-here marker and the route were visible. He kept the map up. "Quick, that way." He pointed with his bare arm.

"Aye aye," PFC Quick said, and went where Dean pointed.

Trees and bushes burned to the platoon's sides, and waves of heat washed over them. Their plasma shields weren't good at deflecting the fire's heat, and the Marines were sweating heavily. If they didn't get out of the fire quickly, they'd be overcome by the heat. As it was, they'd all need medical attention when they reached safety; the hairs on their bare arms grew brittle, frizzled, and fell off as ash; the bare skin reddened and blisters began to rise.

"Angle right," Dean told Quick when his you-are-here on the HUD map reached the first turn in the sinuous passage.

Untouched trees and bushes mixed in with the burning vegetation that lined the fire-free lane the platoon passed through; it provided slight relief from the heat. Where the fire had raged hottest, charred, broken tree trunk stelae smoked and dropped flakes. Dried dirt crunched under the Marines' feet. Ash and dust puffed around their ankles and calves, slowly rose higher, and coated them a visible gray.

"Sleeves down," Bass ordered when the ash coating allowed him to dimly see his men. The Marines gratefully lowered their sleeves, their newly covered arms feeling abruptly cool, but only in relation to how hot they'd been. "Make sure your plasma shields are still on!"

Light and heat suddenly flared to their left flank, accompanied by a riot of loud popping and crackling, and a shower of sparks and embers pelted them. They spun at the unexpected attack and dropped to the dried, heated ground. Blasters slammed into their shoulders and they returned a maelstrom of *crack-sizzle* fire. Plasma bolts struck bushes, trees, and foliage already dried by the fires all about them, pushing them over the edge to blaze themselves.

When the fire turned into a solid wall of flame, Bass suddenly knew no one was attacking the platoon from the flank.

"Cease fire!" he screamed, loud enough so most of the platoon heard his voice through the air rather than the radio. "Cease fire!" He checked the UPUD's motion detector. It showed only the Marines and the rapidly growing fire that was advancing on them.

"Get up!" he shouted, with less volume, his voice carrying over the radio net now. "Move out, at the double!"

"Angle left, around that tree," Dean told Quick as they scrambled to their feet. "Then turn sharp right."

"Left around that tree," Quick said back, pointing with an ash-covered arm. "Then sharp right."

"That's the one. Go!"

As thickening smoke swirled around them, flames leaped, and the tree was suddenly engulfed. Fire spread from it to the surrounding trees and bushes so fast, Quick barely had time to stop before he ran into them—the way was blocked.

Almost frantically, Bass looked around for another route while he made a sitrep to Captain Conorado.

"Use your UPUD visual," Conorado ordered. "Two hundred meter radius."

Bass muttered to himself, calling down curses on the UPUD from every god that came to mind, but he looked at its visual display, set to the radius Conorado said—the damned thing hadn't betrayed him this time; it wasn't the UPUD's fault the fire had jumped to block the platoon's route of egress. He had to blink away the sweat that flowed into his eyes.

"I see something, Skipper," he said. "Fifty meters to my northeast. The fire seems to have burned out there. If we can get there, we'll be out of it." A thin stream ran through the burned-out area; it looked like it broadened into a small pond.

"Damnit, Charlie, you've got a wall of fire between you and the burned-out area, you can't get there!"

Bass glared at the display, as though demanding the UPUD show him another path to safety. All it showed was more patches of fire all around. "That's the thinnest line of fire around us," he said. "It's the only way out of the flames." He coughed and tried to blow the smoke out of his helmet.

There was a beat, then Conorado asked, "How are you going to get through that fire, Charlie?"

Bass remembered what happened scant moments earlier when his men reacted to what they thought was an ambush and choked off a bitter laugh. "We're Marines, Skipper. We'll do it the Marine way—we'll blast our way through!"

"What—" Conorado began to ask, but Bass ignored him.

"Third platoon! We're going to fight fire with fire. On line, on me." He held his arms out to show the angle on which he wanted them lined up. "Forward at a brisk walk," he ordered while they were still getting on line. The platoon began advancing toward the northeast. "Volley fire, right into that fire. *Fire!*" The blasters and guns of the platoon erupted with the *crack-sizzles* of plasma bolts that flamed into the flames they faced. The attached assault gun was silent since the platoon didn't stop to let the gunners set up the tripod.

"FIRE!" Again, they fired. The wall of flame they faced began burning more furiously, lashing them with greater heat. Wood popped and cracked as heated sap expanded and burst its fibrous bonds.

" 'Toon, *halt!*" They stopped, barely more than thirty meters from the flames. "FIRE!" They *crack-sizzled* another volley of star-stuff into the fire, which now burned too hot to make smoke.

"FIRE!" Once more they fired. The flames shot higher, and heated air rushed in, dragging smoke from other blazes with it. Wind beat at the Marines' backs, eager to reach the hottest fire. The snaps and pops became a constant, clattering din.

"FIRE!" And yet again. Overheated air roared skyward, shooting flames ever higher. The highest flames detached from the slower moving fire closer to the ground and fluttered higher on their own before winking out. Husks of trees collapsed into incandescent coals. Flames bent toward them from the rear.

"FIRE!" With a mighty WHOOSH! the remaining combustibles billowed out and up in roiling, overlapping balls of fire and scaled into the sky. Only gray ash and steam rising from glowing dirt remained where the fire had blazed.

"GO, GO, GO!" Bass roared, and sprinted. He looked to his sides to make sure everyone was running, slowed enough to let them pass him, then looked back to make certain nobody was left behind. He saw how close behind him the flames were and sprinted across the burning dirt, feet touching down too briefly for the great heat of the ground to translate through the soles of his boots. Ash rose in clouds at each pounding step.

"Squad leaders report!" Staff Sergeant Hyakowa ordered as soon as Bass and the others crossed the burning ground into the area that had already burned out.

"Fire team leaders, report," Sergeant Ratliff commanded.

"Fire team leaders, report," Sergeant Linsman ordered.

"Gun team leaders, speak up," Sergeant Kelly barked.

"Assault squad, all present," came the first of the squad leaders' reports—the assault squad had only two men to account for.

"First squad, all present," Ratliff reported, panting.

Linsman had to cough his throat clear before reporting, "Second squad, we're okay."

"Gun squad, we're good," Kelly said.

Bass joined Hyakowa, Kelly, and Groth. His breath was ragged from the smoke and his yelling.

"Everybody, turn on your coolers," he ordered. "Turn off your plasma shields." The plasma shields used a lot of a uniform's power. He looked around. The nearest flames were more than fifty meters away; everything between the platoon and the fires had been burned to ash. The flames themselves were distorted by eddies of air wavering in the heat. Smoke moved toward the flames. The Marines were all visible, ghostly in translucent gray, with a flickering red undertone from the heat their plasma shields radiated safely away. Away from the flames, the cooling units in the uniforms would do a better job of keeping them from overheating.

Bass found that the streamlet was dry in places, now that he was close enough to see it, and where it did broaden into a pond, steam rose from the surface. He lowered his head and raised a hand over his eyes so he couldn't see any fire, then dropped his infra into place and examined the ground, looking for a cooler swatch. His lip curled, but he double-checked with his UPUD's infra download. It agreed with what he'd already seen—there wasn't any cooler ground. Even the small pond showed an elevated temperature, but in the infra the water didn't glow as brightly as the ground surrounding it.

"Follow me," he croaked. "I think it's cooler over here."

"Cooler?" MacIlargie laughed phlegmily. "*Out* of here it's cooler." Then he yelped. "Hey! What'd you hit me for?"

"Because I didn't have a rotten egg to throw at you," Claypoole snapped, then doubled over coughing. "You're a lousy comedian," he gasped when he cleared his throat enough to speak again.

"Hey!" MacIlargie yelped again.

"I think you're a lousy comedian too," Linsman said. "Get over there with the boss." His voice was strained from breathing smoke.

Bass knelt next to the pond and splashed some water onto his sleeve. The infra image of his arm glowed less redly where the water evaporated off it. He quickly plunged his arm to the elbow into the pond, and immediately yanked it out. His arm was enveloped in a cloud of steam that rapidly whisked away.

Yes, his lower arm definitely showed less brightly in the infra.

"Everybody, splash water on yourselves," he ordered. "*Don't* stand in the water, it's too hot. But evaporation from the water will cool your chameleons."

The men of third platoon gathered at the side of the pond, splashed water on themselves and on each other, and disappeared in a cloud of steam. When the steam cleared, they were marginally cooler than before, but the atmosphere was still well above body temperature, and they coughed and sweated copiously, even with their climates on the coolest setting.

As soon as the steam cloud dispersed, Hyakowa began assigning fields of fire and Bass reported to Captain Conorado.

"Good thinking, Charlie," Conorado said when he heard what they'd done. "Burning through that fire wall was dangerous, but it worked. And that was smart about the water."

"I didn't see any other choice, Skipper. How's the rest of the company?"

"I've got them moved outside the valley. The flames were too close." He paused. "I'm on top of the saddle, where I can see into the valley. It looks like the entire valley is spotted with fire for three or four klicks in. How far away are you? I'm in a blind spot for UPUD reception."

Bass adjusted his UPUD's display. "A bit more than a quarter klick from the edge of the forest," he replied, then paused to cough. "All I can see from the valley wall to about sixty meters from me is fire."

"How are you holding out?"

"It's hot in here. The smoke is clearing, though. The fire's hot enough that the updraft draws it away from us."

Conorado looked at the flames above the trees. There was smoke down low, and another band halfway up the trees, but not much above that for several yards, where it was caught and whipped away by the growing wind.

"No injuries?"

"Only minor smoke inhalation and heat."

"Is everybody drinking enough water?"

Bass knew his reservoir was empty. He touched his canteens. One was nearly empty but the other was full. "If the fire burns itself out soon enough, nobody'll go down from dehydration. But we're sweating a lot and we'll need a lot of water and electrolytes when we get out of here. Probably oxygen too. We've breathed a lot of smoke."

"Any sign of enemy?"

Bass cut off an ironic laugh; laughing hurt his chest too much. "Anybody in shooting range of us is a crispy critter."

"Keep me posted."

"Roger that, Skipper."

They waited and watched. There was nothing else to do except hack up smoky phlegm and take measured sips of water—those who had any. The pond water, even if it was normally clean enough to drink, was clotting with ash and totally unpotable. Puffs of steam rose here and there as the Marines splashed pond water on themselves and the men next to them.

"You okay, Wolfman?" Claypoole asked after they'd waited half an hour. The air still stank of smoke and it was still way too hot, but the fire was receding on all sides.

MacIlargie cleared his throat and worked saliva around his mouth before spitting. "Yeah, I'll make it."

"H-Hammer? How about you?" Claypoole felt odd asking Schultz how he was, since the Hammer was always better than anybody else in a tough situation.

Schultz grunted and hacked up black phlegm. He'd been the first in the platoon to raise all his screens and let air movement evaporate his sweat, even though he knew that reduced the effectiveness of his climate; he also knew there was no enemy nearby to threaten them. If embers hadn't been drifting through the air, he would have taken his helmet off.

"I guess that means yes," Claypoole murmured. He looked at Schultz more closely. It was hard to tell with his coppery complexion, and the ash and soot coating his face, but the big man looked flushed. Claypoole snorted. They were *all* flushed; they had to be in this heat. How hot was it?

He didn't want to know.

He looked around at the other Marines. It felt strange to be able to see them even though they were in chameleons. Yet they were all clearly visible, an irregular gray from the ash and soot that coated them. He wondered how much longer they'd have to stay in the clearing.

He looked toward the valley wall. The fire was nearly a hundred meters away, and much lower than it had been. He blinked and lowered his magnifier.

Yes! He saw areas that seemed clear of fire—it must finally be burning out.

"Sergeant Linsman!" he croaked.

"What?" his squad leader asked.

"Look there." He pointed. "The fire's breaking up."

Linsman didn't bother using his magnifier. He peered and saw holes in the fire. "Hey, boss! Fire's starting to go out."

Bass looked and grunted, his throat too thick and sore for him to try talking. He lowered his infra and examined the fire and the ground in between it and the platoon. He cleared his throat and hacked.

"Third platoon, on your feet. Follow me." He led them toward another spot, closer to the fire, where the ground had cooled a bit. He nodded to Hyakowa, whose throat was in better shape than Bass's. The platoon sergeant radioed in a report.

"It's breaking up on this side too," Conorado replied. "I've got the corpsmen standing by to take care of you when you get out, and a Dragon is ready to ferry anybody who needs it to the hospital."

Bass checked his UPUD's visual. The fire, which just minutes ago had been almost two hundred meters wide, was less than half that. Maybe another half hour, certainly less than an hour, and they could get out of there.

In twenty minutes the fire thinned farther and there was a path thirty meters wide through it. The only problem with that was, an arm of the fire blocked passage to the saddle where the company waited. Bass reported in.

"I'm going to take a page from your book, Charlie," Conorado said. He'd moved to where his UPUD could receive the real-time download. "Get your platoon into position." He marked his map where he wanted third platoon to go and transmitted it to Bass. "I'm sending a squad back in to heat up that blocking fire. As soon as it burns itself out, come on through. Use your plasma shields."

"Roger, Skipper." Third platoon moved to within fifty meters from the still shrinking fire.

First platoon's second squad went back into the valley. Fire burned less than a hundred meters from the wall; everything between fire and wall was ash and splinters of charcoal. Seventy-five meters to their right a blaze was eating through fallen trees and heavy brush. They got on line and fired volleys into that fire until it *whooshed* up in billows of overlapping balls of smoke-eating fire. Moments later there was a flame-free passage along the valley wall. They passed the word and waited to escort their fellow Marines out of the valley.

CHAPTER TWENTY-ONE

"Shirts off!" Doc Hough shouted as the Marines of third platoon came out of the valley. "Get those boots off. Strip down!"

Panting and gasping, the thirty-two Marines of third platoon staggered into the cool air under the trees. Their chameleons, dried by the heat they'd been in, were coated with ash and crisp with absorbed body salts. Sweat no longer flowed down them in sheets; sweat barely ran at all, they were so dehydrated. Relieved at being out of the fire, most of them ignored the corpsman in favor of finding shady places to drop supine and pant, opening their shirts as they did so.

Corporal Claypoole tried to suck in a chestful of cool air, and his body wracked so violently with coughs he had to roll over onto his hands and knees to hack out his lungs. At least it felt like he was hacking out his lungs. He was only vaguely aware of other Marines from the platoon also bent over, hacking and coughing, or of the shouts of the corpsmen ordering other Marines to assist third platoon.

He staggered as someone began pounding on his back, and more black phlegm erupted from his throat and mouth. A hand clapped a flexible cup over his mouth and nose.

"Breathe through this," a voice said, and cool, refreshing oxygen filled his nose and mouth and made its blessed way into his lungs. Claypoole pushed himself upright and clapped his hands over the cup, holding it in place.

It wasn't until someone started pulling his shirt off, forcing his hands away from his face, that he realized the cup was held on by a band that went around his face and head. He tried to protest the rough hands, but was told, "Just relax, keep breathing." His shirt was off and water sluiced over his head and torso, cooling him.

"Turn around, sit." He rolled off his knees and sat. Hands grabbed his calves and pulled his legs straight, then removed his boots. The words "Lay down" were enforced by a hand on his chest, pressing him back. Then his trousers were tugged off and more water sluiced over him, bare head to naked toe. He tried to focus on whoever was tending him, but the cool, clean oxygen he was breathing, and the cool, wet— so very wet—water, relaxed him so much he couldn't force his eyes to do what he wanted.

Then, "How ya doing, Claypoole?" another voice said, and a face hovered just above his. Fingers touched his forehead, gently raised his eyelids one at a time.

He brought his eyes together, made them focus on the face. "Not too bad, Doc," he said through the oxygen mask to Doc Hough. "How about you?" His voice was rough and muffled, but his words were clear enough.

"Better than you, that's for damn sure," the corpsman said. "You're dehydrated, Marine. Gotta get some fluids into you." He lifted Claypoole's blistered arm. "Gotta do something about this too." Using economical movements, he quickly attached an osmosis fluidizer to Claypoole's left arm, then applied a layer of skin to the blisters on his right. He looked up, and someone helped him lift Claypoole into a sitting position.

Hough lifted the oxygen mask from Claypoole's face and held a squeeze bottle to his mouth. "Here, take some of this. Don't swallow. Swirl it around your mouth, then spit it out. I know you're thirsty, but don't worry, I'll give you more." He gave the bottle a squeeze as soon as Claypoole opened his mouth.

Cool liquid shot into Claypoole's mouth, onto his palette, cutting through caked ash he hadn't realized was there until the fluid hit. Obediently, he swished it around his mouth, forced it back and forth between his teeth, and ballooned his cheeks, each in turn. The fluid quickly began to feel gritty and slimy. He leaned to the side and spat. The stream was gray with flecks of black.

"Again," Doc Hough said, and squirted more into Claypoole's waiting mouth. Claypoole swirled and swished again; it took longer for the fluid to turn slimy-gritty. What he spat this time, it was clearer than before.

"Open up, let me see," Hough ordered. He flashed a light into Claypoole's wide-open mouth. "You're getting there," he said. "Take some more. Hold it this time, let a little trickle down your throat, then rinse and spit again."

Claypoole did as instructed. He didn't know what the fluid was, but it wasn't water. It had the same viscosity and feel as water, but there was a faint taste of something else. Metallic? Salty? He couldn't tell and he didn't care. He wanted to drink it all, but rinsed with the rest and spat it out, then held his mouth open for more.

"Just a little now," Doc Hough said. "Don't gulp it, let it trickle down. I'll give you more later." He filled Claypoole's mouth from the squeeze bottle, watched to make sure he was swallowing the liquid slowly, then patted him on the shoulder and got up. "I've got to take care of someone else now, but I'll be back. Put your oxygen mask back in place when you finish drinking."

Claypoole reached for the squeeze bottle, but Hough snatched it out of reach. "Later," he said. "Lay back down now and rest. You're being rehydrated."

Claypoole lifted his face to the sky and let the not-water slide down his throat. He replaced the oxygen mask over his mouth and nose and lay back, reveling in how much better he was feeling. Then he remembered and sat up abruptly, looking sharply around.

He pulled the mask away and croaked, "Wolfman, Hammer, where are you?" His men, he was responsible for them, where were they? He was sure they came out with him, but his mind and eyes had been so blurry he couldn't remember for sure. Were they being taken care of, were they all right? *Where are they?*

"Schultz! MacIlargie! Where are you?" He struggled to his feet, looking around manically at the prone and supine third platoon Marines who surrounded him—there weren't enough of them. "*Where are you?*"

A hand grabbed his shoulder and yanked him around. He found himself nose-to-nose with Gunnery Sergeant Thatcher.

"You lay yourself right back down, Corporal Claypoole," Thatcher ordered.

"Where are my men? I've gotta take care of my men."

"MacIlargie's right over there, under that tree. Schultz had to be medevacked, but he'll be okay. Now lay back down like you're supposed to."

"Medevacked? Hammer? Gunny, I have to go to the BAS to make sure he's all right."

"He's not at the battalion aid station. He got too dehydrated in there, he went to the hospital. There's nothing you can do now, but he's going to be all right," Thatcher said calmly. Then he raised his voice and fixed the younger Marine with a glower that would have made First Sergeant Myer proud. "Now lay back down and let the fluidizer rehydrate you, or you're going to be standing in front of my desk wishing you had!"

"Ah, lay down. Right, Gunny. Aye aye, Gunny." Claypoole was about to lower himself back to the ground, then turned toward the tree where Thatcher said MacIlargie was laying. "I'll just check on Wolfman first."

"*Belay that!*" Thatcher roared. Everybody who could looked to see who the company gunny was chewing on. "You'll lay right back down right now!" He lowered his voice so only Claypoole could hear, and added, "You're concerned about your men, that's what a good Marine noncommissioned officer is supposed to be. I'm your superior, and I'm telling you your men are taken care of. It's *my* responsibility to take care of my NCOs. You're one of my NCOs. I'm telling you to lay down and rest. Now do it."

Gunny Thatcher had said he was a good NCO! Claypoole exulted. *I'm one of his NCOs and he's taking care of me.* "Aye aye, Gunny." He pulled the oxygen mask back over his face and sat down.

"On your back, Corporal," Thatcher growled.

Claypoole lay back.

"That's better. Now stay there until I, or one of the corpsmen, tell you it's okay to get up."

"Aye aye, Gunny."

Thatcher nodded crisply and moved on.

Claypoole lay there, absorbing fluids through the osmosis fluidizer, breathing clean, cool oxygen. Knowing his men were taken care of. Thinking how Gunny Thatcher said he was a good Marine NCO. Or as close as the Gunny ever came to saying that.

Mike Company had gotten out of the valley's forest fire in better shape than Company L—none of its platoons had gotten trapped, as third platoon had. Kilo Company's corpsmen came to help Doc Hough and Company L's other corpsmen treat the Marines of third platoon. In less than half an hour all had been cared for and were recovering—even the six who'd been medevacked to the hospital in Ammon weren't in severe danger, though they would need a couple days of treatment to fully recover.

Commander van Winkle made the rounds of his companies; he wanted to check on his Marines as well as get firsthand explanations of what had happened.

"We were attacked, sir," Captain Conorado said. "Our plasma bolts set off fires, and the fires grew. It's as simple as that." He looked toward the saddle that led to the valley.

"Just like that, it grew," van Winkle repeated quietly. Captain Boonstra, Mike Company's CO, had told him the same thing—the fire simply started, and it spread as if the forest was tinder dry. Yet the forest hadn't been dry. The ground was damp, the foliage lush, and many tiny streams ran through it. A forest like that shouldn't ignite easily, nor should a fire spread through it so rapidly.

Damn these people, he thought. No one had ever made a proper survey of Maugham's Station. There must be something in the chemical makeup of the forest vegetation that made it more susceptible to fire than forests of other worlds. Even a cursory examination by the Bureau of Human Habitability Exploration and Investigation should have discovered that volatility. Evidently, BEHIND's initial study of Maugham's Station before the colony was established, when it had been an emergency way station, was even more casual than he'd imagined.

But if the vegetation was so highly flammable, why weren't frequent forest fires recorded in the database on board the *Grandar Bay*? The number of forest fires worldwide that the string-of-pearls detected was well within the statistical norm for a world with the area of woody tracts of Maugham's Station.

So what was different *here*?

He needed to secure samples and have Brigadier Sturgeon send them to the *Grandar Bay* for analysis.

"Where's Bass?" van Winkle asked. "I want him to tell me about what happened with his platoon."

"He's over here, sir." Boonstra led the battalion commander to a tree, under which Ensign Charlie Bass was giving a corpsman from Kilo Company a hard time about his treatment.

"—all right, I tell you. Take care of my men!"

"Ensign, maybe you scare your own company corpsmen, but you don't scare me." The corpsman did his best to sound firm, but he didn't sound as tough as his words—Charlie Bass *did* scare him. "They wanted to medevac you, and so do I. Your lungs need to be suctioned to get the gunk out. We can still medevac you, you know. Now suck on this tube if you don't want me to put you on the next Dragon out of here!" He was trying to insert a flexible tube into Bass's mouth and down his throat when van Winkle interrupted him.

"Ensign Bass, are you trying to damage Marine Corps property?"

Bass twisted his face away from the tube and looked up. "Sir!" he said, harsh-voiced, and began to stand up.

Van Winkle clamped a hand on his shoulder to stop him from rising. "Sit, Charlie." He glanced at the corpsman and gestured for him to leave them. When the corpsman was gone, van Winkle squatted next to Bass. "What the hell happened that you got stuck in the middle of a forest fire?" he asked.

"Sir, there were fires all around, but there was a clear path through them that the company was following." He coughed and spat to the side. "The fire jumped into the path and cut us off."

Van Winkle nodded. "I was watching the download and saw that. What I really want to know is, you had fires all around you—how did you think of the tactic you used to get out of it?"

Bass snorted, the snort turned into a wracking cough. Van Winkle slapped him on the back and he spat out a large globule of blackened mucous. "Sorry 'bout that, sir," he said when he was able to speak again.

"Don't apologize. Tell me briefly—and let me know if talking becomes too difficult."

"We heard something to our flank, thought it was an ambush and reacted. It wasn't an ambush, it was a tree going up. Its trunk split and popped, threw out embers. Our return fire put so much more heat in the fire over there it burned out in a hurry. I saw"— he looked at Conorado— "the Skipper and I saw a burned-out area with a screen of fire between us and it. I remembered watching the tree go up, and had the platoon volley fire into the fire until the vegetation got hot enough, flared up, and burned out. We went through and waited." He shrugged; it was simple.

"That was good thinking, Charlie. I knew we had a reason for making you an officer."

Bass snorted again. The coughing it brought on this time wasn't as violent as before and he recovered faster, without having his back pounded. "Nothing any old gunnery sergeant couldn't come up with."

"But an ensign couldn't figure it out for himself?" van Winkle said with a wry smile.

"A lot of ensigns used to be gunnery sergeants." Bass stopped before adding, "Not everyone takes a dumb pill when he gets commissioned."

"Regardless, it was good thinking. Congratulations, Charlie." Van Winkle stood. "Now," he said, looking around for a corpsman, "I want you on the next Dragon out of here—you belong in the hospital. That's an order, Ensign."

"But, sir—" Bass looked to Conorado for help, but the company commander just looked back at him, and he saw no help there.

"I'll have Gunny Thatcher make sure he's on it, sir," Conorado said.

The Kilo Company corpsman who had been trying to work on Bass returned.

"Ensign, let this good corpsman stick that tube down your throat," van Winkle ordered. He nodded to the corpsman and walked away.

"He's one of the best small-unit leaders I've ever seen," van Winkle said to Conorado when they were far enough away that Bass wouldn't overhear.

"Yessir, he is," Conorado agreed.

"But he's sometimes stubborn almost to the point of being suicidal."

Conorado barked out a short laugh. "Yessir, he's that too."

*   *   *

It was the next day before the forest fire finally burned itself out. Brigadier Sturgeon agreed with Commander van Winkle about sending vegetation samples up to the *Grandar Bay* for analysis. He contacted Commodore Boreland, who sent down a three-member science team. The string-of-pearls showed a single stand of trees and brush untouched by the flames, on a small island in the middle of a large pond near the middle of the valley. Kilo Company hadn't been involved in the fighting or the fires in the valley, so Commander van Winkle sent one of its platoons to escort the scientists to the island. They went on foot; the forest leading up to the saddles was too dense for Dragons to get through, and neither he nor Sturgeon was willing to send people in the flimsy civilian vehicles that were small enough to fit between the trees. They didn't know whether Skinks or other enemy were left alive in the valley, or if they had rail guns or other antiaircraft weapons, but Sturgeon wasn't going to risk losing a hopper and everybody in it if there were.

The string-of-pearls' ground-penetrating sensors didn't pick up anything that indicated caves or tunnels under the surface inside the valley, but that didn't mean there weren't any underground formations.

CHAPTER TWENTY-TWO

Corporal Juliete lay between Lance Corporal Rising Star and PFC Bhophar, his point man. They were on top of a different saddle from those Company L and Mike Company had used to enter the valley; its sides weren't as steep and they wouldn't have to rappel to reach the valley floor. They peered into the valley. It was burned for almost its entire breadth and width. Only a few green trees still stood, outside of the sparkling emerald oasis several kilometers away on the island in a small lake near its center.

Juliete heard Staff Sergeant Oconor, his squad leader, slither into position between him and Rising Star to look for himself. Oconor whistled softly at the devastation. A moment later Ensign Zantith, commander of Kilo Company's first platoon, joined them. Unlike Mike Company and Company L when they went into the valley, this platoon could see the lay of the denuded land. It rippled slightly, and rose and fell in longer swells.

The four Marines studied the valley for a few minutes. The floor was mostly shades of gray, with blackened spikes sticking up here and there, the remains of trees. A few thin waterways were discernible as glistening gray ribbons. Nothing moved over the ground that wasn't propelled by breezes. Nothing flew above the dead valley.

Zantith used his magnifier to scan the sides of the valley. "Where does the water go?" he asked softly.

"Sir?" Oconor said.

"All those waterways. They don't flow to any outlet from the valley that I can see. So where does it go?"

Nobody answered, which was all right with Zantith. They knew as well as he did that if the water didn't flow out of the valley on the surface, that meant it went underground. That, in turn, meant there were probably caves under the valley floor, even if the string-of-pearls hadn't found any yet. Skinks liked caves—they must really like caves with water running through them. And those caves would extend well beyond the limits of the valley, which meant Skinks could be anywhere.

When he realized he wasn't going to gain any more advantage from looking at the valley, Zantith projected his map onto his HUD and adjusted the route already drawn on it. He transmitted the revised map to his platoon sergeant, squad leaders, and Corporal Juliete. He also forwarded a copy to his company commander. "Let's do it," he said.

Juliete nudged Bhophar and said, "First fire team, move out," into his fire team circuit.

Bhophar led off, followed by Juliete and Rising Star. Oconor trailed them with a gun team, the rest of first squad behind him, then Zantith and his comm man. The platoon sergeant followed second squad with the three scientists off the *Grandar Bay* and the cargo scoot that carried their equipment, and third squad pulled drag. The cargo scoot was the reason they had to use an easier way into the valley.

Lieutenant Brightly, the *Grandar Bay*'s botanist, looked around in dismay. He'd studied the maps and knew that much of the botany of this isolated valley had to be unique to it. Such a loss! he thought. Why did the Marines think it was necessary to burn it down? He mourned the life-forms that might have been exterminated in the fire.

Well, maybe not completely. As he looked about, he saw individual trees and bushes that seemed almost untouched by the fire, even the occasional clumps of bushes in their brilliant colors. And the island they were headed for didn't appear to have suffered from the flames and heat—at least, no damage showed up in the images from the string-of-pearls. And it was unknown flora, so no one knew what kind of damage it could sustain before suffering irrecoverable stress. Of course, being burned to char was considerably more stress than he thought the plant had evolved to deal with.

Lieutenant Brightly had lived up to his name: no matter how

morose he felt at any time, a negative mood was unlikely to be sustained. He was soon looking forward to examining the flora on the island. Maybe he'd be able to find out what had made the fire spread so rapidly. He began walking more jauntily.

Unlike Lieutenant Brightly, there was nothing jaunty in PFC Bhophar's gait on the platoon point. He neither knew nor cared about the uniqueness of the flora of this valley. What he did know and care about was that Company L and Mike Company had been attacked with acid shooters in this valley. Acid shooters meant Skinks. Skinks liked water and caves, and there was both of them in the valley. He moved cautiously, placing his feet carefully to stir the ash as little as possible. His head moved constantly, checking his front from one side to the other, and halfway to his rear. The muzzle of his blaster pointed everywhere his eyes looked; if he saw a threat, he wouldn't have to waste even a split instant to bring his blaster to bear on it. He paid particular attention to narrow waterways the platoon crossed, looking for signs of anything moving—or waiting—under the surface. As softly as Bhophar stepped, he still raised some ash, and by the time they'd gone a quarter of a kilometer his boots and ankles were coated with ash—in visual, he was a pair of ghostly feet stalking across the valley floor.

Behind and to the right of Bhophar, Corporal Juliete watched almost as broad a front, from his right rear to his left front. He also looked down and, after a while, grimaced. He realized that, like him, everyone in the platoon was gradually becoming visible from the feet up from the ash. He looked closer at the space between himself and Bhophar. Fine ash was suspended in the air. He looked down and saw that his legs were visible higher up than Bhophar's. Even staggered as the platoon column was, each man walked through a low cloud of ash raised by the men ahead of him, and each increased the density of that cloud. The scoot raised even more ash. Juliete looked back along the column. The last men in the gun squad were faintly visible almost to their knees, and the last men in second squad were visible to their waists.

He swore silently. The Marines' chameleons weren't going to provide them with much concealment if they ran into an enemy.

In some places, ash covered the ground to a depth of several centimeters; in others, the surface could be seen through a thin coating of the fiery residue. Ensign Zantith suspected those nearly clear spots must be where small clearings had been. He could have called data down from the string-of-pearls to compare the map of the valley before the fire with the positions of the thinly covered spots, but couldn't think of a possible threat related to them that would justify taking his attention from his men and their surroundings to make the check. He wondered about the squiggly lines of darker, more granular ash that snaked for meters across the valley floor. They looked like they were made by someone pouring streams of water on the burning ground.

He did stop briefly to look at the first streamlet the platoon crossed. The water, clotted with suspended ash, was so viscous it barely flowed. He looked along the streamlet in its direction of flow and lost it to sight before he could see where it went underground. He would have liked to divert his platoon to follow the waterway, but his orders were strict, and he had a timeline to follow that didn't allow for a side trip. He wanted to know if ash buildup had blocked the flow where the water went underground. If it had, nobody traveling between the surface and the caves via those routes would be able to resurface until the ash plugs were broken.

Each waterway the platoon crossed was the same as the first—thick and sluggish with suspended ash. No matter where he looked, he was never able to see where one went. He saw no standing pools that would indicate a blocked entry to an underground stream.

Kilo Company's first platoon didn't encounter Skinks or anybody else in their trek across the undulating valley floor. It reached the small lake in good time.

Like the waterways, the lake was gray with ash, but noticeably less viscous. Other than some scorching, the growth on the island appeared untouched by the fire that had raged around the small lake. It seemed the lake itself was fed by an upwelling from underground, or at least no streams flowed into it in the stretch of bank that the Marines and the scientists could see from where they stood. Neither did water flow out anyplace they could see.

Lieutenant Brightly studied the island from the lakeshore. It sat a hundred meters away across the water. "Ensign," he said after he'd given the bank a quick scan, "I want to take a look at the other side before we go to the island."

Zantith had intended to send a squad on a circuit anyway, to check for enemy threat; if the xenobotanist wanted to go with them, that was fine.

"I'm sending a squad around the lake on a recon in force," Zantith replied. "You can accompany them. Just remember, until we get on the island and have it secured, we're in a tactical situation. That means when you go around the island, the squad leader is in command. If he says you can't stop someplace, you can't stop. If he says move, you move. Understand?"

Brightly made a face. A navy lieutenant outranked a Marine sergeant, but he had to concede that Zantith was right—they were still tactical, even though the xenobotanist was certain there was no danger other than what nature provided, and he believed he was better qualified to deal with that than the Marines were. All he said, though, was, "I understand. I'll be a good boy and do what your sergeant says until you declare the island secured."

"Thank you," Zantith said, and meant it—if Brightly had objected, he would have refused to allow him to go with the squad when it went to scout the island's far side, and he didn't know the botanist well enough to know whether he'd try to make trouble over it later on. He checked the UPUD and saw that his platoon sergeant had already set one blaster squad and the gun squad in a defensive perimeter and left the other blaster squad aside for the recon. "Sergeant Kraeno up," he said into his command circuit.

In seconds the second squad leader joined him. Zantith shook his head; Kraeno was visible. His feet were solid gray, the color slowly fading as it climbed his legs and body until only the upper part of his helmet still had the full chameleon effect.

"I want you to take your squad and scout around the lake," Zantith told the squad leader. "Take Lieutenant Brightly with you. The lieutenant understands you have command."

"Aye aye, sir," Kraeno replied. He looked at the width of the small lake and judged its circumference. "How long should I take?"

Zantith also looked at the lake. It was about four hundred meters across, and the map showed it to be almost circular. With the vegetation burned away his Marines could easily circumnavigate it in less than half an hour. But he wanted more caution than a slow amble would allow. "Give yourself an hour," he said.

That satisfied Kraeno; he thought an hour sounded about right. "Second squad, on me," he ordered into his squad circuit, and slid a sleeve up before he raised his arm for his men to home on.

Lieutenant Brightly was annoyed by the slow pace of second squad when they started off; after all, with all the ash clinging to their uniforms, the chameleon effect was pretty well negated, and they didn't need to move so slowly to avoid being seen. He didn't realize that the slow pace allowed them to thoroughly investigate their surroundings. But he was a navy officer, not an infantryman—he wasn't used to long walks, and the brief stop at the edge of the lake had been enough to let him notice how tired he was. It wasn't long before he was glad they were walking little faster than a crawl. Not even the brilliant greens, scarlets, pinks, ambers, and blues of the foliage on the island distracted him enough to ignore the aches in his muscles and soreness of his feet. By the time they reached the far side of the lake, what he mainly wanted to do was sit under a shady tree and rest for a while. But, other than those on the island, there weren't any trees, shady or otherwise, nearby. Brightly was so tired he barely remembered to watch the sides of the lake for streams.

There weren't any. Curious. He was no geologist, but knew enough about geology to know that running water had to come from someplace and go somewhere. Not only running water, but water in standing bodies.

"Can we stop here for a few minutes, Sergeant?" he asked.

Sergeant Kraeno looked around at the eerily gray landscape on which nothing moved except occasional breeze-driven ash devils. "Will five minutes be long enough?"

Brightly nodded, then remembered that, despite the thin coating of ash that covered his uniform, his head might not be visible, and said, "I think so, for what I want to do right now."

"Take five," Kraeno said into the squad circuit. "First fire team, twelve to three o'clock, second fire team, three to six o'clock. Third fire team, watch the island." Security taken care of, he asked, "What do you want to do, Lieutenant?"

"I want to look for currents." He waved a hand at the lake, his hand and arm coated with enough ash to be fully visible.

"Enjoy yourself, sir," Kraeno said.

The xenobotanist knelt at the side of the lake and leaned forward to study its surface. The water moved in gentle ripples, as in any other undisturbed lake he'd ever looked at. The ash was settling out of it, and the upper several millimeters looked clear, giving the lake a mother-of-pearl shimmer. He tilted his head this way and that, trying to detect the water's direction of movement, but it didn't seem to favor one direction more than any other. He looked at the ground he knelt on, saw a fragile flake that hadn't been turned to fine ash by the fire, and carefully slid his fingers under it and picked it up. He stretched his hand out a centimeter above the water and tipped it to let the flake slide off his fingers. The flake broke when it hit, but two of its pieces were large enough for him to easily watch. He knelt unmoving, his eyes on the two small flakes, until Sergeant Kraeno called for the squad to mount up and resume moving.

Except for slowly sinking as they became waterlogged, the two small flakes didn't move at all—he wasn't able to discern a current in the lake.

"Same-same," Sergeant Kraeno reported when the squad returned to the rest of the platoon—everything looked the same all the way around the island.

Lieutenant Brightly conferred with the other two members of the science team and told them of his experiment with the flake that failed to show a current.

Ensign Szelt, a hydrologist, had also tested the water for a current and hadn't found one. She'd also tested water quality, and found it clear for the top six millimeters. "The only elevated salinity is in the polluted water," she concluded. "It appears that the water is clean enough to drink without purification—once you filter the ash out, that is."

Lieutenant Prang, the team's xeno zoologist, gave the lake a worried look. "There must not have been anything living in this water—there aren't any floaters," he said. Lieutenant Brightly looked at him, not understanding. Prang explained, "All that ash would have clogged the gills of any piscoids and suffocated them. Dead fish float, and there aren't any floating bodies. The samples I took didn't have any microbial life—or any other kind—either. Very odd." He shrugged. "We'll find out more when we get the samples back to the *Grandar Bay*."

The three looked to the island. With its flashy colors and promise of cooling shade, it was inviting. Once they got there, Brightly would be fully in charge of the scientific mission—unless they found animals, in which case Lieutenant Prang would take over.

When the Marines looked at the island, they were less sanguine. They knew other Marines had gone into a very similar forest in that valley and were attacked. UAVs had been knocked out of the air and destroyed, and recon minnies had been destroyed on the ground.

The scientists might have been ready to search for new and fascinating life-forms to study, but the Marines were ready for a deadly fight and intended to come out of it the winners.

CHAPTER TWENTY-THREE

According to the string-of-pearls, from where they stood the pond floor sloped gently and evenly from the bank to its lowest point, little more than a meter down. On the other side it climbed more abruptly to the island, but not so abruptly that they would have to crawl or climb instead of walking to the shore. What the string-of-pearls didn't show was whether the bottom was firm or soft—its sensor suite hadn't had time to check until after the fire; by then, the pond was filled with ash and it couldn't make the determination. Which also meant the string-of-pearls report on the pond's depth was suspect.

The scoot carried a float to ferry the scientists' equipment to the island. The original plan called for a squad to wade to the island and establish security, then for two more Marines to wade across, pushing the float ahead of them. Then the float would be drawn back and forth as needed via ropes attached fore and aft. But Ensign Zantith wasn't willing to risk any of his Marines to what might prove to be a quicksand bottom. The float had a carry rating of three hundred kilos, more than sufficient to carry two Marines, maybe even three, equipped with weapons.

"Sergeant Oconor up," Zantith ordered over the command circuit. The first squad leader joined him in a moment. "Get the float in the water and assign your three lightest men to take it across to the island. We don't know how firm the bottom is, so I want them to rest as much of their weight as possible on the float, just in case. Understand?"

Sergeant Oconor looked at the small lake and the island in its middle. "Yessir," he said.

"As soon as they've got the towline secured over there, I'll have the float pulled back and send more of your squad over with it. Questions?"

"Nossir, that's pretty clear."

"Do it."

"Aye aye." Oconor headed for the scoot. "First fire team, on the scoot," he ordered into his squad circuit as he walked. First fire team wasn't his three lightest men, but he didn't think they would swamp the float. Corporal Juliete and his men got to the cargo scoot at almost the same minute he did. The Marines hadn't packed it; that had been the responsibility of the scientific team. The scoot was loaded with small crates, and smaller parcels were lashed down on top of them.

"Lieutenant, which one of these crates contains the float?" Oconor asked the three navy scientists, all of whom were standing next to the scoot, discussing what they were going to do when they reached the island. Let them sort out which one he was talking to.

"What?" asked Lieutenant Brightly. "Oh, the float."

"It's in there." Ensign Szelt pointed with an ungloved hand, not that the Marines needed to see the bare hand at the end of her ash-coated sleeve to tell where she was pointing.

"Thanks. By your leave?" Oconor didn't wait for the officers to move out of the way before directing Juliete and his men to start unloading the scoot to get to the float. He had an intelligent layman's respect for scientists in most instances, but in the field, in a place where there'd just been significant fighting and he had no reason to believe there wasn't still danger from hostile forces, he saw scientists—even navy officers who were scientists—as nothing more than clueless civilians who would just get in the way and endanger lives when the shooting started.

"Hey, be careful with that!" Brightly yelped, and wrested a parcel away from Lance Corporal Rising Star. "That package has some delicate instruments in it." He carried the parcel several meters away from the scoot and gently laid it on the ground. By the time he turned back, Ensign Szelt and Lieutenant Prang were busily unloading packages with scientific instruments. Brightly joined them, and in moments all the smaller parcels that had been lashed to the crates were unloaded. Once most of the equipment was unloaded, Lieutenant Prang began setting up trid cameras to record the Marines' approach to the island. Ensign Szelt helped him. They also set up two 2-D vid cameras.

"Thank you, sirs and ma'am," Oconor said when the three scientists were through. Just because he thought they were in the way didn't mean he couldn't be polite. "Too bad the float wasn't loaded last." But not polite enough to not get in a jibe about how the navy officers loaded their gear. He ignored the scientists' protests as Juliete and his men opened the crate and removed the float. It was bulky, nearly two meters wide, half again as long, and twelve centimeters thick, but it weighed next to nothing. The four Marines held onto it as they carried it to the lake, not so much to bear its weight as to keep it from blowing away in the gentle winds that gusted through the valley.

"All right," Oconor said once he assured himself that the towlines on the float were properly tied off fore and aft, "the lake isn't supposed to be any deeper than chest high anyplace, but we don't know what the bottom's like, if it's firm or soft. There might be sinkholes in it. I want one of you prone on the bed, the other two, one on each side. Put as much of your weight on the float as you can and still have traction to push the thing across. When you get there, secure the fore-end cable to a tree and we'll bring it back to send another fire team over. I'll come with them. Juliete, talk your way across, let me know what the footing's like and if you feel anything else under the surface."

"Any questions?" Oconor finished.

They did have questions, beginning with, *What can we expect to run into over there?* and *What's going to happen if we run into a whole shitload of Skinks?* But they didn't ask any. The reason they were going was to find out what was over there, and the rest of the platoon would be standing by to give them covering fire to withdraw under if they did run into a whole shitload of Skinks.

"Do you see the tree with the red leaves—there's a yellow bush about a finger to its right?" As soon as Juliete said he had it, Oconor said, "That's your aiming point. Get over there as fast as you can. Keep a low profile while you do it. Don't move out of my sight when you get to the island." Sight, right, he thought. With the ash coating their chameleons, he'd be able to see them with his unaided eye. As much ash as there was suspended in the water two of them would wade through, they'd probably be even easier to see by the time they got there. "I'll join you as soon as possible," he concluded. "Go."

"Roger," Juliete said. "Bhophar, get on, we'll give you a ride. Keep your eyes peeled." PFC Bhophar was his usual point man, and he was good enough at spotting trouble before walking into it that he was on point more often than anyone else in Kilo Company.

"Right." Bhophar stepped into the water and pushed the float out a few meters to where the water was thigh deep before he climbed on to lie down facing the island. He settled his blaster into his shoulder and shifted its aim with every movement of his eyes.

Juliete and Lance Corporal Rising Star took up positions on opposite sides of the float. They lay their blasters on it but didn't let go of the weapons. Each got a firm grip on the float's side with his free hand.

"On three," Juliete said to Rising Star. "One, two, three." The two Marines pushed off.

They didn't lift their feet completely off the bottom as they pushed along, but lifted their heels and slid their toes forward. Rising Star quickly adjusted his pace to Juliete's, and the float didn't waver from a straight line toward their destination. It was easy to keep it going straight since there was no current for them to struggle against. The lake bottom had a soft upper layer, but the soft layer was thin. Their boots barely sank into it before their treads found purchase on firmer ground. The irregularities in the bottom were minor and mostly gentle; only seldom did they have to lift their feet over an obstruction high enough that they couldn't simply slide across. The hardest part was when the water got crotch deep, but the water temperature was close enough to that of the air that there was hardly any discomfort.

Juliete kept up an almost constant chatter about what his feet encountered. "I wish I could see down there," he said when they were almost halfway across. "I don't feel any weeds, but some of the things I have to step over feel like roots, or vines. Nothing's moving, though." He was talking to his squad leader, but was on the circuit that allowed the platoon command group and the other squad leaders to listen in.

He and Rising Star kept pushing when the water reached chest height, where the bottom leveled off. But nothing about the lake changed; no leafy plants brushed against their legs, no swimming life bumped them. There were only the occasional things like roots or vines that they had to step over—and those became more frequent as they neared the island.

Prone on the float bed, Bhophar studied the nearing island through his magnifier screen, occasionally switching to the blaster's optical sight to get a finer view of whatever caught his interest. Nothing moved that couldn't be accounted for by air currents. Two or three times he switched to the infra screen, but nothing showed on it other than the normal background of rotting vegetation. He kept a sharp watch anyway; he was experienced enough to know that lack of visible movement didn't mean no one was there—and he'd fought Skinks before, so he knew they didn't show up easily in infra, especially when there was something to mask their signatures.

The rest of the platoon, prone in fighting positions, anxiously watched the fire team's progress. None of them wanted to change places with the three Marines in the lake; all of them would give them fire support if they ran into trouble. Ensign Zantith didn't assign anybody to watch the platoon's flanks or rear, since he wanted to be able to use the platoon's entire fire power if the three Marines needed help. Instead of eyes to the flanks and rear, he had his comm man watch the UPUD's motion-detector display; he thought that would give just as good a warning as human eyes if anyone approached.

When the first fire team was only twenty-five meters from the island, Juliete reported, "The stuff on the bottom is getting thicker. There's not much in the way of bare bottom now. We have to step on those roots, or whatever they are. And they're loose." A shudder was audible in his voice. "They move when we step on them."

"How firm's the bottom?" Zantith asked.

"It's been firm enough all the way," Juliete answered. "We didn't need to hang on to the float. And there's no current to make you lose your balance."

"Sergeant Oconor," Zantith said into the all-hands circuit, changing the plan for moving the platoon to the island, "get the rest of your squad ready to cross as soon as the towline is secured on the other end. Keep the float there for now. Have everyone keep a hand on the towline."

"Roger," Oconor replied. "You heard the man," he added to his Marines. "When I say go, head for the water. Get a good grip on that line."

"The bottom's rising now," Juliete reported when they were ten meters from the island. "There's a real tangle of roots on the bottom. I believe it could be real easy to get a foot stuck here." He grunted as he pulled a boot free from a tangle.

Seconds later the float butted against the island's bank and Bhophar slithered onto land. Juliete and Rising Star scrambled ashore and the fire team leader quickly tied off the end of the fore towline around the trunk of the tree they'd used as an aiming point.

"Line secured," he reported, and positioned his men far enough away from the tree to allow other Marines to come ashore without crowding. He kept them out of the forest, so they were visible from the lakeshore.

Juliete didn't know what the leaves on the trees and bushes should look like. He hadn't entered the valley before, and so hadn't seen the forest before the fire. But the foliage appeared wilted to him. He reached out and took a large blue leaf between his fingers. It wasn't supple, the way he expected a leaf to be. When he bent it with gentle pressure from his fingers, it snapped.

"Do you see anything?" Zantith asked as the rest of first squad filed into the water.

"That's a negative," Juliete reported; he'd turned up his ears and been cycling through all of his screens even while examining the leaf. He and his men settled in to watch, listen, and wait. All he could see inside the forest were trees and bushes with brilliantly colored leaves, and the vines that trailed along the ground or snaked up the trees to dangle from branches. He hoped they didn't have to fight—if the leaf that broke in his hand was typical, that patch of forest was dry and could easily flare up if the platoon began hammering it with plasma bolts.

The rest of the squad was more than halfway across the lake when Bhophar murmured, "I hear movement, my one o'clock."

"How far?" Juliete asked, shifting his attention and aim to Bhophar's right front. He cycled through his screens without seeing anything.

"Too close," Bhophar said.

Juliete snapped his aim to his direct front when he heard something—something too close. On his other side, Rising Star aimed to his left front. "We hear movement all across our front," he reported, totally forgetting the dryness of the forest.

"Do you see anything?" Zantith asked. In the water, Oconor urged first squad to move faster.

"Negative," Juliete answered. "We hear them close, but we can't see anything. There's another one! I still can't see anything, damnit!"

"I see movement!" Bhophar blurted, then, "No, it was just a vine." After a brief pause he whispered, "What made it move?" His eyes traced the length of the vine where it lay on the ground as far as he could follow it, but he didn't see anything that could have made it move.

"Buddha's balls," Rising Star murmured. "I see a vine moving by itself."

"That's impossible," Juliete said, but he looked where Rising Star's blaster aimed and watched as a vine slowly twisted without anything visible to make it move.

First squad was scrambling to reach the island. Most of the Marines had released the towline and were spreading out. They tripped and slipped on the roots that snaked across the lake bottom, but managed to keep their balance and their blasters pointed into the forest so they could fire on anyone who attacked their squad mates already ashore.

On the lakeshore, first squad and guns looked through their optical sights. The island jumped into sharp focus, the fringe of foliage seeming only ten meters away. Seeking a foe, they looked into the gaps between tree trunks and brightly colored leaves.

"I see a vine moving!" someone in second squad shouted.

"What's moving it?" Sergeant Kraeno shouted back.

"I dunno, it looks like it's moving itself!"

"It can't be!" Kraeno shouted back.

"Great gods," Zantith said, "it is." Looking through his monocular, he watched as several vines twisted, turning themselves so an end—a hollow end—was pointed at the three Marines on the island's bank. "One, get your people off that island right NOW!" he snapped.

"First fire team, pull back!" Sergeant Oconor ordered.

Juliete and his men had heard the platoon commander's order and were already wriggling backward into the lake. They spun around and dove into the water as streamers of greenish fluid shot through the air and splashed down where they'd just lain.

The members of first squad approaching the island didn't see where the streamers came from and began shooting wildly into the forest. The same held for second and gun squads a hundred meters away—only Ensign Zantith had seen the greenish fluid pulse from the vine ends.

"*Cease fire, cease fire!*" Zanith shouted into the all-hands circuit. "First squad, get away from that island!"

Sergeants Kraeno and Morgan took up the "Cease fire" cry, and fire from the lakeshore slowed to a stop. Tendrils of smoke drifted up from bits of plasma smoldering in wood.

"First squad, pull back!" Sergeant Oconor ordered. The members of first squad began shuffling backward, firing into the forest as they went.

"First squad, cease fire!" Zantith shouted.

"First squad, cease fire!" Oconor repeated. "Fire team leaders, report."

Juliete, ten meters away from the island, into the deeper water, looked to his sides and saw both of his men. "First fire team, no casualties."

Second and third fire teams also reported no injuries or missing. Then, as Oconor reported his squad's status to Zantith, two streamers arced into the water and the entire platoon opened fire again.

"Cease fire!" Zantith commanded. This time the fire from the platoon stopped faster than it had before—the Marines on the lakeshore could see that first squad's first fire team was almost at the middle of the lake, near the extreme range of the Skink acid guns—if any Skinks were on the island.

"What are you Marines doing?" Lieutenant Brightly shouted, bounding toward Zantith. He grabbed the Marine commander roughly by the shoulder and twisted him around to face him. "Look at that!" He angrily waved an arm toward the island, where fires were beginning to spread from the blaster bolts that struck the dry wood. "We're supposed to investigate that flora, and you're burning it up!"

Zantith raised his shields so the navy scientist could see his face clearly and pointedly looked at the hand on his shoulder. Brightly saw the hardness of the look and jerked his hand away.

The Marine stood. "Weren't you watching, Lieutenant?" he asked harshly. "My men came under fire. They returned it."

"Under fire?" Brightly squawked. "I didn't . . . I didn't hear any gunfire."

"Acid guns, Lieutenant. They don't make a big bang."

"Acid guns?" Perturbed, Brightly looked at the island. He hadn't been ashore on Kingdom, but he'd seen trids of the fighting, and saw the remains of some equipment that had been destroyed by Skink weapons in that campaign. "Are you sure there are Skinks on the island?" Fear was clear in his voice.

Zantith slowly shook his head. "No. What I saw was, some of that flora you're so anxious to study shot acid streamers at my people."

Brightly swiveled his head toward the Marine. "The flora shot . . . ? But if it was the flora, why did your Marines fire?"

"Lieutenant, when Marines get shot at, they shoot back." He looked at the island. "Besides, they didn't know it was plants shooting at them."

CHAPTER TWENTY-FOUR

Brigadier Sturgeon leaned back after viewing the last of the naval officers' vids and looked toward President Menno and Minister of the Interior Elbrus. "It looks like you were right in interdicting those valleys," he said to them. "Now you know why interdiction was necessary."

The two local officials sat unspeaking, stunned. They knew about the existence of hostile, predatory flora on some planets, but they'd never heard of anything like what they'd just seen—and they had no idea hostile fauna existed on their own world.

Sturgeon didn't share the civilians' shock. He'd had the trid and vids for a full day and had already seen them more than once. As had Commodore Boreland, who came planetside to view them. The two commanders had adjusted to the idea of acid-shooting flora and both were relieved: Sturgeon, because he didn't face losing Marines to the Skink weapons again; Boreland, because he remembered, at the end of the Kingdom Campaign, how he'd turned the *Grandar Bay* from an amphibious landing ship into a combatant ship, and fought orbital battles around two different planets. He didn't relish the prospect of having to do it again.

"President Menno, Minister Elbrus," Boreland said after a couple moments of silence, "I will have my people make a copy of those for you. You have adventurous young people who like to go into places no one has gone before. They should watch these vids, which should discourage them from going into the interdicted valleys."

Menno nodded absently, but Elbrus spoke up with hard-edged anger.

"Why didn't BEHIND tell us about this?" he demanded. "Why isn't there anything in the planetary records about it?"

"Well, sir," Sturgeon said, "the way station here had been in operation for—how long, a generation?—before BEHIND made its investigation. I can only assume that since there hadn't been any serious problems in all that time, they thought Maugham's Station didn't need anything more than the most cursory examination before opening it up for colonization." He shrugged. "When they see these, they might decide to come back for a closer look."

"Y-You're going to report this to them?" Menno stammered.

Sturgeon shook his head. "No, I'll make my report to Headquarters, Marine Corps, as Commodore Boreland will make his to the Office of the Chief of Naval Operations. It'll be up to them to make the decision to forward the report to BEHIND. Actually, I rather thought *you* would make the report."

Menno and Elbrus looked at each other for a moment, then the President said, "I think leaving it to us is a very good idea."

Sturgeon saw the way they'd looked at each other and knew they wouldn't make any report on the hostile flora to BEHIND—they were afraid that Maugham's Station would lose its Certification of Suitability for Human Habitation, and they'd have to abandon the world they'd spent their lives turning into home. But that was their decision, and he wouldn't tell them what they had to do. Sooner or later, if there were reports of continuing deaths, BEHIND's sluggish bureaucracy would notice and send a new team to investigate Maugham's Station. Maybe they'd force the colonists to abandon their world, and maybe they wouldn't. But that was neither his problem nor Boreland's.

But to satisfy his own curiosity, as well as to assist the people of Maugham's Station, Boreland assigned all of his life sciences people to work with local scientists for a week to conduct a brief study of the flora of one of the hidden valleys in which people had died.

What they found was remarkable.

They knew that the flora was carnivorous and no animal life seemed to be extent in the isolated valleys, so the mission into the valley within the Salainen Mountains—where two young lovers had been killed and devoured by the flora—was commanded by Lieutenant Brightly, the *Grandar Bay*'s senior xenobotanist. President Menno and Minister of the Interior Elbrus were happy to let the navy take charge of the scientific expedition—after a fashion.

"Certainly, Admiral," President Menno said, "I'll be happy to lend the resources of Ammon's entire scientific community to assist the navy in conducting a survey of an interdicted valley's life-forms. I'll instruct Dr. Soma to give you and the general every assistance she can."

As unaccustomed as he was to being called "Admiral," Boreland didn't bat an eye at the title. After all, he *was* a flag officer. "Dr. Soma is . . . ?" he asked.

"Osa Soma," Elbrus said sourly. "She's our chief xenobiologist. Ammon's foremost authority on native life-forms."

"Thank you, Mr. President," Boreland said graciously, though he didn't imagine Ammon's "foremost authority on native life-forms" knew any more about the flora of the valleys than his own people.

"We should coordinate security measures between your people and mine," Brigadier Sturgeon said.

The corner of Elbrus's mouth twitched; he disapproved of anyone entering the interdicted valleys under any circumstances, but he'd been overruled by the President and the legislature. He said, "My Director of Public Safety is too busy with other matters. But I can have his deputy, Casper Bilisi, work with you."

Sturgeon knew why Elbrus wouldn't assign his top security person to work with the Marines, and thought he was incredibly shortsighted about the matter, but he didn't let that show on his face or in his voice. "Thank you, Mr. Minister. My people who have already worked with him speak highly of his abilities."

Lieutenant Brightly was even more excited than at the island in the Haltia valley. The Salainen valley was untouched, and this time he knew what he was looking for—not to mention the dangers.

In addition to Brightly, the scientific team consisted of Ensign Szelt and five enlisted life science technicians off the *Grandar Bay*, and four local scientists led by Dr. Osa Soma. One of the other local scientists was Dr. Kara Kum, the first assistant coroner. Dr. Soma selected her because she had the most local experience with the effects on the human body of the carnivorous life-forms in the valleys, and because she had experience working with the off-worlders.

Security was provided by three police officers from the Ammon Department of Public Safety, and Company L's third platoon. The police were in nominal command of security, but everybody understood they were going along merely for form's sake; the Marines were really responsible for everyone's safety.

Second squad went over the saddle first and set markers fifty meters from the edge of the forest on the valley floor. They knew, from K Company's island experience, that the flora could shoot its acid streamers at least forty meters, and tacked on an extra ten as a safety margin. Everyone was wearing Marine chameleons festooned with non-chameleon streamers for visibility, but the Marines didn't trust the locals—or even the navy personnel—to keep their acid-proofed clothing buttoned up, so they insisted on the safety margin and intended to enforce it.

Corporal Rachman Claypoole checked his men's positions for what must have been the ten thousandth time since they finished setting out the markers to limit how close the scientists could get to the forest edge. Lance Corporals MacIlargie and Schultz were right where he'd put them, just as they'd been each of the other ten thousand times he'd checked. Could it really have been ten thousand times? He looked at the time; they'd only been in position for an hour, so he couldn't have checked their positions that often. But it sure felt like it. They were just upslope from the markers, little more than fifty meters from the edge of the forest. Was that far enough? Nobody was sure how far those vines could spew acid.

He slid his magnifier and light gatherer screens into place and peered into the forest edge, looking for the maws of vine ends. Were any of them moving to aim his way? Were any of them pointed in his direction? Were any pulsing, getting ready to spray him with acid? How far away could they sense their targets anyway?

The vines he saw lay limp and unmoving, the way ground-trailing vines should. And the vines that dangled from tree branches did just that, dangled.

He shook himself and wondered why he was so skittery, acting like Corporal Doyle. After all, his chameleons would protect him from acid. Then he looked at his men for the 10,001st time, just to make sure they hadn't edged closer to the forest. Wolfman MacIlargie's screens were all up, exposing his amused expression as he watched the scientists gather floral specimens from the area they were allowed into. Festooned as he was with colored streamers to make him visible to the scientists and local police, he looked odd. He lounged with his back to the forest. Every now and then he'd clear his throat and glare pointedly at a scientist who looked about to wander past the markers. The scientists always seemed resentful, but they always changed direction and stayed in the area the Marines declared safe.

On Claypoole's other side, Hammer Schultz sat with his knees up and his arms resting across them, his blaster held crosswise in both hands. He faced the forest and never bothered looking at the scientists. He seemed relaxed, but there was an undercurrent of tension about him that made the scientists keep their distance. Schultz didn't expect an attack by the forest flora, but he was ready to fight back if an attack came.

At the other end of the protective line, Corporal Joe Dean was much more relaxed. He hadn't seen, experienced, or heard anything to make him think the vines could spray any farther than fifty meters—and he had full confidence in his chameleons.

If some of the scientists gave him dirty looks when he shooed them back from the markers, well, he couldn't blame them. They were excited about investigating unique life-forms. He imagined he'd be excited too, if he were any kind of xenobiologist.

Instead of fretting about the potential dangers around them, Dean wondered when they'd get to the experiment the scientists planned to run.

A few hours later, Ensign Charlie Bass began wondering the same thing. "Mr. Brightly," Bass said when he neared the navy officer. "I thought you said you scientists were just collecting a few samples." He looked at the slope the scientists had been gathering from; there was noticeably less greenery on it than there had been earlier, and the scientists and technicians were still digging and bagging.

Brightly beamed at him. "Oh, but we are, Mr. Bass," he said. "It's just that we want to make sure we've got a sample of *every* life-form. And the navy needs them as well as the locals, so . . ." He looked around and saw how much barer the slope was, and added a bit sheepishly, "I guess it does look like we're taking quite a lot, doesn't it?" He looked downslope at the forest, then up to where the major experiment waited, out of sight on the other side of the saddle. "Maybe we should stop for a bit and compare what we've got. We probably have some duplicates."

"That sounds like a good idea, Mr. Brightly," Bass said drily.

In a few minutes all the scientists and techs, navy and civilian, were gathered, examining each others' samples. They did have quite a few duplicates, and some trading went on until each group had at least one sample of everything they'd collected.

The scientists wanted to continue working, and objected when Bass ordered a meal break, but the Marine insisted and they acquiesced—especially when their technicians made it plain they also wanted a meal break and were going to take one.

The sun was halfway down the western sky by the time the meal was finished and its trash picked up and stored for proper disposal outside the isolated valley.

On an order from Dr. Kara Kum, the major experiment was brought into the valley. A transport scoot was driven over the saddle and onto the valley's inner slope. The techs unloaded several multispectrum trid and vid cameras and briskly set them up, ignoring the supervision provided by the scientists. Once the techs were satisfied with the siting of the cameras and other recording devices, Lieutenant Brightly told Bass they were ready to commence.

Bass and Staff Sergeant Hyakowa inspected Brightly, Kum, and the two techs—both navy petty officers—who were going to set the experiment in place. Then, satisfied that the quartet going to the edge of the forest was properly sealed into the chameleons, Bass gave the go-ahead.

Brightly raced to board the scoot before the petty officer who had driven it into the valley; he wanted to drive it himself. Not that he had far to go—no more than seventy-five meters to the spot at the forest edge where they'd decided to set up.

"*Wait!*" Bass roared as Brightly started the scoot—Bass didn't want him to reach the forest edge before the others. But Brightly ignored the warning and sped the scoot downslope full throttle, jouncing and bouncing along the way. He was going so fast when he reached the forest that he had to twist the controls all the way over and slid sideways into a tree. The impact was hard enough to knock him off the scoot and jarred a loud squeal out of the scoot's cargo, a crate a meter and a half long, a meter high, and a meter wide, with holes cut in its sides.

Bass ran to him, along with Kara Kum and the two techs. Bass got there first.

Brightly lay on his back, grinning inanely up at Bass when the Marine knelt over him to check for injuries. "I'm not hurt," he said, and began to sit up.

"You'll get up when I say you can," Bass snarled, and pushed him back down. He hurriedly checked for cuts, broken bones, and torn muscles without finding any obvious injuries. Then he checked the chameleon's integrity. "*Now* you get up." Bass grabbed him by the front of his shirt and jerked him to his feet. "Are you trying to get yourself killed?"

Other than a brief yelp when he was yanked to his feet, Brightly made no objection to being manhandled. "That was fun!" he exclaimed, still grinning.

"Everybody, keep moving," Bass shouted. "We don't know how long it takes for the vines to react."

"Let's get out of here." Dr. Kum's voice came from behind Bass. "We're done."

He turned around. One of the techs was starting the scoot, and Kum and the other tech were already on it. He grabbed Brightly by the shoulder and shoved him at the scoot. As they rode away, he looked back at the experiment. A seventy-five kilogram hog, watching the scoot depart, strained at a strong lead that anchored it to a tree trunk.

The hog stopped straining after a few moments and began to root around for something interesting to eat. It snorted and snuffled, spat out something it didn't like, then settled down and lay on its side, ribs rising and falling steadily with its breathing.

Nothing happened for three full minutes, and the hog seemed to be sleeping quietly. Suddenly, it lifted its head and looked into the forest. Then its head jerked to the side and it looked in a different direction. It scrambled to its feet and faced the forest, leaning toward whatever had caught its attention, swiveling its head from side to side.

The Marines flinched—and a third of them went prone with their blasters in their shoulders—when a streamer of viscous, greenish fluid arced from the ground ten meters to the hog's right and splashed over its back and side. The hog jumped and twisted, squealing in pain, but before it could pull away, two more streamers struck home, staggering it. Its loud squeals were cut off when a gout of acid spattered on its face, covering its snout. The hog arched its back, as though it was about to buck, but went rigid for a moment before it thudded onto its side.

Nothing more happened for several minutes, then thin vines rose nearly half a meter into the air and flopped down onto the hog. A few dangling vines began rocking back and forth, as though a child not yet big enough to swing them was trying to. The dangling vines twisted and kinked, but soon reached the carcass, where they straightened and their ends fastened themselves to the hog's hide. Other movement was too slow to see with the naked eye, but later became evident in the time-lapse images: low-lying flora crept toward the carcass and punctured its skin with delicate shoots. In little more than an hour, the hog's body was covered by a living mat of fibers and vines.

They left the hog in place for a week while it was slowly devoured. They set up cameras closer to it, to record the plants' activities at closer range, but none of the close-in cameras lasted more than a half hour before being attacked by jets of acid from the vines and assaulted by what the scientists came to call "second wave" carnivores. The scientists and techs themselves moved in for occasional closer looks, but Charlie Bass refused to allow any of them to stay close for more than a minute or two, and enforced a one-hour interval between approaches to the forest edge.

The only mishap occurred when a local was too intent on a tendril that was slowly wriggling its way into a break in the hog's hide. When he refused to back away from the forest edge after being told to, he was hit by two streamers of acid before Marines could drag him out of range. He had to be evacuated for medical attention because he hadn't completely sealed his protective chameleons and a few drops of acid seeped through his shirt to eat at his belly.

After that, the scientists withdrew from the forest edge more quickly when Bass called, "Time's up."

They stayed for a week, cataloging the numerous plants that directly fed on the carcass. The leaves of some plants flopped onto the flesh and absorbed its fluids through osmosis; others injected tendrils into soft tissues; yet others drilled tendrils through bones to get at the marrow, or leached minerals from the bones.

Lieutenant Brightly and the other scientists and techs from the *Grandar Bay* would have spent months studying the flora of the valley, but Commodore Boreland decided they'd gathered enough information to pass on to the Office of the CNO and ordered them back to orbit. Brigadier Sturgeon was in full accord with Boreland, especially after Ensign Bass assured him the local scientists had developed sufficient respect for predatory plants to be allowed to continue their work without Marine security.

It was time for 34th FIST to go home.

CHAPTER TWENTY-FIVE

The We're Here! invasion fleet, scattered over several light-minutes, emerged into Space-3 along the orbital plane, a couple of Astronomical Units out from Maugham's Station. The distance was beyond the incidental reach of most of the sensors of the planet's geosync satellite, which were faced in toward the planet anyway, and outside the observation cone of the outward facing sensors, which were aimed perpendicular to the orbital plane, the customary direction for starships to approach a planetary system. It was a reasonable direction from which to approach the pirate base. After all, Maugham's Station never detected the pirate vessels—unless, of course, the Maugham's Station government sponsored the pirates.

As the fleet began its slow assembly, Admiral of the Starry Heavens Sativa Orange received the message from Captain Main of the deep space tug *Annie* about the arrival of the Confederation Navy's Mandalay-class Amphibious Landing Ship, Force, the CNSS *Grandar Bay*, and her embarked Confederation Marine Corps Fleet Initial Strike Team. The admiral had exclaimed, "We're going to land and wipe out the Confederation's little pirate den. Think they can mess with We're Here!, do they!"

Neither the *Broken Missouri* nor the *Heavenly Mary* was orbiting at the geosync position opposite Maugham's Station's lone satellite. Based on the *Broken Missouri*'s vector when she left Maugham's Station, Captain Main believed that she was back at the Rock. Likewise, the *Heavenly Mary* had left on a vector that could take her back where she'd come from—wherever that was.

Four days standard after the amphibious landing force arrived in the evirons of Maugham's Station, the ships' captains again assembled in the wardroom of the *Goin'on* to be addressed by their commander. Again, two captains stood back to front in close physical contact. Their neighbors, though fully aware of the intimacy of their contact, ostentatiously ignored them; except for Captain Main, who hadn't been present at the previous assembly.

"Ladies and gentlemen," Admiral Orange began, once more standing partly in the wardroom's hatch and partly in the passageway outside it, "the Confederation Navy pirates are ignorant of our presence, and we are going to use that ignorance to our advantage. The fleet will divide into three task forces for the assault. The assault will commence twelve hours standard, after the return of either the *Broken Missouri* or the *Heavenly Mary*." Behind him, Vice Admiral Toke, the We're Here! navy's chief of operations, displayed a chart, which most of the assembled captains couldn't see at all because of its position in the passageway, and none could see completely because Admiral Orange stood in the way.

"Task Force One, code named 'Toke' and under command of Vice Admiral Toke, will consist of the dreadnought *Groovy* and both Freemont-class light cruisers, along with the destroyer escorts. Task Force Toke will board and take command of the CNSS *Grandar Bay*.

"Task Force Two, code named 'Head' and commanded by Captain Head—who for the duration of this operation will be an acting commodore—will consist of the three Mallory-class destroyers." To his rear, Toke flipped over another chart. "Task Force Head's mission is to destroy the Confederation Navy string-of-pearls satellites and take possession of Maugham's Station's geosync.

"Task Force Three, code named 'Crashpad' and commanded by Rear Admiral Crashpad, will consist of the four auxiliary assault-landing ships, infantry, and the heavy cruiser *Goin'on*." Admiral Toke displayed a third chart that nobody could completely see. "The *Goin'on* will initiate the attack by boarding and securing the pirate ship as soon as she settles into orbit. As soon as the string-of-pearls is secured, the two Mallorys that have embarked naval infantry will join Task Force Crashpad, which will then launch a combat assault planetfall and take the pirate base.

"I will initially be with Task Force Crashpad.

"Are there any questions?" Without waiting to see if there were,

Admiral Orange stepped back out of the hatch, knocking over the easel holding the charts Toke had tried to display. Orange shot a glare at his N3. "I hope you aren't so clumsy when you take the *Grandar Bay*," he snarled. He marched down the passageway to his cabin and disappeared into it.

The captains remained standing, looking expectantly at the commanders of the task forces to tell them where to assemble for their briefings. Or, failing that, to tell them when to expect orders. Vice Admiral Toke, Rear Admiral Crashpad, and acting Commodore Head, for their part, stood in the passageway, looking at each other uncertainly. Except for the three charts Toke had been instructed to prepare for Admiral Orange's briefing, none of them had heard anything about the assault plan before the breifing and none of them had the foggiest notion of what they were supposed to do next.

Captain Main was the one who broke the silence.

"Adm'ral," she growled. "D'any o' ya have plans, or do ya want us to help ya make some?"

Vice Admiral Toke, after seeing the other task force commanders look away from her, realized that as the senior officer present, she was the one who had to answer Main's question. She cleared her throat before she spoke. "Ah, yes, ah, Captain Main. That's an excellent idea. The captains for Task Force Toke, please remain in the wardroom. The captains for Task Force Head, assemble at the fore end of the passageway, and Task Force Crashpad at the aft end. You and your respective commanders will immediately commence drawing up plans for your phases of the operation." She moved the easel out of the way so the captains for Task Forces Head and Crashpad could get by, and looked expectantly into the wardroom.

"Adm'ral," Captain Main said before anybody could leave, "some of us captains ain't bin assigned to task forces. Wha'da we do?"

Toke blinked a couple of times. Oh yes, she realized, the supply ships and tugs hadn't been assigned to task forces.

"Ah, Captain Main, ah, I think for the time being, ah, until further disposition the, ah, remaining ships will form Task Force Four, code named 'Main.' If you would be so good as to assemble your captains someplace out of the way and begin drawing up plans . . ." Her voice trailed off. She didn't know what to tell Captain Main and the captains of her "task force" what to plan, and she hoped Admiral Orange wouldn't get furious when he found out a "Task Force Main" had been formed without his permission.

Captain Main hesitated for a moment; she was to command a task force? She was a mere ensign. Not only did all three of the supply ship captains outrank her, but one of the other tug captains was also senior to her. She looked at them. They all looked away.

"Aargh," Captain Main finally said. The order for her to be in command had been given by a vice admiral. Who was she or the other captains to question her? "Ya heard the man. Le's go find a place we can figure out what we're doin'." She bulled her way through the assembled captains, and the other captains of Task Force Main meekly followed in her wake.

Successful combat commanders strive to plan for the unexpected so they can seize any opportunity that arises—or at least so they don't get caught in a situation where they can't respond effectively to enemy action. They do this because they know full well that their plan, no matter how detailed and how good, probably won't work at all once the first shot is fired. Sometimes events totally obliviate the original plan even before the first shot is fired. What it boils down to is, generals (and admirals) don't often win battles with the brilliance of their plans, but they can most assuredly lose them.

As for the plan devised by Admiral of the Starry Heavens Sativa Orange, well . . .

"Admiral? Admiral, sir." Commander Moon Happiness, captain of the *Goin'on*, stepped closer when Admiral Orange didn't respond to his urgent voice and shook his shoulder. "Admiral, wake up, sir. We have a situation, sir." He shook the admiral's shoulder more vigorously. "Sir?"

Lieutenant Shroom, the *Goin'on*'s doctor, rushed into the cabin and shouldered Happiness aside. "Sorry, sir," he said rapidly, "but he insisted on a sedative. You can't wake him that way." The doctor opened the top of the admiral's sleep shirt and exposed his shoulder. "I have to give him a stimulant," he explained. He quickly applied an injector pad to the admiral's bare shoulder, then stepped back.

Happiness didn't need the hint, he'd already stepped away from the admiral's bunk.

In a few seconds the stimulant reached the admiral's bloodstream.

When it did, he abruptly sat up, flailing his arms about and shouting incoherently. After a moment he realized where he was and who was present. He fixed Happiness and Shroom with a baleful stare and roared, "What is the meaning of this?"

"Sir, we have a situation," Happiness said.

"We most certainly do, Captain!" Admiral Orange said threateningly.

"Sir, the *Grandar Bay* is retrieving her string-of-pearls."

"You think a maintenance problem on an enemy ship is a good enough reason to wake me up?" he bellowed incredulously.

"Sir, it looks like she's preparing to leave orbit."

"What? Why didn't anybody warn me of this?" The admiral swung his legs over the side of the bunk and stood, looking around for his uniform.

"Sir, we had no advance warning. I came to wake you as soon as we detected what she was doing."

"Have either of the pirate ships returned?" Admiral Orange asked. He spotted his uniform and began pulling on the trousers and tunic over his sleep clothes.

"Nossir. We don't expect the *Broken Missouri* for another week standard." Happiness didn't bother to mention that they didn't have enough information to know when to expect the *Heavenly Mary* to return.

"Sound battle stations."

"Sir?"

"Have you gone deaf, Captain?" The admiral paused in buttoning his tunic to glare at Happiness. "I said battle stations!"

"Aye aye, sir!" The *Goin'on*'s captain spun about and left the cabin to sound battle stations, even though with the We're Here! fleet as far out of range of Maugham's Station and the orbiting Confederation starship as it was, he knew there was absolutely no need for anyone to head for battle stations for several days to come.

"Incompetents! Why am I surrounded by incompetents!" the admiral muttered as he brushed past Lieutenant Shroom into the passageway. He used his fingers to comb his hair as he headed for the bridge.

The ship's PA system blared out an ear-splitting klaxon, and a carefully modulated female voice crooned, "All hands, now hear this. Battle stations. All hands, battle stations."

"Well, what are you standing around waiting for?" Admiral Orange demanded as he bustled onto the bridge. The members of the bridge crew were all sitting at their duty stations, waiting for orders.

"What does the admiral want us to do, sir?" Happiness asked.

"Stop the *Grandar Bay* from breaking orbit, of course!"

Shortly, Task Forces Toke, Head, and Crashpad were heading toward Maugham's Station under inertial power. They were four days away from a contact position with the *Grandar Bay*, and even Admiral Orange knew the Confederation starship would probably break orbit sooner than that. The admiral began issuing orders to cover all contingencies.

In the absence of any orders at all, Task Force Main followed slowly.

It took a day and a half standard for the Essay to retrieve the string-of-pearls, and another half day for it to return to the *Grandar Bay*. The Essay docked in the starship's welldeck and was locked down, and its crew headed for their berthing compartment. Moments later the *Grandar Bay*'s PA system commenced the final countdown to launch, and the mighty amphibious starship began her gracefully ponderous break from orbit. Her exit took her to planetary north, angled away from the sun. There was no rush. Commodore Boreland ordered a flight path that would take the starship four days to reach her first jump point. Three hours after launch, the commodore ordered gravity restored, and the off-duty crew and embarked Marines were permitted to leave their cabins and compartments. Shortly after, the galleys were in full operation and the first shift was called to the main mess halls. Most of the Marines headed for other open spaces. Boreland sent a steward to Brigadier Sturgeon and Colonel Ramadan with an invitation to join him in his dining salon for a simple repast.

The mahogany dining table in Commodore Boreland's quarters was covered with a snow-white, damasked linen cloth. Four places were set at it. The commodore and Captain Maugli, the *Grandar Bay*'s executive officer, were waiting for Brigadier Sturgeon and Colonel Ramadan when they arrived.

"Gentlemen!" Boreland said, greeting the two Marines and shaking their hands. "I believe you both know Captain Maugli."

"Yes we do, Roger," Sturgeon said. "Good to see you again, Zsuz." He shook Maugli's hand.

"And you, Ted. Ike," Maugli said as he let go of Sturgeon's hand and shook with Ramadan.

"An aperitif, gentlemen?" Boreland asked, and turned to a side table, where a bottle of cognac waited with four snifters. A nearby steward reached for the bottle, but Boreland waved him away and poured himself.

"Gentlemen," Boreland said, when everyone had a glass, "to a strange mission well accomplished."

"Strange indeed," Sturgeon said, lifting his glass. "Mission accomplished."

"Mission accomplished," Ramadan and Maugli agreed, hoisting their glasses in toast. They savored the cognac's aroma and sipped. Sturgeon noticed it wasn't the same Corsican Special Reserve Boreland had treated him to following the Kingdom campaign. But neither was this as special an occasion.

"Have you ever seen anything like that before?" Boreland asked after a moment.

Sturgeon answered, "Carnivorous plants? Several times. Predatory plants, a few times. But that method of carnivorous predation was new to me." He looked to Ramadan for further comments.

"Humanity has encountered a few thousand carnivorous plants," the colonel said. "Most of them eat insectoids, a few specialize in small species of lizardlike animals, mammaloids, or small avians. Only a dozen or so have been found that predate on larger animals—such as *H. sapiens*. I've searched the literature and haven't found another incident where several species cooperate the way the flora of the hidden valleys seem to."

"Then those life-forms are unique?" Maugli asked.

"It does seem so."

"Imagine," the *Grandar Bay's* executive officer said softly. Then, "You Marines sometimes go planetside, into places where you have limited information on local life-forms, isn't that right?"

Sturgeon nodded. "Oftentimes, as on Maugham's Station, we go in with no reliable information."

"And every time you do, you risk running into something like that." Maugli shuddered.

"Maugham's Station had some unpleasant surprises," Sturgeon said, "but I didn't lose any Marines, and that's the most important thing."

Maugli shook his head. "I'm glad I'm a sailor, not a Marine."

Sturgeon and Ramadan chuckled politely and sipped at their cognac.

"Gentlemen—you Marines too," Boreland said with a smile when they finished their aperitifs, "seats, please."

Two of the place-setting napkins were clinched with holders that bore navy emblems, the other two had Marine emblems. They were arranged so Boreland sat at the table's head and Sturgeon at its foot, with their number ones in between.

As soon as the four were seated, a steward poured an ounce of white wine into Boreland's glass for his approval.

"That will do nicely," the commodore said when he'd tasted the wine. The steward poured for all, and at a signal from Boreland, left the bottle on the table. An open bottle of the same sat chilling on a credenza. Sturgeon didn't recognize the label.

"Gentlemen, a toast," Sturgeon said. "To our Corps and Confederation and," with a nod to Boreland, "our navy."

"Corps and Confederation," Ramadan said.

"Confederation and navy," Boreland and Maugli said.

They drank their glasses half down. Before either number one could propose a toast, two stewards appeared. One bore a tray with four dishes on it, the other a tray with two small tureens. He set one down to Boreland's right front, between him and Ramadan, the other between Sturgeon and Maugli. As he put the tureens in place, the other steward began placing the other dishes in front of the diners.

A light repast, indeed, Sturgeon thought as he looked at the dish in front of him, unless it was a very large appetizer. The dish was a large salad plate, on which portions of three different salads of white meats, possibly chicken, were set, along with some sort of pasta salad, all over a bottom of mixed greens, split cherry tomatoes, and diagonally sliced cucumbers.

"I first had this dish in an only slightly pretentious place called Curlie's, in the South District of Melbourne."

"City or world?" Ramadan interrupted.

"The world," Boreland replied, giving the Marine a questioning look.

"On the direct paternal line," Ramadan responded to the unvoiced question, "I'm Australian. Melbourne was only known as the most important city south of the equator on Earth before a planet was named after it."

Boreland nodded understanding. Given Ramadan's looks, he was no more old Australian than anyone else at the table; he looked to be a blend of the old racial types that had evolved before humanity moved into space and most came to realize that, despite superficial differences, all people were human. To be sure, there were those who decried what they called "the mongrelization of racial purity," but most saw that the helter-skelter mixing of human types and lineages strengthened the species.

"But back to the salad," the commodore continued. "You have a sample portion of an Earth chicken salad, a piscoid salad from New Genesee, of all unlikely places, an 'indeterminate meat' salad from Boradu, and a macaroni salad from Dominion. But what really makes this salad worthy of being a main meal is the dressing." He reached out and lifted the lid from the tureen near his right hand. The dressing was a thick liquid of dark olive green in which darker flecks of suspended solids could be made out.

"Gentlemen, I don't know what this dressing is made of, much less where its ingredients come from, but it has made this salad one of my favorite dishes. Please, Ted, Ike, sample it." He handed the ladle to Ramadan, who put a dollop on a corner of his salad and tasted. His eyes opened wide, as did Sturgeon's at the other end of the table when the smiling Maugli offered some to him.

As he ladled more of the dressing on his salad, Sturgeon said, "You say you discovered it in a restaurant on Melbourne. If you don't know what's in it, or where its ingredients come from, how did it come to be on your menu?"

Boreland smiled and drenched his own salad with dressing as he answered. "When I returned to my ship, I asked the chief of mess if he knew the dish. He didn't, but promised to look into it. I don't know what happened when he visited the chef at Curlie's, but when he came back, he had the recipe. He told me what the portions are, but refused to say anything about the dressing." He shook his head. "Chiefs of mess are as bad as civilian chefs when it comes to secrets. I don't know—and don't even want to think about—what the chief had to do to get that recipe."

"Have you been back to Curlie's since then?" Sturgeon asked with a twinkle in his eye.

"Every time I've been to Melbourne."

Then they stopped talking and paid attention to their food, pausing only occasionally to wash a morsel down with a sip of wine.

After the dishes were cleared away, they sat sipping cognac and puffing on Davidoff Anniversario No. 1's provided by Colonel Ramadan, discussing the ways they were dealing with the inevitable morale problems raised by 34th FIST's quarantine and the supposed loss of the *Grandar Bay*. So far there hadn't been many major problems with the junior people; few of the Marines had families on other worlds who were expecting them to come home soon, and the seriousness of their situation hadn't yet sunk into most of the sailors. There were more problems with the officers and middle-level NCOs and petty officers, who saw their possibilities of career advancement by any means other than the death or incapacitation of higher ranking people cut off. As for the commanders themselves, both Sturgeon and Boreland saw themselves frozen in what they considered the best duty a Marine or navy officer could wish for. Colonel Ramadan enjoyed being a FIST executive officer and had no aspirations for a command of his own or staff duty in a higher headquarters somewhere. Captain Maugli kept his own counsel.

"Excuse me," Boreland said when a beep drew his attention. He turned away from the table and spoke into his comm. "Commodore here." He listened for a moment, then said, "I'll be there immediately," and signed off.

"Gentlemen," he announced as he rose to his feet and headed for the bridge, "it appears that Maugham's Station is under assault by an unknown force—and the Combat Information Center reports that a flotilla of unidentified starships is on an intercept vector with us."

The others jumped up and headed out of the salon.

CHAPTER TWENTY-SIX

"The commodore is on the bridge!" the officer of the deck announced.

"Carry on," Commodore Boreland said as he stepped through the hatch, followed by Brigadier Sturgeon. Colonel Ramadan and Captain Maugli had gone to their own duty stations.

The bo'sun nodded at Boreland, then returned his attention to overseeing the petty officers and seamen of the bridge watch. Nobody else so much as glanced in the commodore's direction.

Boreland stood near the left shoulder of the ensign who was serving as the assistant officer of the deck and looked at the navigation radar globe the AOD was studying; the *Grandar Bay* was centered in the globe, and Maugham's Station was a larger dot toward one edge. "That's them?" he asked, using a laser pointer to indicate a cluster of dots to one side.

"Yessir." The AOD didn't shift his eyes from their concentration on the radar globe.

"Show me."

The AOD touched controls and a line appeared, running from Maugham's Station through the dot that represented the *Grandar Bay*, and on to the edge of the globe. Another line ran through the cluster of dots for the unidentified flotilla. The two lines crossed midway between the *Grandar Bay*'s position and the edge of the globe.

"Has CIC identified them yet?"

"No positive IDs yet, sir. Tentative ID is one heavy cruiser, three destroyers, and five smaller starships—the smaller ships might be space-ships rather than starships, but CIC says *that* identification is unlikely." Spaceships, unlike starships, only functioned within a planetary system and were incapable of interstellar travel. Maugham's Station didn't have any spaceships, much less starships."

"Communications?"

"Radio reports there has been no response to broad-spectrum com-munications. If they are communicating among themselves, they're using lasers or tight directionals that we can't pick up."

"Estimated time of intercept?" Boreland asked the quartermaster's mate first class, who was the duty navigator.

"At current velocities and vectors, twenty-five hours, seventeen minutes standard, sir," the navigator replied. "At current velocity, we are twenty-seven hours, forty-eight minutes standard from our plotted jump point. At flank speed we can reach jump point in fourteen hours standard."

"Thank you. Good work, both of you. Keep me informed." Bore-land turned from the nav globe and stepped over to the OOD. "What do we know about the situation planetside?"

"Sir, a starship took out the geosync before local authorities could transmit anything more than that the geosync was under attack. CIC re-ports that at the same time, a flotilla of four ships took position oppo-site Ammon and began dropping shuttles in combat-assault landing mode."

Boreland said softly to Sturgeon, "It looks as if perhaps our mission to Maugham's Station isn't over."

"It does indeed."

Boreland turned back to the OOD. "Contact CIC and request their very latest data, then sound the maneuver alert." He turned to the sec-ond class on the helm. "Notify engines to prepare to reverse course."

"Aye aye, sir," the helmsman said, and began talking into the engi-neering comm.

The OOD finished talking to the Combat Information Center and turned on the ship's PA system. A bo' sun's whistle sounded throughout the *Grandar Bay*. "Now hear this," the officer of the deck said into the PA system. "All hands not at duty stations, retire at once to your berthing spaces and prepare to secure for maneuvers. I say again, all hands not at duty stations, retire at once to your berthing spaces and prepare to secure for maneuvers." He pushed a button, and the whistle sounded again, then he turned the PA off and turned to Boreland. "Sir, CIC reports planetside signals are very faint, but there seems to be fighting going on where the shuttles from the bogies landed. There are still no communications with Maugham's Station. Also, CIC reports they have made tentative ID of one of the approaching starships." He gave Boreland a smile that was half apologetic, half disbelieving. "The one CIC tentatively identified as a heavy cruiser, they now say it might be a King-class dreadnought."

Boreland nodded as though that explained everything. "I want to know every world that might still have Kings in service."

Before the OOD could respond to the order, he returned his attention to his comm. After a brief exchange, he said, "Sir, CIC reports another flotilla of seven ships approaching Maugham's Station. They tentatively ID at least two of them as deep-space tugs."

"Very well." He looked at Sturgeon, who simply nodded. "Sound the alert," Boreland instructed the OOD. "Reverse maneuver in two minutes. Helm, notify engineering." He and Sturgeon strapped themselves into acceleration couches.

The bo'sun's whistle sounded throughout the ship once more, this time followed by the carefully modulated female voice that said, "Now hear this. All hands, now hear this. All hands secure for maneuver. Maneuver will commence in two minutes. All hands secure for maneuver," again followed by the whistle. The voice repeated the alert three times at thirty second intervals, then ten second intervals until ten seconds remained, when it counted the last seconds down.

At zero seconds, side-mounted rockets fore and aft fired, spinning the mighty ship around stem to stern to face back toward Maugham's Station. The *Grandar Bay* shuddered as her main engines fired for the first time in two days. The artificial gravity had been turned off one minute before the *Grandar Bay* began to turn about. Now gravity began to return—as acceleration g-force, directed toward the stern; toward the aft bulkheads throughout the starship rather than the decks. Anyone and anything not secured fell toward the bulkheads as if dropped.

Slowly, slowly, the mighty starship's relative velocity dropped until she stopped receding from Maugham's Station and she reversed her vector. As slowly as she had stopped, the *Grandar Bay* gained velocity.

"What is the intercept flotilla doing?" Boreland asked the AOD.

"Nothing that I can see, sir."

"What does CIC say?" Boreland asked the OOD.

The officer of the deck spoke into the CIC comm, listened, then said, "Sir, CIC reports no action on the part of the intercept flotilla."

"Restore artificial gravity when we reach flank speed. I'm returning to my quarters. Inform me immediately of any change in the disposition of the unidentified ships."

"Aye aye, sir."

Sturgeon stepped off the bridge ahead of Boreland. "How long will it take for us to get back to Maugham's Station?" he asked.

"At flank speed? About a day and a half. With violent deceleration at the end."

"I'm going to assemble my staff and inform them of what's happening. You'll keep me informed? We'll need to know something of what's going on planetside in order to make any plans."

"I'll even keep you informed of what's going on in space."

"What is that pirate doing?" Admiral of the Starry Heavens Sativa Orange shrieked when he saw the change in the track he was following in the radar globe.

"Sir, she's reversed," the radar officer answered. "She's heading back toward Maugham's Station."

"Going back?" Admiral Orange squeaked. "She can't be going back. Why would she go back?"

The navigator opted for the better part of valor and said nothing. Neither did anyone else on the bridge.

Admiral Orange fretted and scowled, trying to decide what to do about his quarry's unexpected maneuver. None of his primary staff was present for him to hector for advice, they were all in their own flagships, leading task forces—except for Vice Admiral Toke, who commanded the task force led by the dreadnought *Groovy*, on which he also had his command center. But Orange had lost all confidence in Toke's advice; besides, the flotilla commander wasn't on the bridge to offer advice if he did decide to ask her.

Task forces, that's it! he suddenly realized. Task Force Crashpad was already on station at Maugham's Station. The gator ships wouldn't be able to do anything against the Mandalay headed toward them, but the *Goin'on* was an Omaha-class light cruiser, the most modern and powerful starship in We're Here!'s navy; she should have no trouble killing or disabling the pirate. And she was right there, with two task forces of warships!

"Captain!" he barked. "Communicate with all ships of Task Force Toke and Task Force Head. Instruct them to change vector to pursue the pirate at flank speed!" When he didn't get the immediate reply he expected, he looked around. The *Groovy*'s captain wasn't on the bridge. "OOD, did you hear me?" he barked.

"Yessir!"

"Well, what are you waiting for? Communicate with the other ships!"

"Aye aye, sir." The OOD spoke into his comm and instructed the radio shack to order all starships of the two task forces to change direction and head for Maugham's Station.

Of course, Admiral Orange hadn't given any instructions regarding the timing of the turns, or about maintaining formation. So the nine starships of the two flotillas each immediately began turning, which meant no two of them turned at the same time. And, being of various classes and ages, they weren't all able to change vector at the same rate. In the two hours it took for the nine starships to receive the order and complete their turns, the tight formations they had been in disappeared, and they were spread out over such a large portion of planetary space that few of them were in position to support any of the others.

If that wasn't enough, the different classes of starship had different flank speeds. As the nine starships of the two flotillas raced after the *Grandar Bay*, they spread out farther. The spread was exacerbated by the fact that most of them could only run their engines for a limited time before they had to turn them off, either to cool them or to conserve fuel.

Either Admiral Orange didn't notice the increasing spread or he didn't realize the significance. Or, just possibly, he didn't care.

Commodore Boreland, on the other hand, knew full well the significance of the lack of formation on the part of the still unidentified and presumably hostile fleet. There were half a dozen worlds that might still have King-class dreadnoughts in service. None of them was known as a naval power, so the evident lack of intelligent command behind the nine pursuing starships was no hint as to which of the six they might be from.

"They're falling farther behind, sir," the assistant officer of the deck reported.

Boreland grunted. He wasn't surprised; if the King was typical of that fleet, none of them could come near matching the *Grandar Bay's* speed in Space-3. So unless they had weapons to match those of the Skink starships he'd fought in orbit around Kingdom and Society 419, they didn't worry him at all yet.

Of far greater importance just then was the situation on Maugham's Station.

"I'll be in the radio shack if anybody needs me," he told the OOD.

Captain Wilma Arden rose to her feet but didn't come to attention when Boreland entered the radio shack.

"Have you established comm with anyone on Maugham's Station?" he asked.

"Nossir. Either the geosync was destroyed or it's been occupied and turned off—or it's not replying to our signals for other reasons. But we are picking up transients. Here's the log." She leaned over and touched a control on her console.

Boreland sat at her station and skimmed the log entries. "Do you have transcripts?" he asked when he saw that the log only noted messages sent and messages intercepted.

"Yessir. Highlight the entry you want to read and click."

The commodore didn't bother to look at any of the *Grandar Bay's* attempts to contact Maugham's Station, he went straight to the intercepts. There were two groups—one from Ammon, the other from the opposite side of the world. Not many had broken through the ionosphere, and those that had were fragmentary.

"Does intelligence have these?"

"I don't know, sir, I didn't want to risk missing any transients, so I didn't take the time to check with them."

"What about from the unknowns on station?"

"Either they aren't transmitting or they're using tight beams."

The intercepts from the populated area of Maugham's Station were fragments of normal commercial broadcasts, and a few freak police transmissions. None indicated any awareness that an invasion force had landed on the opposite side of the world. The most significant intercept was a commercially broadcast message from President Menno, who said they had no idea who the starship was that had attacked the geosync or why they did it. Neither did he know where the starship went after the attack.

The intercepts from the far side were even more fragmentary. All Boreland could tell from them was it appeared that heavy ground combat was going on, but it was impossible to tell from the transcripts whose forces were involved.

"Are these translated?"

"No, they spoke English." That told Boreland nothing. Some worlds preserved old languages, but English was the common language of the Confederation of Human Worlds and the primary language spoken on many of its member worlds.

"How many different units could you identify?" he asked.

"Sir? I don't understand."

"Did you hear the intercepts?"

"Yessir," she said, realizing what he meant. "There were many different voices, but they all seemed to have the same accent. None of them sounded like the accent I heard on transmissions from Ammon."

"Let me hear one."

Arden pressed a control, and the speaker next to the console's main display emitted a static-filled voice. "Over there, they're over there! Get them!" the half-panicked voice shouted.

Boreland leaned back and listened as the intercept was replayed. Though the accent was distinct, with drawn-out vowels and many mushy consonants, he didn't recognize it. "They all spoke like this?" he asked.

"Everyone I listened to."

He looked at the log again and found a longer intercept that wasn't broken up too much with static. "Send this one to the bridge," he ordered, and stood to leave the radio shack.

"Aye aye, sir." Arden resumed her seat, to send the recording to the bridge.

"Good job, Wilma," Boreland said on his way out.

Back on the bridge, he picked up the PA comm and nodded for the bo'sun's whistle to be sounded. After the whistle trilled, he said, "Now hear this. All hands, now hear this. This is the commodore speaking. I am about to play a radio intercept from Maugham's Station. Listen to it carefully. The voice has a distinct accent. If anyone recognizes the accent, inform your section chief immediately. Officers and chiefs, if anybody recognizes the accent, I want to be informed as fast as you can get the information to me. Stand by for the transmission." He looked at the OOD and nodded.

The officer of the deck had prepared the intercept for broadcast as soon as he realized Boreland's intent and sent it. The intercept was nine seconds long. He repeated it twice, then Boreland took the comm again.

"All hands, this is the commodore. If anyone recognizes that accent, I want to know immediately. That is all." He nodded at the OOD, and the bo'sun's whistle sounded once more before the PA clicked off.

Boreland settled back and waited, but nobody reported recognizing the accent.

The *Grandar Bay* was twelve hours standard from deceleration, and the main thrusters had been off for several hours when she turned about so her stern was pointed at Maugham's Station. Normal gravity was restored as soon as the turning maneuver was completed. Radar showed that the distance between the *Grandar Bay* and the trailing fleet was still increasing, and that the followers were stringing out even farther. In the radio shack, Captain Wilma Arden and her crew were intercepting more fragmentary transmissions from Ammon and the fighting at its antipodes. Still, none of the intercepts gave any indication of awareness of the invasion, and the destruction or capture of the geosync satellite was still a mystery—at least for public dissemination. The intercepts from the antipodes continued to indicate intense fighting, though all the transmissions seemed to be from one side of the battle.

"Perhaps it's an internal conflict," Commander van Winkle, the infantry battalion commander, commented after listening to the most recent batch of intercepts.

Brigadier Sturgeon made a gesture for him to explain what he meant. He, his top staff, his primary subordinate commanders, and their top staff were in the FIST command center, where the combat intercepts were piped to them.

"Invaders or illegal colonists are there from another world," van Winkle said. "Their own government wants them to leave, but they refuse and prefer fighting to leaving."

Commander Wolfe's face bore a bemused expression. "An off-world civil war? What a novel concept," he said.

Van Winkle shrugged at the comment, acknowledging that his suggestion had been bizarre. "The only other explanation" he said, "is either the other side has no radio communications or their comm is so low-powered none of it can break through the ionosphere."

"That's just as likely a premise," Commander Usner, the FIST operations officer, interjected. "More likely even." He looked at Commander Daana, the intelligence officer.

"*No* comm doesn't make sense," Daana said. "*Weak* comm does."

"We don't know who the combatants are," Sturgeon said, "but what can we tell with some degree of certainty from these intercepts?"

"They don't seem to be using aircraft," Wolfe said.

"How positive are you?" Sturgeon asked.

Wolfe shook his head. "I'm not positive, but I haven't heard anything that indicates aircraft."

"They're using projectile and explosive weapons," van Winkle said. He looked at Captain Likau, his logistics officer.

"Between what we have and the stores on board, we have enough body armor for everyone in the battalion, so that's no problem," Likau said.

Captain Rhu-Anh, the infantry battalion intelligence officer, was next. "So far, we've identified thirty different voices in the intercepts. Unfortunately, for the most part we have been unable to distinguish among them vertically. At least one seems to be battalion level, but most of the rest could be anywhere from squad to brigade level."

"Spotters?" asked Daana.

"Negative." Rhu-Anh shook his head. "If they're using any indirect fire weapons, they're so short range they don't need forward observers."

"That's the read from here also," Daana said. "It sounds like light infantry without air, armor, or artillery support on either side."

"What does the Surface Radar section report?" Sturgeon asked.

"We're still too far out for them to see anything," Daana answered.

"Then what we are faced with is probable unsupported light infantry of unknown size and strength," Sturgeon summed up.

Nobody had anything to say. They all knew that wasn't enough information on which to make any plans.

CHAPTER TWENTY-SEVEN

The bo'sun's whistle shrilled throughout the *Grandar Bay.* "Now hear this. Now hear this. The ship will commence deceleration in five minutes. All hands not at duty stations, report to your berthing compartments. Secure all objects. Null-g will commence in four minutes. That is all." The whistle blew again.

Throughout the *Grandar Bay* rapid footsteps echoed off bulkheads as sailors and Marines left what they were doing and rushed to their compartments. Thanks to the maneuvers the starship had made during the previous day or so, even the greenest Marines knew how important it was to be securely strapped in when the ship's gravity was turned off and the main engines fired.

The warning was repeated at regular intervals until it reached the final countdown, then "zero." The thrusters fired far more powerfully than after the *Grandar Bay* reversed direction, and null-g was replaced by g-forces that quickly increased back up to one gravity and then all the way to three g's, where they leveled off and remained. Throughout the starship, acceleration couches swung from deck-down orientation to the aft bulkheads.

Among the occupied duty stations were those of the *Grandar Bay*'s Surface Radar section, where Lieutenant (j.g.) McPherson was the duty officer and Chief Radarman Nome rested in his couch between and behind the two radar analysts on duty. In orbit, there would be more than two analyzing the mass of data flowing in from the string-of-pearls. But, still hours from geosync, and under fierce deceleration, with only the ship's integral sensors in use, Nome used only his best analysts—SRA2 Hummfree and SRA2 Auperson. And he didn't expect results until after the main thrusters stopped and the starship began maneuvering against the flotilla of unknown ships hovering in geosync above whatever was going on planetside.

Hummfree and Auperson had other ideas.

"We up on ship ID, sir?" Hummfree asked McPherson. Talk was difficult. The helmet mike that under one g would stand millimeters above his lips, bobbing with every breath he took, now lay heavy against his lower lip, an extra annoyance he didn't need. He already felt as if a mess chief were sitting on his chest and as many messmen as could fit were lounging on every other part of his body. His eyelids were so heavy they didn't know whether to slide all the way open or close completely. Not long before deceleration began, they'd identified the classes of the ships they were headed toward: an obsolete Omaha-class light cruiser and four troop ships of even greater vintage. If they could identify the ships, they'd know which human world the invasion fleet was from, which might also give the commodore a handle on *why* they were invading. Of course, if the Skinks were using human starships or were copying human designs, all bets were off. But if the ships couldn't be specifically identified, it might indicate that they weren't human at all—which was a very important thing for the commodore and the Marines to know.

"Last year's *Jane's*," McPherson replied. He would have said more, but many messmen were using him as a couch, and he had just as much trouble talking. He wasn't sure the *Grandar Bay* had the most recent edition of *Jane's War Starships of Human Space*, but she likely had an edition recent enough to identify the ships ahead of them if they'd begun service in the Confederation Navy. He knew the ship had the most recent *Jane's War Starships of the Confederation of Human Worlds*.

"Let's try." Hummfree couldn't dislodge the messman using his right arm for a settee, but he was able to lift the guy far enough to reach his console. He flipped on the aft radar, infra, UV, and visual displays; he didn't bother with X and gamma rays. Charts and graphs sprang to life; bar, line, scatter, high-low, running averages, along with the image displays—and looked like they were going crazy as he turned the sensors to face into the *Grandar Bay's* direction of movement. Then he had to make further alignment adjustments to keep the sensors from being blinded by the back scatter of the thrusters.

Nome and Auperson both watched Hummfree with interest. The aft sensors were sometimes used while the main engines were on, but the thrusters threw out so much electromagnetic radiation that in the hands of all but the most skilfull technicians, useful data was buried in electronic noise. Chief Nome himself had never managed to get a truly accurate read through a starship's thrusters, and Auperson had never tried. After several minutes the displays gave data that Nome could almost make sense of, and that looked to Auperson like they might mean something, even though they made no sense to him.

Hummfree studied the displays for a long moment, then said, "Doppler."

Auperson grunted as he struggled to twiddle the dials that adjusted the displays to correct for relative motion. The displays jerked a couple of times, then became intelligible to Chief Nome. Even McPherson and Auperson were able to make enough sense of the displays to identify the class of the light cruiser and one of the transports they were approaching. The image only held for a second before it began jerking about, in and out of focus, as the amount of noise overwhelmed Hummfree's computer and made it impossible to suck intelligible data from the overheated electronic soup it was being fed. But it was on screen long enough to impress everyone who saw the image.

Nome toggled on his command comm and murmured into it, "Why's he only a second class?"

McPherson, who was also surprised by what Hummfree had accomplished, murmured back, with awe in his voice, "I'll find out."

Hummfree wasn't satisfied, though. "Stedcam," he said. Auperson struggled against the g-forces to turn on the motion-compensation motors for the cameras. Hummfree kept brushing and tweaking the controls that refined the filtering of the radiation of the *Grandar Bay's* thrusters. Suddenly, the light cruiser popped into view on a visible light display. The image was small, and when he enlarged it, grainy, but the markings on the starship's port bow were obviously block Roman alphanumerics. He switched his attention to the comp that controlled the stedcam motors and worked it until the jittery image steadied.

"Is that one-five-six-six?" Hummfree asked. "I can't make out the last number."

"Can't tell," Auperson replied. "Maybe five."

"First number's a seven," McPherson said. He couldn't make it out any better than the two petty officers, but he could tell the cruiser was too recent to have a hull number that began with "one."

"Six-five," Nome said.

The image blurred and cleared again as Hummfree kept working his controls, but he couldn't refine it—the g-forces interfered too much with his fine movements.

"Ease up," Nome ordered. "Wait for it."

Hummfree let his hands drop back to rest on the arms of his acceleration couch and watched the displays.

Commander Moon Happiness stood on the bridge of the *Goin'on* and watched the approach of the *Grandar Bay* on the bridge displays. The Confederation amphibious landing ship was braking hard. Their best calculations were that she would come to relative rest with the *Goin'on* close to the extreme range of the *Goin'on*'s main batteries. Happiness knew that Mandalay-class ships were armored and shielded well enough to survive an attack by an Omaha-class light cruiser—it didn't matter that the *Goin'on* was a heavy cruiser in We're Here!'s navy, she was still an obsolete light cruiser by Confederation Navy standards, and her weaponry hadn't been upgraded. He knew the *Goin'on* posed no severe danger to the Mandalay.

In which case, why was the Mandalay headed for relative rest at the extreme range of the *Goin'on*'s main batteries? The obvious answer was her weapons had greater range. But the Mandalay class wasn't like Crowe-class amphibious battle cruisers, armed with planet-busting weapons—the Mandalay's weaponry was strictly defensive. Yet now, when the Mandalay found herself being approached by a fleet of warships, instead of taking evasive measures or even attempting to jump prematurely to get away, she turned about and headed back to Maugham's Station in what looked like nothing so much as an attack attitude.

Conclusion: this Mandalay was far more heavily armed than the normal starship of her class.

Happiness looked to his right, at Rear Admiral Crashpad, who was slumped in the captain's acceleration couch, staring at the displays. "Sir, the enemy ship will be on us in little more than two hours standard. What does the admiral recommend we do?"

Crashpad didn't respond, he simply continued staring.

"Admiral, sir?" Happiness said, more forcefully than a wise commander ever spoke to an admiral. Several of the officers on the bridge turned to look. The enlisted bridge crew kept their eyes on their duties.

"Hmm? What?" Crashpad tore frightened eyes away from the displays and turned them toward Happiness. He didn't look like he really saw the *Goin'on*'s captain.

"Sir, the enemy ship will be here in little more than two hours. She appears to be in attack posture. What does the admiral recommend we do?"

"Ah," Crashpad said hesitantly, "what would you normally do, Captain?"

"Sir, I have reason to believe the approaching starship is more heavily armed and armored than we are." The rest of the bridge officers and crew turned to look at their captain. "She's too close for us to recover the landing force before she arrives. The first thing I would do is order the troop transports to break orbit and head for jump points so we don't lose them when the fighting starts."

"Fighting, yes, there's going to be fighting," Crashpad rasped. Like the Admiral of the Starry Heavens, he'd never been in an actual space battle. Unlike Admiral Orange, he didn't relish the prospect of correcting that deficiency against a starship that was likely more heavily armored and armed than his own. He cleared his throat and, in a stronger voice, asked, "How would you handle the fighting, Captain?"

"I wouldn't stand around and wait for it, Admiral. I'd begin maneuvering so I don't make an easy target, and attempt to get a telling strike against my opponent that would put her out of action. If I couldn't accomplish that, I'd have to take measures to save my ship."

"Yes, yes. Sound thinking, Captain." Crashpad levered himself out of the couch. "Take care of it. I'll be in my cabin if you need me."

"The admiral has left the bridge," the officer of the deck announced when Crashpad staggered off the bridge.

"What are you standing about gaping at?" Happiness snapped at the bridge officers and crew. "I want the transports to move out of harm's way right now. Break orbit, let's see if we can do anything against that Mandalay."

"They're moving, sir."

Commodore Boreland grunted; he could see that for himself. The transports were headed toward planetary south, he guessed on course to a jump point. But he wasn't concerned with them; they didn't pose any threat to the *Grandar Bay*. The Omaha light cruiser, on the other hand, was moving north at an angle to his own course—and the *Grandar Bay* was still moving too fast to turn to meet the threat the cruiser posed.

"Do we have an ID on that Omaha yet?" he asked.

The officer of the deck murmured into his comm, listened to the reply, then said, "Nossir. Radar's got her narrowed down to four different ships, but they don't have a positive."

If he remembered correctly, when the Omaha class was decommissioned, the cruisers were sold individually to various worlds. It didn't do him much good to know she might be from one of four different worlds. He said, "Maintain course and deceleration."

He waited, and watched the deceleration process. When the *Grandar Bay*'s relative speed was low enough he ordered, "Thrusters off in two minutes. Sound the alert."

The assistant officer of the deck reached out a heavy hand and touched his console. Immediately, a whistle sounded throughout the starship, and the female voice intoned, "Now hear this. Now hear this. Main thrusting will terminate in two minutes, followed by null-g." The voice repeated the alert at thirty second intervals until ten seconds remained to the cutting off of the thrusters, then gave a countdown.

Abruptly, the shuddering of the starship ceased and the background of engine roar vanished. Acceleration couches throughout the *Grandar Bay* swiveled back.

"Gravity on," Boreland ordered.

The AOD carefully reached for his console. The whistle sounded again; the voice ordered all hands to secure themselves for the return of ship's gravity. Seconds later normal weight returned to everyone and everything.

"Damage report," Boreland said. The bridge officers and crew were already talking into their comms, getting reports from around the ship.

"Sir, no damage or injuries reported," the OOD said when the last report came in.

Boreland then spoke more formally into his own comm: "Commander, Landing Force, this is the commander, Amphibious Task Force." Some task force, he thought—just one amphibious starship. When Brigadier Sturgeon answered his call just as formally, he continued, "Ready the landing force, Code Gamma. Launch will commence in sixty-one minutes." Code Gamma; the *Grandar Bay* would not come to rest relative to the planet, but would keep moving throughout the launch—which would make the launch more difficult than usual. Command of the launch would remain with the CATF and not pass to the CLF, as it would under a normal launch. Boreland put his comm aside when Sturgeon acknowledged the order. And they still didn't know what the situation was planetside.

"Notify weapons," he ordered the OOD. "Ready all defensive shields and missile countermeasures. Ready lasers to take out the *Omaha*'s weapons and engines."

"Ready defensive shields and missile countermeasures. Ready lasers to take out weapons and engines, aye," the OOD repeated, then gave the order into his comm to the weapons division.

The *Grandar Bay* continued her plunge toward Maugham's Station. The Omaha-class light cruiser continued on her course, to a position where her weapons would have their best chance of damaging the *Grandar Bay*.

Five minutes after Commodore Boreland gave the order to ready the landing force, the Marines of 34th FIST lined up in passageways outside their berthing compartments. There, the squad leaders and then the platoon sergeants inspected them to make sure each man bore his full combat load, had on his body armor, and that everything was attached securely. The men shifted about, uncomfortable with the unaccustomed weight of the body armor. Elsewhere, the officers of the infantry battalion and artillery battery were given a final briefing by a staff that had little idea of what they were heading into. The pilots, crew chiefs, and controllers of the composite squadron's Raptor and hopper sections were in ready rooms, receiving final mission orders from staff officers who had no more idea about the situation planetside than the ground combat element staff. With so little information to impart, the briefings were short and the officers and air crews were quickly dismissed to head for their assigned positions.

"Attention on deck!" Staff Sergeant Hyakowa ordered when Ensign Charlie Bass entered the passageway.

Bass, like his men, was dressed in body armor covered with reinforced chameleon fabric. Like them, he carried his helmet in his hand, so his head was fully visible. Had he not been so accustomed to it, the sight that presented itself would have unnerved him—twenty-nine disembodied heads floating in midair. Ungloved hands fluttered about between the heads and the deck. But Bass was a salty old Marine, and bodiless heads and hands were exactly the sight he expected to see.

"At ease!" he snapped. He gave his men a couple of seconds to relax from attention, and quickly swept his gaze about to see everybody looking intently at him. "Here's the situation. Nobody knows *what* the situation is planetside. We're going in blind. So we had best be ready for anything. Even then, 'anything' is liable to jump up and bite us on the ass. But if we don't let things turn into a cluster fuck down there, we'll make it through all right.

"One more thing." He smiled grimly. "We aren't going to cross the beach on Dragons, we're going in on hoppers. We'll swing in around the fighting and set up as a blocking force. I know few of you have crossed the beach in hoppers recently, but we're Marines, we do what we're told, and we do it right the first time.

"Questions?"

"Yessir," Corporal Dean asked. "Who are we fighting?"

The lights dimmed before Bass had a chance to answer. Their lumination rose and fell for several seconds before returning to normal.

"If anybody doesn't know," Bass said to the platoon when the lights returned to normal, "that was the *Grandar Bay's* defensive shields blocking energy weapons being fired at us." He paused for a few seconds to let that sink in, then went on, "To answer your question, Corporal Dean, offhand I'd say we're going to be fighting the ground forces of whoever it was that just took a shot at our ship. Seeing as how we don't know who they are to begin with, we'll just take on whoever wants to fight us when we get planetside." He looked about once more, then said, "Squad leaders, with me," and turned to lead Hyakowa and the squad leaders to where he could brief them.

"I've never crossed the beach on a hopper," Corporal Claypoole muttered nervously when Bass and the senior NCOs had gone.

Corporal Chan heard him. "I have," he said. "It's just like on a Dragon, except we exit the Essays at a thousand meters instead of on the deck."

"It's that thousand meters that bothers me," Claypoole muttered.

Corporal Kerr, third platoon's most experienced fire team leader, overheard the exchange. He was one of the few members of the platoon who had crossed the beach in a hopper, and he knew from their looks that most of the Marines were nervous about the prospect of riding into combat in a way they'd never rehearsed. Since nervousness could develop into fear, he decided to deal with it immediately.

"We've all made combat assaults on hoppers," he said to Claypoole, loud enough for everyone to hear. "What we're doing here is called an 'envelopment.' That means we don't go in hot, we go to someplace where the enemy will come to us. I've done it before—believe me, it's safer than riding the Dragons across the beach."

Lance Corporal MacIlargie, voicing Claypoole's concern, said, "Don't the hoppers leave the Essays at a thousand meters? Is that *safe*?" He ignored the look Lance Corporal Schultz gave him.

"Sure it is," Kerr answered calmly. "It's been done thousands of times; the navy knows how to drop hoppers without breaking them. And if anything does go wrong, the hopper's got a thousand meters to recover in. I've done it, and I'm still here." His visible hands patted his invisible chest and hips.

"I've done it too," Corporal Pasquin growled. "Not only is it safe, riding in a hopper is more comfortable than in a Dragon pounding across the water."

Quickly, Corporals Dornhofer, Barber, and Taylor spoke up, reassuring the other Marines that they'd made planetfall on hoppers and everything would be copacetic. Most of the Marines began to feel a little better. Of course, had they known what the corporals really thought about launching hoppers from Essays . . .

It wasn't long before the Marines were headed for the welldeck. They began filing in by company, where the FIST's Dragons, hoppers, and

Raptors awaited them, already in Essays. The Marines lined up at the Essays' ramps and awaited the order to board.

When the order to embark came, third platoon and Company L's assault platoon boarded one Essay and filed into the three hoppers that waited inside to receive them.

Corporal Claypoole looked at the webbing cocoons stretched across the interior of the hopper and felt like backing out and finding an Essay with a Dragon that had an open slot for him to slip into. He was accustomed to the web couches Marines rested in during assault landings in Dragons. The cocoons in the hoppers didn't look strong enough to take the violent shaking the Essays experienced during their descent down the rocky road of the atmosphere. Intellectually, he knew hoppers made landings all the time. Emotionally, he had trouble believing hoppers could stay in the air at all, much less be flung out of Essays at altitude and not injure or kill the Marines riding in them.

And the cocoons . . . Straps attached them to the overhead, straps attached them to the side walls, and more straps anchored them to the deck. Nothing held them from moving fore and aft. They looked like they'd make a very unstable ride. He looked, but didn't see the cupped tubes Dragons carried for Marines to regurgitate into if their stomachs got too queasy to hold their contents down.

"Secure your men, Corporal," Sergeant Linsman said harshly into Claypoole's ear.

Claypoole jumped. "Aye aye, Sergeant."

Lance Corporal Schultz had paused to help Lance Corporal MacIlargie into his cocoon before casually climbing into his own. With their weight in place, upchuck tubes dropped from the overhead and settled on their shoulders. But they were supine, and Claypoole knew that if someone threw up in that position, he could choke to death on his vomitus. He swallowed to keep his own gorge from rising.

He checked the webbing and saw that both of his men were properly strapped in. At least, he thought they were. He'd been oriented on hopper webbing, but had only used the webbing on ground-to-ground hops. Then he climbed into his own cocoon and found the straps easier to lock in place than they appeared. Sergeant Linsman came around to check everybody in his squad.

"See, it's not so hard," he said when he reached Claypoole.

Claypoole didn't respond; he didn't believe the worst was past.

Shortly, the alert came to stand by for null-g. The atmosphere was sucked out of the welldeck, then the great doors slid open, exposing the Essays to space. On signal, the Essays were plunged out of the welldeck. They maneuvered away from their still-moving home to group in formation, then began their straight-down descent to the surface of Maugham's Station. The "rough ride on a rocky road" had begun.

CHAPTER TWENTY-EIGHT

The ride down through the layers of the atmosphere wasn't as bad as Corporal Claypoole had feared, it was merely as rough as the ride was for the Marines in the Dragons inside other Essays—until the Essays dropped to an altitude of five thousand meters. Then they flared into a wide breaking spiral, slowing their descent as well as their airspeed, and flipped about so their front-facing ramps were pointed to the rear. The Essays' engines fired in short bursts, *tap-tap-tap,* slowing them more, and the small attitude thrusters on their bottoms fired, further slowing their descent. When the Essays passed two thousand meters, they lowered their ramps, their cargo holds filled with the roar of air rushing past, and, sucking the air out of the holds, the hoppers strained against their tie-downs. At fifteen hundred meters the attitude thrusters changed their pattern of fire and the main engines cut off. The Essays tipped nose downward. At a thousand meters the Essays fired their forward attitude thrusters to increase their airspeed, and the tie-downs holding the hoppers in place released their grips.

The hoppers rolled out of the Essays and began to plummet uncontrolled toward the ground. As soon as they dropped the hoppers, the Essays spun about, fired their main engines, and headed back to the *Grandar Bay.*

The hoppers didn't drop for long. Every aircraft commander had performed that maneuver many times in the past, as had the copilots. Before the hoppers dropped a hundred meters, their engines were firing and the pilots were bringing them under control. They worked their way into formation by the time they reached five hundred meters. The flight commander ran a comm check with the other hoppers and with the Dragons, which were already speeding westward across the ocean to the shore, which was over their horizon. The land was visible from the altitude of the hoppers.

Assured that everything was in order, the flight commander turned his ten-hopper formation to the north and sped off. Fifty kilometers on, the hopper flight swung through a ninety degree turn and sped west another two hundred kilometers before swinging through another ninety degree turn south. Not much more than half an hour after being flung from the Essays, the hoppers touched down, well inland from the fighting forces that were being approached by the rest of the battalion from the coast.

"Say again?" Commodore Boreland said incredulously.

"She's the *Goin'on*, sir," McPherson repeated, "of the We're Here! navy. We're Here! is—"

"I know what We're Here! is, Mr. McPherson," Boreland interrupted. "That's why I'm surprised. We're Here! is one of the least aggressive worlds in the Confederation. Why in the cosmos would they be making war on Maugham's Station?"

McPherson was equally baffled, so he said nothing.

"Does she show any sign of coming back for another pass?"

"Negative, sir. After her first salvo, she changed course to planetary south and followed the transports. She's still receding. Looks like she's running away."

"A wise move," Boreland murmured. An Omaha-class light cruiser had neither the fire power nor the armor to stand up to an unmodified Mandalay, much less to the weaponry the *Grandar Bay*'s engineers had modified to fight the Skink starships at Society 419 at the end of the Kingdom campaign. "What about the starships coming behind us?"

"Sir, we've resolved them well enough to know the class of most of them."

"Tell me."

"In addition to the King-class dreadnought, there are two Mallorys and three Freemonts, along with three smaller starships we haven't identified yet."

"The Mallory cruisers are even older than Omahas, I know that, but what is the Freemont class?"

"Three-generation-old destroyers, sir. The last of them was retired before my parents even met." McPherson couldn't hold back a short bark of laughter.

"Have you ID'd the King yet?"

"We think she was the *Trefalgar* before she was retired."

"Let me guess, sold to We're Here!"

"Yessir. And our records show that We're Here! also bought two Mallorys and three Freemonts."

Boreland could hardly believe it. The *Grandar Bay* was being attacked by a task force of ships so old they'd all been retired before he joined the navy. The *Trefalgar*, or whatever she was called now, was the only one that stood a prayer against the *Grandar Bay*'s weapons as they were now configured. The only threat the task force altogether posed was in strength of numbers. And that was only if their weapons and armor had been well maintained, which he seriously doubted. He knew that if he fought them, he was going to feel like a bully. But he couldn't simply let them regroup, cross his T, and fire broadside after broadside into his shields where he couldn't fire back. Could he?

Corporal Claypoole hadn't been the only member of third platoon's second squad to find out how the regurgitation tubes in the hoppers worked. The webbing sensed when a Marine's abdominal wall rippled in the pattern typical of pending regurgitation. When the regurge tube sensed it was being placed over the Marine's mouth, some of the web cocoon's straps shortened and others lengthened, turning the man facedown, allowing him to vomit without choking.

By the time the hoppers settled into level flight, Sergeant Linsman, Corporal Kerr, and Lance Corporal Schultz were the only members of the squad who hadn't vacated their stomachs, but far more of them lost it during the violent maneuvers after the hoppers were thrown out of the Essays than during the plunge down from the *Grandar Bay*. The interior of the hopper stank for a while, until the air scrubbers did their job, but the tubes managed to catch all the ejecta, so the aftermath was less unpleasant than it might have been.

All were relieved when the hoppers set down and they were able to scramble off into an open landscape that was broken up with treelines. Low mountains rose a couple of kilometers behind the company.

"Third platoon, squad leaders, check your you-are-here," Ensign Charlie Bass called on the platoon's command circuit. The squad leaders synchronized their HUD maps with their platoon commander's map; their you-are-here icons were all in the right place. "Put your people in the treeline here," Bass told them. He transmitted an overlay that he had already marked on his HUD map to the squad leaders. The squad leaders led their men to the trees and set them in place facing east.

"Wolfman, are you linked with second fire team?" Corporal Claypoole called.

"I'm in contact with Corporal Doyle," Lance Corporal MacIlargie answered.

"Good. Cover from ten o'clock to two o'clock," Claypoole said, assigning MacIlargie his primary field of fire. "Make sure you're overlapped with Doyle."

"Roger," MacIlargie said, and turned to his right to ask Doyle what his field of fire was.

"Hammer!" Claypoole turned to his left, then paused. He had to lower his infra screen to find his other man; Lance Corporal Schultz wasn't in the treeline area facing east. Claypoole finally found him just behind it facing south. "Ah, right," Claypoole said aloud to himself, "watch the flank, good idea." Then to Schultz, "Hammer, watch the flank."

Schultz raised his helmet screens and languidly spat to his front. He was on the company's extreme left flank, where else was he going to watch?

"I'll cover to my nine. Does that overlap with your field of fire?" Claypoole asked, trying not to sound nervous. He took Schultz's grunt to be an affirmative. "Right. Now we wait." He silently groaned, hoping that didn't sound too dumb.

"Everybody linked here?" Sergeant Linsman asked as he dropped to a knee next to Claypoole.

"Sure are, Rat," Claypoole said. "Wolfman's overlapping with Doyle, I'm overlapping with him and Hammer. Hammer's watching the left flank."

"Good." Linsman clapped a hand on Claypoole's shoulder and started to rise.

"What's the situation out there?"

Linsman paused. "Don't know. The last I heard was when we were still on the hoppers and the rest of the battalion hadn't made contact yet. So we wait." He thought for a moment. "There's no string-of-pearls, so we're pretty much blind beyond eyeball range. Tell you what. Until I get other word, one-third alert." He patted Claypoole on the shoulder and left before the corporal could ask another question.

Claypoole swore about the lack of information, then realized nothing was developing fast, otherwise Linsman wouldn't have told him only one man at a time in the fire team had to keep watch.

"Hammer, Wolfman, one-third alert. Who wants first watch?"

There was a long moment's silence, then MacIlargie said, "I'll take it."

"You got it." Claypoole relaxed. If Schultz didn't want first watch, trouble must still be some distance off.

Corporal Doyle didn't think going off one hundred percent watch was such a good idea. There was an unknown number of unknown enemy soldiers out there somewhere. He knew those enemy soldiers badly outnumbered Company L. Worse, he knew he was smack in the center of their advance. Who were they? Nobody had told him, all everybody said was, "We don't know." Were they Skinks? Thirty-fourth FIST came to Maugham's Station in the first place looking for Skinks. Instead of Skinks, they found acid-spitting vines and flesh-eating plants and wound up almost getting killed in a forest fire. But they were looking for Skinks—were the Skinks here now? Is that why everybody kept saying they didn't know who they were up against, so the troops who had to fight them wouldn't get too scared while they waited for the enemy to show up?

No, that didn't make any sense; if they were waiting to intercept Skinks, they could prepare, because they knew that's who was coming. He wasn't sure how they could prepare for the Skinks, but he knew they could do something. So what was really going on?

Worrying was tiring, and Doyle's guts were still unsettled from the ride down. He realized he was too tired and unsettled to keep worrying about it all. Corporal Kerr said he'd take the first watch. If Corporal Kerr was watching, Doyle knew, they were all right, he wouldn't let any bad guys sneak up on them. Corporal Kerr was just about the best Marine Doyle had ever seen. And he knew Lance Corporal MacIlargie was on watch to his left. MacIlargie wasn't as good as Kerr, but he was still pretty good.

Doyle relaxed and rolled onto his back to rest, maybe catch a quick nap. His eyes slipped slowly closed, then snapped open again.

Right in front of him, only a couple of kilometers away, were some low mountains. He sat up to take a better look at them. It wasn't a long range, only a few kilometers from end to end. But the ends weren't ends, they curved as if they formed an arc of a circle, or an oval. They looked just like that circle of mountains where the company had run into the killer plants that shot streams of acid that were like the Skink acid guns.

Corporal Doyle whimpered.

The Dragons carrying Kilo and Mike Companies hit the beach at a densely forested estuary and sped upstream on the river until the forest thinned out enough to allow movement on land, where the long column split into three. One column remained on the river, the other two flanked it to either side on land. A hundred twenty-five kilometers inland the three columns made a quarter left turn and left the river behind. A few kilometers beyond, they spread out on line. Minutes later the Raptor section of FIST's composite squadron roared by low overhead in the same direction.

Commander van Winkle was the very image of calmness as he sat in his racing command-and-control Dragon. He had to project image; everybody was nervous about rushing blind into harm's way. He knew that as long as he appeared calm, his presence calmed his men—even those who thought his calmness was because he didn't understand the seriousness of the situation.

But van Winkle understood the seriousness of the situation better than any of his subordinates. They were blind, absolutely blind, beyond what they could see and hear with their own eyes and ears, and the limited organic equipment they could use on the move. Just then, he couldn't even communicate with the *Grandar Bay*; the starship was over the horizon, dropping into a lower orbit that would allow her to communicate with the planetary government as well as the Marines.

At least, van Winkle hoped that's where the *Grandar Bay* had gone—she'd moved off and dropped out of sight without getting a message through to the Marines of the landing force. She'd tried to, but a heavy burst of static broke up the message so much that it was unintelligible.

Where had that static burst come from? An unpredicted solar flare? That didn't seem likely. It reminded him more of the jamming he'd encountered when he was humping a radio as a young lance corporal on . . . on . . . It was so long ago he couldn't even remember what campaign it had been when the Marines went up against someone with jamming equipment strong enough to knock out even Force Recon communications.

He didn't know, but his best guess was that the unknown forces locked in combat ahead of the Marines had pretty good electronics.

He looked at his map. Without real-time satellite guidance from the string-of-pearls, his plot on it was inertial, as was the movement of the Raptors. He saw where the Raptors were; right where the intelligence he had before launch said the fighting was going on. But he didn't hear the weapons of the Raptors; he should have heard them since they weren't at all quiet when they attacked ground targets. But he heard nothing above the rumble of his Dragon. For that matter, the Dragons were close enough that he should have been able to hear the sounds of the ground combat. He turned up the volume on the Dragon's ears. All he heard was the line of Dragons crashing through the forest. What happened to the fighting?

"Sir." Captain Uhara, his executive officer, got van Winkle's attention. "Heaven's Hell One reports all ground combatants are in full flight to the west. He requests instructions." Heaven's Hell was the call sign for the Raptors on this mission; Heaven's Hell One was the section commander.

Van Winkle calmly looked at his XO. "Thank you, Captain. My compliments to Heaven's Hell One. Request that they maintain contact but stay outside small-arms range, and keep me informed of what the ground contacts are doing. Ask if the ground forces are mounted or on foot. Then order the Dragon formation to slow down and keep pace with the forces ahead of us."

"Aye aye," Uhara said, and relayed the orders into his radio.

Van Winkle wasn't supposed to give those orders. He didn't have command over the squadron; Brigadier Sturgeon was responsible for coordinating the operations of the FIST's ground and air combat elements. Sturgeon was supposed to follow on planetside when the Raptors came down, but van Winkle hadn't heard from him yet—and evidently neither had Commander Wolfe, who was likely flying as Heaven's Hell One. Without Colonel Ramadan or Commander Usner, the FIST operations officer, on the air, joint command fell onto the ground combat element commander—Commander van Winkle.

Van Winkle turned up the gain on his FIST command circuit. All he got was faint static. Either the FIST commander was still aboard the *Grandar Bay* or he was planetside with his comm knocked out. Or the enemy had better jamming equipment than any van Winkle was familiar with.

They paused briefly at a landing zone where a hundred or more shuttles sat, presumably abandoned by their crews after the troop transports that landed them fled orbit. A few kilometers farther, the Dragons passed through an area built up with industrial-looking structures and piles of debris that moments before had been the site of fierce fighting but now seemed abandoned. Van Winkle didn't want to waste time on it, and ordered Kilo Company to drop half a platoon and a Dragon to investigate the site.

"Vision by thirds," Staff Sergeant Nu ordered. Kilo Company's first platoon left him to inspect the industrial site, along with one squad and a gun team. "Ears up. Motion detectors and sniffers—if you got 'em, use 'em."

The Marines of first squad and the gun team adjusted their helmet screens so one man in each team was using his infra, one his magnifier, and one his light gatherer. They turned up the "ears" on their helmets so they could hear better. The few who had motion or scent detectors activated them.

"What are we supposed to be sniffing for?" PFC Bhophar asked as he turned on his scent detector.

"How the hell do I know?" snapped Corporal Juliete. "I'm only a fire team leader, nobody tells me anything."

Sergeant Oconor was close enough to hear the exchange. "Sniff for anything that isn't forest or Marine," he said. "Put the graph on the side of your HUD so you don't have to take your eyes away from what you're supposed to be looking at." Then he went to make sure his other man with a sniffer knew what he was supposed to be alert for.

Bhophar gave the sniffer the right command and tucked it into its pouch on his shoulder, where air could circulate through it, then gave the vertical graph on his HUD a quick glance to make sure he could read it easily, before returning his attention to the landscape.

"First fire team, check out that slag," Oconor ordered. He slid a sleeve up to expose his arm and pointed to where he wanted them to go.

"Right," Juliete replied. "First fire team, let's go." He used his infra to make sure his men were with him, then headed for a ten-meter-high pile of what he assumed was industrial leavings.

Footing was uncertain on the pile, which consisted of irregular stony granules, mostly smaller than the last joint of a man's little finger. Climbing it was like ascending a dune of coarse-grained sand.

"This is refinery tailings," Lance Corporal Rising Star said when they reached the top and paused to look around. Nobody questioned him, they all knew his family were metal workers and his own degree was in metallurgy. "Look." He pointed up, to where an inverted funnel hung over the top of the tailings heap. The funnel was at the end of a wide pipe that led from a domed building built around a large smoke-stack. No smoke rose from the stack.

Bhophar turned his sniffer to sample the air currents. "I'm not pick-ing up any living bodies but us," he reported. "No animal decay either. There is something odd I can't identify, though."

"Could it be metal?" Nu asked. "Rising Star, check it."

Rising Star took the sniffer and hooked it in to his own jack. "Anti-mony, lead, zinc," he said as he read the display. "Cobalt, copper, iron." He whistled. "Rare earths and transuranics, lots of them." He unhooked the sniffer and handed it back. "This has been a very active refinery. But I don't pick up any sign of current activity."

"Movement?" Oconor asked.

Juliete was carrying a motion detector. "Only normal background noise. If there's anybody out there, they've got good movement disci-pline."

"Come on down, let's look inside," Staff Sergeant Nu ordered.

"Very strange," Lance Corporal Rising Star said, looking around be-fore he ski-footed down the trailings.

"Got that right," Juliete agreed.

Projectile and explosive weapons had been used there. The bark was torn off trees, branches were broken and splintered—some small trees had fallen, their trunks shattered. Craters pocked the ground. It was the first time Juliete had been on a battlefield that had seen such heavy use of projectiles and explosives. In its own way, he found it more horrifying than the burned-out landscape of the Haltia valley.

"Does anybody see any blood on the ground?" Nu asked on the platoon circuit. Nobody answered. "Well, look for some! With all the metal that flew around this place, we should be finding body parts everywhere we step."

They should have, but they didn't. It was a very strange battlefield indeed.

Then they entered the first of the structures.

Every external wall was pockmarked by hundreds of fléchette hits. The high windows on the structures were similarly scarred, and some were shattered.

Nu ordered Oconor to keep one fire team and the gun team outside for security while he went inside with the other two fire teams. The interior was huge and filled with machinery that nobody but Rising Star could identify, and even he didn't know what all of it was. After standing for fifteen minutes, they decided the building was vacant and probably had been for a week or more.

"It takes several days for the furnaces to cool down this far," Rising Star said, "and these are cooled down to maintenance temp."

Nu raised his screens and looked a question at him.

"Warm enough to keep them from reaching ambient air temp," Rising Star explained. "If they get that cold, it'll take too long for them to come back to working temperature. It's economical too—it takes more energy to raise the furnaces back from ambient temp than is needed to keep them warm."

Nu grunted; someone planned to come back and use the installation again. But who?

They entered the other industrial buildings, but stayed in each only long enough for Rising Star to determine that they hadn't been used for several days. They saved the administration building for last.

Unlike the other buildings in the complex, power was still on in the admin building. Lights went on in each room as the Marines entered, so they went very cautiously, blasters at the ready and fingers on the firing levers. They found plenty of evidence that somebody had been there recently—somebody other than the invading troops.

One wing of the admin building was living quarters. There was fresh produce and fruit in the pantries and unfrozen meat in a cooling box. Five sleeping chambers had beds that had recently been slept on.

"Got something!" Corporal Juliete called when he entered a sleeping chamber.

"What ya got?" Staff Sergeant Nu asked as he joined him.

Juliete didn't bother to answer. Nu saw the blood as soon as he reached the room's doorway. There was a spray of blood about chest high on the wall above a small desk, and a smear on the floor between the desk and the door. The blood didn't trail out into the hallway.

"They took the time to bandage him before they took him out of here," Nu observed.

Juliete nodded. "Probably wasn't badly wounded; there isn't that much blood."

But search as they might, they found no bodies or other signs of casualties from the fierce fighting around the industrial site. The only other thing they found of interest was a lightly camouflaged shuttle landing field two kilometers southwest of the buildings. But no shuttles were on it, and it looked like it hadn't been used for a couple of weeks or more.

CHAPTER TWENTY-NINE

"Look alive, people, company's coming," Ensign Charlie Bass said softly into third platoon's all-hands circuit. All along their line, third platoon and the rest of Company L got into position.

"Where are they, Rabbit?" Corporal Joe Dean asked on the squad circuit. "I don't hear any fire."

"Your guess is as good as mine," Sergeant Ratliff answered. And he didn't have any good answers. If the rest of the battalion was chasing the enemy toward the anvil that Company L formed, the other companies should have been hammering them. So should the FIST's Raptors. But Ratliff heard no sounds of combat.

Dean turned his ears to maximum, but all that did was make the buzzing of the insectoids and cries of the avians so loud that the noise numbed his eardrums. When he used his magnifier screen, he saw the specks of Raptors circling and darting in the distance. He could tell none of them was attacking; they looked more like they were herding.

Then he saw them. Flickers of tan and brown camouflage flashed through the treelines ahead of him. He slid his magnifier screen into place and made out armored vehicles crashing through distant tree-lines. He couldn't make out their formation; they seemed to be moving independently of each other. And they were small. They didn't look big enough to hold an entire squad in addition to their crews.

"Great Buddha's balls," Lance Corporal MacIlargie swore on the fire team circuit. "We don't have any antiarmor weapons!"

"What do we do when they get here?" PFC Quick asked.

Dean heard the uncertainty in his junior man's voice. Quick had fought bravely against the Skinks on Kingdom, but he'd never fought armor. Dean had. He wanted to dig a deep hole to crawl into and haul the entryway in after himself.

The Marines in the path of the armor still didn't hear any pursuing fire, and the Raptors buzzing above were not firing at the vehicles. The armored vehicles crashed closer until there was only one treeline area left between them and Company L. Then the Raptors shot high up into the air, rolled over, and plunged back toward earth, firing their guns—

—into the ground to the right front of the armor.

The vehicles veered to their left to avoid the monstrous plasma bolts as the Raptors clawed for altitude to dive again. That was when the hoppers returned, all armed and firing assault guns, creating a barrier of plasma to the armor's right front. The leading enemy vehicles burst and scattered through the final treeline area. They were not in formation; they seemed to be in panicked flight.

Company L was no longer in their path, they were going past, still headed west at high speed. The aircraft stopped firing and continued circling.

Moments later the armored mass reached the foot of the forested mountains behind Company L. Before they could skirt the mountain flanks, the aircraft opened fire again, making a fence of plasma to pin them against the mountains. The vehicles milled about, slamming into each other and crashing into trees. Some stopped. Several turned and raced uphill, away from the corralling fire.

The forest canopy hid the climbing vehicles for a few seconds. By the time they were visible again, they were more scattered than they'd been on the flat. Some of the hoppers fired blocking bursts from their assault guns, but the vehicles wouldn't stop their scramble for altitude—they climbed up and over, into the valley.

The oncoming dreadnought opened the fighting with a salvo of mixed energy weapons and missiles before the *Grandar Bay* could launch the last wave of the landing force. The starship's shields and defensive weaponry had no trouble absorbing or destroying most of the incoming fire; the rest missed, but some of it could have hit the Essays.

Brigadier Sturgeon was in a bind. He needed to be planetside with his FIST, but Commodore Boreland couldn't risk any of his Essays by launching them while enemy weaponry might hit the shuttles.

"You can't do much even if you are down there," Boreland told Sturgeon when the Marine commander insisted on taking his chances. "Without the string-of-pearls in place, you can't see the battlefield, you'll have to rely on internal communications and trust in the accuracy of everybody's inertial maps."

Sturgeon took a deep breath and said, "We're Marines. We fought using paper maps long before we had access to rings of satellites. We can do it again."

Boreland gave him a wry smile. "Ted, that was way back in the twentieth century. I suspect you're rusty."

Sturgeon pursed his lips; Boreland was all too right. It was probable that none of the officers of 34th FIST had participated in an exercise without satellites since they were in Officer Candidate College.

Boreland looked at the display that showed the approaching fleet. "I think we've got a little bit of time," he mused. "We'll slingshot around Maugham's Station and drop a couple of Essays to lay a string-of-pearls. You and your staff go with them. When the satellites are in place, they'll take you planetside."

"Oh, gods," Commander van Winkle sighed when he got the report of twenty-five of the fleeing armored vehicles going into the valley. "Two, do we have any reason to believe that valley isn't like the valleys near Ammon?" he asked Captain Rhu-Anh, his intelligence officer.

"Sir, we have no data at all on the flora and fauna on this side of the planet," Rhu-Anh answered.

Van Winkle swore softly again, then ordered Captain Kitchikummi, "Tell air I want eyes-in-the-sky over that valley, but high enough so they don't spook the people in it."

"Aye aye." The battalion operations officer got on the radio to the squadron to pass the order along.

"Have we established contact with them yet?" van Winkle asked Rhu-Anh.

"Negative, sir. We know their freqs, but they haven't answered any of our calls."

"Give me." Van Winkle reached for the radio and checked the display that showed him his forces deployment. Kilo Company, in Dragons, was moving into position on the south side of the armored mass, as was Mike Company to the east of the enemy. Hoppers were picking up Company L to take it to the north flank.

"Armored force commander," van Winkle said into the radio, "this is Commander van Winkle of the Confederation Marine Corps ground forces facing you. Over." He waited, then repeated his message when he got no response. And a third time. Finally he said, "We have your force surrounded, north, east, south, and overhead. There are only two things you can do: talk to me, or go over the mountains. My forces have not fired on you except to redirect your movement away from my units. There may be serious danger to your forces on the other side of the mountains. Your better course is to talk to me.

"What do the eyes-in-the-sky say?" he asked Rhu-Anh.

"The vehicles in the valley tried to go into the forest, but it's too dense. Now they're circumnavigating it."

Van Winkle grunted and sat back to wait for a reaction from the still unidentified armored force.

As soon as the Essay carrying Brigadier Sturgeon finished laying its arc of observation and communications satellites, it heeled over and fired its main thrusters, sending it into a planetward plunge. The coxswain didn't aim for an over-ocean touchdown, he headed for a landing a scant two kilometers behind the Marine line west of the mountains— with all the satellites and their launch system, there hadn't been room in the Essay's cargo bay for Sturgeon's command Dragon. The Marine commander, his staff, and their most essential equipment were secured in webbing normally used by people making the more sedate, spiraling landings favored by everybody but the Marines. Commodore Boreland had assured Sturgeon the webbing was strong enough to withstand the stresses of a combat assault landing. That hadn't dissuaded Sturgeon from double-checking with the Essay's coxswain.

"Sir, I'd trust this webbing to keep my own granny safe," the coxswain assured him.

Sturgeon cocked an eyebrow and sardonically asked, "Ah, but then the question is, do you *like* your granny?"

The coxswain laughed. "My granny Troycott, I do, sir. And she's the one I'd trust the webbing with."

"That's good enough for me."

"Sir," Captain Rhu-Anh said excitedly, "we have string-of-pearls!"

"Show me," Commander van Winkle said, turning to the S-2 comm team.

"Here, sir," Lance Corporal Striker said, leaning out of the way so the infantry battalion commander could look at the satellite communication displays.

Van Winkle saw a welter of displays: images in visual, infra, radar, and several others; graphs and charts and scrolling strings of numbers. "Give me a visual of the inside of the valley," he ordered.

Striker leaned back in and worked the controls on his station. "Upper right, sir," he said. A large screen morphed from an array of smaller screens and gave a sharply angled overhead view of the valley. The string-of-pearls was equatorial, so not all of the valley was visible; the mountains on the south side occluded part of the view of the valley's southern edge, and the tall trees to the north blocked vision of the northern edge of the valley's bottom.

"Overlay infra," van Winkle said. Suddenly, bright red showed through the trees a quarter way around the valley floor on the north— the signature of the engines of the We're Here! vehicles. They weren't moving. "Get me an eye-in-the-sky over that, I want to see why they stopped." The distant shriek of a landing Essay barely registered on his consciousness.

The air liaison immediately got on his comm to order one of the orbiting Raptors to overfly the north side of the valley.

"Sir, do you want the sky-eye view alongside the string-of-pearls, or replace it?" Striker asked.

"Alongside."

The display to the left of the string-of-pearls view enlarged. At first all it showed was static, then a wildly careening visual resolved. Van Winkle studied it intently until he understood what it was and the location and direction of the viewpoint. He ignored the sudden increase in communications at all the staff points; if his staff was receiving anything he needed to know, they'd tell him.

The view on the display closed on the northeast quadrant of the valley walls, then swerved and ran along the northern edge of the valley floor until it reached a cluster of vehicles haphazardly stopped in front of a large rockfall. The Raptor went into hover over the vehicles.

"Tighten the image, let me see what the people are doing."

Striker touched his controls and the image sprang into a smaller scale, enlarging the landscape below and showing soldiers running from their vehicles into the forest.

"Oh, no. No, no, no! Do we have comm with anybody in the We're Here! unit yet?" He looked away from the display when nobody answered. All of his staff were on comms, none had heard him. "Three!" he shouted. "Do we have comm with We're Here!?"

Captain Kitchikummi jerked as though struck. "Sir? Nossir, nobody has replied yet to our comm."

"Broadcast on all freqs they might be using, tell them to order their people in the valley to get out of the forest—and tell them why."

Kitchikummi's face registered surprise that the We're Here! soldiers had left their vehicles, but he didn't ask any questions, instead he immediately began giving orders, then spoke urgently into his comm.

"Sir," Captain Uhara, van Winkle's executive officer, said, "the brigadier is planetside. I just dispatched two Dragons to pick up him and his staff."

"What's wrong with his C-squared Dragon?"

"I don't know, sir. He just said he needed transportation."

Van Winkle let it go; he knew he'd get an answer soon enough. He looked at Kitchikummi and saw that the ops officer was still trying to establish comm with the We're Here! commander. "Get a platoon ready to go in and haul those people out of there before they get themselves killed," he ordered Uhara. Brigadier Sturgeon might have a different idea of how to deal with the situation, but he would have his own solution ready to go.

"Aye aye, sir." Uhara replied. He glanced at the display that showed the status of the battalion's companies and platoons, then got on the horn.

"Third herd, saddle up!" Ensign Charlie Bass ordered into third platoon's all-hands circuit.

"Saddle up, first squad."

"Saddle up, second squad."

"Guns, saddle up," the third squad leader echoed.

"Where are we going?" Lance Corporal MacIlargie asked as he checked to make sure he had all his weapons and gear.

"Someplace," Corporal Claypoole snorted. "How the hell am I supposed to know, Wolfman? You heard the same all-hands I did. What say *you* tell *me* where we're going?" He busied his hands checking MacIlargie's weapons and gear, double-checking his readiness. He turned to Lance Corporal Schultz to check his readiness and hesitated with his hands inches away from the big man. "Ah, you all ready, Hammer?" he asked.

Schultz slid up his infra screen and spat a streamer into a thorny bush.

"Ah, yeah, I guess you're ready." Claypoole turned back to MacIlargie and snapped, "What are you doing just standing there, looking like a lost kwangduk? Check your body armor, make sure it's secure."

"Are we going to need it?" MacIlargie blurted. Before he could say more he noticed the you're-too-stupid-to-live look Schultz was giving him, turned away and checked his body armor.

The Marines turned and looked at the five Dragons that roared up. They wondered who else was joining them when the Dragons dropped their ramps to show they were all unoccupied.

"Squad leaders up," came Hyakowa's voice over the command circuit. The squad leaders assembled with him and Bass to be given their orders.

"Give me an update," Brigadier Sturgeon said when communications were established with the infantry commander.

Commander van Winkle gave it all to him concisely: there had been no actual combat, most of the We're Here! force was contained in one unprepared position, twenty-five of their armored vehicles had entered the valley, he had no communications with the We're Here! commander or anyone else in the invasion force, and he had a platoon standing by to go into the valley to rescue the dismounted soldiers who were fleeing into the forest. The telling took less than two minutes.

Sturgeon briefly studied his own displays, then asked, "Do you plan to send them over the saddle where the We're Here! forces are?"

"Yes, that's the only way I can get them in fast enough to do any good."

"Send them in." Then he had his radios set to broadcast on all known frequencies used by the We're Here! forces and delivered a message to them.

"This is Brigadier Theodosius Sturgeon, Confederation Marine Corps, Commander of 34th Fleet Initial Strike Team. You have people in trouble on the other side of the ridge behind you. I am sending Marines in to help them. These Marines will be passing close by you. Do not, I say again, *do not* fire on them or otherwise attempt to impede their passage."

He left the "or else" unsaid.

"Second squad, on me," Sergeant Linsman called when he returned from the squad leaders' meeting. He removed his helmet and raised an arm, letting the sleeve slide down. His expression was that of a man who didn't know whether to laugh at the joke being played on him or to tear the head off the jokester. The Marines of second squad also removed their helmets as they approached.

"These *people* we're stopping are from We're Here! Before you ask, it's a back-space world with a comic opera army and navy that has never gone to war. I have no idea what they're doing here, and neither does anybody else up the chain of command. What we do know is, about a company of them went into the valley. We're going in after them." He hurried on before anybody could comment on that. "To rescue them, not to fight.

"First and second fire team, get in Dragon Four. Third fire team, you'll be in Dragon Five with a gun team. We pull out in zero-two. Move."

"But . . ."

"What . . . ?"

"You gotta . . ."

The Marines threw questions and objections, but they went to the Dragons they were directed to, and Linsman ignored the questions and comments.

The Dragons crossed the saddle without incident and sped at top speed after the armored vehicles stopped at the rockfall. They got there a lot faster than the Marines of third platoon wanted; they'd already dealt with the dangers of the forest and didn't want to do it again. They found a couple dozen We're Here! naval infantrymen huddled in terror behind their vehicles or up in the rocks. Nearly as many more lay on the ground in front of the forest, tendrils already probing their way inside their corpses.

None of the frightened men looked like he was in charge, but one of them had epaulets with what looked like officer rank insignia on the shoulders of his dull green shirt. Ensign Charlie Bass spotted him as soon as he dismounted and headed toward him. The officer jumped when Bass removed his helmet and his head suddenly appeared suspended in midair.

"I'm Ensign Bass, are you in command here?"

"S-Sir?" The officer was so wide-eyed-shaken, it seemed he hadn't understood Bass's words.

Bass looked around. Including the bodies at the edge of the forest, there wasn't anywhere near a company there. If the vehicles held five men each, plus crews, there were well over a hundred of them missing. "Where are the rest of your people?"

"S-Sir, in there." The officer pointed toward the trees. His whole arm shook.

"Mohammed's pointed teeth," Bass muttered. "How many?" he asked.

"I heard sc-screaming. Th-Then nothing." The officer's voice trembled.

"How many went into the trees?" Bass repeated firmly.

"I don't—I don't know," he said plaintively.

"Get your people back in the vehicles and get out of this valley. Now! Rejoin your command."

"The—The trees and flowers, they killed us!"

Bass snarled at the officer's helplessness and spun about. He redonned his helmet as he headed to where his infra screen showed his men were assembled.

"More than a hundred of these 'soldiers' went into the forest. We're going in to see if any of them are still alive, and bring them out. Enter the forest in columns of squads. We'll get on line once we're under the trees. Dial your blasters down to minimum power. If we have to shoot, I don't want to start another forest fire." He wanted to spit in disgust, but would have had to raise his infra screen and didn't want to expose any part of his body so close to the forest. "Move out, and keep moving. Those plants need time to fix on a target, they won't shoot at you if you don't stop long enough to give them a target."

Third platoon entered the forest in three columns fifty meters apart, and spread out farther once they were inside.

"Get on line," Bass ordered when they were twenty-five meters inside. "Ten meter intervals." The squads spread out on line, with ten meters between men.

They found the first body moments after they formed on line.

"Leave it," Bass ordered. "We're looking for live ones, the dead can wait."

Soon after that they heard gunfire to their right front. Not the *crack-sizzle* of blasters, but the staccato chittering of fléchette rifles firing on automatic.

"Platoon, half right!" Bass ordered. "Keep on line. Step it out. Make sure your armor is sealed. Remember, we're here to rescue those people, not fight them." He resisted another urge to spit.

Screams punctuated the gunfire.

Their body armor did what it was supposed to do—it stopped every fléchette that hit them. But there weren't many hits; nobody was shooting at them, and only some were shooting in the Marines' direction. Thirty of the We're Here! naval infantrymen were massed in the middle of a clearing, and twenty more lay moaning or still. The clearing was barely large enough to hold the soldiers. They were yelling, screaming, crying, and firing wildly at every movement.

Two more went down in agonizing pain from acid strikes between the time the Marines first spotted them until they had the naval infantry surrounded and began firing low-power plasma bolts at the acid-shooting vines. The survivors in the clearing were so panicked they didn't notice the blasts of fire around their position, or that the floral movement was slowing, until Bass turned on his external speaker.

"We're Here! forces, don't stand there. These things will kill you. A platoon of Confederation Marines is here. We'll lead you to safety. Don't panic if someone you can't see grabs you, we're wearing chameleon uniforms. Pick up your casualties and bring them along. We'll handle defense."

The disembodied voice panicked them. Some fired long bursts into the forest, others bolted. The fléchettes bounced off armor or flattened against it. Every man who ran was grabbed or knocked down by a Marine he couldn't see.

"Pick up your casualties, we've got to get out of here! Do it NOW!" Bass switched to his platoon circuit and gave orders. The Marines began moving into the clearing and manhandling the naval infantry into a rough formation, making them pick up their dead and wounded. Then they headed back to the edge of the forest. Only a few acid streamers came toward them on their way out, and most of them either hit Marines or missed everybody.

Still using low power on their blasters, the Marines burned the edge of the forest back from the valley side. When Ensign Charlie Bass decided it was safe enough, he had his Marines herd the dejected We're Here! naval infantry into their armored personnel carriers and directed them back to the saddle over which they'd entered the valley.

"Pretty pathetic, aren't they?" Corporal Claypoole commented as he watched the rescued soldiers boarding their small vehicles.

Lance Corporal Schultz hawked and spat. "They never fought," he said. "Fighters didn't train them." Those seven words were almost a speech from the taciturn big man. But Claypoole was able to fill in the rest easy enough. The We're Here! naval infantry might have been full-time soldiers; nonetheless, they were pretend soldiers. None of them had any combat experience before whatever they'd seen on Maugham's Station, and they hadn't been trained in warfare by anyone who had combat experience. Claypoole knew that unless you've got experience, you don't have a clue what combat is really like, or how to fight when lives and more are on the line. The best people to train an inexperienced army were combat veterans. We're Here! didn't have any, and didn't contract with anyone who did to train their troops. So of course they were pathetic.

Later that day the seventy-one Marines and sailors of the artillery battery were left planetside to guard the prisoners when the rest of the FIST was abruptly ordered back to the Grandar Bay.

CHAPTER THIRTY

While the Marines were planetside dealing with the We're Here! ground forces, the *Grandar Bay* fended off the We're Here! fleet by letting it cross her T.

What Commodore Boreland knew that Admiral of the Starry Heavens Sativa Orange didn't was that before the Confederation Navy sold its obsolete warships, it downgraded their weaponry. Not that it mattered in this case—Mandalay-class Amphibious Landing Ships, Force, had shields designed to defeat naval guns a generation beyond those the King class had *before* its weapons were downgraded. The only danger the *Grandar Bay* faced was if the entire We're Here! fleet concentrated its fire on the same spot. Or if the King or one of the Mallorys rammed her; she could easily withstand a collision with one of the Freemonts or the smaller ships.

But the commander of the We're Here! fleet refused all communication with the *Grandar Bay*, and repeatedly crossed her T, salvoing with all lasers and missile batteries on each pass.

After three passes it got tedious.

"We could knock out the King's guns, sir," Executive Officer Maugli suggested. "That could make them reconsider talking to us."

"I already thought of that, Zsuz. But her shields have probably degraded, and our lasers and missiles would do severe damage to the ship, likely kill her." Boreland shook his head. "I can't help feeling like I'd be a schoolyard bully picking on the class runt if I fired on her."

Maugli chuckled. "She can't hurt us, but if we disengage and leave her unhindered, she can do damage to Ammon, is that it?"

Boreland nodded. "I think we're going to have to take her. The Marines have the planetside situation under control, right?"

"Yessir."

"Send a message to the Commander, Landing Force. Secure prisoners, and reembark all landing force personnel not needed to maintain planetside security."

"Aye aye, Skipper."

"We need to board that King," Commodore Boreland told Brigadier Sturgeon. "Otherwise, we'll have to keep playing this monotonous game until that fleet runs out of power and missiles, or decides to disengage and go away. If they do that, we'll have to follow them to We're Here! and deal with planetary defenses."

Sturgeon nodded. "You've got a Tweed hull breacher?"

"It's even been modified so it doesn't explode."

"It was one of my Marines who came up with the modification, did you know that?"

Boreland shook his head. "I knew it was a Marine who figured it out, but I didn't know a FIST had that level of engineering expertise."

"A FIST doesn't. It was a Corporal Doyle. He was a company clerk then, now he's a blasterman. He'd studied some mechanical engineering in college and figured it out on his own."

"I'm impressed. What operation was it on?"

"I was impressed when I found out too. But the operation it happened on is classified 'Ultra Secret, Need to Know.' As it is, I know more about it than I'm authorized to know. Sorry."

Boreland let it go; he understood about secrecy. Though why he and Sturgeon should bother about secrecy between each other in their current circumstances . . .

"How are we going to do it?" Sturgeon asked. "I don't like the idea of sending my Marines across any distance to get to the dreadnought."

"Something only moderately risky. We're going to make a close pass—hopefully, close enough so the King won't be able to fire on the THB while it closes. I don't have any information on the internal security of that ship, but before the Confederation Navy retired the Kings, they carried a compliment of twenty-five Marines. You'll need a boarding party that can handle that many, plus whatever deck crew is armed to repel boarders."

"I have a blaster platoon that has actually boarded a starship with a Tweed hull breacher—the third platoon of Company L. I'll suggest to Commander van Winkle that he use that platoon as the point of the spear, and the rest of the company to complete the boarding party. How much time do we have to prepare?"

The Marines of Company L sat hip-to-haunch in a troop lounge designed to accommodate half their number. They listened intently as Captain Kitchikummi, the battalion operations officer, and Staff Sergeant Nelflare, the operations chief, briefed them on the boarding mission. Most of them had spent enough time on different classes of starship to be able to find their way about fairly easily, but only a few had ever boarded a starship against resistance.

A trid model of the former *Trefalgar* rotated to one side of the briefing stage. A miniature Tweed hull breacher was mounted on the model's side, nearer the after compartments than the bow.

"Third platoon's first objective is to secure the breach head," Kitchikummi said, "so the follow-on platoons can get in to build up strength quickly. First platoon, your objective is main engineering." A section of the trid enlarged and morphed to a cutaway view, showing the entry chamber, the passageways outside it, main engineering, and the route between them. "It's not far, that's why we chose this chamber for entry. The comm shack is adjacent to main engineering; you will secure it as well."

"Second platoon, you will go by squads to neutralize the main laser and missile mounts." The trid changed again, showing all the weapons points. "You'll have the FIST sapper platoon with you. They'll neutralize the guns."

"Third platoon, a platoon from K Company will relieve you once first and second platoons have passed through your position. You will then move forward to take CIC—the Combat Information Center—and the bridge. CIC is colocated with the bridge.

"Captain Conorado will be with third platoon, Lieutenant Humphrey with first platoon, and Lieutenant Rokmonov will command the reaction group from K Company."

Nelflare then went into the details of coordination between the platoons, and Kitchikummi finished the briefing. "King-class dreadnoughts are double-hulled," he said, "with water and nonvolatile stores between hulls, so you don't need to worry about accidentally punching holes through her skin." He smiled grimly. "That means you can use your blasters on full power if you meet stiff resistance."

Corporal Kerr flashed back to the *Marquis de Rien*, the single-hulled ship third platoon had used the Tweed hull breacher to board as she tried to escape them at Avionia. His fire team had taken the bridge, and a stray shot punched a hole through the hull in the fight. Two crewmen died of decompression. That was a mess he'd rather not see repeated.

Kitchikummi released the platoons so their commanders could give them more detailed instructions.

The We're Here! fleet maneuvered to cross the *Grandar Bay*'s T again. Commodore Boreland ordered his starship to commence her countermaneuver.

The THB hung at the end of an umbilical a hundred meters to the aft port side of the *Grandar Bay* as the mighty starship closed with the King-class dreadnought. The Marines and sailors attached to tethers trailing from the THB couldn't see the King; she was off the starboard bow. The two ships weren't on a collision course, or not quite. Unless one made a course change, they would be no closer than five hundred meters at their nearest approach.

Led by Chief Petty Officer Young, ten sailors were positioned around the box of the THB, eight of them at its forward edge. Young and Engineering Mate 3rd Resort were at its rear, Resort at the THB's flight controls. The Marines of Company L and the first platoon of K Company were attached to short tethers strung out behind it.

"Zero two," came a voice into the helmets of everyone outside the starship—the signal that two minutes remained before the maneuver that would fling the THB to the dreadnought. The officers and NCOs repeated the orders a final time and everybody stood ready.

The voice came back to count down the final seconds, and the *Grandar Bay*'s attitude rockets fired, sending her into a spin along her long axis.

"Go," Chief Young said. Resort fired the THB's side thrusters, sending it in the same direction as the starship's spin. Centrifical force pushed the THB out to the full length of the umbilical that held it to the starship, the Marines tethered to the THB arcing after it.

The *Grandar Bay* and the THB spun slowly at first but quickly increased velocity. The THB swung over the starship, and the King-class dreadnought rose into view broadside, some six hundred meters distant. Chief Young gave a rapid series of commands to Resort. The engineering mate cut the side thrusters and briefly fired the thrusters on the opposite side to neutralize the THB's angular momentum, then he fired a short burst from the main thrusters. The THB headed straight on an intercept course for the dreadnought.

Vice Admiral Toke nervously cleared her throat. "Admiral, sir?" she said to Admiral of the Starry Heavens Orange. She waited several seconds for the furiously stewing CNO to respond. When he didn't, Toke said, "Sir? We have an anomaly."

"I heard you the first time," Orange snapped. He blinked, then spun on the task force commander. "What anomaly? Why didn't you bring it to my attention earlier?"

Toke nervously fingered her collar. "Sir, it just happened. The *Grandar Bay* fired a new weapon at us."

"What?" Orange squawked. "Fired on us? At this range? She's too close, she'll be hit by fragments or backwash!" He grabbed handholds and prepared for the impact.

"Ah, sir? We—We still have a minute before impact."

Orange stared at Toke in disbelief. "Nonsense, Admiral. Sound the collision alert! A missile should already be here!" He blinked, hearing what he said, and straightened up. "We've been fired on from extreme close range and haven't been hit yet? What are they shooting at us?"

"I don't know, sir. They—They sort of flung it at us."

"Flung?"

"Sir, if you will look . . ." Toke gestured vaguely toward the vid bank.

"What am I supposed to be looking at?" Orange demanded, peering at the bank of vids showing local space around the *Groovy*.

"Here, sir," an ensign said, pointing at one of the displays. It showed a boxy object with strings of something trailing behind it. The object drifted aft as it grew.

"Enlarge," Orange demanded when he didn't recognize it. The ensign obeyed. Orange peered more closely, then asked, "What are those things trailing it?" The ensign enlarged the view of the stringers. Orange's eyes popped when they resolved into vacuum-armored figures.

"Sound general quarters!" he shrieked. "Prepare to repel boarders!"

"Repel boarders, sir?" Toke croaked.

"Look at it!" Orange slapped the display. "Those are Confederation Marines. That's a hull breacher and a boarding party!"

Nobody on the bridge moved for a moment. The We're Here! navy had never run repel-boarder exercises, and nobody knew what to do.

"Do I have to do everything myself?" Orange shrilled. "Sound general quarters, have the chief of ship break open the weapons locker and issue weapons to the deck crew. Get ready to defend the ship and repel the boarders!"

The officer-of-the-deck belatedly responded to the first command and sounded the general quarters alarm—needlessly, since the *Groovy* was already at general quarters.

The alarm jolted the *Groovy*'s captain out of his shock and he grabbed his comm to order the chief of ship to issue arms to the deck crew. "You heard me, Chief," he snarled when the surprised chief of boat requested clarification. "Issue arms and prepare to repel boarders."

It hadn't yet occurred to anybody to determine what part of the hull the boarding party was going to breach.

Resort fired the breaking engines and the THB gently *thunked* onto the plating of the King's hull less than four meters from its aiming point. The sailors stationed around the THB's forward edge immediately activated the magnets that held it against the hull until the sealant pumped in and took hold.

"Reel in the boarding party," Chief Young ordered.

"Reel in the boarding party, aye," Resort repeated, and engaged the motors that took up the tethers.

The first Marine to reach the back of the THB was Ensign Charlie Bass. "We're ready anytime you are, Chief," he said.

Young checked his instrument panel. It showed some ambers but no reds. Even though he'd never been involved in a hull breaching, he knew time was of the essence in the beginning of a boarding operation. "Open it," he ordered.

Resort touched the control that slid open the hatch to the interior of the THB, and squeezed through as soon as it was open far enough.

"Go!" Bass slapped the shoulder of the next Marine in line. Lance Corporal Schultz grasped the edge of the open hatch and propelled himself through, followed immediately by Corporal Claypoole. Between them they held a two and a half meter ram. Bass pointed at the next pair, Corporal Kerr and PFC Summers, and they went through, armed with a second ram.

Bass turned off his helmet comm and touched helmets with EM2 Resort. "Are you sure you know what you're doing?" Bass asked the sailor as he guided Sergeant Linsman and Lance Corporal MacIlargie through the hatch.

"As many times as Chief Young drilled me on this, I better know." He shut and dogged the hatch as soon as MacIlargie was through.

Bass knew there was nothing more he could do until the Marines inside the THB breached the hull. The next Marine on the tether was Corporal Doyle. Bass touched helmets with him. "This is a lot different from the last time, isn't it?" he said.

Doyle, pallid face invisible behind the reflective screen of his helmet, nodded, then remembered his nod couldn't be seen. He swallowed and replied, "A lot different, boss." The other time third platoon had used the THB, breaking into the *Marquis de Rien* when she was attempting to slingshot around a star, fleeing the Marines on the *Khe Sanh* at Avionia, Doyle was the first Marine into the THB and had operated the burner controls on the inside—which Chief Young was doing this time.

Young saw that the hatch was secured and the six Marines in the THB with him anchored to the deck by their magnetic boots. He moved the inner hatch lever from side to side to make sure the two halves of the hatch butting against the hull worked, then activated the start sequence.

Gases flowed at high pressure into mixing chambers, then shot through the ring of valves on the face of the hatch combing and ignited with blue flame. The nozzles swiveled and the tips of the flame touched the hull of the dreadnought. The metal snapped and popped as the cutting flames bit into it. The cutter frame began to turn in a slow circle, and a ring of metal turned red, then white, and began puddling.

Chief Young kept his attention on his console, watching for the indication that a pinhole would be cut through the burning ring. It came, and he slammed the inner hatch shut, simultaneously cutting the pressure that mixed the burning gases. He turned the valve that pumped atmosphere into the THB. Behind the closed hatch, he heard sizzling and metal cracking, which grew louder as the THB filled with air and began to carry sound waves.

"Stand steady," he said into his comm, and looked to see that the Marines had firm grips on handholds. He opened the hatch a crack, and water from between the double hulls of the starship shot through. The hatch halves shuddered from the force of the water forcing its way between them, but they held. He eased them farther apart. Water swirled and balled in the chamber, bubbles bouncing off each other, off the bulkheads, off the armored Marines, melding together to form larger bubbles.

"Stand by for three," he said on his command comm.

"Standing by, aye," Resort replied, and signaled Bass to make sure his Marines were clear.

"Three . . . two . . . one . . . mark." Young turned off the air cock to prevent more atmosphere from entering the THB.

Resort slid the outer hatch open and atmosphere and water boiled out into the vacuum.

Inside, water continued to shoot through the slit between the inner hatch halves. Now it didn't bounce or bubble, but continued to hose toward the outer hatch. Resort opened the outer hatch farther, and the water flowed faster for a minute or more before it slowed to a trickle.

"Secure it," Young ordered. He closed the inner hatch at the same time Resort closed the outer, and pumped the chamber full of air again, then reopened the inner hatch.

Schultz swung his ram back and forth so fast he caught Claypoole off guard and nearly yanked it out of his grip, but Claypoole recovered quickly. The ram slammed into the cracked and weakened circle of hull and shattered it. Kerr and Summers didn't need to use their ram.

Young turned on a floodlight in the THB's overhead, filling the space between hulls with light. The inner hull was two meters away, through a tangle of struts. He used the extension controls, and the cutting ring slowly telescoped from the inner wall of the THB until it was almost at the first struts. He repressurized the gas flow and reignited the cutters. The cutting ring began turning and the chamber was filled with the sound of cut struts clanging as they fell free. "Stand by with the rams," he ordered when the flames reached the inner hull and began cutting.

On an order from Kerr, the two pairs of Marines awkwardly walked forward. They stopped when the lead Marines were in the middle of the now empty water storage tank between the hulls. Their balance precarious, they could feel the starship's artificial gravity in the tweenhulls space. The inner hull pinged, snapped, and popped. It glowed red, then white. Threads of ship's atmosphere visibly mixed with the air in the tweenhulls.

"Now!" Young shouted.

Schultz and Claypoole, Kerr and Summers, lunged forward and slammed their rams into the circle inside the burned ring. The thin armor shivered, then fell away. The four Marines charged through and dove to the deck, rolling away from the hole they'd just made, dropping the rams and readying their blasters in their shoulders. Linsman and MacIlargie followed on their heels.

As soon as all six were through, Young closed the inner hatch and Resort opened the outer. Bass sent first squad into the chamber, then waited while the outer hatch closed so the newly created airlock could cycle full of air again and the squad could enter the ship.

While he waited, Captain Conorado joined him.

"You're next, Charlie," the company commander said, touching helmets.

"I should have gone in first."

"Going first isn't your job. You have to take care of your whole platoon."

"I know that. Still—"

He didn't get to say anything more because the hatch reopened and he shoved himself through at the head of the rest of third platoon.

"Good hunting," Conorado whispered after him.

The compartment the THB opened into was a berthing space, empty of crew now because everybody was at battle stations. Bass found that the Marines inside had already shed their vacuum suits, but he had to use infra to see them in their chameleon-covered body armor. Sergeant Ratliff was at one of the two hatches that led to the passageway outside the compartment, listening. Corporal Dean and his fire team covered Ratliff and the hatch. Corporals Claypoole and Doyle covered Lance Corporal Schultz, who was at the hatch on the right, ready to fling it open and plunge through to the interior of the starship. Everyone was ready, and first platoon was already filling the compartment.

"Open them."

Ratliff and Schultz opened the hatches and dove through, rapidly followed by the Marines covering them. There was no firing.

Bass ran through the right hatch and found himself in a passageway whose ends seemed to disappear in the distance. It looked long enough to run the entire length of the dreadnought. Closed hatches lined the passageway on both sides at about ten meter intervals. He knelt next to Schultz.

"Anything?" he asked.

"Nothing close," Schultz said.

Bass looked to Claypoole.

"My motion detector doesn't show anybody but us," he said.

Bass turned the other way and went to where Ratliff waited with his third fire team. They also had detected nobody nearby or coming their way. He spoke into his platoon circuit: "Secure the next compartments."

Corporal Kerr raced through the right hatch, followed by Doyle and Summers. He flattened himself against the bulkhead next to the first hatch on the left, beyond third fire team, and undogged it. He flung it open and tossed in a canister, then slammed it closed.

Corporal Pasquin led his fire team out the left hatch and did the same in the other direction. After a moment, Kerr reopened the hatch and waited. Nothing. The same with Pasquin.

"Go," Bass ordered.

Kerr spun through the hatch and across the compartment it opened into—another empty berthing compartment.

Summers checked his sniffer when he came through. The knockout gas from the canister Kerr had thrown in had already dispersed.

"Passage secured," Bass reported as soon as Kerr and Pasquin gave the all clear.

"First platoon, go," Conorado ordered. First platoon raced out of the entry compartment and headed aft for the passageway that led to Engineering. By then, second platoon was crowding its way through the THB.

On Bass's command, third platoon's remaining fire teams came through and checked the next compartments up. They were also empty berthing compartments. He continued leapfrogging the fire teams from compartment to compartment until Captain Conorado came to tell him K Company's first platoon was ready to take over.

"Third platoon, let's head for the bridge."

They heard the occasional *crack-sizzles* of blaster fire from second platoon as it took the weapons stations.

CHAPTER THIRTY-ONE

Lance Corporal Schultz took the point, sprinting along the passageway toward the bridge. Corporal Claypoole followed; he had trouble keeping up while watching for danger and keeping an eye on his motion detector, so he gave it to Lance Corporal MacIlargie to carry. He figured MacIlargie, as third in line, didn't need to watch his surroundings as carefully. Besides, rank has its privileges.

Narrow passageways branched off to the left every fifty meters; they led a short distance to a parallel passageway, most didn't have hatches opening into compartments. Schultz stopped and carefully peered around each corner, then sprinted for the next, with the rest of third platoon following. At the sixth, he stopped and asked for confirmation before turning onto it. The passageway was as wide as the one they were on and led all the way across the dreadnought. Almost midway along it was a two-way lift to other levels. That passageway was the first place third platoon saw crew—a gaggle of sailors under the command of a chief petty officer scrambled out of the lift when Schultz was still fifteen meters from it.

They spun and pointed their weapons at the sound of approaching footsteps. Schultz opened fire as he dove for the deck and rolled to one side of the passageway. He got off two shots before Claypoole fired from the passageway's other side. Half a second later MacIlargie fired over him. All four shots hit. None of their blasters were on low power, so those first four shots took down seven sailors, three dead. The unwounded scrambled back into the lift, their panicked voices fading as they traveled away. None had returned fire.

Schultz pushed himself up and bolted for the lift. Claypoole and MacIlargie went with him. MacIlargie thrust the motion detector between them, into the lift; it showed the sailors going down.

"Let's convince them to keep going," Claypoole said, pointing his blaster down the lift shaft. He fired a bolt so it ricocheted off the shaft wall. Schultz grinned behind his chameleon screen and fired off two bolts.

Screams from below answered the bolts, and they heard the sailors scrambling out of the lift.

Another shaft was next to the lift. It held a ladderway, stairs so steep they could barely be descended by an agile person.

Claypoole gave a quick report of the action and got the order back, "Climb the ladder."

"Going up," Claypoole told his men.

Schultz headed for the ladder and started up.

Bass ordered first squad to bandage and secure wounded sailors, then follow second squad and leave the prisoners in place.

Two levels up they ran into more sailors. Schultz had just turned the corner to climb to the next level when three members of the deck crew ran by. They heard footfalls on the ladder; they couldn't see anything but fired anyway. Fléchettes pinged off the Marines' armor. By the time Schultz turned around to fire back, Claypoole and MacIlargie had already killed the three.

"Go, go, go!" Ensign Bass shouted over the helmet comm.

They resumed climbing.

Three levels higher—the bridge level—Schultz stopped without exposing any part of himself through the ladderway exit. "Give me," he growled into the fire team circuit. He held his hand back and Claypoole passed the motion detector to him. The big man held it near the ladderway entrance for a moment and studied the display, then tucked the detector into a belt pouch.

"A squad to each side, more straight ahead," he said.

Claypoole eased around him and took a look. In addition to the cross-ship passageway, a three-meter-wide passageway led straight away from them. He saw a small group of armed sailors clustered near its end. They seemed scared, ready to start firing at any sound. The passageway looked like it opened into a large compartment where the armed men were. A double-wide airtight hatch was on the far side. A lighted sign said, ADMIRAL ON BRIDGE.

Claypoole pulled back and reported what he'd seen and what Schultz read on the motion detector. Before he was finished with the report, Sergeant Linsman pushed past him for a quick look. Charlie Bass and Captain Conorado joined them seconds later and took a quick look for themselves.

When the two officers pulled back, Bass pulled his gloves off and used his hands to tell Conorado what he wanted to do.

Conorado raised his screens and nodded. He approved of Bass's plan.

"Rat," Bass said, "get two fire teams ready. Send one left, the other right. Take out anybody they see. Hold your other fire team ready to help if either of the first two need it. Rabbit, get first squad in position to charge for the bridge as soon as second squad is out of your way. Questions?"

There were none; his orders were clear.

The Marines moved fast. They were ready to go in less than a minute. So far, they hadn't been detected on this level.

"On my mark. One, two, three, GO!"

Schultz went first, with Claypoole and MacIlargie right behind. They spun left through the entry and began firing even before they acquired targets. Corporal Kerr led the first fire team past them to the right, and they also began firing immediately. First squad was on their heels, with Corporal Dornhofer, Lance Corporal Zumwald, and PFC Gray in the lead, firing as they raced to the end of the facing passageway.

The passageways filled with the *crack-sizzle* of blaster fire and the shouts and screams of frightened, wounded, or dying sailors.

Only a few of the sailors were able to return fire. Those who survived the first few seconds dove for cover, threw their weapons away, and raised empty hands in surrender to the enemy they couldn't see.

Corporals Pasquin and Dean raced each other to be the first to the entrance to the bridge. They reached it simultaneously, but Dean's hand fell on Pasquin's when they both reached for the button that opened the hatch. Pasquin's fierce grin was wasted behind his screens.

"Wait one!" Bass snapped before Pasquin pressed the button. He stood at attention, left of the hatch, and raised his helmet screens to show his face. Conorado stood to his right; his screens were still up.

Conorado listened to the reports coming in on his helmet radio, then nodded and said, "Now."

Dean pushed on Pasquin's hand, and together they pushed the button to open the door to the bridge.

"Sir, a berthing compartment on level eight has been breached," the officer of the deck announced in a shrill voice.

"Why haven't the boarders been repelled yet?" Admiral of the Starry Heavens Orange demanded.

The OOD spoke into his comm, then reported, "Sir, the chief of ship has just begun issuing weapons to the deck crew."

"Just now? What took him so long?" Orange screamed, his face turning red.

Nobody answered. The OOD suspected the admiral and his staff were the only people on board who didn't know that the weapons locker was forward on level two, above the bridge and closer to the bow. The chief of ship had been in the comm shack, three levels below the bridge and farther aft. The deck crew was scattered all over the starship. The OOD was surprised that the chief of ship had reached the weapons locker and begun issuing weapons this quickly.

"What's going on?" Orange shrieked. "What are the boarders doing?"

The Assistant OOD reached past the ensign manning the vid bank and began pushing buttons. Displays showed 2-D images of the interior of the starship. One showed the breached compartment. Nobody was in it.

Then the compartment's hatches flew open and there was a hint of movement, as though bodies were darting through them.

Another display showed the passageway outside the breached compartment. Hatches along it began slamming open. There were more flickers of what might be moving bodies coming out of the first compartment, except nobody was visible.

"Buddha's hairy balls," the Assistant OOD murmured, "it's true."

"What's true?" Orange demanded.

"S-Sir." He stood and faced the furious admiral. "The Confederation M-Marines are invisible."

"What? That's impossible!"

The Assistant OOD gestured helplessly at the display that showed hatches slamming open for no visible cause. "S-Sir, I have no other explanation for that." He sounded like he wanted to curl into a ball and hide.

"Nonsense!" Admiral Orange snapped. He'd heard the same rumors, but he didn't believe them then and wasn't about to start believing now. The Marine detachment at the Confederation embassy on We're Here! certainly never turned invisible; he'd know if it had!

Vice Admiral Toke didn't say anything, even though she knew the Confederation Marines *did* have chameleon uniforms that made them invisible. She'd read about them in the *Proceedings of the Naval Institute*.

The bridge hatch popped open and a chief petty officer stepped in. "Sir," he said, addressing the *Groovy*'s captain, "I have a security section here. They're stationed to defend all approaches to the bridge."

Captain Hemp cast a nervous glance at Admiral Orange, then said, "Thank you, Chief. I know I can rely on you. Carry on."

"Aye aye, sir." The chief stepped back into the passageway and closed the hatch.

Admiral Orange glowered at the closed hatch, turned his basilisk gaze on Captain Hemp. *He* was the senior admiral present, the report should have been given to *him*, not to Hemp. But this wasn't the time to address issues of protocol. There were Confederation Marines somewhere on the starship and they needed to be found and dealt with.

"Where are those Marines?" he demanded of Hemp. "Why haven't they been found and dealt with yet?"

Hemp had barely opened his mouth when the weapons officer broke in.

"Sir, comm has been lost with laser banks four and five!"

"What?" Orange shrieked.

The vid-bank ensign tapped buttons and two displays showed the interiors of laser banks four and five with the laser crews jerking around as though they were being manhandled. Wrist ties appeared on them and they fell as though pushed into a pile in a corner of the bank spaces. Panels fell open on their own, unidentifiable objects came from nowhere, were placed inside, and the panels replaced. After a few seconds the panels buckled violently.

"What is happening?" Orange shrilled.

"Comm lost with missile turret two," the weapons officer reported.

"Comm with the fleet lost," the OOD shouted.

The vid-bank ensign showed the interior of the comm shack. Its crew was trussed up and the comm banks were warped, as though something catastrophic had happened inside them.

"Medical alert," the Assistant OOD reported. A display splashed the picture of seven sailors sprawled on the deck outside the mid-centership lift on level eight. Three of them were bandaged and bound, the others were still, possibly dead. Almost immediately the Assistant OOD's voice rose as he announced another medical alert, and the display showed three sailors down outside the lift on level six—they were obviously dead.

"We've lost engineering!" the OOD screamed.

"What is going on?" Admiral Orange shrilled. "Where are they?"

Blaster fire and shrieks from the passageway just outside told him and everyone else on the bridge where they were.

The hatch *whooshed* open and two faces appeared in the opening. Suspended in midair.

"I am Captain Lewis Conorado," the face on the left said in a firm, confident voice, "commander of Company L, 34th Fleet Initial Strike Team, Confederation Marine Corps. Who is in command here?"

All eyes turned to Admiral Orange. Orange stood dumbstruck, staring at the hovering faces.

"Sir, my Marines have disabled your starship's main laser and missile batteries, and your communications center. Every crew member who resisted has been killed or wounded. Those we encountered who didn't resist have been secured as prisoners. We now have complete control of the starship, or will momentarily. I respectfully request that you surrender yourself and the officers and crew of your bridge to avoid further bloodshed."

Orange slowly drew himself up. He glared at the suspended faces for a moment longer, then announced, "I am Admiral of the Starry Heavens Sativa Orange, Chief of Naval Operations of the We're Here! navy. I demand that you and your pirates put down your arms and surrender!"

Conorado removed his gloves and helmet and patiently shook his head. "Sir, I don't think you understand the situation. My Marines have control of your starship. At this moment, officers and crew from the Confederation Navy Amphibious Landing Force starship *Grandar Bay* are on their way to take the controls in Engineering. Your alternatives are: surrender peacefully, resist and die needlessly, or be locked helpless on the bridge. Which will it be, Admiral?"

Behind him, more suspended faces appeared as the Marines of third squad raised their screens to expose their faces.

There was a thud. Someone had fainted and fallen to the deck.

"Sir," Vice Admiral Toke said timidly, "I don't think we have a choice."

Captain Hemp cleared his throat. "Admiral, I'm sorry, sir, but I must surrender my ship before she or my crew suffer any further injury."

Moments later the Marines of Company L owned the We're Here! dreadnought *Groovy*. Minutes later they handed her over to the crew that came from the *Grandar Bay*, and a squad from second platoon escorted the two admirals and Captain Hemp to the Confederation starship, where Commodore Boreland convinced Admiral Toke to order the surrender of the rest of the fleet.

Admiral Toke needed very little convincing.

EPILOGUE

The *Grandar Bay* couldn't stay in orbit around Maugham's Station waiting for the return of the *Broken Missouri* and the *Heavenly Mary*. Commodore Boreland was under strict instructions to leave as soon as his primary mission was accomplished—which it had been once the Marines discovered the cause of the Unexplained Expirations in Ammon. So via drone, Boreland sent everything he knew about the mining operation on the Rock, as well as the refinery and transit station on Maugham's Station, in the afteraction report he filed with navy headquarters on the battle with the We're Here! fleet.

Filed and forgot, he thought. The navy didn't care who mined what where.

His cynicism was justified. Many reports that might have been of extraordinary interest to other government agencies got sucked into the bureaucratic morass of the Heptagon and never again were seen. And even those that were, sometimes got lost in another agency's bureaucratic morass.

But once in a while . . .

This was an instance where one world committed acts of war against another and, by attacking the *Grandar Bay*, effectively declared war on the Confederation of Human Worlds.

When the drone arrived, the duty communications officer in the drone message center on Confederation Navy Base Gagarin, the military space station in orbit around Earth, was a brand-new ensign by the name of Lit. Ensign Lit was anxious to make a positive impression on his superiors, so when he saw an incoming message over the signature of an officer he knew had been on the *Grandar Bay*, which he also knew had been lost in a Beamspace jump, he became so excited he read it, even though it was marked at a higher security clearance than he held. He then bypassed his local chain of command and queued the message "Urgent" to the office of the Chief of Naval Operations.

Later that evening Ensign Lit was led from the Officers' Club, where he was expounding to several other very junior officers about the message he had routed that afternoon, and placed under arrest in solitary confinement.

In the meanwhile, the message had been taken to Admiral K. C. B. Porter, CNO, within minutes after its arrival in his office. He read it, grimaced, and placed a call to Marcus Berentus, the Confederation Minister of War.

Minister Berentus agreed with Admiral Porter that the matter required immediate Confederation attention. On his own authority, he instructed Porter to dispatch a task force to Maugham's Station, both to defend it against any possible resumption of hostilities from We're Here! and to intercept the *Broken Missouri* and *Heavenly Mary* on their return.

Admiral Porter instructed Admiral Rasumbrata, his N3, to assemble a task force for that purpose, and within a day orders were on their way to the heavy cruiser *Kiowa*, a light cruiser, and three destroyers. En route, the *Kiowa* picked up a company from 29th FIST to secure the planetside facilities.

Task Force *Kiowa* was on station only three days when the *Heavenly Mary* arrived to pick up a load of refined metals. She immediately surrendered two days out from Maugham's Station when her captain was informed she was surrounded by three Confederation Navy destroyers.

The *Broken Missouri* showed up ten days later. She tried to make a run for it, relying on her cloaking to get away. But the starships of the task force had superior detection devices and were much faster in Space-3. The *Broken Missouri*'s crew nearly mutinied after the *Kiowa* put a laser across her bow, forcing her captain to surrender.

The officers and crews of the two starships were locked into their berthing compartments and the ships were crewed by navy personnel for the voyage back to Earth.

Following an investigation by the Ministry of Justice, seven midlevel functionaries of the St. Helen's government were sentenced to life imprisonment on the penal world of Darkside. Even though the investigators tried very hard, they couldn't come up with convincing evidence that any upper level members of the government were involved in, or even aware of, the piracy that stole the *Broken Missouri* or the *Heavenly Mary*. The President and several other high-ranking politicians and industrial moguls were, however, convicted of lesser offenses and given lighter prison sentences, fined, and banned from holding Confederation or planetary office.

Admiral of the Starry Heavens Sativa Orange was tried both in Confederation and We're Here! military courts on a variety of charges ranging from conduct unbecoming an officer to interstellar piracy and incitement of interstellar war. He was found guilty on enough counts to assure he'd spend the rest of his life in prison. The entire upper staff of the We're Here! navy was reduced in rank and retired.

A board of inquiry found Commander Moon Happiness innocent of any wrongdoing. He got his expected promotion to captain and was assigned to shore duty, but retired two years later when he realized he was never going to be given another starship command.

President Menno of Ammon finally had the proof he needed to pass legislation making it a criminal offense to enter the interdicted areas without presidential approval. Which legislation did absolutely nothing to dissuade the more adventurous young citizens of Ammon from heading for the planet's wild places anytime they felt like it.

Ensign Lit, who knew things he shouldn't and couldn't keep his mouth shut about them, found himself assigned to the *Grandar Bay*. It was a close call, though—the *Grandar Bay* didn't have use for any more ensigns and he could just as easily have gone to Darkside.

The *Grandar Bay*, lacking other orders, settled in orbit around Thorsfinni's World, and most of her officers and crew took to spending their free time planetside, enjoying the hospitality of the 'Finnis.

The Marines of 34th FIST returned to a peacetime routine, preparing for their next deployment by training for the last. They didn't know when their next deployment would come, nor where it would take them, but they were determined to be ready and give worse than they got.

Both Maugham's Station and We're Here! were so remote and insignificant that any rumors from them about being visited by the "lost" *Grandar Bay* would take quite some time to reach the general population of the Confederation of Human Worlds.